ALSO AVAILABLE FROM
CATHERINE COWLES

The Tattered & Torn Series
Tattered Stars
Falling Embers
Hidden Waters
Shattered Sea
Fractured Sky

Sparrow Falls
Fragile Sanctuary
Delicate Escape
Broken Harbor
Beautiful Exile
Chasing Shelter
Secret Haven

The Lost & Found Series
Whispers of You
Echoes of You
Glimmers of You
Shadows of You
Ashes of You

The Wrecked Series
Reckless Memories
Perfect Wreckage
Wrecked Palace
Reckless Refuge
Beneath the Wreckage

The Sutter Lake Series
Beautifully Broken Pieces
Beautifully Broken Life
Beautifully Broken Spirit
Beautifully Broken Control
Beautifully Broken Redemption

Standalone Novels
Further to Fall
All the Missing Pieces

For a full list of up-to-date Catherine Cowles titles,
please visit catherinecowles.com.

Secret
HAVEN

CATHERINE
COWLES

Secret HAVEN

CATHERINE COWLES

Copyright © 2025 by Catherine Cowles
Cover and internal design © 2025 by Sourcebooks
Cover design © Hang Le
Internal design by Champagne Book Design
Cover images © Kharkhan_Oleg/Getty Images, Ingaga/Getty Images, Pobytov/Getty Images, ioanmasay/Getty Images, Elena Medvedeva/Getty Images, Elena Feodrina/Getty Images, jirawut seepukdee/Getty Images

Sourcebooks and the colophon are registered trademarks of Sourcebooks.

All rights reserved. No part of this book may be reproduced in any form or by any electronic or mechanical means including information storage and retrieval systems—except in the case of brief quotations embodied in critical articles or reviews—without permission in writing from its publisher, Sourcebooks.

No part of this book may be used or reproduced in any manner for the purpose of training artificial intelligence technologies or systems.

The characters and events portrayed in this book are fictitious or are used fictitiously. Any similarity to real persons, living or dead, is purely coincidental and not intended by the author.

All brand names and product names used in this book are trademarks, registered trademarks, or trade names of their respective holders. Sourcebooks is not associated with any product or vendor in this book.

Published by Sourcebooks Casablanca, an imprint of Sourcebooks
1935 Brookdale RD, Naperville, IL 60563-2773
(630) 961-3900
sourcebooks.com

Originally self-published in 2025 by Catherine Cowles.

Cataloging-in-Publication data is on file with the Library of Congress.

Printed and bound in the United States of America.
LSC 10 9 8 7 6 5 4 3 2 1

FOR EVERYONE WHO FEELS LIKE THEY DON'T BELONG.
I SEE YOU. YOU'RE BEAUTIFUL, GOOD, WORTHY.
AND YOU WILL FIND OTHERS WHO SEE IT, TOO.
DON'T EVER GIVE UP.
FINDING YOUR PEOPLE WILL BE ALL THE SWEETER
BECAUSE YOU WALKED ALONE FOR A LITTLE WHILE.

A NOTE FROM CATHERINE

Hello, dearest readers,

Thank you for picking up this book and wanting to embark on this journey with me. It means a little something extra because this story is my favorite journey yet.

The Sparrow Falls series follows a group of foster siblings, and *Secret Haven*'s storyline dives deeper into the foster care and child welfare systems. I'm lucky to have worked with two incredible social workers who helped me portray these subjects as accurately as possible. That said, this is a work of fiction, and while I did my best to reflect real-life procedures, some details may differ for the sake of the story.

My goal was always to remain as true to life as possible while honoring Fallon and Kye's unique journey.

It has been a privilege to learn more about the foster care system through writing the Sparrow Falls series, and I am incredibly grateful to all those who have helped me on that path. If you'd like to explore ways to support foster youth, I encourage you to visit the following organizations' websites:

Foster Love: fosterlove.com

CASA: nationalcasagal.org

National Foster Youth Institute: nfyi.org

If you are looking for a list of sensitive topics covered in this story, you can find them on my website at the bottom of each book page.
catherinecowles.com/secret-haven

PROLOGUE

Fallon

AGE FOURTEEN

"IF YOU JUST FINISHED THE LAST OF THE LUCKY CHARMS, I AM going to hack into your Instagram and post that picture of you streaking downtown the night before graduation."

I didn't look up at the sound of my brother Cope's threat. My pencil kept right on scratching across the paper, the sound inaudible above the din in the kitchen. But growing up the way I had, I was used to noise and chaos. The good kind. The kind that came from my mom taking in foster child after foster child—anyone who needed her—even after my dad had passed away. It was just the kind of woman she was.

Sometimes, kids came for only a night or two. Other times, they stayed forever. But there were always a lot of us, which meant noise and chaos.

Shep shot Cope a grin, his amber eyes twinkling with mischief. "Good thing I've got a great ass. Nothing to worry about there."

"Your ass is so pale, it gives *mooning* a whole new meaning," Cope fired back.

"Watch your language. Both of you," Mom warned, eying the newest member of our crew.

Arden was twelve and had only said about two words since coming to live with us a few months ago. But the way she watched everyone with her gray-violet eyes said she picked up on more than someone might expect.

My grandma, Lolli, made a *pssh* noise as she walked into the kitchen wearing a bedazzled workout outfit, tie-dyed in every color of the rainbow. "Foul language is honest."

Mom pinned Lolli with a hard stare. "Foul language is not welcome in this house."

"Just like my naked yoga isn't?" Lolli huffed.

Cope's face scrunched as he shook his head, making his light-brown hair flutter in a way I was sure the high school girls would sigh over. "Please do not remind me. I'm scarred for life."

Lolli stuck out her tongue at him. "It's called a sun salutation, and it's your fault for coming over to my guesthouse unannounced."

Shep chuckled as he lowered himself to the stool next to me. "Bet he won't do that again."

"I'm staying at least two hundred yards away at all times," Cope said with a shiver.

Rhodes ambled into the kitchen, her deep-brown hair a little wild. "Don't let them dull your sparkle, Lolli."

"Never, my babycakes," Lolli called back.

Shep set his bowl of cereal on the island next to me, making his milk slosh over the side. He quickly moved to mop it up as I lifted my journal out of its path. "Sorry, Fal."

"When do you go back to college again?" I asked, my lips twitching.

He made a face. "This morning. And you're gonna miss me like crazy."

"Not when you take the last of the Lucky Charms," Cope called from the opposite side of the kitchen.

"You snooze, you lose," Shep shot back.

Mom looked up from the stove, giving them each a look that said she was exasperated. "You both need protein, not to mainline sugar."

Rhodes sent my mom a smile. "I'll have eggs, Nora."

My mom's expression turned gentle. "Have I told you that you're my favorite today?"

"Kiss-ass," Cope called as he tried to get the last shreds of Lucky Charms into his bowl.

"Copeland," Mom chastised.

"Sorry, Mom." He grinned at Rhodes. "Sorry, Rho Rho."

My best friend was newer to our bunch. She'd come to live with us a year ago after her family was killed in a fire. And even with as much time as she'd spent here growing up, she was still finding her footing in the sibling pack.

"That's pretty good," Shep said, leaning over to look at what I was drawing.

I quickly closed my journal, hiding my sketch of a house. "Not as good as yours, future contractor extraordinaire."

He sent me a lopsided grin. "Let's hope."

"Only if he's not distracted by all the girls chasing after him on campus," a new voice called. Our eldest brother, Trace, ambled into the kitchen, his new deputy uniform looking perfectly ironed.

"I thought you moved out," Shep shot back.

"I'm out of coffee," Trace muttered.

"Move out of his way," Cope ordered. "Trace without coffee is a dangerous beast."

Trace leveled him with a stare. "I don't get my coffee, and I'm much more likely to write you a speeding ticket when you're doing thirty-five in a twenty-five."

Mom straightened, leveling a glare at my biological older brother. "Copeland Colson. I am entrusting you with precious cargo. Tell me you are not speeding."

There was a slight edge to her tone, and I knew why. When I was ten, a car accident left Cope and me in the hospital, and our father and brother, Jacob, dead.

Trace winced and quickly wrapped an arm around Mom. "I'm

just giving him a hard time. He's only doing like two miles over the speed limit."

It was a lie. Cope was a speed demon on skates *and* behind the wheel. Always looking for that next thrill. Maybe because we'd come so close to losing it all.

I stood, putting together my things and shoving them into the backpack at my feet. Once that was done, I moved around the kitchen, gathering supplies for lunch. I quickly glanced around to see if anyone was watching before making two turkey sandwiches. But I got caught up making sure they were perfect and didn't notice my mom moving in beside me.

She brushed some hair back from my face in that easy way of hers. "Did you get enough for breakfast? You've been bringing a lot for lunch lately."

My muscles stiffened; I couldn't help it. A mixture of anxiety and guilt washed through me at hiding my mission from her. But if I shared, she'd get involved. I loved her for it, but I also feared it might make things worse.

"Sometimes, I want a snack on my free period," I hedged. It wasn't a lie. I did occasionally want something to eat during my free periods. It just usually came in the form of candy—strawberry Sour Patch Kids, if I had my way.

Cope sent me a look that told me he was about to be a shit-stirrer. "Eating for two, Fal?"

My jaw dropped, and Mom whirled on him. "That is not something to joke about."

"Oh, please," Cope muttered. "Fal's never even kissed a boy. I think you're safe."

My cheeks heated because he was right. Cope's words stung, but he was right. Everyone else in my family seemed to find relationships easily—or at least offers for them. Trace had been dating the same girl since he started college. Shep had endless female interest. Girls waited by Cope's locker every day. Even Rhodes had plenty of boys paying her attention. And I was sure even Arden would have her share of interest if she ever ventured off our property.

But it was never easy for me. I was a little awkward. I didn't care about the same stuff most kids in my class did. It just...didn't seem important. And it didn't help that I was shy around people I didn't know well. More often than not, I faded into the background.

Grabbing the sandwiches, I stuffed them into my backpack and bolted out the front door. My feet hit the boards of the front steps, and I felt the sting of tears in the corners of my eyes. It was so stupid.

"Fal, wait," Cope called from behind me.

I didn't stop—not that I had anywhere to go. Colson Ranch was miles from town, and my only escape would've been into the pastures with the horses or cattle. I slowed at the fence line, staring out at the horizon. The Monarch Mountains were stunning in the morning light, and their staggering beauty and power were reminders of just how big the world was beyond our fences.

Cope moved in next to me, not saying anything for a moment. "I'm a dick."

I didn't respond.

"A dick of epic proportions. And I'll give you my Lucky Charms for the next two weeks as restitution."

My mouth curved slightly at that. "The ultimate penance."

"No kidding," he muttered. He knocked his shoulder into mine. "I'm sorry. Any boy would be lucky to have you at his side. But I'd also kick his ass if he made a move on you."

I made a face at Cope. "And how many girls have you kissed?" I challenged.

"I'm seventeen. It's different."

"Whatever," I muttered.

Cope looped an arm around me. "Forgiven?"

I glanced up at him. "I don't know. You going to get me a milkshake after school?"

"Lucky Charms *and* a milkshake?"

"You were a dick of *epic* proportions."

Cope burst out laughing but tugged me back toward the line of family vehicles. Trace watched us approach, the edges of his expression hardening. He didn't like anyone around him feeling less than, especially those he loved. It likely came from the events of his life before he came to stay with us. But he'd taken that hardship and turned it into something good.

"Want me to put him on a most-wanted list?" Trace asked, Shep and Rhodes standing next to him.

"I'll settle for Lucky Charms and a milkshake payment," I called back.

Cope pulled me tighter against him and gave me a noogie. "She drives a hard bargain."

"Cope!" I squealed.

"Not the hair," Rhodes yelled. "That's adding insult to injury."

I struggled to get free. "I'm going to put glitter in your hair gel."

Cope laughed. "I don't use hair gel."

"Your body lotion, then."

"Turn him into a fairy nymph," Rho encouraged.

Cope released me. "Brutal."

I tried to right my hair. "And don't you forget it."

The second bell rang, and more students flooded the halls. Kids stopped to offload books in their lockers and grab lunch money or food they'd brought from home. Nearly everyone but me. I kept my backpack on and dodged kids darting this way and that while trying to avoid any teachers who might question why I wasn't headed for the cafeteria.

Who was I kidding? None of them would stop me. They'd assume I was working on a school project or logging some extra hours of homework. They wouldn't be completely wrong. But they wouldn't be totally right either.

"Fal!"

My muscles stiffened at the sound of Rho's voice above the crowd. I could've pretended I didn't hear her, but Rhodes was determined, and she would've followed me. I slowed in the side hallway, stepping out of the flow of traffic.

"You're fast for how tiny you are," Rhodes said, struggling to catch her breath.

"What's up?" I asked, feigning nonchalance.

Rho's eyes narrowed on me the way only a best friend's could. "Where are you going?"

"I have something to do this lunch period."

"And that is?" she pressed.

I didn't say anything right away.

Rhodes let out a long breath. "You've been MIA at lunch for weeks. What's going on?"

I twisted the strap of my backpack around my fingers and pulled it tight. "I'm tutoring someone."

Rho's brow furrowed. "Why didn't you just say so?"

"He doesn't want people to know he's struggling. That's all."

One corner of her mouth quirked up. "*He*, huh?"

My cheeks heated. "It's not like that." No matter how much I wanted it to be. But even if there were no stolen kisses or anything of the like, we shared something deep—an understanding I'd never had with anyone else. Not even Rhodes.

"I'm just giving you a hard time," Rho said. "I'll cover for you if anyone asks."

I grinned at her and started down the hall. "You're the bestest bestie," I called.

"I know I am!" Rho shouted.

Keeping an eye out for any faculty members, I ducked out the side door and jogged across one of the soccer fields toward the forest. The moment I stepped into the trees, I breathed a little deeper. The clean mountain air, the pine scent clinging to everything, the sound of the creek in the distance...it all put me at ease.

I wound through the trees, following a path I knew by heart. It had been my escape route since high school started a few months ago. I just hadn't realized at the time that it wasn't only mine.

My heart stuttered as I caught sight of him sitting on a log. I recognized him instantly, even from behind, and with the hood of his sweatshirt pulled up. Kyler Blackwood was just that kind of boy. Bigger than most of the guys at Sparrow Falls High, it wasn't only his size that made him so easy to identify.

It was the energy that emanated from him, wafting off him in crackling waves. He seemed to prowl through life in a way that made others keep their distance. But I was never scared of Kyler. He was *real*. He didn't paint on a smile when he didn't feel it. He didn't pretend that everything was okay when it wasn't. He simply was. And I was in awe of it.

Fallen leaves crunched under my feet, and Kyler turned, revealing one side of his shadowed face. Even half-covered, I instantly knew something was wrong.

"Hey, Sparrow."

I didn't say anything right away; I just kept moving, needing to get to him. I lowered myself to the log next to him and let my backpack fall to the ground. "Tell me."

Kyler shrugged off the request, asking a question of his own. "Got any new house drawings?"

He was the only one I'd ever shown my drawings to by choice. Sometimes, living in an imaginary world—one where parents and siblings didn't die, and kids weren't neglected or hurt—was easier. So, I'd repeatedly draw a whimsical house: a place where no bad things happened. It was a cross between a Craftsman and a Victorian, with teal siding and bright blooms covering most of it.

I wasn't especially good at drawing, but I'd gotten good at this one thing. It was my escape. Except that escape had shifted over the past few months. Changed. Because Kyler had become a part of it.

I could feel the anger and pain swirling around Kyler. I took him in. His hand lay on the log, pressing against the rough bark. His knuckles were torn, which wasn't unusual given the number of fights he got into, both inside the ring and out of it. But some of the tears were fresh.

The urge to clean them gnawed at me. I'd taken to carrying a first-aid kit in my backpack for exactly that reason. But it wasn't time.

Not yet. Because something was hurting him a hell of a lot more than those knuckles.

I moved, linking my pinky with his and squeezing. It was our sign that we were there for each other. If I needed to rage about how unfair it was that I'd lost Dad and Jacob, or how worried I was about one of my siblings... If Kyler needed to let loose the ugly stew of feelings regarding what he faced at home each and every day: his father's fists, his mother's vitriol. We were always there.

"Tell me." My words had a slight pleading edge.

Something about that made Kyler turn. And that's when I saw it. A sick feeling swirled inside me as I took in the side of Kyler's face. It was bruised and swollen in a way that could only come from someone hitting you over and over again when you were down.

My pinky tightened around Kyler's as if my grip on him was the only thing keeping him with me. "The fights?" I croaked. Kyler was a hell of a mixed martial artist, but he'd started taking some fights for money, and I'd never had a good feeling about them. Looking at his face now, I realized it was more than just the physical toll of those fights.

The light in Kyler's amber eyes swirled, turning darker. "No."

My throat constricted. Worse than fights for money with no protective gear? Worse than getting mixed up with guys who wore motorcycle club vests and Trace said were dangerous?

"Your dad?" I could barely get the words out, my throat weaving into intricate knots I didn't think I'd ever get undone.

Kyler looked at the creek below us. The dogwoods that had been in full bloom months ago when we first met here were now bare, like bony fingers that had been starved of food and affection for far too long. Like Kyler himself.

A muscle along his jaw pulsed in time to a beat only he could hear. "He got the jump on me when I got home. Drunk or high. Maybe both. He got me down, and I couldn't get up. Woke up on the floor this morning."

The pressure of unshed tears was instant, but I shoved them and the rage swirling inside me down as far as they would go. "Your mom?"

The two words were strangled, barely audible, but he heard them. "You know she doesn't give a fuck about me. She's still pissed that I ruined the best years of her life. Sometimes, I think she'd rather he finish me off."

Tears filled my eyes, cresting up and spilling over as I kept hold of Kyler's pinky. But I couldn't speak. Didn't have the words for him living through something so awful.

He turned then, taking in my face. "Fuck, Sparrow. Don't cry."

Kyler tugged his hand from mine. Not holding his pinky made me feel a little sick. Like I could no longer protect him. Kyler covered his thumbs with the sleeves of his hoodie and swept them under my eyes, clearing away the tears. "I'm okay."

"You're not." The words were barely a whisper. "They can't get away with this. We can't let them."

Kyler's hands dropped from my face. "I'm gonna take off. Maybe try to make it to Portland."

Panic flooded my system, fear fast on its heels. Kyler was two years older than me, but sixteen wasn't old enough to make it on your own in a huge city. Anything could happen to him. And the idea of not seeing Kyler every day? Not knowing he was all right?

It made me feel like I couldn't breathe.

"Don't," I croaked. "I can talk to Trace. He's a deputy now. He can help—"

"No." Kyler was on his feet in a flash, pacing. "You can't. I could end up in a group home or, if my dad rats me out for fighting, juvie. I can't risk it, Sparrow. Promise me you won't tell anyone. Promise."

Each word wound the panic tighter. But I knew I couldn't betray the gift Kyler had given me.

Trust.

For the boy who had nothing, he'd given me everything. His trust. His kindness. He'd seen me doing battle with my grief and had come alongside me in the most beautiful way.

"I won't tell," I whispered.

The tension in Kyler eased a fraction, like someone had dialed down an electrical current. "Okay."

I stared at the boy who'd become my haven, taking in his beaten and bloodied face. "I can't stand you hurting," I rasped, pushing to my feet. "I want to fix it. I want to *kill* them. I want to take away all the pain and make it better."

"You do," Kyler said, cutting me off as he moved into my space and linked his pinky with mine again. "You bring me food. You make sure I don't flunk out of my classes." His finger traced the arrow necklace I wore every day. "You make me feel…not alone. And, Sparrow? I've been alone for basically as long as I've been breathing. But you? You make it all better."

My breath hitched as Kyler's hand lifted to cup my cheek, his thumb sweeping away the last of my tears. My pulse thundered in my ears as his head dipped. But he just hovered there, not closing the distance, waiting for me. Like he always did.

And because it was Kyler, I wasn't afraid or even nervous. I just wanted. To know what his lips felt like, what his tongue tasted like, what it would be like to be kissed by this boy.

I closed the distance, my mouth meeting his. The boy everyone thought of as a brute was heartbreakingly gentle as his mouth met mine. Heat hit my lips, spreading out, moving through my whole form, waking me up as if I'd been sleepwalking through life. Kyler tasted like peppermint and a hint of smoke, and his scent was stronger now, too: oakmoss and amber, but with a twist. As though when those scents connected with Kyler's skin, they changed. Just like I did.

His rough palm slid along my jaw as I pressed into him, wanting more of the magic that was only him. His tongue stroked in, just barely. Hesitant, waiting for that permission again. I met his kiss awkwardly at first, but then I found my footing. His long fingers slid into my hair as I opened for him.

"Well, well, well. What do we have here? I knew there was something more goin' on than studying."

At the sound of the voice, Kyler and I jerked apart. He instantly moved me behind him and glared at his friend.

Oren snorted. "Please. Like I'm interested in the little mouse."

Kyler's hands fisted, and the already bruised knuckles cracked.

"It's a good thing you're not. Because if you lay a finger on her, you know I'd snap your neck like a twig."

Oren held up his hands, but I saw a flare of anger in his brown depths. "Touchy, touchy. Save it for your fight this weekend."

That had anger washing through me, hot and fast. "He's not fighting this weekend. Look at his face. He probably has a concussion."

Oren sent a glare in my direction. "You're a real buzzkill, mouse. You know that? He'll be fine by Saturday."

I stepped to Kyler's side, letting my anger burn out any fear. "If I find out you pressured Kyler into fighting, I'll have my brother put you on every sheriff's department watch list imaginable. I'll let the air out of your crotch rocket's tires every day. And I will find a way to sneak pink hair dye into your shampoo."

"She's got a vengeful streak," Jericho said, stepping out of the trees. "I like it."

I wasn't crazy about either of Kyler's so-called friends, but Jericho seemed to have a soul, at least.

Oren's jaw worked back and forth, his gaze flicking to Kyler. "You'd better keep your bitch on a shorter leash and stop telling her our business."

Kyler moved forward lightning-quick. The only thing saving Oren from a knockout punch was Jericho grabbing his jacket and pulling him back.

"All right, all right," Jericho said, getting between them. "Let's just take a breath. Ore, you know Fallon's a no-go zone for you and anyone else. Kye will break you in two. Kye, no hitting the home team, remember?"

"He earned it," Kyler growled.

"Maybe. But Oren's never *not* gonna be an asshole. So, we just gotta deal."

"You're both pricks," Oren muttered.

The school bell rang in the distance, and it felt a lot like a clock striking midnight. I was about to turn into a pumpkin. Kyler turned, his gaze roaming my face like he was trying to memorize it. "You'd better go. You don't want to be late."

I moved in, not caring that his friends were there. I linked my pinky with his. "You gonna be okay?"

One corner of his mouth quirked up. "Always am, aren't I?"

"Be careful," I whispered.

Kyler stared down at me for a long moment. Then he dipped his head and pressed a kiss to my forehead. It was like he was trying to memorize that, too. My insides churned because it felt a hell of a lot like a goodbye.

"Kyler—"

I swung my backpack around and pulled out the extra lunch I'd made, shoving it into his hands.

"Go," he said quietly. "Not letting you be late because of me."

So, I went. But I regretted it for the rest of the day.

A ringing sounded from down the hall and the kitchen below as I stared at the ceiling in the dark like it held all the answers to my problems. Two rings later, it cut off.

My bedroom was two doors down from my mom's, but I could still hear her muffled voice as she answered the phone—not the words but her familiar, sleepy tone. Then I listened to the floorboards creak as she made her way down the hall and the stairs.

It likely meant one thing: a newcomer. And one coming in the middle of the night meant it was bad. An emergency placement.

I tossed off the covers and sat up, sliding my feet into my fluffy unicorn slippers that matched my PJs and padding down the hall. Mom already had the kettle on by the time I made it downstairs.

"Hey, sweetie. Did I wake you?" she asked as she tightened the sash of her flannel robe. It was the one Dad had gotten her a decade ago. She said putting it on felt like getting a hug from him. She'd patched holes and restitched seams, and I had a feeling she'd wear it for the rest of her days.

I shook my head. "Couldn't sleep."

Mom brushed some hair out of my face. "Everything okay?"

No, everything was not okay. But I'd made a promise, and Kyler had given me his trust. I wouldn't ever break that. "Just a lot going on at school."

"I'm making some Sleepytime tea. Drink some of that."

"Okay." I watched as she expertly removed the kettle before it could make a sound and poured hot water into a teapot before pulling out three mugs. "Who's coming?" I asked softly.

Mom's face got that troubled look it often did when we were about to get a bad case. Like when Arden had arrived and couldn't bear to sleep with the lights off. Or when Trace went to the cemetery to visit his mom on her birthday. "A boy's coming to stay with us for a while."

I watched her face for more clues. "What happened?"

She placed a hand-sewn tea cozy over the pot, then rested her hand there. "He was hurt, and he needs a safe place to stay."

My stomach cramped. How were there so many people in the world who wanted to inflict pain? "Did they get who did it?"

Mom nodded. "Trace said the man's in lockup."

"Good." The force behind the word had my mom raising her brows.

She reached out and cupped my face before tapping the arrow necklace Dad had given me. "Always my little warrior for justice." A soft knock sounded on the door before she could continue. "That's probably Trace."

Mom was already on the move, and I followed behind, wanting to see if I could do anything to help. But as the front door opened, my whole world dropped away. It wasn't the weary look on Trace's face that did it, or the sad look on his partner, Gabriel's. It was the boy whose gaze was cast at the ground. The same one who'd given me everything.

I must've made a sound because Kyler's head jerked up. The second it did, pain filled his expression. His dark brown hair looked black under the dim porch light, mirroring the shadowy circles under his amber eyes.

"Careful," Trace said quietly. "The stitches will smart for a while."

Stitches?

My gaze jumped around Kyler's form, taking in new flashes of information: an arm in a sling, taped gauze peeking out from under scrubs, a bandage across his brow, and the side of his face even more swollen.

"Hi, Kye," my mom said gently. "I'm Nora Colson. You're most welcome here. I've got a room ready and some tea brewing in the kitchen. Fallon can show you the way. You might know her from school."

My heart hammered in my ears. A tingling sensation erupted in my fingers, and it felt like the whole world might drop away. Kyler. *My* Kyler was the one who'd been hurt. The one who needed shelter.

"No," Kyler rasped. "I don't think we've met."

It felt like the most brutal blow—worse than waking up in the hospital after the car accident with broken ribs and a concussion.

"Fal?" Mom asked.

"Sorry," I squeaked. "I can show you." I scurried like the little mouse Oren always accused me of being, but Kyler wasn't nearly as quick. Every step he took looked like it cost him, and I couldn't stop the tears that gathered in my eyes.

Mom spoke to Trace and Gabriel in hushed tones as I led Kyler to the kitchen without saying a word. When we finally reached it and had some privacy, I focused on the tea. I couldn't look at him. It hurt too much. In every way.

"Tell me," I croaked.

Kyler didn't say anything for a long moment. "He caught me packing a bag to leave." Kyler's words were rough like sandpaper and full of pain. "Grabbed a knife. Never seen him so mad." His voice caught. "I think he was going to kill me."

I had to look at him then. The shock and fear were too much. "Kyler," I breathed.

His tears came then, running down his face in streaks of agony.

"My dad tried to kill me. And my mom didn't do a damn thing to stop him. She just watched like I was nothing to her."

I wanted to touch him, but I didn't know where. Every place I looked seemed like it would cause him pain. Still, like always, I moved for his pinky and hooked it with mine. "You're safe now. We've got you."

A new sort of fear and pain slid into his expression like they were wrapped in panic. He gripped my pinky harder. "You can't tell them we know each other. That I kissed you."

I frowned, trying to understand.

"They'll never let me stay here if they know. Your brother pulled strings to get me in here. They wanted to put me in a group home in Roxbury. If they boot me from here, that's where I'll go."

Pain ripped through me. Kyler didn't deserve that. He deserved to be somewhere he wouldn't have to watch his back. A place he could heal. And he would be. Even if I had to erase the fact that he knew me better than anyone. Even if I had to hide that I'd fallen in love with him the moment he found me screaming in the woods.

Kyler let go of my pinky, and it felt like someone was ripping my still-beating heart from my chest. But he didn't look away when he spoke again, saying the words that broke me. "Sparrow," he croaked, "you were always too good for me anyway. It's better this way."

CHAPTER ONE

Fallon

FOURTEEN YEARS LATER

Cupping my hands around a mug that read *World's Best Aunt*, I inhaled deeply. The scent of dark roast filled my nose, deep and rich with hints of dark chocolate and almonds. Or maybe I was imagining that. It didn't matter. Only one thing did. "Do your job, sweet, sweet caffeine," I whispered into the cup as if to manifest some sort of wakefulness.

Taking a long pull of coffee, I closed my eyes—eyes that felt like they were full of acid-coated sand. But I felt slightly more human after a few sips.

I opened my eyes and set the mug on the dresser. Countless rings littered the surface from endless mornings just like this one. It drove my mom crazy. She was constantly giving me coasters or offering to refurbish the top. But the coasters got lost in the chaos of my minuscule cottage on the edge of town, and the dresser had character. Or as Lolli said, *"It's seen some things, baby girl."*

Moving around my room, I pulled up the covers on my bed and winced at the stack of file folders and the laptop on my nightstand.

Paperwork. There was never-ending paperwork when you worked for the child welfare arm of the Department of Human Services. And nine times out of ten, it was the reason for my two a.m. bedtimes. I reached for my coffee and took a sip at the reminder of just how little sleep I was going on.

My phone dinged, and I reached over to swipe it from the charging dock, nearly upending the Leaning Tower of Paperwork in the process. I muttered a curse as hot coffee sloshed onto my hand but managed not to do any serious damage. My sibling group chat flashed on the screen.

Shep has changed the name of the group to Cope's Tighty-whities.

I frowned at the screen. My siblings were always trying to one-up each other by changing the chat name, but this was a new one.

Shep: *Look what I spotted at the grocery store this morning...*

A photo of a magazine filled the screen. *Sports Today* had one photo on the cover. My brother, the hockey star, shirtless with some sort of oil on his chest and his hair slicked back. He wasn't in his underwear, thank the gods above, but he was in workout shorts that left little to the imagination. My nose scrunched up.

Me: *I really didn't need to see this before breakfast. I feel a little ill.*

Cope: *Rude. Sutton said I look great.*

Rhodes: *Your fiancée can't exactly be trusted to be impartial.*

Kyler: *Did they dip you in a vat of olive oil for this? Give you a rubdown with a tub of Crisco? I need to know the background.*

Everyone in my family called Kyler by his nickname, Kye, but I could never find it in me to switch his name in my phone. Like so many other things, it was a reminder of what could've been. A brand of something I could never let go, even though it would never be mine.

Trace: *That photo is obscene. It's like gray sweatpants but worse.*

Rhodes: *Ah, gray sweatpants. Men's slut clothes. I think it's cold enough for me to leave a few pairs out for Anson to wear.*

That had a smile tugging at my lips.

Me: *Let me know how the hater of sunshine and bright colors responds to having to walk around in lingerie.*

Rho's fiancé was a notorious grump who'd communicated in mostly grunts and scowls until she came into his life. But everything had changed when the ex-profiler found her—when they'd found each other. A pang lit along my sternum. I set my phone on the dresser and rubbed the spot.

Arden: *It's too early for Cope's junk to be in my face. But I'm sure the puck bunnies will be thrilled.*

Cope: *Don't say puck bunnies around Sutton. She gets a little stabby.*

Arden: *I think I'll get her a switchblade for Christmas.*

A soft sound of amusement left my lips as I started on my makeup. In our family, Arden was known for pulling a knife first and asking questions later—which was exactly how she'd met her now-fiancé, Lincoln.

Cope: *Please, don't. I'm not sure I can afford the lawsuits.*

Shep: *You'll all be happy to know that I sent this photo to Lolli, and she said she's going to turn Cope into a fairy prince in her next art piece.*

A grin finally found my lips as I struggled to keep the cover-up where it was supposed to go. Lolli was infamous for her inappropriate diamond art creations. They all had some kind of phallic or sexual bent to them. And no matter how hard a time Mom or my siblings gave her, she never stopped gifting them.

Cope: *There will be payback, hammer boy. She's probably going to have me mounting a poor, defenseless fairy.*

Rhodes: *You could luck out and be part of one of her throuple creations. Remember the elf queen Eiffel Tower piece?*

Trace: *My eyes still haven't recovered.*

I studied my face in the mirror and winced. My dark circles would need two coats of makeup today.

Kyler: *I'm demanding to know her artist's vision at dinner tonight.*

A curse slipped past my lips as I glanced at the stack of work on my nightstand.

Me: *I might have to miss tonight. Sorry, guys. Give me the play-by-play if I do.*

Rhodes: *What's going on? You've been totally MIA lately.*

Guilt pricked at me because she was right. I'd missed more family dinners over the last month than I had in the past five years.

Me: *Sorry. Work's nutty right now. We're down a caseworker, and things have just been...a lot. But I'll try to make it. Promise.*

Kyler: *Let me guess who's picking up the slack.*

I scowled at my phone, both because he was right and because he knew why this was so important to me. Not just because I knew how deep the need for social workers and support systems was for these kids, but because of *him*.

Kye was an invisible brand on my bones. Something I carried with me wherever I went, in whatever I did—even if no one ever knew.

Trace: *You need to take care of yourself, or you won't be able to help anyone.*

That only deepened my scowl. Trace had retained the overprotective-big-brother role for all of us. Now, he was also the sheriff, extending that protectiveness to the entire county.

Me: *I know what I can handle. Love you all.*

Cope: *That's Fal-speak for fuck off.*

Arden: *You'd all better watch your backs, or you're gonna get glitter-bombed.*

I wanted to smile at her reference to my favorite version of retribution but couldn't quite get my mouth to obey. I was too tired. Instead, I locked my phone and finished getting ready. I donned my typical slacks and button-down and wove my blond hair into a braid.

There was only one piece missing. My hands moved to my jewelry tray and the necklace there—the arrow I'd worn every day for as long as I could remember. I fastened it around my neck and stared at the tiny charm. Tracing it with my fingertips, I swore I could still feel the echo of Kye's fingers doing the same thing.

I squeezed my eyes shut and let myself remember those days for a fleeting handful of moments. I called on the ghost of Kyler, letting the memory wrap around me, allowing myself to recall what it had felt like to be his.

When I opened my eyes, he was gone. No more Kyler. Only Kye. The only foster brother I'd never see as what I should: a sibling and nothing more. Because it didn't matter if it had been fourteen seconds or fourteen years, he'd always be the boy who'd given me everything.

My hatchback sputtered slightly as I parked in a spot at the end of a row. I grimaced and turned off the engine, giving the dashboard a little pat. "Just make it through this winter, and I'll retire you somewhere nice and sunny." *Like the junkyard.*

Climbing out of my car, I moved to the back and grabbed my overflowing tote bag. While the rear seat was tidy, the back was littered with a second set of basically everything I might need since I practically lived out of my car some weeks: countless water bottles, workout gear, changes of clothes for court or jeans to go riding with Arden and Keely, even a pillow and a blanket.

It had also become home to my backups for everything I could possibly need for the kids I worked with: clothing, books, toys, snacks, and a first-aid kit. It was a chaotic disarray, but it worked.

I closed the back door and beeped my locks. Even that sounded a little sad and tired. "Me, too, buddy. Me, too."

Rolling my shoulders back, I started toward the office. Mercer County Child Welfare served five different towns and the surrounding areas. Including the support staff, five of us worked here. We could've used at least twice that number.

As a caseworker, it was recommended that I work on no more than twenty-five cases at a time. I currently had thirty-two. The past few months had shown me exactly why so many social workers got burned out. The work could be hard on your soul, and when you were overtaxed on top of it? It was a recipe for disaster.

But it was also the most rewarding job I could imagine doing. There was no better feeling than helping families on their way to healthy reunifications or getting kids into new environments where they could finally soar. There were always cases where it didn't feel like a win was possible, and the best you could hope for was survival. But that didn't mean I would stop fighting.

Every single child's file that crossed my desk deserved my best. And that's what they would get. Even if I had to go without sleep to give it to them.

A buzzer sounded as I entered the office, and Mary Lou looked up from her reception desk. "Morning, Fal."

"Morning," I greeted. "How's Ginny? Her cold any better?"

"Much. Unfortunately, Tom caught it, and you know what that means."

I shuddered. "Not the man flu."

Mary Lou chuckled. "You know it."

"May the force be with you."

"I'll take whatever I can get."

I headed inside the small office area I shared with the other caseworker, Mila, and our investigator, Noah. The only separate office was for the head of Mercer County Child Welfare, Rose.

"Morning," Noah greeted, looking up from his laptop and adjusting his glasses. "I brought donuts." He gestured to the kitchenette along the far wall.

"Thanks. I will take any and all sugar and deposit it straight into my bloodstream."

Mila shook her head, her dark hair cascading around her in waves that only accentuated her stunning Eastern European features. "I'm not sure how you two are even alive with how you eat."

I glanced at her green juice and wrinkled my nose. "I'll keep my greens in a salad, thank you very much."

"When you're crashing at one p.m., you'll wish you'd had my green juice."

Mila might've been right. She had four years on me in both age and experience on the job. But I was keeping my head above water the best I could. "Pry sugar from my cold, dead hands," I muttered as I crossed to my desk.

Noah chuckled as he leaned back in his chair. "Sugar is energy. It keeps us going."

"I'm taking that as evidence-based proof because Noah's been at this job for longer than either of us."

At thirty-four, Noah had been at DHS for a decade. And hitting the ten-year mark usually meant it would stick.

I slid my tote bag to the floor and pulled back my chair, stilling as a package and note caught my eye. A bag of strawberry Sour Patch Kids and a folded piece of paper with *Fallon* in artful, colorful letters.

My throat tightened as I sat, my fingers hovering over the paper in a battle of both wanting to open it and not.

"She wanted to read it," Noah said, refocusing on his computer.

"Way to throw me under the bus," Mila shot back.

My gaze flicked to her, my eyes narrowing.

She held up both hands. "I didn't. Geez. I'm just curious what the bad boy of Blackheart Ink has to say today."

I fought the urge to shift uncomfortably. It wasn't uncommon for Kye to stop by on his way to his MMA gym, Haven, or the tattoo studio he also owned, and leave something for me. Candy was the most common treasure. But it wasn't always that. I had a collection of things he'd left strewn across my desk.

A Chevy Impala key chain from the show *Supernatural*. A stuffed velociraptor from Kye's and my favorite movie, *Jurassic Park*. A snow globe of New York City from when he had flown out there for some huge tattoo expo. A drawing he'd done of my dream house.

The last was my favorite. He'd taken what I'd doodled over and over again and turned it into something beautiful. It didn't matter that I'd never make enough money to afford that kind of house. It was more than that. It was a symbol of hope.

I flipped the note open to find more artful script inside.

Can't have you passing out on the job. A little fuel to keep you going. Don't work too hard.

Below the text was a drawing of a sparrow. It was how he signed every note. I struggled to swallow as I refolded the paper and opened my bottom desk drawer to tuck it safely away. I had to empty the drawer every so often, but I never threw the notes away. I kept them in boxes in my closet. And when I really wanted to torture myself, I'd pull them out and read them.

"That bad, huh?" Mila asked. "He tell you he murdered someone last night?"

I scowled in her direction. Mila wasn't being intentionally cruel, but she saw the world in black and white. Right and wrong. Kye's record and his sometimes-surly demeanor put him in the *wrong* category for her. And I was sure him being covered in tattoos and wearing scarred motorcycle boots instead of cowboy ones didn't help.

"Leave it," I warned.

She opened her mouth to say something else, but Rose's door opened. "Oh, good, Fal. You're here. I want to go over the Andrews' placement with you."

I pushed back my chair and stood, grateful for the interruption. If anything tripped my trigger, it was someone insulting Kye. Thankfully, Rose and I had plenty to go over.

I lost myself in the rhythm of the day. I had two home visits. One was to check on a reunified family after the mom had gone to rehab. She was doing great, working her program and getting some additional support from a sister who'd decided to move closer to help out with the kids. I was cautiously hopeful.

The second was to check on a set of brothers in their foster placement. The younger boy was flourishing under the newfound attention and care, doing better in school and making more friends. But the older boy was struggling. At fifteen, he'd built up walls, and his foster parents would have to work to break them down. But the Moores were up to the task. I knew because I'd seen them do it countless times before.

By the time I made it back to the office, I was fading. As I glanced at my watch, I cursed. One-thirteen in the afternoon. Damn Mila for being right. Instead of taking time to make something in the office, I beelined for my desk and ripped open the bag of strawberry Sour Patch Kids.

Noah looked up from his computer. "That bad?"

"If you tell Mila that I had a sugar crash exactly when she said I would, you're dead to me." I shoved the strawberry gummies into my mouth, closed my eyes, and moaned. "Sour strawberries, you're all I need in this world. You never abandon me in my time of need. You're always there just when I need you."

When I opened my eyes, it was to find Noah's attention zeroed in on my mouth. He cleared his throat and quickly averted his gaze. "While you mainline sugar, want to go over the Cooper case?"

"Sure," I mumbled around my gummies as I sat at my desk and pulled out my laptop.

When I opened the window that housed my files, Noah stood and moved in behind me. "The prosecutor is going to file charges for child neglect and endangerment tomorrow. With the evidence and testimonies, I think the parents will do some time."

My stomach twisted the way it always did with these kinds of cases. It didn't matter how many times I'd gone through situations like this one. Some people at DHS said they had to turn off their emotions to get through the day and do the work they did. And I understood that. But I couldn't. I wasn't built that way.

"The kids' grandmother would like to assume permanent custody. She has good support around her and a steady income with a work-from-home job. Do you think we can file to terminate the parental rights?"

Noah made a humming noise, his hands gripping the back of my chair as he thought about his answer. Instead of Noah's voice, I heard a deeper one. One that held a rasp that felt like fingertips skating down my spine.

"Not sure what you're looking for, but I can tell you where it's fucking not. And that's in Fal's cleavage."

Oh, hell.

CHAPTER TWO

Kye

I'D GOTTEN GOOD AT FIGHTING OFF TRIGGERS TO MY TEMPER over the years, learning to deal with the monster that lived inside me. But some things were always a tripwire: someone harming those more vulnerable than them, anyone hurting an animal, and Fallon.

Nothing could send my temper flying quicker than someone messing with Sparrow.

I wasn't an idiot. I saw how Fal's so-called coworker looked at her. The way he'd always looked at her. The only one who seemed oblivious to it was Fallon.

But he was getting bolder. Like the way he'd been hovering over her, guarding her like a precious toy he didn't want any of the other kids to play with. Or how his gaze wasn't on her computer screen but down her shirt.

My hands fisted, the ink on my skin rippling with the move. It took everything I had not to let my temper grab hold. I didn't have room for fuckups. Not with my history.

It didn't matter that it was a juvenile record; it still had the potential to bring the hammer down if I took a wrong step. Assault. An illegal fight ring. Getting mixed up with what the courts called *organized crime*. It didn't matter that I'd had my reasons at the time; they were all black marks on my record. And on my soul.

Noah made a startled sound and whirled around. "I'm not looking at her cleavage."

I simply stared back at him, unmoving.

Fallon sighed—the weary kind that said she didn't know what to do with me. "Ignore him. His overprotectiveness knows no bounds."

"Not sure that's what it is," Noah muttered, returning to his desk.

I eased a bit as his distance from Fallon grew. It wasn't that I didn't know that Fal would meet someone someday. Fall in love. Truly move on with her life in a way that was more than a handful of dates here and there. It would kill me, but I'd be happy if the man was truly worthy of her. Because she deserved all the good things this world had to offer.

"Kyler," Fallon said, arching a brow as she swung her chair around. "What are you doing here?"

My dick twitched at the use of my formal name. I lived for those moments. The way they reminded me of what had almost been. Of the few fleeting seconds she'd been mine. Even if she only said it now if I was in trouble. Sometimes, I wondered if I purposely pissed her off just so she would call me Kyler.

I lifted a bag with *The Mix Up* in teal lettering across it. "Thought you might need more than sugar to get through the day."

Fallon's expression softened. She unfolded from the desk chair as a smile tugged at her mouth. "Tell me it's the spinach and artichoke grilled cheese."

"Not gonna go out of my way to bring you lunch and do you dirty."

Her lips twitched. "I can always count on you."

She could. Always. It didn't matter if she needed me in the middle of the night or from a million miles away. I'd be there.

"Picnic tables?" I asked, knowing it was her preferred lunch spot, even when it was freezing.

"Yup." She shrugged on her jacket, pulling acres of blond hair from under the collar.

My fingers twitched, dying to reach out and tangle in the strands, every part of me so damn attuned to Fallon's beauty. It was the kind that only grew the longer you looked at her. The way the curve of her smile turned her mouth into a perfect bow I wanted to tug on with my teeth. How the deep blue of her eyes turned stormy with any heightened emotion—good or bad. And her shape—how she fit perfectly against me any time I dared to wrap an arm around her.

Fuck.

I shoved all of that down like I always did and headed outside.

The November temperatures hovered in the mid-forties, but it was cold enough that I'd opted for my truck instead of my bike today. At least Central Oregon had the sun to take the edge off.

Fallon took a deep breath as we headed for one of the picnic tables. "Smells like snow."

"Bite your tongue."

She laughed as she settled on one of the benches, and the sound rattled around in my empty chest, making itself at home there. "You never were one for the white stuff," she said, pulling her jacket tighter.

"People think it's all enchanting, but it's really just a cold, wet, broken bone waiting to happen."

One side of Fallon's mouth kicked up. "Okay, Grinch."

I opened the bag and pulled out her sandwich, drink, and a few cookies. "I am not a grinch. Christmas movies? Hell, yes. Especially *Die Hard.*"

Fallon rolled her eyes. "*Die Hard* is *not* a Christmas movie."

"Then *Little Women* isn't either," I challenged.

Fallon unwrapped her sandwich. "You fight dirty."

"I'm also a fan of Christmas cookies, presents, and forced time off work," I continued.

"Okay, okay. You're Santa's secret elf. Happy?"

"Been called a lot of things. Can't say Santa's secret elf has been one of them."

Fallon grinned. "A supersized elf?"

I grunted and pulled out my turkey sandwich. "So, how's everything going?"

Fallon eyed me carefully. "Is that what this is about? A checkup?"

I shrugged, but the truth was I'd always check on her. Until we were old and gray and cursing at kids to get off our lawns. "You've been pushing pretty hard."

"You're one to talk," she muttered.

I grinned. "Work hard, play hard."

That had a scowl twisting her lips. "I do *not* need to know about your extracurricular activities."

A sour sensation swept through my gut, but it was better this way: letting Fallon believe countless women were warming my bed, when the truth was the damn thing was as frigid as the Arctic tundra.

"You're not answering my question," I pressed.

Fallon took a bite of her sandwich, buying time. "I just have a larger-than-normal caseload."

"How many?"

She moved to take another bite, but I caught her wrist, stilling the motion. The feel of Fallon's skin scalded me the way it always did, leaving beautiful burns in its wake. "How many, Fal?"

"Thirty-two," she whispered.

I cursed. "You're going to work yourself into the ground."

A little fire entered those deep blue eyes, darkening the irises and turning them to glittering sapphires. "I know what I can handle."

"Do you? Or are you just willing to hurt yourself for the sake of others?"

That fire burned brighter. "They're worth it, and you damn well know it. Nothing's more important than making sure they have someplace safe to rest while their worlds are upended."

"*You're* more important. How many kids can you help if you end up in the hospital from exhaustion?"

Hurt flickered in Fallon's eyes. "I'm not weak."

Hell.

I set my sandwich down and did something I rarely allowed myself to do anymore. I curled my pinky around hers and squeezed.

"The last thing I think you are is weak, Sparrow. But we miss you. Your family misses you."

If anything happened to her, I wouldn't survive it. And I knew all too well how much vile cruelty and violence lived in the world—just as I knew that Fallon placed herself right in the middle of it, time after time.

My truck rumbled to a stop in my parking spot outside Blackheart Ink. Everything about it was black on black on black. The wood façade of the building on the outskirts of Sparrow Falls had been stained a shadowy tone that Shep hadn't been all that sure about at the time. But my contractor brother had used the color on several renovation projects and new builds since. The sign for the shop was a matte black you could only see in certain light.

Jericho said it was moronic not to have a sign you could read easily, but I thought it added to the mystique of the place. And I'd been right. After an article in *The New York Times* titled "The New Face of Ink" came out, business in my little corner of the world exploded. The fact that it felt like a secret speakeasy with a hidden name only added to the allure.

I hated the attention that article—and subsequent ones—had brought, but I didn't hate the resulting cash. Lines of ink, tools, and even apparel meant I was more than comfortable. And when I discovered I had a penchant for the stock market, that comfort had grown to a sum I'd never spend in this lifetime. It was so far from what I'd grown up in and with, and something my so-called father never would've believed.

Climbing out of my truck, I slammed the door and headed toward Blackheart. I flexed my hand, my pinky still tingling from where it had been linked with Fal's. I wanted to burn it into my flesh forever—and forget it at the same time. I shoved the battle for supremacy down and tried to focus on what came next.

Walking past a row of vehicles, I cracked my neck: Penelope's bright-pink Caddy, Bear's and Jericho's bikes, and a couple others I didn't recognize. A bell jingled as I opened the front door, and Bear looked up from the reception desk.

The grizzly grandpa of a biker grinned at me. "Runnin' a little late, boss man. Get distracted with Miss Fal?"

I scowled at him. "You look like you need more work to do."

He leaned back in his chair and patted his leg, which had a prosthetic for its lower half. "I dunno. Feels like snow. You know my leg acts up when it snows."

I scoffed. "You could take on a two-ton grizzly in a snowstorm and still bring us cookies."

"Don't forget the cookies," Jericho called from one of the tattoo chairs, where he was inking some delicate lotus flowers on a very attractive redhead.

Jericho had been with me since the day I opened my doors. Together, we'd managed to extricate ourselves from the Reapers' hold—and I had Trace to thank for that. He'd put enough fear into the motorcycle club for them to steer clear. Having law enforcement permanently parked outside their clubhouse wasn't exactly ideal. And they'd wanted it gone badly enough to free us and end the underground fights.

"Cookies are the only thing keeping you employed," I called as I headed for my station. I also had a closed room in the back, but I liked knowing what was happening in the shop. Getting a feel for what was going on and who was coming through its doors.

Bear leaned back on his stool and crossed his arms over his barrel chest. "This shop would fall apart without me."

He was right, and we knew it—even if he had an organizational system no one else could understand.

I grabbed my sketching pencils and notepad and kicked up in the empty chair at my station. I needed to work on an addition to a client's sleeve. He'd given me a couple of touchstones, but beyond that, I had free rein. It was my favorite way to work: knowing some things that had meaning and bringing my artistry to it all. The client's trust meant something.

"Priest, you want to hit Haven later and spar?" Jericho asked from next to me.

I needed a sparring session desperately. It didn't matter that I'd left behind the more nefarious aspects of mixed martial arts; it was still one of the few places I felt free. Art, MMA, and Fallon. That was my trifecta, and it always would be.

My fingers moved, the pencil skimming across the page in delicate strokes. "Can't. Family dinner."

I felt eyes on me but didn't look up. I knew it wasn't Jericho. He was too focused on his work. And it wasn't coming from Bear's direction. It had to be the redhead. I was proven right when she spoke. "You're Kyler Blackwood, aren't you?"

My gaze flicked over to her briefly, but it was long enough to see hers fixed on me. "That's me."

Her eyes lit then, the green sparking. "I tried to get in with you, but they said you were booked out for six months."

"You're welcome," Bear called.

Jesus.

Jericho lifted the tip of the tattoo machine from her skin. "What am I? Chopped liver?"

The redhead giggled and sent heart eyes in his direction. "Never."

A little of the tension weaving around me eased. All sorts of people came in for ink. Those who truly loved the art, those looking for a thrill, those wanting to memorialize a loss or something they'd lived through... And then there were those who used it for the high.

The redhead seemed to be the latter. But it wasn't just women. Men could be ink addicts, too. People who wanted to be as close as possible to the culture of it—the artists, the buzz—but either didn't want to put in the work to become artists themselves or didn't have the skill.

I refocused on my drawing, but footsteps soon sounded down the hall. "Here's your aftercare kit. Make sure you follow the directions and all the steps. If anything gets red or hot to the touch, it's time to see a doctor."

Penelope appeared, leading a woman who looked to be in her mid-forties with a new septum piercing out into reception. "Thanks, Pen."

Penelope hugged her, her unicorn hair of light pinks, purples, and blues swishing around her. "Take care."

As the woman checked out, Penelope turned to me, assessing. "You look tired."

What was new? My demons had been riding me extra hard the last few months. And everything Trace went through with his douchebag of a father recently had stirred them up even more. Sometimes, it felt like I was waging war with them every night.

Memories of my father coming at me with that knife. My mother's voice swirling around and around in my head. *"Worthless. Everything you touch, you ruin."*

"I'm fine," I bit out.

Penelope let out a scoff. "Want me to get you lunch?"

"Already ate with Fal."

Penelope's mouth tightened—the barest amount—but I didn't miss it. Just like I didn't miss her subtle invitations. They never crossed a line, and I did my best to let her know the door wasn't open, but she never quite seemed to get the message.

Jericho looked up from his lotus flower, his blond beard glinting in the studio lights. "How come you never offer to get me lunch?"

"Because I have a modicum of taste," Penelope shot back.

"You crush me."

She just shook her head, but did it with a grin. "Going to grab something at The Mix Up. Be back."

She headed out the door with her client just as the sound of a motorcycle lit the air. It didn't matter how much time passed; that noise always had me on alert until I knew the owner was a friendly. I swiveled my chair around and grimaced as I caught sight of the bike through one of the front windows. I knew it in a single glance.

The flames encircling the skull were so over-the-top and cliché

I couldn't help the way my lip curled. But it wasn't just that. It was what it signified. The Reapers. And the small emblem on the fuel tank marked the rider as an enforcer for the MC—one I knew all too well.

The bell over the door jingled as Oren stepped inside. "Afternoon."

I stared at the man I'd once thought was a friend but realized never was. "What are you doing here?"

He shrugged, his leather cut shifting with the action. "I missed you assholes. I can't come say hello?"

"No." The answer was simple and to the point. All I needed. He'd lost that privilege when he tried to keep Jericho from calling the cops the night I nearly lost my life in that damn fight circle.

Oren's brown eyes narrowed as he turned to Jericho. "He speak for you now, too?"

Jericho glanced up from his work and then looked back down. "In this case, yes."

"Look. I wanted to give you an opportunity. Prez is putting together a fight. One-hundred-K purse. Thought you might want in."

My gut tightened. Apparently, the fights weren't as dead as I'd thought. Or they were making a comeback. That was risky as fuck for the Reapers. "Pass," I clipped.

"Ditto," Jericho said.

Lines of strain bracketed Oren's mouth like an endless chain of parentheses. "You should be honored he extended the invite."

It was my turn to scoff. "It's an *honor* that he wants to get us mixed up in the same shit that got us arrested? Got me beat to hell? Almost dead? Thanks, but no thanks."

Oren took one step toward me. "Remember you made this choice."

"Boy," Bear called from behind the reception desk. "Get gone before I set Trace on your ass. Or worse, I handle you myself."

Oren sent a scathing look in his direction. "You think I'm scared of some weekend warrior? Please."

Bear wasn't fazed, even for a second. "The measure of a man

doesn't come down to the amount of stupid shit he gets into. Might do you well to remember that."

Oren's gaze swept the room. "Could've been friends of the club. Remember that, too." And then he stalked out and started his bike.

"Fuck," Jericho muttered as he set down his tattoo machine.

"He's all talk," I assured my friend.

But I wasn't sure I completely believed that. Oren came around now and then, trying to needle us. I got the sense it was mainly because he was bored or lonely. But he'd never asked us to come back or to fight. Which meant something was going on.

Memories of that time in my life swirled, trying to dig in their icy claws: my bare knuckles striking someone's jaw, a fist smashing into my ribs, falling to the cement floor, feeling all the pain until I felt nothing at all.

And waking up in the hospital with a pale-faced Fallon at my side, seeing the tears welling in her eyes. *"You can't leave, Kyler. Promise me you won't leave me."*

I'd promised. And it was one I intended to keep. Even if I'd only ever have pieces of her. Those tiny shards were better than anything else.

CHAPTER THREE

Fallon

It had been hours since I'd sat at that picnic table with Kye. Hours since I'd felt his pinky curved around mine. Hours since I'd heard those words. But I could still feel the heat of his finger, the buzz it left beneath my skin. And that single sentence still haunted me.

"The last thing I think you are is weak, Sparrow."

I fought the urge to close my eyes and trace his face in my mind. That dark scruff tipping almost into beard territory. The even darker hair that was just a little wild. The scar that ran parallel to his eyebrow. The way those amber eyes burned into me.

Dumb, dumb, dumb.

I tried to shove the image of Kye down as I flipped on my blinker to turn onto the gravel road that would take me to Colson Ranch. Take me home. But the words still echoed in my mind. And I couldn't help but hold tight to one in particular.

Sparrow.

He'd told me once that he called me that because he'd found me singing. Though he likely meant screaming. Letting loose everything

I'd been holding on to so tightly inside. But the nickname had come to mean so much more to me.

Just thinking it had me struggling to suck in a breath. Kye rarely used the nickname these days. But when he did, it felt like a knife to the heart and the most precious gift imaginable. It didn't matter that it caused me pain. I still clung to it with everything I had.

Sparrow.

I pressed a palm to my chest, rubbing the spot between my breasts, the one that always ached when I missed Kye—especially in the way I used to have him.

The closer I got to the ranch, the more I tried to shove those thoughts away. They had to go back into that secret compartment in my heart where I always kept them. It was better that way for everyone—everyone but me. But I could make the sacrifice.

As the house came into view, warmth spread through me, the kind that came from countless beautiful memories. It eased the sting of my sacrifice a bit. It also reminded me that I needed to prioritize my family, even when work got busy.

The white farmhouse had been around for generations, but Mom and Lolli had made sure it remained in perfect shape. They painted it every few years, oiled the rockers and porch swings every spring and fall, and maintained the gardens with a single-minded focus—even if Lolli's personal garden had a few so-called *herbs* that were far from just medicinal.

I passed Trace's sheriff's department SUV that I knew housed his daughter Keely's booster seat and likely a few painting supplies from his girlfriend Ellie's new interior design gig. I grinned as I saw Anson's black truck with a new flower bumper sticker that read: *Stop and smell the roses.* He'd *hate* it. And I needed to know if my bestie-sister, Rho, was responsible or if it was Shep's doing since Anson worked for him.

I spotted the Range Rover I knew belonged to Arden's fiancé, Linc, and Shep's truck with the Colson Construction logo on the side. The only missing vehicle was Cope's over-the-top SUV since he, Sutton, and Sutton's son, Luca, were in Seattle for the hockey season.

I did my best not to focus on the second black truck in the

lineup. The one with the artful, matte-black accents I knew Kye had drawn himself before having them detailed onto his precious baby. Everything Kye had was so…him.

My hatchback sputtered slightly as I pulled into the final makeshift parking spot. I gave her another pat. "Just one more winter."

I was saving as much as possible, but it wasn't like my salary would make me a millionaire. So, it took careful adjustments here and there: less takeout, more meal prep, cutting my cable—even though I loved movies. At least I still had Kye's Netflix password. There were countless tiny concessions, but it would all work out.

Climbing out of my car, I was grateful I'd taken the time to change into jeans, boots, and a flannel. The November air had gotten even cooler this afternoon, and it was downright cold now. Grabbing my bag, I headed for the steps but came up short at the towering, tattooed mountain of a man standing in front of them, a scowl on his face.

I let out a tiny yelp of surprise. "What are you doing out here?" I hadn't had time to shore up my defenses or put up all my walls. So, I found myself tracing the tattoos on his neck with my gaze: the sparrow tucked just behind his ear and the anchor with artful script around it. Every tattoo had a story, and I couldn't help but wonder if that sparrow was for me. But then again, we did live in Sparrow Falls. It could've been a nod to that just as easily.

"You're late," Kye grumbled.

I glanced at my watch. "Fifteen minutes. I wanted to change."

His scowl only deepened. "What's wrong with your car?"

I rolled my eyes and tried to sidestep him. "It's older than dirt."

"Fallon," Kye growled as he blocked my path.

"It'll be fine. Just one more winter, and I can get a new one." Or a new-to-me one. I'd never had a brand-new car in my life. But I'd take one that didn't sound like a chain smoker after their fifth pack of the day.

"I'll look at it this weekend."

I sent Kye a look that should've had him stepping back. "I don't need you to look at it."

His amber eyes flashed with something I couldn't identify. "You don't want to get stranded somewhere. Or break down on the side of the road. It's not safe. Especially given some of the places you go."

That last sentence sounded like he'd ground it out through gritted teeth and a world of frustration.

"Kye—"

"Please."

Damn it all to health food hell. The one thing I was powerless against—Kye asking. And worse than that was seeing the worry in those amber eyes.

"Fine. But I cover the cost of any new parts it needs."

A grin curved Kye's mouth, and I felt it in that spot along my sternum that belonged only to him. "Thank you," he said, wrapping an arm around my shoulders and guiding me toward the house. "Did that creeper leave you alone for the rest of the day?"

"Creeper?" I asked, confusion furrowing my brow.

"Noah," Kye ground out.

I sighed. "He seemed slightly terrified of me for the rest of the day, so thanks for that." Every time Noah needed to ask me something, he looked over my head instead of at me.

"Good."

"You traumatized the poor man," I shot back.

Kye scoffed. "If that traumatized him, he needs a little more life experience."

"Whatever," I muttered.

As we trudged up the steps, the front door opened, and my mom appeared. "There's my baby girl."

Kye's arm slipped off my shoulders, and I went straight for her. Mom wrapped me in a tight hug, the scent of cinnamon and apples swirling around me. "Apple pie?" I mumbled into her neck.

"I had some sort of sixth sense that my girl needed some comfort food."

"You are the bestest mom ever. Do you know that?"

She laughed. "It never hurts to hear it once in a while."

"Do I get some of that apple pie, too?" Kye asked hopefully.

Mom arched a brow at him. "That depends. Are you and Lolli going to start trouble?"

The grin on Kye's face widened. "Of course."

Mom threw up her hands and moved back into the house. "I give up."

"We just like to keep you on your toes," Kye said.

"You like to give me gray hair," Mom shot back. There was a little more silver woven through the light-brown strands now. It looked beautiful, but it reminded me that she was getting older, and that wasn't something I was fond of thinking about.

Voices and sounds of chaos filtered out of the living room. We moved in that direction, passing countless familiar landmarks along the way. Family photos. The vase that had been glued back together after Cope and Kye broke it during a round of indoor football. A painting of our house and land that Arden had done for Mom. A frame that Trace and Shep had gotten her one Christmas, complete with a chaotic family photo. A potted plant Rho had nurtured from a seedling just for Mom. A clock that had been passed down through the Colson family for generations.

I loved that the house was a patchwork of memories, just like our family—brought together in unexpected ways but with heart. The familiar sounds of chaos got louder as we approached the living room.

"She made it," Rhodes cheered as I walked in, her newly acquired engagement ring flashing in the light.

"Auntie Fal!" Keely yelled, jumping up from where she'd been coloring with Ellie and Arden. She ran at me, and I caught her on the fly, stumbling back a few steps until Kye steadied me. Keely hugged me tightly. "I've been missing you."

I rocked her back and forth, realizing that Trace's daughter had somehow grown since I'd seen her last week. "I've missed you, too. And look at these braids. Aren't you fabulous?"

Keely grinned as I set her down. "Ellie's teaching Daddy some new ones. It's an infinity braid. Isn't it the coolest?" Keely spun in a circle, sending her hair flying.

Trace lifted a beer from his spot in the kitchen where he was helping Mom prep a salad. "I think this one is above my pay grade."

Kye's lips twitched as he moved to sit in one of the overstuffed chairs. "Never took you for a quitter."

"He's right," Lolli said from her spot on one of the stools at the kitchen island. "If I would've quit my diamond paintings because of how hard those damned little gemstones are to maneuver, you all wouldn't have the gorgeous works of art you have now."

Shep started choking. "Gorgeous works of art?"

His girlfriend, Thea, thumped him on the back as she struggled not to laugh. "I love my diamond painting."

"Penis pumpkins," Trace argued. "She made you penis pumpkins."

Kye lifted his beer. "I really prefer dick gourds."

Linc chuckled from his spot on the couch. "It does have a certain ring. But it'll never beat my dick sticks diamond painting."

Keely looked around the room. "What's a dick stick?"

Trace set down his knife and sighed. "Seriously? Keely's teacher is already concerned because she suggested riding cowboys instead of horses on their field trip to the animal rescue."

"Supergran said it was a good idea," Keely argued.

Lolli lifted her cocktail glass. "It's the best idea."

It was then that I fully took in her outfit. She wore tie-dyed bell bottoms in every color of the rainbow, bedazzled high-top Chucks, and a T-shirt that made me blink a few times. Across the front was a rhinestone heart with a pot leaf in the center, and below it, in artful script, were the words: *Keep Blazing Stay Amazing*.

"Lolls," I said, struggling not to laugh as I made my way to her. "You *are* amazing."

She beamed at me. Once I was within arm's reach, she pulled me to her and kissed my cheeks. "You've always been my favorite."

The room erupted with shouts of protest. Lolli just winked at me.

I carried plates into the kitchen with Shep's help as everybody else talked over pie in the living room. That was the thing about our family. We had a good cadence. Whoever cooked never cleaned, everyone helped out with whichever kids were around, and no one left a family dinner feeling like the rest of the crew hadn't checked in on them.

So, it wasn't surprising when Shep asked, "How's the caseload?"

"Kye say something?" I grumbled.

"He might've mentioned that you're almost ten cases over the recommended number."

Of course, he had. I knew he was only concerned, but having my entire family on my case wouldn't help.

Shep knocked my shoulder with his. "Go easy on him. He's worried about you." Shep's gaze flicked to where Ellie was curled into Trace's side, Keely at their feet. "And I think what happened to Trace triggered him."

Only a handful of weeks ago, Trace had been targeted by his father—recently out of prison and hell-bent on revenge. Trace and Ellie had nearly lost their lives, thanks to Jasper and the people working with him. I'd seen the toll it took on Kye, but as I searched him out now and noticed the shadows beneath his eyes, worry gnawed at me.

"He's not sleeping," I mumbled.

Shep handed me a plate. "Not much. He talk to you?"

I shook my head as I rinsed the dish. "No. I've tried. He just won't go there." The most Kye would give me was quiet, where the two of us simply...were. A trip out to the river or a nearby creek. Anything with water, nature, and peace. He occasionally let something slip. But lately? He wouldn't say a word about what was actually swirling in his head, and he disappeared often, sometimes for days.

"Give him some time," Shep encouraged. "If he talks to anyone, it'll be you."

An invisible fist ground into my sternum. I wanted to believe that. But more than anything, I wanted Kye to be okay. "How are you and Thea doing?" I asked, trying to steer the conversation away from things that might have me revealing too much.

A soft smile overtook Shep's face as he searched out Thea in the room. Her brown hair was slowly giving way to her natural blond tone now, and her green eyes shone as she animatedly talked with Rhodes. "We're good. Better than good. She's been helping me more and more with landscape designs for my builds. It's been great to have her input."

"Love that you guys can do that together." But it was more than that. I loved that they had each other. The two of them had brought healing where neither had thought they would find peace.

"Me, too," Shep agreed.

My cell phone buzzed in my back pocket, and I pulled it out, glancing at the screen before swiping my finger across the device to answer. "Hey, Rose."

"Sorry to bother you after hours," Rose said.

"That's okay." It was the nature of the job. You were rarely off the clock. "What's up?"

"Remember the little girl and her sister that you flagged for us? Gracie and Hayden Jensen?"

I stiffened. "Sure. You said Noah didn't find anything." Gracie was a friend and classmate of Keely's, who had always seemed on the shyer side. The fact that her older sister always picked her up from school had flagged something for Trace. When Cope was in town this past summer to teach a hockey camp, he'd gotten to know Hayden, who played girls' hockey. He'd mentioned that it seemed like she was more a mother than a sister to the little girl.

"At the time, he didn't," Rose said. "Teachers said homework's always done for Gracie, Hayden, and their middle sister, Clementine. Clothes aren't the nicest, but they're always clean. They have lunches. No one has seen any physical injuries on the girls, besides one or two bruises on Hayden that she said were from hockey. And we know she plays the sport."

"But?" Because I knew there was a *but*.

"There was an incident tonight," Rose went on.

My stomach pitched. The word *incident* could mean anything. But it was never good. "What happened?"

"Mercer County Sheriff's Department got a call about a fight in one of the trailers at The Meadows." The RV park and cabins were in an area of Sparrow Falls that wasn't always the greatest. There were hardworking people struggling to get by, but there was also a fair amount of drug activity in the area.

My fingers closed tighter around my phone as I moved away from the noise of my family. "What'd they find?"

"Lieutenant Rivera is on the scene, but he didn't tell me much other than it's clear Hayden's mother hit her."

I bit the inside of my cheek so hard that the metallic taste of blood filled my mouth. "I should've pushed harder. Both Cope and Trace knew something was off."

"Fallon," Rose said gently. "You know it doesn't work that way. You can't remove a child from a home just because you have a bad feeling."

"I could've asked Noah to stop by the home again. Keep checking in," I pressed. He might not have been able to get inside without due cause, but we could've worked harder to find it.

"And opened us up to a harassment suit? You know better than that."

An invisible fist squeezed my heart. Sometimes, it felt like there was no winning in this career. Like you were trying to help with a blindfold on and both hands tied behind your back.

"What can I do?" I might not be able to go back and change the past, but I could do whatever I could to help now.

"I know you're already over your max caseload, but do you want to be their caseworker?"

"Yes." The word was out of my mouth instantly.

"Case is yours. Noah's on his way. As I said, the sheriff's department is on the scene."

"Okay. I'm leaving the ranch now. It'll take me about twenty minutes to get there."

"Sorry to interrupt your family dinner."

I shook my head, even though she couldn't see me. "You know it's worth it every time."

"Call me if you need anything."

"Thanks, Rose." I hit end on the call and turned around, only to come face-to-face with two hulking forms sporting stormy expressions. I might've been intimidated if I didn't know them and hadn't seen them playing tea party with Keely or nursing an orphaned calf. But I had. So, instead, I simply said, "I need to go."

"What was the call?" Trace asked, his worried brow furrowing deeper.

It would cut him the same way it had me. I wanted to save him that. But I knew he'd find out first thing in the morning anyway. "There was an incident at Gracie's house. Her mom struck her older sister, Hayden."

Energy crackled through the air like tiny whips of pure electricity lashing at my skin. Kye's hands fisted, making the ink on his knuckles ripple while Trace's dark green eyes deepened to a stormy shade.

"I'm coming with you," Trace said instantly.

Kye jerked his head in a nod. "Me, too." But those two words were wound so tightly, I knew he was battling his demons. His memories.

That place between my breasts, the bone that kept me together, ached like something was eating away at the marrow. Because I couldn't handle Kye being in pain. Would do anything to stop it. But I had to deal with Trace first.

"Gabriel's got this. You know you can't work the case, given you have a personal relationship with one of the potential victims." My words were gentle, but I didn't lose Trace's eyes.

He let out an indiscernible grumble, then his gaze moved to his daughter, who was blissfully ignorant about what was happening. Ellie cast a concerned glance our way every so often, though.

I squeezed Trace's forearm. "Go be with your family. I'll call as soon as I'm done so you can prep Keely. Gracie's going to need her."

"Okay." The word was more an expulsion of air than anything else. But he was already moving. Heading back to his girls—the ones his whole world revolved around. And wouldn't that be nice? To be someone's anchor in that way.

My fingers twisted in my necklace as I turned to Kye. His whole body almost vibrated, and I had to fight back the instinct to touch him. "Tell me."

It was always my gentle command. Not a question, but a deep need to know what swirled inside Kyler's mind.

"Don't want you walking into a volatile situation," he ground out, his pinky curling around mine.

"I'm not," I assured him. "The sheriff's department is already there. I'm just going to support the girls and get them settled in their temporary emergency foster placements."

Kye's jaw clamped tighter, and a muscle pulsed like an early warning system. "You never know when something could turn."

My brows pulled together as I tried to look deeper. As if I could peel back every layer of this man and uncover what he was truly feeling. "Talk to me. What's going on?"

He opened his mouth to say something but closed it again. He just stared at me like he was searching for something, too. Like I was his lifeline, and he needed to make sure I was still there. "It's been bad lately."

My fingers twisted tighter in my necklace. "I know."

"I don't know how to silence all the darkness. It's just…it's drowning me."

The ache in my chest turned into a blazing pain, and I couldn't hold back any longer. I locked my pinky with his, squeezing tightly. "I'm here." It was all I could give him. I couldn't erase his pain or stop the demons that had flared to life after everything Trace went through. All I could do was weather the storm with him.

"I know." Kye's eyes held mine, and for a moment, I thought he might pull me closer. He didn't. "Thank you."

"I'll call you after I'm done," I promised. "And I'll be with Gabriel the whole time."

He jerked his head in a nod. "I'm going to Haven. Get a workout in."

Trying to fight back those demons.

"Okay. Don't push yourself too hard." I didn't want him to get hurt or worse.

He ignored that and said, "You have your location on?"

"You'd yell at me if I didn't."

He tried to smile but didn't quite get there. "I like knowing where you are so I know you're safe."

I gave his pinky another squeeze. "Trust me to take care of myself."

Kye's amber eyes swirled with varying hues of gold and rich brown. "There's no one I trust more."

CHAPTER FOUR

Fallon

DARKNESS HAD DESCENDED BY THE TIME I DROVE THROUGH The Meadows. There was a wide array of dwellings—everything from cabins and manufactured homes to trailers and RVs. There was also a wide array of care. Some houses were kept with pride and attention to detail—fall mums and decorations for Thanksgiving dotting the lawns and front steps. Others had broken-down cars and trash in the yards, and it didn't look like anyone had taken care of the homes in years.

I saw at least half a dozen vehicles in the distance, gathered around a trailer at the end of the street, including a few sheriff's department vehicles, an ambulance, and Noah's sedan. My stomach sank when I saw Dr. Avery's SUV.

I forced myself to sweep my surroundings, Kye's voice in my head. *"Always know what you're walking into. Eyes on every angle so you're not surprised."* While he hadn't been willing to train me in self-defense, he had drilled the rules into my head.

I took in the residents' various reactions to the presence of law enforcement and emergency personnel. Some stood out in their front yards, looking concerned. Others looked pissed off that someone had infiltrated their oasis. Still more only peeked out of blinds and from behind window coverings.

A group of young guys wearing baggy jeans and tank tops or T-shirts despite the temperature being in the mid-forties gathered in one yard, talking animatedly and gesturing at the sheriff's department presence with clear annoyance. We needed to keep an eye trained there. But I also needed to watch the man who sat stone-faced, viewing the action like a hawk. It wasn't always the people you expected. Sometimes, the quietest ones held the most danger.

I parked my hatchback next to Noah's sedan, and my vehicle made that sputtering noise again. I didn't have it in me to worry about it at the moment because I'd seen the gathering behind the trailer: a group crowded around a picnic table.

Still, I forced myself to take in my surroundings again. This time, it wasn't to look for threats. It was to try to read the story the Jensens' home told. The trailer was dilapidated. Siding peeled in places, and the paint was dingy. But I saw where someone had tried to put the siding back into place using nails and duct tape.

The front yard was full of long grass and rusted lawn furniture that likely hadn't been used in years. There were no fall decorations or signs that kids lived in the area at all. Until I looked past the trailer and into the backyard. I could see part of it from my vantage point and realized that someone had cleared an area to put in a swing set.

The equipment was simple but looked as if it had been cared for and used often. It had a slide with scuffs and two swings with worn seats. *Someone* here cared for these girls, and I needed to know who.

I climbed out of my vehicle and reached for my bag and coat before locking my car. I pulled my jacket on and headed for the huddle in the backyard. I recognized Dr. Avery by his white hair as I approached, spotting an EMT holding a bright light so the physician could see what he was doing. The moment the sight came into focus for me, I nearly stumbled.

The oldest girl, who I knew was Hayden, had an angry gash down the side of her face that Dr. Avery was meticulously tending, with what looked like liquid stitches. The girl, only fourteen, didn't even flinch as he held her flesh together. And all the while, she held little Gracie in her arms.

Gracie clung to her sister like Hayden was her lifeline. The little girl's eyes were rimmed in red, and tearstains streaked her cheeks. An invisible fist squeezed my heart. Next to them sat a girl who looked to be about ten or eleven. She didn't have dark hair like her two sisters. Hers was red, and freckles dotted her nose. They stood out because of how pale she was. An officer had obviously given her a jacket, and she clutched the edges of it like a vise.

"Fal."

Noah's voice shook me out of my heartbreak. "Sorry," I croaked.

Pain streaked his face, too. "I'm the one who's sorry. I should've pushed harder. Made a second pass. But everything checked out—"

"Don't," I said, quickly squeezing his forearm. "We're here now. Let's do what we can. Do you know what happened yet?"

He shook his head. "We wanted Hayden to get treated first. We tried to get her to go to a hospital, but the girls lost it at the idea of being separated."

Of course, they had. My stomach churned, and nausea rolled through me. "It's better to keep them together as much as possible." But I knew that would be a challenge if they entered the system. Keeping two siblings together was tough. Three would be even harder.

"Dr. Avery got here about twenty minutes ago. He's almost done. Once he is, we can talk to them. A neighbor called it in. Heard the screaming and glass shattering. Crying."

I nodded, taking in each blow of information but desperate to get to the girls. Gabriel was hovering nearby, and Beth Hansen, who'd just been promoted to sergeant in the department, sat opposite the sisters. Gabriel gave me a chin lift as I approached. "Fallon."

Hayden's gaze instantly cut to me, assessing the newcomer. All the while, she didn't move an inch.

I sent her a smile and a nod but didn't get any closer. I wouldn't until Dr. Avery was done. I didn't want to put any more stress on Hayden while she was compromised. Instead, I hovered nearby.

"All done, Miss Hayden," Dr. Avery said and straightened. "How's your pain level?"

"It's fine," she said quietly. Gracie gripped her tighter.

Dr. Avery's mouth thinned into a hard line. "I'm going to give you some Tylenol and ibuprofen now, but I'll also write you a prescription for something stronger in case you need it."

"I can get it filled for her," I said, using that as my excuse to move in.

"Fallon," Dr. Avery greeted. "Good to see you. How are Arden and those babies doing?"

My sister was a few months along, and her stomach was just starting to swell. I smiled at the doctor. "I tried to see if they'd kick at their favorite aunt today, but no dice."

Dr. Avery chuckled. "I think it's still a little early for that."

Gracie's head lifted from her sister's shoulder, her eyes searching me out. Recognition from the various school events I'd attended for Keely flashed across her features. "Miss Fallon?"

"Hi, Miss Gracie. It's so good to see you."

Gracie's lower lip trembled, and I had the sudden urge to break something. Hayden's gaze narrowed on me. "Who are you?"

I lowered myself to the picnic bench, and Noah sat beside me. "I'm Fallon. And this is Noah. We work with the state and look out for the best interests of kids when they need some additional support."

"You mean you work for CPS." Her gaze flicked to Noah. "You were the one checking into us before."

Noah's Adam's apple bobbed as he swallowed. "That was me, yes."

"Miss Fallon is Keely's aunt," Gracie told her sister.

Hayden's eyes widened a fraction. "Cope's sister?"

I knew she and my hockey star brother had made a connection during the hockey camp he'd taught, but it was clear there was hero worship in her whiskey-colored eyes. "One of many," I said. "He talked a lot about you. Said you have a killer wrist shot."

Pure pride filled Hayden's expression, but she quickly covered it. "When can we get back in the house?"

Noah and I shared a look, but it was Noah who spoke. As an investigator in the Child Protective Services arm of DHS, his role was to examine all the angles. "Can you tell us what happened, Hayden?"

Her gaze slid to the side. "It was an accident—"

"No, it wasn't!" the redhead burst out. "She threw the glass at your *head*."

"Stop it, Clem," Hayden hissed, then looked at us. "It was an accident. It slipped."

Clementine glanced at Noah. "Mom slapped Hayden because she said she sassed her, and then she tried to come for me, but Hayden got in the way. Mom was so mad she threw her glass at her."

"She had a little too much to drink. It was an accident," Hayden gritted out.

Gracie started to cry again, her tiny shoulders shaking. "Please, Hay Hay. I don't want her to hurt you anymore."

The *anymore* had my hands fisting at my sides. This hadn't been the first time.

Clementine's eyes filled with tears. "What if she hurts you worse next time?"

Hayden's mouth pressed into a thin line, and I saw a weight in her eyes that no fourteen-year-old should be shouldering.

"Ms. Jensen is under arrest. We'll be taking her to the station shortly," Gabriel cut in.

I knew he meant to comfort the girls, but I saw real fear slipping into their expressions at his words.

Noah nodded, looking up from the notepad he was scribbling in. "We'll talk about next steps once we have all the facts."

"Next steps?" Hayden's voice cracked like a whip. "You can't separate us."

"I'm going to do everything I can to keep you guys together," I said quickly. "You'll be staying with a foster family for the next few days to start. We'll take it one step at a time. And you can tell me if something doesn't feel right at any time. Okay?" I kept my voice as gentle as possible, but I knew my tone didn't lessen the heaviness of my words.

The girls were all silent. The younger two looked terrified, and Hayden's face had gone completely blank.

I leaned forward, my arms resting on the picnic table. "I know this is really scary. But my number-one priority is making sure you're safe. I'm going to do everything I can to make that happen. I will also listen to anything you tell me. What you want and don't want. What you think is best for you. And I'll make sure the judge hears that, too. It's my job to be your microphone. Okay?"

Hayden looked dubious at my promise, but Gracie and Clementine nodded.

Gabriel sent me a look. "I'll take you guys into the house so you can get some clothes for the girls."

I looked back at Hayden, Clementine, and Gracie. "Do you guys have any favorite outfits you want me to grab? Any stuffed animals, blankets, special treasures?"

"My squishy Hay Hay got me," Gracie said softly.

Clementine blinked a few times, her face still pale. "Can you get my books for school and my *Hunger Games* book? I was right in the middle."

"Of course. I'll get all your backpacks." I sent Clementine a small smile. "I *love* that one."

"Really?"

My smile widened to a grin. "Team Gale or Team Peeta?"

A hint of pink hit Clementine's cheeks. "Peeta. He's quiet, but he's always looking out for her."

"Sometimes, the quiet ones are the best ones. You know, I think I might need a reread. We can have our own book club." I felt eyes on me, and my gaze flicked to Hayden, who didn't seem thrilled with the idea. "Be right back."

Gabriel led me and Noah toward the house. "I had the officers do a search, and it wasn't pretty."

A hollow feeling settled somewhere deep inside me. "What'd they find?"

"An unsecured thirty-two. Loaded."

My back teeth ground together, but I stayed silent, sensing there was more.

"A stash of meth in one of the drawers in the mom's bedroom. That'll get her a possession charge. The gun isn't registered, and—"

"It's enough to support removing the children from the home," Noah finished.

Gabriel nodded. "I've got a deputy running her criminal history to see if anything else can nudge this into something a judge will move on more quickly. I know nothing popped in earlier searches, but we're just doing our due diligence. And I need you to see the house. It paints a picture. And it's not a fuckin' good one."

I saw it then: the anger Gabriel had been trying to cover so he wouldn't scare the girls. He was furious. And the moment I stepped into the trailer, I saw why.

The scent of stale air and rotting food swirled. Plates were piled high in the sink, and a half-eaten meal had bugs crawling all over it. The carpets in the living room were soiled with who knew what, and countless piles of debris littered the couch. The only empty spot was a recliner in the corner, where empty glasses and some hard seltzer cans sat.

Nausea rolled through me as I covered my nose with my shirt. I couldn't believe the girls had been living like this.

"Primary bedroom's that way." Gabriel headed in the opposite direction. "This is the girls' room."

I stepped inside, and my eyes widened. The small room held a set of bunk beds, a single twin, and two mismatched nightstands that had seen better days. There was a dresser on the far wall near a closet. The entire room was spotless. No marks on the carpets or piles of trash. Other than a handful of dolls and a few stuffed animals that were obviously mid-tea party, even the toys were put away.

My throat constricted, and I struggled to swallow. "Hayden's taking care of them."

Gabriel lifted his chin in assent. "Look at this."

He moved to the closet and opened the doors. At first glance, it looked normal: hanging clothes, shoes, and some boxes. Then Gabriel pushed the clothes and a box aside, revealing a mini fridge tucked into the corner. Opening it, he stepped back so we could see. Milk, cheese, and turkey. Sitting atop the fridge were two boxes of cereal and a sleeve of bread.

"There are other items in the boxes. All hidden under layers of clothes," Gabriel went on.

"They're hiding it from their mom." The fact that the girls needed to do this made me want to rage. Instead, I took a deep breath and started planning. "Noah, we need to file to terminate parental rights. Do we know if there's a father in the picture?"

A muscle in his jaw ticked. "There's a Les Jensen listed on their birth certificates. But none of the teachers I spoke with were familiar with him, and Ms. Jensen said she was a single parent." Noah looked at Gabriel. "Your deputies take photos?"

"I've got every angle you could ask for. Made sure to get the rat droppings, too."

I bit the inside of my cheek and then pulled the empty duffel from my tote bag. We didn't get much funding for extras like travel bags for the kids we worked with. Sometimes, nonprofits stepped in to help, but other times, kids could be left transporting their things in garbage bags. I wasn't about to let that happen. I always bought duffels in bulk whenever they went on sale on Amazon or other similar sites.

"Noah, will you get their school stuff?" I asked.

"On it." He moved around the room as I gathered clothes and shoes and Clem's books. Knowing the girls might never return, I took more than I usually would and included some things that looked like keepsakes. A single framed photo of the three of them. A drawing. A jewelry box filled with beaded bracelets.

Noah lifted two backpacks onto his shoulders and handed a third to Gabriel. "Got everything but the squishy." He said the word *squishy* as if it were foreign.

I moved to the bunks, thinking Gracie would likely be on the bottom. My gaze roamed over the stuffed animals on the bed, settling on one. I bent and picked up the round, purple creature. "A

Squishmallow. They're all the rage with kids these days and very huggable."

I tucked it under my arm and turned back to the group. "Let's get out of here."

"Don't have to twist my arm," Gabriel muttered.

Steeling myself to pass through the rest of the house, I followed Gabriel into the hall. We wove our way back outside, and I sucked in fresh air the moment we passed the threshold.

The sound of cursing had my gaze searching out the source. A woman was struggling against Deputy Fletcher's hold as he tried to guide her toward a squad car. Her hair was a mix of brown and gray, her amber eyes were dull, and her skin was sallow. But I would've known the face anywhere.

I'd only seen a crumpled photo of her and a man once, but the image was burned into my brain. How couldn't it be? It didn't matter that they were younger in the photo or that she looked less ravaged by drugs and hard living. I'd never forget her face. Not when I knew the damage she'd done.

My hand lashed out, gripping Gabriel's arm with a force that had him jerking his head in my direction. My heart hammered against my ribs, and blood roared in my ears. "W-what is she doing here?"

Some part of my brain recognized the confusion on Gabriel's face. "That's Renee Jensen. The girls' mother. You know her?"

"Those girls," I croaked, my brain rapidly putting the pieces together, a sick feeling sinking into my gut. Gracie's, Clementine's, and Hayden's eyes were amber. It was a color I knew better than any in existence. Those girls were Kye's sisters. And he had no idea they existed.

CHAPTER FIVE

Kye

My headlights swung over Haven's nearly empty parking lot, illuminating the mural I'd painted on the outside wall of the building. It blended a few different styles. The lettering was a nod to the role ink played in my life, while the creatures peeking out from behind the letters represented my hometown and nature's role as a calming force. And, of course, there were countless sparrows among it all.

I pulled into a spot near the door, taking stock of who I would find inside. Everyone here tonight had a key to the building—people I trusted to come and go as they pleased. I cared about all of them, but I honestly just wanted them to stay out of my way at the moment.

Climbing out of my truck, I headed to the front door, which was unlocked since my manager was still on the premises. As I stepped inside, I came face-to-face with her.

"What are you doing here?" Serena asked. "I thought you had a family dinner."

"Came from there," I grumbled. "Just need to blow off some steam."

Serena's head tipped to the side, her box braids swinging with the movement. "You need the bar or the bag?"

"You're a good friend." I scrubbed a hand through my hair. "The bag."

"You know where those are. I've got some Jim Beam in my office if that doesn't work."

I saluted her and headed down the hallway to the men's locker room. I changed quickly, not even bothering to lock up my belongings. By the time I made it out to the gym, Serena had retreated to her office. She ran the day-to-day operations of Haven and handled the schedules and hiring. I just signed the checks.

I was damn lucky to have her as my right hand and knew it. And it didn't hurt that she didn't bristle when I got cantankerous. She never took it personally, but she wasn't afraid to put me in my place when I needed it either. And the fact that she'd been a professional MMA fighter for five years meant she could do it.

Rock music spilled out of the speakers as I took in the massive space. The room was a mix of black and gray, except for two walls I'd used as my canvas for additional pieces. There was an infinite array of colors there. *HAVEN* branded the longest wall with all sorts of images springing from it. The murals had taken me months, but when it all came together, it felt like they made the place *mine*.

"Well, look what the cat dragged in," a voice greeted.

I looked at the twenty-one-year-old restocking towels. "Hey, Ev."

Evan's brows rose. "Shit. Who messed with you?"

"I need to work on my poker face," I mumbled. "I'm fine. Just a long-ass day."

"You need anything?" he asked, concern pulling his dark brows together.

I lifted one of my boxing gloves toward a heavy bag. "Just a date with that beauty."

"All right. Holler if that changes," he said, getting back to work.

I'd discovered the kid at barely eighteen, trying to tag my tattoo studio. He'd been drunk and angry at the world. Instead of calling Trace, I'd made him a deal: work off the damages and get a chance at a real job in the end. He'd made it through and now helped Jericho run the youth program at the gym. He also assisted Serena with whatever she needed.

A loud thwack had me looking at a ring, where Jericho and one of our top fighters, Mateo, sparred.

Mateo was on a tear tonight. He was easygoing every moment of the day except when he was in that ring. It was as if it was the one place he truly let his demons loose—demons he kept under lock and key. I understood that. I searched for the same release half the times I walked through the door.

Mateo moved with panther-like grace as he took Jericho to the mat in a single-leg takedown. A handful of seconds later, Jericho tapped out. "Jesus," he grumbled, climbing to his feet and spitting out his mouthguard. "I'm gonna feel that for a week."

But Mateo was already back to his easygoing self, grinning at our friend. "Gotta motivate you to work a little harder."

"Good luck with that," I muttered, dropping my gloves and moving to the jump ropes to begin warming up. Nice and easy to get the muscles warm. I might be itching for the heavy bag, but I wouldn't risk an injury to get to it.

"Not everyone wants to work out five hours a day," Jericho shot back. "Some of us have lives and can still make this look good."

I picked up the pace on my jumps, tossing in a skip step here and there.

Mateo scoffed as he hopped down from the ring. "We all know who looks best around here." He turned to me. "And speaking of looking good, how's my girl, Fal?"

The rope caught on my foot, making me nearly trip.

A grin spread across his face, his eyes twinkling. "She tell you she misses me?"

Jericho slapped him on the back. "You want to get dead? Keep it up. You know no one messes with Fal."

"Especially not someone who gets around as much as you do," Evan called from his new vantage point on the far side of the room.

Mateo sent a scowl in his direction. "I got issues making decisions, that's all."

I grunted, moving toward one of the heavy bags and pulling on my boxing gloves. "Call it whatever you want. Just keep that *indecision* far from Fal."

I felt eyes on me, and my gaze flicked to Jericho, finding him assessing me. He and Oren were the only ones who knew that Fallon and I had a history. Oren was too caught up in his own bullshit to even remember, and Jericho thought we'd moved to a simple friendship. But nothing about Fallon would ever be simple for me.

My gloves tapped the bag in a few testing jabs as the guys smack-talked each other. I tuned them out as I started in on the bag in earnest. Some part of me was aware of them leaving and Serena telling me she was locking up. But it only broke through for a scattering of seconds here and there. Otherwise, it was just me and the bag.

Serena had turned off the stereo when she left, knowing the music I loved most was the sound of my gloves hitting the bag. The tap, tap, thwack. The cadence I could make be whatever I needed. I kept going until my lungs heaved and my muscles ached. Until I felt like I might not be able to stand any longer.

And it still wasn't enough. None of my old tricks were numbing the swirling darkness like they used to. It was as if I needed more and more.

Stepping back from the bag, I bent at the waist, struggling to catch my breath. As I stood, I caught sight of her: blond hair gleaming beneath the gym lights, the strands so long I knew I could get lost in them as I got lost in her. And, God, I wanted that. But as I took in more of Fallon, I instantly went on alert.

Her face was pale. Eyes rimmed with a hint of red that told me she'd cried at some point in the past couple of hours. I didn't wait a goddamned second. I crossed to her in five long strides, tossing my gloves to the floor as I went. "What happened? You're white as a sheet."

I wasn't particularly fond of touch. When you'd experienced

it as nothing but pain for so long, it made you wary of letting someone into that sphere. But Fal was the exception. She always felt safe.

I tried not to let myself do it often. Didn't want to give in to temptation. But without fail, the need for connection—for her—built inside me until I could do nothing to stop it. Only now, I didn't even consider holding myself back.

My hand reached out to cup her face. Her skin was so smooth. Delicate. Like a petal that had never once been exposed to the elements. "Fal."

I searched her dark blue eyes. I'd memorized the countless shades long ago, but I tracked each one now, knowing they'd tell a story. The shades changed with her mood and emotions, and I'd studied every single arrangement.

"It's not me," Fallon whispered, her voice barely audible.

Fuck. Keely's little friend and her sisters. It must have been bad. "We'll talk it through," I promised. "I'll take you to get a double-chocolate Oreo shake, and we'll sit by the river until we've figured it out."

My sparrow was a deep feeler. It was as if the whole world affected her more than most other people. But she didn't run from those feelings. She met them head-on. She'd take all the pain if it meant helping someone along the way.

Fallon shook her head, her cheek still pressed to my palm. "It's about you," she croaked.

My brow furrowed, and confusion swam. "What do you mean?"

Pain swirled in those dark blue irises. No...it was deeper than pain. Agony. "Your mom," she finally rasped.

I stilled, my blood running cold as my hand slowly dropped from Fallon's face.

"She had more kids. You have three half-sisters, and DHS just took them into custody."

CHAPTER SIX

Fallon

I didn't want to tell him. Would've given anything to make the truth disappear. So, I'd stayed in the gym for far too long, simply watching him move. My beautiful everything. I took in the way his body bent and bowed. The infinite power he held within him. I hadn't wanted to break the spell. Hadn't wanted to break *him*.

Because I knew the fact that he had siblings who had been raised in possibly the same environment he had would kill him. That they had moved through the world with no one to look out for them when he lived less than five miles away.

"No." There was a finality to Kye's voice. A certainty. "That's not possible." I stepped toward him, and he instantly took a step back. "No."

I stayed where I was, not wanting to heap on even more pain. "I'm so sorry."

"How do you know for sure?" Panic laced every word—a desperate plea for me to be wrong.

"I saw her."

Kye jerked back as if I'd slapped him.

"I'll never forget her face. You showed me a picture once, and I'll never forget it. Because I know how much she hurt you." Hurt him and had all but gotten away with it after the sob story she gave the judge. She'd gotten nothing more than a slap on the wrist in the form of three months in jail and a revocation of her parental rights with Kye. And now, she'd hurt others, too. Had done untold damage to those tiny humans—tiny humans who were pieces of Kye.

His face paled, making the ink on his neck stand out more as if it were strangling him. "She has my eyes," he rasped.

My knees nearly buckled, but I wouldn't let myself fall. Kye had been strong for me countless times. I needed to be strong for him now.

"Gracie," he choked out. "Keely's friend. She has my eyes."

"They all do," I whispered.

His jaw tightened so much I could see every one of the bones. "Tell me."

I knew he'd want to know. Need to. "They're amazing. Three girls. Gracie's six. Clementine, who goes by Clem, is eleven. And the oldest, Hayden, is fourteen. She's the one Cope was coaching on the side last summer. She plays hockey."

Kye's breaths grew more ragged with each fact I gave him. "Trace and Cope know my sisters better than I do." He jerked a hand through his hair, tugging on the strands. "How is that even possible? She would've had to be pregnant when she was arrested. Or right after—" He halted. "They were always fucking around on each other. Toxic to the core."

"They have a different father. A man named Les Jensen, who doesn't seem to be involved in their day-to-day lives."

I had to explain in case he was worried that Rex Blackwood was back after getting out of prison. But that coward had never returned to Sparrow Falls. At least as far as I could tell.

"You're sure? Sure they're hers? That they're my...my sisters?" Kye choked on the word and then started pacing. "I've seen that callous bitch around town and haven't once seen her with a kid."

Another dagger to the heart. Another nail in the coffin. As far as

I could tell, Renee hadn't been a mother to those girls in a long time. Then I watched as realization dawned.

Kye's hands fisted, his forearms flexing with the motion. "Because she doesn't take care of them. Probably not goddamned once." His gaze jerked to me. "What happened? Why the callout?"

True terror was grabbing hold of him now, cutting him open. I knew I had to stanch the flow. And there was only one way to do that: the truth.

"A neighbor called in the sounds of a fight. When the sheriff's department arrived on the scene, it was clear that Hayden was injured. Renee slapped her and threw a glass at her head." I got out the worst of it as quickly as I could.

Kye had gone stock-still. There was no expression on his face now. No anger. No fear. Just blankness. "What else?"

"Deputies found both a loaded gun and a stash of meth," I said quietly. I would've given anything for the words to be lies. For the girls. And for Kye.

"In a house with a six-year-old." Kye's voice had a quiet lethality now. One I'd only heard once or twice in my life. "She could've killed someone or been killed."

"Everyone's okay. Hayden had to get liquid stitches, but she's all right. She's been taking care of her sisters so well. Now, she'll have some help doing that."

Kye's amber eyes flashed, more golden tones threading through them. "Taking care of?"

I swallowed, knowing he needed to hear it all and that it would be better to tell him now. "The trailer was in bad shape. Filthy. Hayden had food hidden in their room. Even a mini fridge. She's kept them fed, their clothes clean, their hair washed."

"She's fourteen fucking years old," Kye bellowed.

I let his rage hit me, but I didn't brace because I knew it wasn't for me. "And now she'll get to be a kid."

Kye's spine snapped straight. "Where are they? Tell me you're not letting that bitch keep them."

I didn't let that one land, knowing he wasn't thinking straight.

"Renee is being charged with several offenses, including child abuse, assault, child endangerment, and drug possession. Now that I've flagged the connection to her past charges, we'll be able to file a lawsuit to terminate parental rights. The girls were born in a different state and have a different father than you. That's why it didn't come up right away."

None of that mattered to Kye right now. Nothing but the girls being safe did. "Where are they?" he growled.

"With one of my most amazing foster families. I promise. They're together, and they're safe. With time, they'll heal," I assured him.

Kye's pacing started up again. He moved back and forth as he tried to make sense of the unthinkable. "They got pulled from a nightmare, and now they'll get shuffled from one place to the next. Ripped apart. Thinking it's their fault that no one wants them."

"Kyler," I whispered, hoping using his full name would reach him. "You don't know that. Look what happened to you."

His gaze cut to me. "My situation was a fucking miracle. A one in a goddamned million chance. Three girls? And none of them infants or toddlers? They'll never keep them together."

The problem was, I knew he had a point. If a family member didn't step forward, keeping the girls together would be an uphill battle, though one I'd never stop fighting. But I wouldn't lie to Kye and say it would be easy.

"They've been all fucking alone." The words tore from his throat with an animalistic tone that had me instantly on alert. He moved so fast I didn't have a prayer of getting in his way. He went for the equipment rack first, upending it and hurling the shelves at the wall.

"They've been living through hell, and I didn't know." He dove for the towel stand next, grabbing that and throwing it with all his might. It shattered into countless pieces on the floor.

I moved then. I knew it was stupid, but I couldn't let Kye hurt himself even worse than he already was. I did the one thing I thought might pull him out of it. If even just for a moment. A fraction of a second where I could reach him.

Pushing off my feet, I launched myself at Kye as he stormed toward a rack of weights. I saw his brief moment of surprise before he caught me. Just like he always did.

The moment my body hit his, I held on for dear life, hoping I could keep Kye from detonating or at least put the pieces back together after the trigger had been flipped.

His whole body shuddered, and for the first time, I felt how massive he truly was. Not just tall, but broad. And the power coiled inside him was like a wild animal poising to strike.

"Let go." Kye's command vibrated with fury.

"Can't do that, Kyler."

His entire form shuddered with everything he'd been holding inside. "I'll hurt you. Look what the fuck I just did," he snarled.

I gripped him tighter. "You're not going to hurt me."

"You don't know—"

"I do. I know that you are the kindest soul I've ever known to walk the Earth. I know that a rage lives inside you, but it's only matched by your gentleness. And I know that you will never do a damn thing to cause me any sort of harm."

It was as if all the fight drained from Kye in a split second. Every ounce of tension, every speck of rage…it all just collapsed, and Kye sank to the floor with it, taking me with him.

I still didn't let go. I kept holding on. And then Kye was holding me, too, the two of us curving around each other as his entire body started to shake. I held on as the tears came—not holding him together but telling him I was there no matter what.

"I wasn't there when they needed me." The words were choked, escaping through the sobs he so desperately tried to hold back.

I pressed my face to his neck, the scent of oakmoss and amber stronger there. "You didn't know."

Slowly, the sobs abated, but a bone-deep grief remained. "It doesn't change that they were alone."

I pulled back and brushed a lock of hair from his face, feeling his agony. "They won't be now."

Kye searched my eyes for a long moment. "I want to take them.

I want to give them a home. I want to make sure they're never scared again. I want to make sure they always know they're wanted. That someone *chose* them."

My jaw went slack. I had known Kye would want to be involved in the girls' lives. I'd even thought about seeing if Mom might consider becoming a kinship placement of sorts, even though I knew it was a stretch. But Kye taking custody and possibly becoming their guardian? He lived in a one-bedroom apartment over his tattoo studio. He worked long hours and hated getting up early.

But I also knew that if he was truly ready to make that choice, no one would give more to be everything to those girls.

His amber eyes swirled darker. "Can you help me file for custody, Sparrow?"

CHAPTER SEVEN

Fallon

THE *SUPERNATURAL* THEME SONG CAME THROUGH MY PHONE'S speakers, and I groaned, rolling over and inhaling deeply. The scents of oakmoss and amber filled my nose as I pressed my face into the pillow. Clinging to it, I slowly opened my eyes to all things Kye.

Bedding in shades of gray. Textured cement walls. Industrial bookcases filled with books on the art of tattooing, mixed martial arts, and the occasional sci-fi novel. Knickknacks that marked different things and times in his life, like a snow globe that matched the one he'd given me from New York. Various family photos. Pictures of Kye with the kids from his youth program at an MMA fight.

I gripped the pillow tighter and breathed in Kye's scent again. As I closed my eyes, memories from last night returned in flashes: the girls, Kye losing it, the words he'd spoken.

"I want to take them. I want to give them a home. I want to make sure they're never scared again. I want to make sure they always know they're wanted. That someone chose *them."*

Those words would haunt me for the rest of my days. Especially the pain that lived in them—the pain that lived in *Kye*.

My phone dinged, and I forced myself to release the pillow that smelled like him and roll to sitting. I snatched my phone off the nightstand and unplugged it from Kye's charger.

A group text illuminated the screen, one I'd started last night when I asked Serena and Evan if they could handle the mess at the gym before opening.

Serena: *What the hell happened?*

She'd obviously made it in early. I worried the corner of my lip. It wasn't my place to share.

Me: *It's a long story. But Kye's okay.*

That might be a lie, and I knew the gossip mill would put the pieces together before long, but I wouldn't help it along.

Evan: *Already at the hardware store, Ser. Getting stuff to patch the wall and some paint.*

Me: *Thanks, guys.*

Serena: *Let me know if he needs anything. I'm here.*

Evan: *Me, too.*

For everything Kye had been through, he'd found himself an amazing community. Built it with people who each had a story. I knew Serena had found MMA after escaping an abusive relationship, and Evan had run away from home at sixteen. Kye found people who shared elements of his pain and helped them heal. I just hoped I could do the same for him.

Me: *Thanks again, guys. You're doing it.*

Standing, I stretched, Kye's oversized T-shirt riding up my thighs. My whole body ached—probably from throwing myself at the six-foot-five mountain of a man last night. But I'd do it again if it meant soothing even a little of his pain.

The sounds of movement in the apartment's small kitchen had

me heading in that direction. As I crossed the threshold, I found Kye wearing a faded Haven T-shirt with low-slung gray joggers. The tee was so old it was worn in places and hugged his chest in a way that had my eyes lingering there, my fingers tightening into fists at my sides.

"Morning," Kye said, his voice still gritty from sleep as he set two mugs on the counter.

My gaze jerked to his face. It wasn't unusual for me to spend the night here. It happened from time to time when we stayed up too late having a movie marathon or when I talked Kye into a re-watch of *Supernatural*. He always made me take his bed and opted to sleep on the couch.

But today was different. I searched his face, tracing the dark shadows beneath his eyes. "Did you sleep at all?"

He ran a hand through his hair and shook his head. "Maybe a couple of hours."

I moved then, drawn by some invisible tether between us. As if his pain called to mine. I went straight to him, wrapped my arms around his waist, and pressed my face to his chest. But I didn't say a word. Anything I offered now would be a useless platitude. Instead, I just held on. Like I always would.

Kye's chin rested atop my head, and his arms encircled me. "Can I see them today? I need them to know…to know I'm here."

My body stiffened ever so slightly, and I forced myself to pull back. "Because you don't have an existing relationship with them and haven't been cleared by a background check, regulations won't allow visitation just yet."

A muscle in Kye's jaw fluttered. "They need to know."

"They will. When the time is right, they will. In the meantime, I'll be there for them."

Kye's hold on me tightened, those tattooed fingers stressing his point. "I still want to file."

It was the decision I was waiting for. "You're sure?"

His amber eyes searched mine. "You don't think I can do it?"

My fingers fisted in his tee. "I *know* you can do it. I know those girls will be beyond lucky to have you in their lives. But I want you to take the time to make sure this is what you want."

Kye's hand slid to the back of my neck and squeezed gently. "This is what I want. Tell me what I need to do."

I watched his face as he spoke, looking for any signs of doubt. There were none. God, he was such a good man. But he tried to hide it beneath layers of shadow and humor. As if he didn't want anyone to see just how amazing he truly was.

"Okay." I let out a long breath as I reached for the coffee mug and took a sip. "First things first. You'll never be approved with this as your residence. A home visit is required, and there isn't enough room here for the girls."

Kye reached for his mug, his large hand engulfing it as he stared into the black liquid. "I've got another place. There's plenty of room there."

I blinked back at him a few times. "You have...another place?"

A foreign feeling nibbled at my chest. Something that felt a lot like betrayal. As if Kye had some secret life he hadn't told me about.

Kye's gaze lifted to meet my eyes. "It's not like that. I had it built years ago. I just...it never felt like the right time to move in."

"You built a house and didn't tell me? Did Shep do it?"

"I didn't tell *anyone*," Kye stressed.

The feeling of betrayal morphed into pure hurt. "I'm not just anyone."

"Sparrow," he whispered.

That only made it hurt worse.

Kye closed the small distance between us and set his coffee on the counter before hooking his pinky with mine. "You're my person. Always."

Pain and pleasure warred inside me in equal measure as tears pressed against the backs of my eyes. "I'm here. Whatever you need."

He leaned forward and pressed a kiss to my forehead, letting his lips linger. "I know you are."

My poor little hatchback sputtered as I pulled to a stop outside the McKenzies' house, and I started to doubt my girl would make it through the winter. Sighing, I grabbed the massive bag from The Mix Up and climbed out of my car. As I did, I saw a familiar figure getting out of an SUV ahead of me.

Trace wore a somber look as he pulled bags out of the back seat of his vehicle. I recognized the name of a bigger store from a town over—one of the few that would be open this early. God, my brother had such a good heart. And I knew by his presence that Gabriel had filled him in on *everything*.

He caught me looking and grimaced. "It's dumb. It's not like toys and books will fix what's going on."

I shook my head. "It shows you care."

Trace searched my face. "How is he?"

"Not good," I said honestly. When I left Kye, he still had shadows swirling in his eyes but was no less determined to get the ball rolling on custody. "He wants to file for custody of the girls."

Trace's brows all but hit his hairline. "Seriously?"

I nodded.

"I knew he'd want to be involved, but custody?" Trace let out a low whistle.

"Don't say anything to them. Not until we know what's what."

The expression on Trace's face morphed into an assessing one. He would forever be the brother who saw...*more*. "You're not sure he'll get it."

I shifted my weight from foot to foot. "He has some things to overcome."

"His record?"

I nodded. "He'll need to prove that he can provide a safe and stable environment for the girls. And he needs a bigger place. But he said he already has one."

Trace stared at me, and his jaw slackened the slightest bit. "I always wondered where he went when he did his disappearing acts."

I had, too. Only my mind had invented something that made me sick to my stomach to think about. Something that involved shacking up with a woman for days on end.

"I guess we'll find out soon enough," I muttered.

Trace scrubbed a hand over his stubbled cheek. "I guess."

"Come on. I don't want our breakfast getting cold," I said, starting up the front walkway to the adorable Craftsman.

Trace peered at my bag. "You got an extra in there? I left before I could make myself breakfast."

I grinned at my brother. "I didn't know what the girls liked, so I brought lots of options. But you pick last."

Trace chuckled. "Fair enough. Just don't tell Keely and Ellie that I got The Mix Up for breakfast. They'll be jealous."

My lips twitched. "I'll take it to the grave."

I knocked lightly on the front door. A few moments later, a gray-haired woman with countless laugh lines opened it. "Fallon. Morning."

I held up the bag. "I come bearing gifts."

Her mouth curved. "You're too good to us."

The McKenzies were in their seventies and no longer did long-term fostering, but they were still able to do emergency short-term placements. And the home they'd created was the perfect place for kids to rest and begin the healing process.

"Morning, Edith," Trace greeted.

"Good to see you, Trace," she said as she stepped back and ushered us in.

I peeked around the living room and into the kitchen but didn't see the girls. "How are they doing?"

Edith's lips thinned, and I saw worry in her eyes. "I heard the little one crying last night. I checked on her, but I don't think my presence helped."

That ache flared to life in my chest again. "They're pretty used to going it alone, I think."

"That's what I figured. I'll never rush them, but I'll try to let them know I'm here if they need me. Ron is keeping his distance for now. I think they're a little wary of men."

My stomach twisted at that tidbit of information. From what I'd gathered, the girls' father was in and out of their lives but hadn't been present at all since they moved back to Sparrow Falls. I reached out and squeezed Edith's shoulder. "Thanks for all you're doing."

"You know I'm happy to help," she said. "I'll just let them know breakfast is here. You know where everything is."

I moved in the direction of the kitchen I'd been in countless times. The McKenzies were always my first choice for emergency placements if they had the space. I pulled out the different breakfast options, along with the half-dozen cupcakes I'd gotten them for later. By the time I heard footsteps, I'd stacked the plates and silverware buffet-style.

Turning, I took in the three girls, all dressed for school. Gracie's hair was arranged in pigtail braids with colorful ties at the ends, while Clementine's was fixed in a French braid that hung down her back. I had a feeling Hayden had done both.

"Morning," I greeted, sending them all a warm smile. "I brought breakfast from The Mix Up."

Gracie's eyes went wide. "All that's for us?"

"I wasn't sure what you liked, so I got a little bit of everything." I motioned to Trace. "Plus, my brother, Trace, eats as much as three people do, so he'll finish whatever we don't."

"Hey," Trace protested.

"What's he doing here?" Hayden demanded, her gaze hard. The area around her wound was starting to bruise, showing just how hard the glass had been thrown at her.

Trace didn't take offense. "I'm not here as the sheriff. I'm here as Keely's dad. I just wanted to check in on you guys and see if you needed anything. I brought a few things to tide you over, too."

"We need to go back home," Hayden said.

Gracie moved closer to Hayden, and the older girl instantly wrapped an arm around her.

Clementine looked at them both and then at the floor. "I don't want to go back home."

"Clem," Hayden hissed.

The redhead's gaze snapped up to her sister. "I don't. I don't wanna go back there. I don't want to live with Mom. Or have to hide our food. Or put the dresser in front of the door when she drinks. Or listen to her scream. Or—"

Hayden's face paled, cutting off her sister's words.

"I know it's scary," I said softly. "The unknown always is. But we're going to get through this together, and I'm going to do everything I can to help. Is there anything you want to know right now?"

Gracie looked up at me with glassy eyes. "Where's Mom?"

"She's at the sheriff's station." I'd never lie to my kids. Even if you were trying to soften a blow, it had a way of coming back to bite you.

Amber eyes, so similar to Kye's, widened. "Like she's in jail?"

Trace took this one. "Not jail. We have a couple of cells with beds at the station. She's staying there."

A muscle in Hayden's cheek pulsed. "When is she being charged?"

"Today," Trace said. "I spoke with the prosecutor on my way here."

"Will she go to jail?" Clementine asked.

Trace looked at me, and I nodded to give him the go-ahead. He turned back to them. "I'm not sure yet."

"What's going to happen to us?" Gracie's voice was so quiet I almost couldn't hear it. But as soft as it was, it still broke my heart.

Crouching low, I met her eyes. "That's what we're all going to figure out together, okay?"

Hayden scoffed. "Like you're going to listen to us."

My gaze lifted to hers. "You're the first person I'm going to listen to. And I'm going to ask your opinion on *everything*. That's a promise."

"And Fal never breaks her promises," Trace assured them. "When she was nine and I left for college, she promised to take care of my horse for me, and you know what happened?"

Gracie looked up at him, her lower lip trembling a bit as if she were fighting the movement. "What?"

"She took such good care of him, he still loves her more to this day. He totally ditched me for her."

"Hey." I shrugged. "He just has good taste."

Gracie giggled as she looked at me. "What's his name?"

"Buster. He's sweet as can be, and he loves sugar cubes. If you want, I can take you out to meet him one day."

"Really?" Gracie asked, suddenly excited. "Keely said she goes riding all the time, but I've never been."

That phantom ache was back, but I forced myself to keep smiling. "I'd love to teach you. And I know my mom would love for the horses to get some exercise."

Hayden's amber eyes flashed with a gold that spoke of fury. "You can't buy us off with breakfast and horseback rides. Only one thing matters, and that's us staying together. Can you do that?"

A lead weight settled in my gut because I knew she was right. At least when it came to what mattered. So, I met Hayden's angry eyes and held nothing back. "I'm going to do absolutely everything I can."

As I trudged up the steps to the child welfare offices, it felt like my tote bag weighed a thousand pounds. But I knew one thing: I'd sell my soul to make sure those girls stayed together. Just one breakfast with them, and I could already tell they all carried wounds from how they'd grown up. Gracie was timid and unsure of herself. Clem tried to hide her brilliant mind as if showing how smart she was would make her a target. And Hayden... She'd become a fierce protector, giving up her dreams to make sure her sisters were safe and cared for.

Mary Lou waved at me as I walked inside, the phone pressed to her ear. It took everything I had to give her a half-hearted wave in response.

Noah looked up as I made my way into the offices. "That bad?"

"It's been a long twenty-four hours."

He grimaced. "Talked to the prosecutor just a few minutes ago. He agrees with the motion to terminate parental rights given the previous charges."

That was a good thing. I knew it. But it was still heavy. "Good. That's good."

"You find any possible kinship placements?" Noah asked as I dropped my bag to the floor next to my desk and shrugged out of my coat.

I knew he wasn't even considering Kye filing for custody, which had my temper flaring. I shoved it down. "I'm working on it."

Mila looked up from a report she was reading. "I've got an extra green juice in the fridge. You look like you could use a pick-me-up."

"I appreciate you and your glowy skin, but the only thing that will save me now is pure, unadulterated sugar." I snatched the half-eaten bag of strawberry Sour Patch Kids Kye had left me and started for Rose's office.

I knocked softly.

"Come in," she called.

I slipped through the door and closed it behind me, just as Rose looked up from her computer. Her office had a comforting vibe with a couch in the corner and décor that gave little glimpses of Rose herself. The basket she'd told me her sister had woven held toys for when she needed to occupy little ones. A Pollock-esque splatter painting adorned one wall and brought an endless array of color to the room. And the collection of figurines her kids had given her over the years adorned her desk, including a trophy that read *World's Best Mom*.

Settling into one of the chairs opposite hers, I finally met her gaze. She still hadn't said a word. But Rose was good at waiting until you were ready—just another reason she had a way with the kids whose cases crossed her desk.

"Kye didn't know about his sisters," I began.

Rose leaned back in her chair, grief settling into her eyes. "Noah said."

"He would like to file for custody."

Surprise lit her features. "Did you contact the birth father, Les Jensen?"

A parent would always be given the first chance to take custody. "I've left three messages. So far, nothing. I'll move on to serving him if I don't have any luck contacting him personally."

Rose nodded slowly. "Is Kye ready for that kind of responsibility?"

"Is anyone?" I asked.

Rose let out a soft chuckle. "When I had my Lucy, I was lost. I didn't know up from down. If not for my sister, I would've been royally screwed."

"He has us. All of us. My mom, Lolli, everyone in the whole Colson crew." Which was made up of many more people than just those with the Colson last name.

Rose tapped her fingers on the edge of her desk. "I adore that boy. You know that. I've got a soft spot for the ones who turn their lives around."

"But?" I prodded.

"You know what I'm going to say. The fact that he has a record, even just a juvenile one, hurts him. He'll be a single parent, and as far as I can tell, he doesn't have an especially predictable schedule. And I hate to say it, but some judges are stuck in the past. They'll see the tattoos, hear that he works in a tattoo studio and that he's still involved in the MMA world, and they'll be concerned."

Everything in me cramped and twisted. "But he also runs a free program for youth in our county. He owns and operates two successful businesses. He has a family who supports him."

Rose's sympathetic expression deepened. "I know that. But a judge might be concerned placing three young girls with a single man they don't know."

"So let them get to know him. Start building the relationship now."

"I already placed an order for Kye's background check. That will get us started," Rose assured me.

"I'm sorry," I mumbled. "It's just so unfair. He's the best person I've ever known."

"It is unfair." Rose tapped her fingers on her thigh. "Does he have a partner at all? I've never seen him with one. But having someone else in the picture, especially if they are another safe and stable set of hands, might help."

My stomach twisted. The last thing I wanted to think about was the women coming in and out of Kye's life.

"It would have to be a serious and committed relationship," Rose went on. "But if they filed for domestic partnership or were planning to get married, it might help."

As Rose arched a brow, my mind started swirling, tendrils of an idea gathering at the edges of my thoughts. One that was likely stupid and more than a little reckless. Something that could end up with me losing my job or even getting charged with fraud if I were found out.

I shoved the chair back and pushed to my feet. "I need to check on something. I'll be back in a couple of hours."

I was already headed for the door, but Rose's voice stopped me in my tracks. "Fallon?"

I turned and looked at her in question.

Rose's deep brown eyes met mine. "Make sure you're ready to walk down the road you're thinking about."

She knew me too well. But I also knew she'd made the not-so-subtle suggestion for a reason. My eyes burned. "I'd walk through fire for him."

Rose's face softened. "He's lucky to have you."

I shook my head. "I'm the lucky one."

CHAPTER EIGHT

Kye

I TURNED TO REACH FOR A COLORED PENCIL AND KNOCKED MY coffee off the corner of the shelf. Cursing, I pushed to my feet and went in search of some paper towels.

Jericho grabbed his roll and moved toward the spill, mopping it up. "You okay?" he asked, lowering his voice.

"Fine," I grumbled, picking up the broken pieces of the mug.

"Real convincing," Jericho shot back. His gaze flicked up to mine as he continued to soak up the coffee. "This about Oren showing up yesterday?"

Any other day, Oren trying to loop us into some fucked-up fight ring again would've been my top concern. Now, it didn't even rate. I'd spent the morning calling a cleaning service to get the house in shape for a home inspection, pulling financial records in case Fallon needed that for my case, and putting a call into my lawyer so she could adjust my will accordingly.

"It's not Oren," I finally said.

Surprise lit Jericho's features, but I also saw worry. I felt like the biggest ass.

"Are *you* okay?" I pressed.

He shrugged as he tossed a wad of paper towels into the trash and tore off more. "I can't risk getting mixed up with him again—or even the appearance of it. I didn't pull my shit together as quickly as you did."

Jericho had a few dings on his record for stupid shit after he turned eighteen. But he was sober now, working a program and toeing the line.

"You've done great for years. No one's going to think anything other than Oren's an asshole."

But as I said the words, I thought about the risks I was taking. If word got out to the people deciding custody of Hayden, Clementine, and Gracie that an MC member was hanging around my studio, it could have serious repercussions. *Fuck.* I might need to have a word with Trace.

"I hope you're right," Jericho muttered.

"Whatcha doing on your knees, boys?" Penelope called. "Waiting for me?"

Bear let out a snort. "Doll, you are nothing but trouble."

She clasped her hands under her chin and blinked up at him with faux innocence. "Little ole me?"

Jericho chuckled. "You're going to send some man to an early grave."

"And he'll thank his lucky stars," Penelope shot back, crossing to my station and hopping up onto the counter, swinging her legs as she lifted my sketchpad. "This is looking good."

I fought the urge to rip the drawing out of her hands. Only one person got to see my stuff before it was done, and that sure as hell wasn't Penelope. I crossed to the trash can and poured the shards of mug into it.

Penelope's nose wrinkled. "You're extra grumpy today. Didn't sleep well? You know I could help with that."

This time, I did jerk the sketchpad out of her hands. She was getting bolder, and I needed to shut that shit down. "Not interested. And I think I've made that clear."

Hurt bloomed on Penelope's face as she slid off the counter.

"Shit," I mumbled. "I—"

"No. I get it. Message received."

I gritted my teeth as she hurried back down the hall. "I am the world's biggest asshole."

"Sometimes," Jericho agreed.

Bear just shook his head. "It needed to happen. Better to have one moment of pain than to keep stringing her along."

"I wasn't stringing her along," I argued.

Bear simply arched a brow. "You're the king of avoidance. Don't like to hurt others, so you just dodge and weave."

"You mean he's the priest of avoidance," Jericho corrected.

"Oh, fuck off," I muttered. But he was one of the few who knew the truth of just how empty my bed had been the past fifteen years.

The bell over the door jingled as a woman who made me feel distinctly un-priestlike walked in. Fallon had her blond hair piled into a messy bun, tendrils of it spilling out and cascading around her face. My fingers itched to snap the band and let it all fall free.

She had on wide-legged black pants and a button-down shirt peeking out from beneath a tan sweater, but the real Fallon shone through in her choice of footwear and the bracelets on her wrist: a pair of white sneakers decorated with little pink hearts, and beaded bracelets in every color under the sun—ones I knew Keely had made for her.

She was a knot of contradictions, and it captivated me. But as I looked deeper, I saw the strain—the dark circles just visible beneath her makeup, the tight grip she had on her tote.

"Fal," Bear greeted, a huge smile on his face.

She answered with one of her own, even if it was tense around the edges. She leaned across the reception desk and kissed his bearded cheek. "I've missed you."

Bear's smile only widened. "Made gingersnaps last night if you want one."

"You've been holding out on us?" Jericho accused.

Bear simply shot him a look. "You heathens would have already eaten every single one, leaving nothing but crumbs for the rest of us."

"I am partial to gingersnaps," Fallon said, her lips twitching.

Bear opened one of his desk drawers and handed her a resealable bag. "Here you go."

"You are the best."

Jericho scowled at the biker. "This is cruel and unusual punishment."

Bear chuckled and fished out another bag. "This is only because I don't want to hear you moaning and complaining for the rest of the day."

Jericho jumped on the bag as if he hadn't eaten in months.

"Jesus," I muttered.

Fal broke off a piece of cookie and popped it into her mouth. "I don't blame him. They're worth it."

That was about as much of an offer of friendship as Jericho would get from Fallon. Because in her mind, he was linked to something that had almost cost me my life. She might be glad he'd pulled his life together but she'd always harbor a resentment that he'd been part of the fight ring that had almost taken me out.

I moved toward her as if some invisible tether pulled me in. "You got something?" I asked quietly.

She nodded. "Out back?"

The urge to reach for her hand was strong, but I simply pressed my palm to her back and guided her down the hallway. The contact scalded as if Fal's heat could burn through layers of clothing. But I didn't pull away.

Penelope's door was open, and she looked up from where she was eating lunch over her desk. Her gaze locked on Fal and me, taking in our closeness, but I didn't drop my hand.

Fallon raised her hand in a small wave that Penelope didn't return, and a stream of mental curses ran through my head. I knew I'd end up paying for my earlier comment—and I had zero time or energy for the drama.

"Everything okay with her?" Fal asked as we stepped out onto the shop's small back patio. There was an outdoor table, some chairs, and a couple of aspen trees.

"Everything's fine. Just had a little dust-up earlier," I explained.

Fallon arched a brow at me in question.

"It doesn't matter. What'd you find out?"

Fal's grip on her bag tightened, and my stomach dropped.

"It's not good," I surmised.

"It's a mix," she said quickly. "So far, the girls' birth father hasn't returned my calls. I called in a request to have him served. We're just waiting for a response. But we have to wait for the allotted time to pass to see if I can speak to him."

"But..." Because I knew there was a *but*. It felt like there always was. As if my life were made up of a series of almosts.

Fallon slipped her bag from her shoulder and deposited it on one of the chairs. "I talked to Rose. She's all for you filing for custody, but she thinks we could run into issues getting final approval for placement from a judge."

My back teeth ground together. "Because of my record?"

A wince tightened Fallon's features. "That and she was honest about the fact that some may not see your job setup as the most stable. It's stupid and prejudiced, but some of the judges in this county are stuck in the past."

I started to pace, my motorcycle boots hitting the stone patio with more force than necessary as I raked a hand through my hair. All the stupid things I'd done in the past. All the things I'd been forced into. And now my sisters might pay the price.

Fallon moved into my path, halting me by placing her hands on my T-shirt-clad chest. "You are the most amazing person I've ever known. And Hayden, Clem, and Gracie would be so lucky to have you looking out for them."

Each sentiment was like a hot poker sliding through my chest: the belief Fal had in me, the way she saw things no one else did... "If the judge doesn't think so, it doesn't really matter. And my fuckups could keep them from staying together."

Just speaking the words out loud hurt. Admitting to another failure.

Fallon reached up and cupped my cheeks. The contact lit another beautiful burn in me, scorching me like lava. I wouldn't have traded it for the world.

"You did what you had to do," Fallon said quietly. "What you thought was right at the moment."

Only it wasn't. It was so far from right it wasn't even funny. "Tell me what to do, Sparrow."

Her tongue darted out, wetting her bottom lip as she dropped her hands from my face. I couldn't help but track the movement. The memory of her taste flooded my mind: spearmint and fresh, clean air. It was as if her taste could cleanse all the badness right out of me.

"I have an idea that might work," Fallon began. "But it is completely unhinged."

Energy and something that felt a lot like hope crackled through me. "What? I'll do anything. Hell, I'll cover my tattoos with body makeup if I have to. Wear polo shirts and take up golf. Whatever you think will make me acceptable in the court's eyes."

Fallon's delicate throat worked as she struggled to swallow. "Marry me."

CHAPTER NINE

Fallon

K YE'S ENTIRE FORM FROZE. HE DIDN'T MOVE, DIDN'T BREATHE, and for a second, I thought his heart might've stopped altogether. "Marry you?" he croaked.

I couldn't deny that his total and complete shock stung a bit. I understood it logically, but some part of me was still that fourteen-year-old girl Kye had given her first kiss. And some part of me, more than I wanted to acknowledge, was still in love with him.

It didn't matter how hard I'd tried to move on—dates, boyfriends—none of them ever felt right. Eventually, I'd given up. Because I realized I'd rather be alone than keep searching for something that could never be what I'd had, even for that flicker of a moment.

I stared into those shocked amber eyes. "Yes."

The single word startled Kye into moving again. He paced across the patio, his scarred boots threatening to wear a path in the concrete. "Explain."

It was a command, not a question, but I didn't blame him for it. "Rose said having a partner could help. Two caregivers in the home instead of one. Another stable force for the girls."

Kye's dark brows pulled together thunderously. "Okay..."

My fingers twisted in the hem of my shirt, trembling as they did. "Well, everyone knows we're close. And I'm kind of what they'd be looking for on paper. I majored in child psychology in college, have a master's degree in social work, work for DHS, and have plenty of experience with kids."

"And you come from the most well-respected family in town," Kye finished for me.

I stiffened. "So do you."

Kye stilled mid-stride. "You know it's not the same. People don't see me as coming from the Colsons. They see me as someone the Colsons took pity on."

Anger and sadness warred in equal measure, but anger quickly won out. "The hell you are. You were dealt one of the worst hands I've ever seen. Your family betrayed you in ways I wouldn't wish on anyone. Yet you found a way to overcome it. You turned your life around. You built two incredible businesses. You give kids a safe place to grow and gain confidence. You've taken everything you've been through and turned it into something good."

My breaths came in ragged pants as I struggled to get enough air into my lungs.

"Sparrow..."

"Let me do this for you. For them," I pleaded.

Kye searched my eyes. "And what? Give up the rest of your life?"

I shifted from foot to foot. "It doesn't have to be forever. Just until you have permanent custody. Maybe a little longer so neither of us gets charged with fraud."

Kye stared at me for a long moment and then shook his head. "No. I'm not putting you at risk like that."

"You're not putting me at risk. This is *my* idea. *My* choice. And you have to trust me to make decisions for myself." A little of my anger returned.

"Your family will freak," he muttered.

"*Our* family. And no, they won't. Be a little shocked? Sure. But no freaking involved."

"Okay, *our* family. Which people will see as twisted and weird."

I couldn't help but roll my eyes. "You came to live with us when you were sixteen, not six. We went to school together before then. We tell people we knew each other back then but downplayed our connection."

So much swirled in Kye's eyes—pain and faintest flickers of hope. "Sparrow…"

Pressure pulsed along my sternum, and I struggled not to rub the spot. "We just need to tell them the truth, and no one will think twice about it."

God, it hurt to say that. To voice what had almost been and think about letting people into that.

"For my sisters," Kye rasped.

"For your sisters," I echoed.

His hands fisted at his sides, the ink rippling across his fingers. "If we do this…*nothing* can happen between us. Not a damn thing."

Kye might as well have reached out and slapped me. It would've hurt less. That the idea of touching me was so disgusting to him that he needed to place such a harsh barrier between the two of us.

"You're killing me, Sparrow." He stepped forward, and I moved back. The thought of him touching me now—out of pity—was more than I could bear.

Kye halted any forward movement, his hand flexing, then clenching at his side. "It's not because I don't want to. I've been dreaming of you since I was sixteen. You've been my one spark of light in the hellish dark. The *only* good thing in my life. But I won't risk losing you or the family you gave me. Because I'm sure of one thing: I'll fuck this up. And I'm not ruining the only good in my life because of it."

And with that, he stalked back inside the studio, leaving me alone with the bomb he'd just detonated, blowing up everything I thought I knew.

CHAPTER TEN

Kye

I PROWLED BACK INTO THE STUDIO, THE DOOR SLAMMING BEHIND me. But the vicious bang had nothing on the darkness that roiled inside me. The oily blackness that felt like it was eating my insides.

Jericho looked up from the artful sleeve he was working on for a man in his mid-fifties. "Everything okay?"

I didn't answer. Instead, I cast a quick look at Bear. "Reschedule my appointments for the afternoon."

Bear's gray brows nearly hit his hairline, and I knew why. I never bailed on clients. But I couldn't trust myself to ink anyone, not with where my head was at. Not waiting for an answer, I kept moving—right out the front door.

Instead of heading for my truck, I moved to the carport around the side of the building. It gave my other pride and joy protection from the elements. I'd done the Triumph's custom paint job myself, mirroring countless tattoos on my body, but they were so interwoven it was hard to identify any one thing. But I knew all their hidden meanings.

I pulled out my keys and started her up. Within seconds, I had my jacket and helmet on and was flying out of the parking lot. I couldn't think about the fact that I'd left Fallon alone with my mess of emotions without giving her a chance to say how she felt about it all.

God, I was a selfish prick. The wind hit me hard as I leaned into the turn that would take me out of town and toward the Monarch Mountains. I needed both—the cold bite of the air and the peace those peaks could bring.

A million questions and fears swirled in my mind as I twisted the throttle. There were times I swore Fal and I had never moved on from the bond we'd shared as teenagers. But there were others when I was convinced that she saw me as nothing more than an annoyingly overprotective brother figure.

One outcome hurt like hell—thinking it was easy for her to move on when I never could. The other? It had the potential to be lethal. Not just for me. For both of us.

I couldn't help hearing Renee's voice in my head, the tone swirling with the vitriol that coated her every move. *"You ruin everything you touch."* I gripped the handlebars tighter, and Rex's taunting face flashed in my mind, right along with the knowledge that he was walking free after less than a decade inside.

I turned onto a mountain road, taking switchback after switchback until I reached the spot I was looking for. I pulled my bike into the overlook and slowed to a stop. The spot was completely empty, which wasn't a surprise in November. Tourist season had ended, and we'd yet to get the folks who braved the icy roads for the snow sports the area had to offer.

Swinging my leg over my bike, I pulled off my helmet and rested it on the seat. A blaze of energy still coursed through me as I walked toward the stone wall at the edge of the overlook—a surge of anxiety and sheer terror I wasn't sure could be snuffed out. I stepped up onto the wall and just breathed deeply for a moment, letting myself teeter in the wind. Then I sat on the cold stone ledge.

The frigid feel helped somehow. Just like the air swirling around me. I stared out at the horizon, taking in the steep drop-off into the forests and fields below, and the golden faces of Castle Rock in the distance. If I squinted, I could almost convince myself I could see Colson Ranch out there.

I swallowed hard as I scrubbed my hands over my face. Such a goddamned mess. And it was all of my own making.

My phone dinged. I didn't take it out right away, but when two more dings sounded, I twisted to pull it from my pocket. It was probably Fallon reading me the riot act I deserved.

Instead of glitter bomb threats, I found our sibling chat activated.

Cope has changed the group name to Middle Child Mafia.

Cope: *Who told Lolli I needed diamond art for our new house in Seattle?*

A laugh bubbled out of me. It was the last sound I expected to make at the moment, but it was everything I needed.

My finger flew across the screen as I sent three raised hands emojis.

Cope: *Damn it, Kyler. Look what just showed up. It's so big it had to be delivered by FREIGHT.*

A grin spread across my face as I waited.

Rhodes: *The suspense is killing me.*

Cope: *It's Kye who's in danger of getting dead.*

Finally, a photo appeared. No laugh bubbled out of me this time. Instead, my jaw went completely slack. The piece had to be at least seven feet by five feet, covered in thousands of glittering gemstones.

Trace: *Is that a fairy orgy?*

It couldn't be anything but. And there were more sexcapades than could be found in the dark recesses of the internet.

Arden: *Lolli has truly upped her game. I'm pretty sure that's a fairy sex club.*

Shep: *I thought the penis pumpkins she gave Thea were bad.*

Cope: *What the hell am I supposed to do with this?*

> **Trace:** *Burn it and claim it got lost in the mail?*
>
> **Cope:** *She paid for some expensive tracking. The delivery team took a photo of its arrival, and I had to sign for it.*

A full laugh came this time.

> **Me:** *You're welcome, Copeypants. I just wanted you to have a reminder of us all while you're away.*
>
> **Cope:** *A fairy sex club is supposed to remind me of you?*
>
> **Arden:** *I already have first-trimester morning sickness that lasts all day. I don't need to think about you degenerates getting it on.*

The chat devolved after that, everyone one-upping each other. The only one who didn't join in was Fallon. And that only had my guilt mounting.

I needed to tell them all about the discovery of my sisters. And I had to apologize to Fal.

I stared down at my screen, watching every member of the chat other than Fal shit-talk each other. I'd already dropped one bomb today. Why not another?

> **Me:** *I've got some news. Fallon found out yesterday that I have three half-sisters. Hayden, Clementine, and Gracie. Their home situation hasn't been good, so I'm filing for custody.*

I didn't let myself wait or angst over word choice. I just hit send. Whether I followed through with Fallon's ridiculous idea or went another route, I was fighting for those girls.

Staring at the screen, I waited. There was nothing for a long stretch, and then the texts came in all at once.

> **Arden:** *The Gracie in my art program?*
>
> **Cope:** *Fuck. I knew there was something up with Hayden. Are they okay?*
>
> **Rhodes:** *What do you need, Kye?*
>
> **Shep:** *We can all write statements about what a good guardian you'd be. Do you need those?*

Trace: *We've got your back. They're so damn lucky to have you.*

Arden: *You made Trace curse. He must really believe in you.*

Then, finally, another name. The one I could never bring myself to change.

Sparrow: *We're here. Whatever you need.*

Pressure built behind my eyes. I didn't deserve her. After everything I'd pulled over the years, she should've run for the hills. But here she was, still offering me everything.

Me: *Thank you. I don't know what I'd do without all of you.*

It was the only thing I could say. I might not deserve any of them, but they were my lifelines. And I couldn't risk losing any of them.

CHAPTER ELEVEN

Kye

I PULLED MY BIKE INTO A SPOT AT HAVEN AND CLIMBED OFF. Nora had called on my way here, obviously having gotten word from one of my siblings about what was going on. She'd offered the same sentiments of support everyone else had, but I heard the worry in her voice. She knew this would stir shit up for me.

It was another reason I'd come to Haven instead of going home. The sounds of children's voices lit the air as I headed for my office. Checking my watch, I saw that the youth after-school class would just be finishing up for the day.

I grabbed workout gear from my office and quickly changed, feeling the call of the gym. But I wasn't sure the heavy bag would be enough for me this time. I needed to spar.

I nearly collided with Evan as I left the locker room. He did a quick sweep of my face. "You okay?"

I swallowed back the urge to lie. He didn't deserve that. And because he'd grown up like I had, he'd know I was lying anyway.

"No. But I will be."

Evan lifted his head in assent. "You need something, you holler. I've got your back."

I clapped him on the shoulder. "Thank you. How were the kids today?"

Evan grinned. "Fuckin' funny. That Benny kid thinks he's the next Anderson Silva."

That had me fighting a smile as I looked up to where Benny was heading out with his dad.

"Mr. Kye!" he called, his cheeks bright red from class. "Did Mr. Evan tell you that I kicked booty today?"

I bit back a chuckle. "He did. Keep up the good work."

"I've been practicing. Like all the time," Benny informed me.

His dad sent me an exasperated look. "He has. Our couch cushions will never be the same."

"Might be time for an at-home punching bag," I suggested.

Benny's whole face lit up. "Can I, Dad? Then I can practice defending Miss Arden's honor."

A choked sound escaped me. The kid took art classes from Arden and had been enamored with her from day one. "She's in good hands."

Benny's dad pinched the bridge of his nose. "God help us all."

As they headed out the door, I turned back to a grinning Evan. "I'm not sure anyone has ever called me *Mr. Evan*. Ever."

I chuckled. "Should I get you a nameplate?"

"I'll hang it with pride," Evan shot back.

As he headed for the locker room, I moved to the gym. The last of the kids were leaving with their parents as Jericho put the final pieces of gear away. His gaze instantly cut to me. He didn't ask how I was—he just checked silently. Whatever he saw seemed to ease him, at least slightly.

That was good. The last thing I needed was to feel more guilt for making Jericho worry. I held up my MMA gloves. "You wanna spar, or did those kids wear you out?"

Jericho grinned. "They ran circles around me, but I can still kick your ass, Priest."

I scowled at him. "Just for that, I'm not holding back."

Jericho cracked his neck. "I can take you any day of the week."

"Dude," Evan called as he strode back into the gym, pulling on some boxing gloves. "Benny handed you your ass today."

I barked out a laugh. "The truth comes out."

Jericho glared at both of us. "I'm helping his confidence."

"Sure, you are," Evan said as he began hitting the heavy bag.

I moved to one of the treadmills to do a quick warm-up, taking stock of the half-full gym: Serena was working with Mateo in one of the practice rings, a few guys were at heavy bags, and a woman was working a speed bag like it was her job. This was typical for this time of day, but when the workday ended, the place would be packed.

As soon as my muscles were loose, I slowed to a walk and then turned the machine off altogether. I crossed to the closest ring and began moving through my stretching routine, but as I studied Jericho, my brows pulled together. "You okay?"

I'd been so caught up in my own shit that I'd missed how tightly wound he was. Jericho moved from foot to foot as if he had boundless energy. The moment I asked the question, his gaze shot to me. His jaw worked back and forth. "Oren showed again after you left. It was clear he was watching. Waiting for you to leave so he could get me alone."

A muscle pulsed in my jaw. "Thought he could get you to go down."

Jericho jerked his head in a nod. "Pushed all the usual buttons. Offered money. Then made some vague threats."

"Fuck," I muttered. "I can't have him coming around right now. I'm gonna have to talk to Trace."

All it would take was one rumor of me being mixed up with the Reapers MC for me to lose all hope of getting custody of my sisters. I rubbed at a phantom pain taking root in my chest like I was having a heart attack.

Concern lit Jericho's features. "Are you going to tell me what's going on? You've been a wreck. Then you took off on Fal, and she looked like she'd seen a ghost when she left the studio."

More guilt ground into me. I cracked my knuckles on one hand

and then the other. Jericho knew everything that'd happened to me as a kid. So, I knew he'd get the gravity of what I was about to say. "Renee. She's got three girls. I have three half-sisters."

Jericho's jaw went slack. "Fuck, man. That bitch should never be trusted with a child."

"I know." I raked a hand through my hair. "They were removed from her care, and I'm trying to get custody."

The color drained from his face. "They okay?"

"As okay as they can be. But I'm not letting them live with the fear I did. I'm gonna give them something stable. But I can't do that if Oren's hanging around."

"Oren? Oren with the Reapers?" Mateo asked, his eyes hardening as he and Serena moved in our direction. "Tell me you're not getting mixed up with that asshole."

"Trust me, I'm doing everything I can to get him gone," I muttered.

Concern lit Serena's dark eyes. "Something I need to know about?"

"Not right now. I'm gonna let Trace tackle it." It was the only thing I could do. I couldn't risk trying to deal with Oren personally.

A little of the tension eased from Serena's shoulders. "Good. And if he tries coming in here, *I'll* handle it."

My mouth pulled into a grin. "He's scared shitless of you. He won't set foot in here."

"Anyone with half a brain is scared shitless of Ser," Evan called from the nearest heavy bag.

Serena's lips twitched. "And don't you forget it."

Mateo sent Serena a mischievous grin. "You can beat me up anytime, Ser."

She swatted a towel in his direction. "Hit the showers, Casanova."

Mateo began jogging in that direction. "I love it when you spank me."

Evan started choking on a laugh while Serena just shook her head. "I'm gonna go catch up on paperwork. Holler if you need me."

As she headed down the hall and Evan started up with the heavy bag again, Jericho and I climbed into the second practice ring. I put in my mouthguard and set my water bottle on the edge of the ring, pulling on my gloves.

Jericho's gaze swept my face again. "You sure you're in a good enough headspace for this?"

"I need it." It was as simple as that. I had to get the buzzing energy in me out. And this was the most constructive way—this or getting another piece of ink. But I was running out of space there.

Jericho waited for a second longer as if he needed to see something to decide one way or the other. "We talk as we spar."

I scowled at him. "What are you, my shrink?"

"Some days." Jericho rolled onto the balls of his feet and started moving.

He had a point. And he probably understood better than most. Not the shitty home life, but the things we'd seen and done. He got that piece of it. He understood what put me at risk of losing everything.

I moved to the center of the ring and sent out a few testing jabs that Jericho easily blocked. Then he answered with a few of his own. "You sure you're ready to take on raising three girls? You live in a one-bedroom apartment."

My teeth tightened around my mouthguard. "Got another place. A house."

Jericho's brows rose at that. "You do?"

I lifted my chin in assent.

"You have a house, but you live in that shitty apartment?" he asked. "I never did understand why you didn't buy a place. Because I know you've got the funds for it."

There was no way Jericho couldn't know. He worked too closely with me. Knew what I charged. Saw all the deals I signed for licensing.

"My apartment isn't shitty." I landed a blow on his ribs to punctuate my point.

Jericho let out a sound of protest. "Dude. That place is like seven hundred square feet. And the bathroom is more like a closet."

"Whatever," I muttered.

Jericho moved in, trying for a leg sweep, but I dodged it easily. He retreated, keeping his hands up in a defensive guard. "You ever think you never got yourself something better because some part of you thinks you don't deserve it?"

Fuck.

The words hit harder than any blow could. But that wasn't it. Not entirely, at least. I didn't know what I'd do with some massive house. When I finished the project with the builders out of Portland, I knew I'd never be able to live there. As perfect as it was, every time I walked around in it, I felt...empty. As if it made me more aware of what was missing in my life. What I'd never have.

"It's not that," I said, throwing a hook that Jericho dodged.

"Whatever you say." He landed a punch to the kidney that stung.

"What's the process like? Filing for custody, I mean."

My teeth clamped tightly around my mouthguard again.

Jericho didn't miss the movement. "What?"

"Might be a challenge with my history. What I look like on paper."

He sent a cross to my shoulder that I dodged. "Fuckers."

"Fal had an idea," I said, lowering my voice to make sure no one else could hear. I shouldn't even be telling Jericho, but I had to let it out. Needed to tell someone. And he knew Fal's and my true history.

Jericho grinned, revealing his black mouthguard. "Of course, she did. I'd vote for that girl for president."

"She thinks we should get married."

Jericho halted, his hands dropping to his sides and his jaw going slack. "She what?"

I jerked my head in a nod. "Said it'd make the home look more stable on paper. Just until I can get approved for adoption."

Jericho scrubbed a hand over his face. "And how do you feel about that?"

"I'd do anything for my sisters." It didn't matter that I hadn't even met them yet. I knew what it was like to be raised by Renee. I knew what they'd likely lived through. And I'd do anything to make sure they never had to experience it again.

Jericho straightened and pinned me with a stare. "That wasn't what I asked."

"It's playing with fire," I rasped. But it was so much more. It was already a daily battle to keep myself in check with Fal. Living with her? Having her in my space day in and day out? It would tempt a saint. And worse, the emptiness would be so much worse when she left.

"I don't get it. You're both grown now. I see how she looks at you. She didn't stop loving you for a single second. And I can't imagine a better woman. She's kind and fierce. Fucking funny. And she's sure as hell easy on the eyes. Why aren't you going there for real?"

A burn lit in my gut, the pain of hope I couldn't hold on to, knowing I'd never have her the way I wanted. Like I craved with every last piece of me. "I can't," I croaked.

Jericho just stared at me.

That fire intensified, spreading through me like lava, leaving third-degree burns in its wake. "I'll fuck it up. And I can't lose her. I can't lose Fal. I can't lose the family she gave me. I wouldn't survive it."

"Kye—"

"Don't," I clipped. "I just can't, okay?"

Jericho was quiet for a moment. "Okay. But you gotta know she's gonna move on someday."

"I know." And that would kill me, too. But at least I'd still have pieces of her. The tendrils of friendship and the bond we'd always share. That was better than taking the chance of losing her altogether.

One corner of Jericho's mouth kicked up. "You marry her, that'll delay things a little bit."

"Oh, fuck off." I shoved him. But he wasn't wrong. I'd be able to keep Fal from moving on for just a little longer.

Jericho's half smile turned full. "I really wanna see you all respectable. Ball and chain. Kids."

Hell.

But it would be worth it to give my sisters the home they deserved.

Sisters.

I let that truly land. I had sisters. A family I hadn't known about.

That would change. I might not have been there when they needed me before, but I would be there for them now—and every day for the rest of my life.

My hand flew across the sketchpad I had leaning against the steering wheel of my truck. I'd only slept for maybe an hour or two, and I felt it in the burn behind my eyes. But it had given me time for this.

I'd tried countless concepts, starting with traditional and expected. But it didn't fit. If I was going down this road, I had to do it as me. And I would give Fal everything she deserved.

I pulled the pencil back and stared down at the paper. My hand was covered in dark smudges from all the different incarnations I'd drawn, but I thought I finally had it.

The center stone was a black diamond. Thorny vines cast in rose gold curved around it, and the band was made up of those vines woven together. I let out a long breath as I let the sketchpad drop against the wheel. This was the one. Me. Her. Us.

I stared at the storefront, tracing the scripted font with my gaze and studying the window displays shining in the early morning light. Movement caught my eye, and I took in a woman with red hair pulled back into some sort of knot at the base of her head and a trench coat covering her curvy form. It was time.

I slid from my truck, taking the sketchpad with me. Melinda's eyes widened in surprise as she took me in, but a smile quickly tipped her lips. "Morning, Kye."

"Morning," I greeted, my voice sounding rusty from lack of sleep. The nightmares were getting worse and worse.

"You stopping by the shop?" I heard the surprise in her voice. Melinda was a few years older than me and had worked at Sparrow Falls Jewels & Gems since graduating high school—managing the place for the last few. She'd also started making some of the pieces they carried. But I had never, not once, set foot inside the store.

I cleared my throat. "I wanted to see if you could make a custom piece for me. But it's a bit of a time crunch."

Curiosity and interest sparked in Melinda's features. "Come on in." She unlocked the door and held it open. It took her a few moments to get all the lights on and turn off the alarm. "Why don't we go to my desk? We can talk it through there."

There was a small, antique desk on the far wall that gave Melinda a place to sit while she kept an eye on the store. She gestured to a chair opposite it, but I wasn't sure it would hold me without breaking. I lowered myself slowly, exhaling when the chair didn't buckle.

"Now, tell me what you're looking for," Melinda said, shrugging off her coat.

My throat worked as I struggled to swallow. "A ring."

"All right. What kind are we talking?"

Flipping open the sketchpad, I slid it over to her.

Melinda's gaze traveled over the page as she lifted the book. "Kye, this is stunning. Is this...?"

"An engagement ring."

A surprised smile slid over her face. "Congratulations."

"Could you make it this week?"

"This week?" she squeaked.

"I can pay a rush fee. Whatever you need. But this needs to be a black diamond. Four carats. The best clarity you can get. An accompanying band. One for me, too."

Melinda's jaw slackened a bit. "We're talking quite a bit of money here, Kye. Are you sure—?"

I pulled out my wallet and slid a black credit card across her desk, one I knew she'd recognize the label on. "Take whatever deposit you need to get started."

She blinked back at me a few times before handing me the sketchbook and opening her laptop. "I know a gemstone dealer in Los Angeles. He just got a shipment of stunning black diamonds in.

I'll see if he can deliver one today or tomorrow. It'll mean paying for a courier's flights, though."

"That's fine," I said quickly.

"I can do the setting as soon as it arrives. I'll call you when it's ready."

My heart gave a jerking thump against my ribs. "Thank you."

"Do you know her ring size?" Melinda asked.

I slid a hand into my pocket and came up with a dainty band covered in colorful wildflowers. "She wears this on her ring finger sometimes. Can you base it on this?"

Fal had left it at my house after one of our movie nights, and I hadn't given it back. I didn't want to look too closely at the reason for that. But now, I figured there was an upside to my creeper tendencies.

Melinda's lips parted as she took the ring. "This is Fallon's, isn't it?"

I nodded, waiting for her reaction.

A smile spread across her face. "She's a lucky girl."

"I'm the lucky one."

It didn't matter that it was all for show. I'd cherish every moment I got with her. Because they'd have to hold me over for eternity when I was forced to let her go.

CHAPTER TWELVE

Fallon

MY PHONE'S GPS CALLED OUT A TURN THAT LED ME INTO A rundown part of Roxbury, a few towns over from Sparrow Falls. I could practically hear Kye's voice screaming in my head that I shouldn't be here alone. But it was broad daylight, and he hadn't exactly been present the past few days. I'd gotten one text from him.

"I'm sorry, Fal. I'm an ass. Thanks for always having my back. I'll gather the references and other documents if you can start the paperwork. I'll bring everything to you as soon as I have it all."

What the hell did that mean? Did he want to get fake married or not? But despite the ambiguity when it came to me, he had no such confusion regarding his sisters. I'd already received statements from all my siblings, Mom, and Lolli, and a letter from Anson, pulling out all his fancy psychology terms to make the judge feel like an idiot if he didn't choose to put the girls with Kye. Even Jericho had given a statement that had my chest constricting, talking about how Kye had inspired him to turn his life around.

Maybe Kye didn't need me after all. It was probably for the best. Because now that I knew I wasn't alone in my feelings for him, I was closer than ever to breaking. His words had been playing on repeat in my mind ever since he'd stalked off that back patio.

"I've been dreaming of you since I was sixteen. You've been my one spark of light in the hellish dark. The only good thing in my life."

Pressure built along my sternum—the bone that held my chest together when it felt like everything inside was shattering. The place that was only Kyler's. Nothing killed more than realizing the person you'd loved for fourteen years might just love you, too. Only to find out the love you could almost taste was still so painfully out of reach. Because how could I ask him to risk the only support system he had?

My phone told me to take the next right, and my grip on the wheel tightened as the neighborhood got a little rougher. I saw a group of guys sitting on a broken-down porch, waiting as a car pulled up. The youngest one, who looked no older than sixteen, ran down and slipped something to the driver, taking cash in return.

My back teeth ground together. I'd call Trace on my way home. See if he could call Roxbury's chief of police and have them do a drive-by.

"Your destination is on the left," my phone announced.

I searched for the right house, and my gaze landed on a house with peeling siding and patchy grass. A grizzled man was working on a motorcycle in the driveway. I pulled up to the curb opposite the house and grabbed my phone from its cradle. I might be stubborn, but I wasn't an idiot.

Me: *Making one last attempt to contact Les Jensen. Neighborhood's a little rough. I'm at 133 N Spruce St.*

My phone dinged with a reply before I could even reach for my purse.

Noah: *I would've come with you.*

Noah: *Want to wait? I can drive over.*

I glanced over at the man who was now watching me, wariness in his gaze. It was too late now.

Me: *I'm good. He's outside, so not much risk.*

Noah: *Text me the second you're done. No, CALL ME.*

I winced. It wasn't fair to put that sort of pressure or responsibility on him. But I'd do the same for him if needed.

Grabbing my bag, I climbed out of my hatchback and beeped the locks. I recognized Les Jensen from his mug shot. He'd been charged with a lot over the years: Drug possession, grand theft auto, armed robbery, and assault. He'd been in and out of jail for most of his life and painted a similar picture to Renee's previous partner, Kye's birth father, Rex Blackwood.

Renee had a type. And it wasn't good.

Les pushed to his feet and surveyed me from head to toe, making me feel like I was wearing nothing despite my wide-leg trousers and thick sweater. It might be sunny, but it wasn't even fifty degrees out.

"Help you?" Les asked, his voice gravelly.

"Les Jensen?"

"Depends."

I knew it was him, but I still needed the formalities. "I'm Fallon Colson. I work—"

Les's green eyes narrowed on me. "You're that social worker who won't quit callin.'"

"Guilty. I—"

"Mighta picked up if I knew you were a looker."

My jaw clenched, a muscle there fluttering with my heartbeat. "I wanted to talk to you about your daughters, Hayden, Clementine, and Gracie. They've been removed from their mother's care."

Les's grease-streaked fingers tightened around some sort of wrench I couldn't identify. "What'd that cunt do now?"

Clearly, there was no love lost between the two ex-partners, but I did my best to keep my expression blank. "She's been charged with child abuse, child endangerment, assault, and drug possession."

"Sucks for her." He crouched and began working on his bike again, not bothering to even ask about the girls.

I adjusted my grip on my tote bag. "We are filing to terminate Renee's parental rights."

"Prolly a good idea," Les muttered.

"In situations like this, we look to the next closest relatives to see if they're interested in taking custody."

Les looked up at me. "Don't got time for no kids. Don't got the space or the funds."

I couldn't deny the relief that coursed through me at his words. There was no way I would have felt good about Les Jensen as a candidate for guardianship. I dipped my hand into my bag and pulled out a folder. "Would you like to relinquish your parental rights? It means that if another relative takes custody, they won't be able to request child support."

Les pushed to his feet again, scowling at me. "Ain't nobody takin' my money."

"This would ensure that. But it also means you won't be able to file for custody in the future. You will just have to appear in court to confirm your decision."

Les jerked the folder from my hand. "Gimme a goddamned pen."

I offered him one but couldn't disguise the trembling in my fingers as I did.

Les scribbled his signature across the pages and thrust them back at me. "Don't you look down on me, bitch. You don't know what I've lived through."

I swallowed hard, trying not to cower. "You're right. I don't."

"Those girls are better off in foster care. Trust me."

That's when I saw that he was trying to do the right thing in his own way. I let out a shaky breath. "I'm going to do whatever I can to make sure they get the best possible placement."

Tiny divots appeared in the corners of Les's jaw, telling me just how hard he was clenching his teeth. Then he looked away and dropped down to his bike again. "Whatever."

My heart cracked. For all Hayden, Clem, and Gracie had missed out on in their lives. And even a little for Les and how he would miss out on seeing his girls grow and all the amazingness that came with that.

I tucked the folder into my tote bag and headed for my car.

Within seconds, I was inside, turning the key. I silently prayed for the struggling engine to start—this was the last place I wanted to get stuck.

Air whooshed from my lungs as it rumbled to life. As I drove out of the neighborhood, I hit a button on the side of my phone. "Call Noah."

"Calling Noah Myers," my phone said in its mechanical voice.

He answered before the second ring. "You okay?"

"Fine."

"Don't exactly sound it."

I flipped on my blinker. "He signed away his parental rights."

Noah was quiet for a moment, knowing the double-edged sword this could be. "It's probably for the best, given his record. And this gives Kye a shot."

I heard the skepticism in Noah's voice about that second piece of the puzzle. "Any updates on Renee?"

"Charges have been filed and so has the motion to terminate her parental rights. That's the good news. The bad news is that she's out on bail."

My fingers tightened around the wheel. "You think she'll seek out the girls?" It didn't matter that it would go against a court order. Some parents didn't give a damn.

A phone rang in the background before someone silenced it, and Noah began speaking again. "I don't think she cares enough. I could be mistaken. I gave the schools a heads-up. And Mrs. McKenzie, too."

"Good. That's good. I'm going to see the girls now. I want to check in and keep them in the loop."

"You sure that's a good idea?"

Every caseworker handled this sort of thing differently. Some wanted to shield their clients from everything; others thought complete transparency was vital to building trust. I sat somewhere in the middle, always considering the child's age when deciding what to share.

I always tried to thread the needle in a way that built trust but didn't make kids who'd often been in volatile situations worry unnecessarily. But with Hayden, Clem, and Gracie…they needed honesty. At least the older two did. They'd lived a life beyond their years, and they'd know if someone was lying to them.

"Hayden has been a mother to Clem and Gracie for…I don't even want to know how long. If I cut her out of this process, I'll lose any hope of gaining their trust."

Noah sighed. "I hope you know what you're doing."

I did, too. Because I was holding the fate of Kye's sisters in my hands. I'd never forgive myself if I screwed up. And I didn't think Kye would forgive me either.

CHAPTER THIRTEEN

Fallon

I walked up the McKenzies' front path to find Ron in the front yard, deadheading flowers. When he heard my footsteps, he looked up from his work and sent me a smile. "Good to see ya, Fal. How are things?"

"Pretty good," I lied. My life felt like it was coming apart at the seams. "How about you?"

"Can't complain, other than these old bones not keepin' up with all I want to be doing."

I chuckled. "I don't know. You look pretty spry to me."

"Tell Edith that. She's always on me to take it easy."

"I'll make sure to let her know."

"Girls are inside workin' on their homework."

I nodded and glanced through the front windows, getting a peek at Hayden helping Gracie with something while Clem scribbled furiously in a notebook. "How have they been the last few days?"

A look of sadness settled into Ron's gray eyes. "Well-behaved. Quiet. Always do as they're asked."

"But?" I pressed.

"They're *too* well-behaved. Turns my stomach. Kids that age should get into mischief now and again."

I agreed. What these girls needed most after safety was the chance to truly be kids. "We're gonna work on that."

"Good," Ron chuffed. "You go on inside. Edith's in the kitchen, I think. She made cookies."

"Double chocolate?" I asked hopefully.

"You know it."

"She's too good to me." I headed for the door, opened it, and called out, "It's Fallon."

Edith appeared with a warm smile. "Good to see you."

"You, too. I heard there might be some double-chocolate cookies on the premises."

She laughed. "I must've had a psychic premonition you were coming. There's a plate in the living room with the girls. Go on in."

I knew she was giving me an easy approach, and I squeezed her arm in thanks as I passed, headed for the living room. When I walked in, I found three sets of amber eyes locked on me. The sight of those eyes still knocked me sideways. Because they were all Kye.

Gripping my bag a little tighter, I called on a smile but didn't force it, knowing they'd see right through me if I did. "I heard there were cookies."

Gracie let out a soft giggle. "I already had three."

"Oh, I can totally beat three," I said, heading deeper into the room. "I can do five at least."

Clem's mouth curved as she looked up from her spot on the rug, where she was writing in a notebook. "Chocolate has addictive qualities. There have been studies."

I lowered myself to the floor and let my bag drop. "Don't tell me that. I'm already hooked."

Gracie let out another giggle. "Me, too."

I turned to Hayden, who watched me carefully. "What about you? Chocolate fan?"

"Who isn't?" she hedged.

Clem rolled her eyes. "It's her favorite thing on the planet."

I grinned. "I happen to be a sugar fiend myself. Strawberry Sour Patch Kids are my number-one favorite. I'm a sucker for gummy bears, too. Gummy candy of any kind, really. But chocolate is my second love. We'll have to get double-chocolate Oreo shakes from The Pop. They're amazing."

A hint of interest flared in Hayden's eyes at the idea, but she quickly squelched it. "Sure. Are you here to tell us something?"

Right to the point. Smart. Astute. With the proper support, Hayden would soar in this world. "I wanted to update you on what's going on and what might happen next."

Hayden instantly straightened from her spot on the couch next to Gracie. "Did Renee get charged?"

I didn't miss the fact that Hayden hadn't called her *Mom*. "She did. She's out on bail right now as the court decides what's going to happen. But if you see her around, let me, the McKenzies, or your teachers know, okay?"

Gracie moved closer to Hayden, and the older girl wrapped an arm around her sister. But Clem's eyes sparked with anger. "We don't have to go back to her, right?"

"We are working to make sure you don't. But a judge has to make the final decision. They may ask to talk to you. If you're comfortable," I explained.

Clem's hold on her pencil tightened. "I'll talk to them. I'll tell them how awful she is and—"

"Clem," Hayden said softly. Gracie sniffed.

"It's true. And I'm not lying about it anymore," Clem shot back.

Hayden held out a hand. "Okay. But let's not talk about it now." Her gaze moved back to me. "What about Les? We don't have to go with him, do we?"

An image of the grizzled man crouched in front of his bike flashed in my mind. "No. No, you don't."

"Because he didn't want us, right?" Hayden demanded, her voice going hard.

Everything in me hurt at hearing those words. No child deserved to feel unwanted—especially by the people who were supposed to care about them the most. "He knows he's not equipped to give you the life you deserve."

Hayden scoffed. "So, we're going into the system."

"There are several possibilities. One is me finding a long-term foster family for you to live with. But there is another possibility."

"What?" Hayden pressed.

My heart hammered against my ribs as I braced to possibly turn the girls' world upside down. "We discovered that you have a relative who would like to file for custody. A half-brother. Kyler Blackwood."

The reaction wasn't what I'd expected. No gasps or shock. Hayden's face went stone-cold. Gracie stared down at her lap. And Clem hunched in on herself.

"He won't take us. Mom said he doesn't want anything to do with us," Clem whispered.

Fury like I'd never known blazed through my system. It felt as if someone had replaced my blood with lighter fluid and then lit a match. It took everything I had to beat it back and swallow the rage so the girls didn't see it.

"That couldn't be further from the truth," I said quietly.

Hayden scoffed. "Sure. That's why he comes around so often."

I turned to her, trying to let her see my truth. "He didn't know you existed. If he had, he would've been there. Trust me."

Hayden's face twisted. "He'd rather be with your perfect family than us. He's probably just saying he'll file so people don't think he's an asshole."

"Hayden." I kept my voice low. "I've known Kyler since I was fourteen years old. I have never, in the past fourteen years, seen him as devastated as when I told him that he had sisters he didn't know about. Sisters who *needed* him. He's never even met you, and he would already lay down his life for any of you. And that's a fact."

Gracie peered around her sister. "I like his drawings," she said quietly. "The one on the wall outside the gym is really pretty."

A phantom fist squeezed my heart. This little girl had been taking stock of Kye's creations, thinking he was a brother who didn't want to know her. "That will mean a lot to him when I tell him."

"Can we meet him?" Clem asked hesitantly.

I breathed through the pain. "He's dying to meet you. But we have to wait until he gets all his approvals."

Hayden's face hardened. "What do you want to bet one of them conveniently doesn't go through? Renee told us she asked him for help when Clem needed to go to a doctor, and he said he didn't want anything to do with us."

"He's giving his everything to make sure he's approved. And even if he isn't, he'll still want to be in your lives—as much as you'll let him. And I can guarantee that Renee never told him anything about Clementine. Because he would've taken her to the doctor himself."

Disbelief swirled in Hayden's expression. It was the sort of mistrust built on years of being lied to and manipulated. There wasn't a damn person in her life who'd proven they had her back. "Maybe we don't want to go live with him. Maybe we choose the foster system."

I went quiet. So many worries gnawed at me. I wanted to give Hayden a choice, to empower her when so much of her agency had been ripped from her. But I knew the chances of keeping the girls together long-term in the system were damn slim. And there was also a greater chance of upheaval as time went on—placements could change at the drop of a hat.

Hayden's face paled. "You don't think you can keep us together in the system."

"We always try our hardest—"

"But you don't know for sure."

Gracie started to cry and climbed onto Hayden's lap, holding her tightly as if she thought I would rip her away from her sister right then and there. "Don't let them take me, Hay Hay! Please, don't let them take me."

Hayden wrapped her arms around the little girl. "No one's taking you. I've got you. You're safe, okay? You're safe."

Gracie only cried harder. Clem looked at Hayden. "We have to try," she whispered.

Hayden sent a furious look in my direction. "Fine. Tell him to file. And when this all falls apart, remember whose idea it was."

A monster tension headache bordering on a migraine pulsed through my skull. It was as if the pain started there but radiated through my entire body. And it wasn't just physical. The agony living in Hayden, Clem, and Gracie had made a home in me, too. As it should. Because if I didn't feel that pain, I wouldn't fight nearly hard enough.

I flipped on my blinker, making the turn into the DHS parking lot. I nearly ran into a parked car when I saw the familiar black truck and the man resting against its back bumper. The battered leather jacket covering a black tee told countless stories, just like the scarred motorcycle boots that adorned his feet. His broad shoulders and thick thighs spoke of someone people didn't mess with often. The scruff on his angular jaw was thicker than the last time I'd seen him, and his nearly black hair looked like he'd been running his hands through it nonstop. But it was his eyes that stopped me in my tracks.

Those amber eyes were darker than I'd ever seen them. Heavy with the weight of responsibility and the demons all this had kicked up. I would've given anything to soothe the war inside him. But I wasn't sure where to start.

I eased my foot off the brake and pulled into a parking spot at the end of the row. Little flickers of shadow danced across my vision as my headache intensified. Not what I needed.

Grabbing my jacket and bag, I climbed out of my hatchback. Kye was already waiting at the end of the parking spot. He didn't get any closer, as if he weren't sure what sort of welcome he'd receive.

"Hi." It was all I could say. So much swirled in me, between us, and all around, I didn't trust myself to say anything more.

Kye was quiet as he studied me for a moment. No one could read me better than he could. He opened his arms. The urge to cry was strong, but I beat it back and walked right into that familiar embrace.

Kye's arms engulfed me the second I reached his chest. I breathed him in, oakmoss and amber, with a hint of leather. His lips grazed the top of my head. "I'm sorry. Sorry I dragged you into all this. Sorry I fucked up where we're at."

"You didn't do any of that," I croaked. "I'd walk through fire for you, Kyler."

His arms tightened around me the minute his full name left my lips. "Want to keep you from any pain, Sparrow. Never want to be the cause of it."

I pulled back so I could look into his eyes. "Pain means we care. Means we love. Means we live. I wouldn't trade any of that just to avoid some suffering."

He stared down at me, searching for something only I could give him. "So damn brave." His brows pulled together as he traced a tattooed finger over my brow. "Headache?"

"It's been a day," I said by way of answer.

"You eat lunch?"

It was after four now, but I couldn't remember having anything but cookies after the bagel I'd scarfed down on my way to Les's house. My gaze slid to the side.

"Fallon," Kye growled.

The demand in that one word had my gaze returning. "I might've missed it."

A scowl twisted Kye's beautiful mouth. "Come on." He began leading me toward his truck.

"I need to go in, tackle a mountain of paperwork, and—"

"And you can do it later. First, you need some food. And I want to show you something."

Curiosity niggled. "What kind of something?"

One corner of Kye's mouth kicked up in that mischievous half grin I loved. "You'll only find out if you eat something first."

"That's blackmail," I muttered.

Kye opened the passenger door of his truck. "Is it still blackmail if a double-chocolate Oreo shake is involved?"

I climbed into the cab. "No. That's bribery, and I'm very amenable to that."

He chuckled, and the sound skated over my skin in the best way. "Good to know."

Kye shut me in and pulled out his phone, speaking words I couldn't hear as he rounded the vehicle. He hovered outside the truck, finishing his call, then climbed behind the wheel. "First, The Pop. Then I'll take you to what I want to show you."

"Blackmailer," I muttered.

"Briber," he corrected as he navigated out of the parking lot and headed for downtown.

"Potato, potahto," I grumbled.

Kye reached over and slid his hand under my hair to massage my neck. "Bad enough headache to make you grouchy."

He wasn't wrong, and as he hit an especially tender spot, I couldn't help the little groan that slid from my lips.

"Gotta take better care of yourself, Fal," he whispered.

"Things have just been busier than usual."

"Because of me."

I shook my head. "Because I want to make sure Hayden, Clem, and Gracie get the home they deserve."

Kye pulled into a spot in front of The Pop and turned to me, his hand still lingering on my neck, his thumb digging into a pressure point there. "Every kid that comes across your desk is so damn lucky."

I swallowed hard. "I saw them today."

Kye's thumb stilled as pain filled his amber eyes. "Bad?"

"The McKenzies are taking great care of them. They were eating their fill of double-chocolate cookies when I got there."

"But?" Kye knew there was more. He always knew.

"Renee told them you knew you had sisters and wanted nothing to do with them." I said the words as quickly as I could because he needed to know, but it was also the last thing I wanted to level him with.

Kye's fingers spasmed on my neck before he jerked his hand away as if he was terrified he might hurt me. "I hate her," he ground out. "I don't want to hate anyone because I know it eats you up inside, but I *hate* her. With every fiber of my being."

"I told them she lied. That you'd do anything for them."

Kye shook his head, the action violent. "Won't matter. Not until they see. Until they can feel the dedication. Words mean nothing. Not to kids who grew up like I did. Everyone lies, cheats, hurts. They gotta see that I won't do that to them."

I reached over and hooked his pinky with mine. "I know. And they will see."

Kye stared down at our joined fingers. "Won't stop until they do."

"I know that, too."

"Gotta get the food, Sparrow."

I didn't want to let him go, but I forced myself to—like I'd had to do time after time. I should've been good at it, watching Kye walk away. But it never got any easier.

My nerves ratcheted up with each moment he was gone. As if some part of me feared he'd never return. But as Kye exited the restaurant, a laugh bubbled out of me. It was the last sound I thought I'd make at the moment. But, of course, Kye made it happen.

His arms were laden with two jumbo-sized bags and two drink carriers. It was a miracle he didn't trip on his way to the truck. I pushed open my door and reached for one of the carriers. "What did you do?"

Kye shrugged. "You needed ginger ale for nausea, Diet Coke for caffeine, water for hydration, and a double-chocolate Oreo shake for your reward."

Something shifted uncomfortably in my chest as if my heart didn't quite know what to do. "Kye."

His amber gaze met mine. "Always going to take care of you."

That familiar pressure built under my sternum, in Kye's spot. But I couldn't say anything because I wasn't sure those words were something I should trust—for both our sakes.

He handed me the second carrier with his two drinks and then slid the bags in at my feet. "Wasn't sure what you were in the mood for. Got you a cheeseburger, a grilled cheese, and a turkey club."

"Your picture is next to over-the-top in the dictionary," I muttered.

"You can take the leftovers home," he argued.

"Thank you."

He didn't say anything in response, simply closed my door and rounded the truck to get behind the wheel. We ate as he drove, slipping into the familiar routine of me unwrapping a burger for him and setting up his fries so he could reach them more easily. We kept the conversation light as Kye steered the truck toward Colson Ranch.

We talked about Lolli's diamond art for Cope and the sonogram photo Arden had sent via our group chat as I nibbled on the grilled cheese sandwich and drank copious amounts of my liquid options.

Kye cast a quick glance at my lap. "You haven't eaten enough."

"I'm working on it. Slow and steady. The last thing you want is me upchucking in your precious baby."

"Wouldn't be the first time," Kye said wryly.

My face twisted. "Do not remind me."

Kye had picked me up after a particularly potent girls' night, and I had vomited all over the front seat of his truck. He hadn't yelled or made me feel bad. He'd simply taken me home, cleaned me up, and watched over me all night to make sure I didn't get sick again.

Kye patted the dash. "She recovered. After back-to-back detail jobs."

I covered my face with my hands. "I still can't handle the smell of Jack Daniel's."

Kye laughed as he turned onto a gravel road across from Colson Ranch. "I will keep that in mind around you."

"Where are we going?" I asked as I sat up straighter, trying to see.

"Gotta eat more of your sandwich if you wanna find out."

I took a big bite, chewed, and then swallowed. "Okay, tell me."

"I wanted to show you the house I built."

I looked over at Kye, his eyes fixed on the road ahead. "And Shep didn't build it?"

Kye had said he hadn't, but the possibility still stung. That he might have shared something with one of our siblings and not me. But he quickly shook his head. "No. I didn't want…I needed this to be mine. I wasn't ready to share it."

My brow furrowed as I studied him, trying to figure out why building a home would be such a secret.

We bumped down the gravel road for a mile or so before Kye turned onto a drive. A massive gate stretched across it, but everything about it was Kye. The design was artful, a blended style like tattoos on metal—a mountainscape with sparrows flying around the top and a single word carved into the middle: *Haven*.

"It's beautiful," I whispered.

"I'm glad you like it." Kye rolled down his window and punched a code into an intercom. A second later, the gates swung open to a paved drive lined with an array of evergreens.

The trees made it hard to see anything ahead, and I found myself holding my breath as we made our way deeper onto the property. "How many acres?"

"A little over a hundred."

I swallowed, my throat sticking on the motion. "Could get lost on that." I also knew it would've cost a pretty penny, especially with more people moving to Central Oregon, trying to soak up all the beauty it had to offer.

"Sometimes getting lost is exactly what you need."

Kye's words hit, and my gaze moved from the path ahead to him, trying to read what it was he was looking for in getting lost. I was so distracted by trying to find my answers that I didn't notice the house had come into view. Not until Kye stopped the truck.

I turned then, and what I saw nearly knocked me sideways. The house was a blend of Victorian and Craftsman, painted a deep teal blue with dark wooden accents. It felt like part castle and part farmhouse, coming together to create something that was out-of-this-world perfect. Something I'd doodled countless times on paper, but also somehow more.

"Kye," I rasped. "That's my house."

CHAPTER FOURTEEN

Kye

I TRIED TO SEE THE HOUSE THROUGH FALLON'S EYES. TRIED TO pull the pieces together like she might. I couldn't help shifting in my seat, wondering if she would think me an obsessed fool. But if she did, she wouldn't be wrong.

Fallon pushed open her door and slid out of the truck, moving toward the towering creation. It had magic and whimsy—something rare and extraordinary, just like the girl who'd dreamed it up. She was full of the same magic. As she took in the three-story structure, complete with three rounded towers and countless balconies, her jaw dropped.

"Kyler...how is my house real?"

I held tightly to that name—the way her mouth curved around it and made it sound like something uniquely hers. In so many ways, it was.

"Because I built it." My voice was rusty like I hadn't spoken all day.

Fallon didn't look at me when she spoke her next question. "Why?"

Here was the moment of truth. I could give it to her as it was, or I could bend it, hiding what lay in every board and nail. I didn't want her to know. Didn't want her to hold all those cards for many different reasons. But I didn't want lies between us either. Not when I was about to ask her for the ultimate sacrifice.

I followed her line of sight, trying to discern which detail she was picking out. "When I lost you, lost what we were, I needed something to hold on to. I thought if I built the house, if I lived in it, I could still have you with me—the you that you were to me back then. But when they finished it a few years ago, it didn't feel right…living here without you."

I turned then, only to see tears glistening in Fallon's eyes. "Kyler."

For so long, I'd wanted her to think I'd moved on. That she mattered to me in the most vital way but that I didn't ache for the version of us we'd almost been. That we were friends, siblings, and nothing more. But it was a lie.

I called the rest of the Colson crew "brother" or "sister," but never Fal. Because she was as far from a sister to me as you could get. My mouth rejected the word, right along with the rest of me.

"Was going to give it to you, but then you'd have known," I rasped.

Those beautiful dark blue eyes cut to me. "Known what?"

"Everything I've buried deep for fourteen years."

A tear tracked down her cheek. "It doesn't have to be that way."

"It does. You know it. I know it. I'm not built for it—for what you deserve. There are too many demons around every corner."

"Bullshit," she spat.

"Please." I wasn't above begging because if she pushed the right lever, everything would come crashing down. "I can't fight you and fight for my sisters. I can't be worried about wrecking your life when I need to be focused on giving them what they deserve and helping them heal."

Fallon's hands fisted at her sides, delicate fingers far more powerful than they looked. She stared at me for a long moment as she let every word land and realized the truth in them. "Okay."

It wasn't fair. What I was asking of us was the farthest thing from it. But I would do it for my sisters.

"Thank you," I said. What I didn't say was that I'd give it to her when this was done. When it was time to end our game of make-believe, I'd leave Fallon in the house of her dreams. She—her imagination—had built it, after all.

She nodded. There was a sadness to it that nearly broke me, but my sparrow was strong, and I watched as she summoned that strength and steeled her spine, looking for the good like she always did. "It's beautiful. More than I could've dreamed."

That was something. It wasn't nearly enough, but it was something. "Want to see the inside?"

The wind caught Fallon's white-blond hair as she turned, and the smile on her face nearly brought me to my knees like it always did. Even more now because I'd put it there. "I want to see everything," she said.

I could give her that, too. "Come on."

I didn't dare touch her. Not now—not after letting so many truths slip free. Not when it would be so easy for us to lose ourselves in what could've been. I kept my distance as I led her up a stone walkway surrounded by landscaping just starting to go bare as winter approached.

Lifting my keys, I unlocked the front door and stepped inside to the alarm beep echoing in the empty house. I plugged in a code and moved to the temperature control, dialing up the heat.

"Kye?"

Kyler was gone now. Good. We were putting the walls back in place like we needed to. "Yeah?"

"You don't have any furniture."

I chuckled, and that felt good, too—more of the normal returning. "Never did get around to that. Think we could talk Ellie into helping us out?"

Trace's girlfriend—Linc's sister—had worked as an interior designer in New York for years and had a gift. The fact that she reveled in rainbows and whimsy made her the perfect person for this job in particular.

Fallon grinned as she moved deeper into the entryway. "She would love to get her hands on this place. I know it."

"You never talked much about what you saw for the inside, so I went on instinct there. I wanted open spaces. Lots of light."

Fallon moved past a massive staircase that curled off into opposite sides of the house. "It's perfect." Her throat worked as she swallowed. "There's even a pond."

I followed her into the open living, dining, and family space, taking in the wall of windows framed with wood to add character. The way the house was positioned made it feel like we hovered over the pond, the structure spilling onto a patio that dipped right in. There was even a little dock you could sit on.

"Told the realtor the property had to have one, and a site where I could build right on top of it. Told the architect and builder it had to feel like we were floating."

Fallon walked farther into the space as if the water pulled her. "It feels like the magical land I always wanted it to be. You know, I always dreamed of it being full of kids who needed a safe place to land. And now, it will be."

Fuck. She was too good. Too pure of heart. This world was too dark for her to even be a part of. But she never let it stop her. She just kept shining that light, taking on people's pain.

Fallon turned back to look at me, acres of blond hair cascading around her. "Can I see everything else?"

She looked so perfect framed by the beams of light streaming in through the windows as the sun set. Like a goddamned angel who'd fallen to Earth. "Yeah, you can see everything."

I took her through the house room by room. I showed her the basement, complete with a screening room, a gym, and something I knew could be a playroom. Then we went upstairs into a room off the side of the house that could be an indoor greenhouse of sorts.

"Rho will have a field day with this," Fallon mumbled as her boots clicked across the brick floor. "We need to let her pick plants for it."

My mouth curved. "I think she'll be up to the challenge."

Fal chuckled. "Especially if you don't give her a budget."

"She's gonna gut me."

"Oh, I have no doubt." Fallon wandered through a door deeper in the conservatory. "What in—oh, my God. This is gorgeous. A library."

The walls were a deep teal similar to the exterior paint, and the built-in bookshelves were so dark they were almost black. The shelves were empty, but it would be fun as hell to fill them.

"We need books," she mumbled. "I think Mom still has my epic Nancy Drew collection from childhood. I feel like Clem might like those. She's a reader."

An invisible vise tightened around my chest, holding me in place, when all I wanted to do was reach out and learn more about my sister. Who was she? What made her light up? "Maybe we can take her to the bookstore and fill this place."

Fal's deep blue eyes sparked with light at that. "And to the secondhand store. They have tons of books there you can buy for like a nickel. And they're all well-loved and have character."

"Will you tell me more about them? My sisters?" I asked quietly.

A little of Fallon's light dimmed, turning soft as if she understood my longing. "I can tell Gracie has quite the imagination. She's quiet, but there's always something going on behind it."

I'd never met the little girl, but I'd seen her a handful of times at Keely's birthday parties and school performances.

"Hayden...she's the fiercest defender," Fal began. "But I won't lie. It'll be a battle to win her trust."

"That means she's smart. World-wise." But I hated the reasons she'd had to become that way.

"And with time, she'll get her chance to be a kid," Fallon said softly.

My back teeth ground together. "She will."

"Come on. Let's pick bedrooms for them." Fallon shot me a smile as she headed for the stairs. We walked from room to room, trying to place my sisters in spaces that would speak to them.

Fallon stood in the hallway, her fingers drumming against those perfect, pink lips. "They'll want to be as close as possible." She spun in a circle, studying the layout as if she were doing an equation in the air. "I think we should put Clem and Gracie here. The two rooms share a Jack-and-Jill bathroom. And Hayden can be across the hall. She'll have her own bathroom but will still be close if they need her."

I nodded, trying to picture it all. "I want Ellie to really make their rooms come to life. Maybe you can ask them what some of their favorite things are."

"Of course. I'll get a list and give it to Ellie." Fallon pulled her phone from her pocket, making a note.

I shoved my hands into the pockets of my leather jacket, too scared they'd give me away. "You want to see the primary suite?"

Fallon looked up at me, that phantom energy crackling between us. "Sure."

I started toward the opposite side of the house and led because I wasn't sure I could look at Fal when she saw the space. Those gorgeous sunset rays beamed into the large room, casting it in pinks and golds. The whole far wall was windows, and it looked out over the pond and to the Monarch Mountains and Castle Rock in the distance.

The view was enough to demand silence. Reverence. I could imagine a bed in this room, facing the windows that would make it feel like you were sleeping in the clouds.

"Kye?" Fallon asked, her voice quiet.

"Yeah?"

"Respectfully. Get the fuck out."

It was the last thing I'd expected her to say, and it had me barking out a laugh as I turned to look at her. Fallon's whole face was alight with shock, awe, and pure pleasure.

"This is a room fit for a princess," she mumbled as she turned in circles.

"No," I countered. "It's fit for a queen."

That stilled her. The spinning stopped, and her gaze cut to me. I saw infinite questions in her eyes.

I moved then, slowly crossing the space. The setting sun danced across Fallon's face as she tracked every move I made. I stopped just shy of her, the scents of jasmine and coconut wrapping around me like a familiar embrace.

My fingers wrapped around the tiny piece of metal in my pocket as I met her hypnotic gaze. "You're the last person I should be asking to do this with me."

Fallon's breath hitched, halting on a jerky inhale.

"It's not fair. And it's so damn far from what you deserve," I continued.

Those blue depths sparked, and I saw a hint of temper there. "Shouldn't I be the one to decide what I deserve?"

I stared at her for a long moment, trying to find the words. "You're my person. The spark in the shadows. You carried me through when I didn't think I'd survive. So, I'm never going to stop demanding that this world give you everything."

Fallon's delicate throat worked as she swallowed. "Kye..."

"This might not be a real marriage, and I might not be able to give you what you deserve, but I can give you this."

I pulled the ring from my pocket, and Fallon sucked in an audible breath. The sunset rays made the rose gold glow in the fading light and brought the black diamond to life in a way I'd never seen.

"I've never..." Fallon struggled for words as she lifted her hand. "It's perfect. Raw and real and stunning beyond measure." Her gaze lifted to mine. "It's you."

Taking Fallon's hand, I slid the ring onto her finger. "I will honor you every day of this marriage. And every day after it's done. And no matter what comes, my battered and blackened heart will always be yours."

CHAPTER FIFTEEN

Kye

THE SUN HOVERED FOR A MOMENT BEFORE IT SANK BEHIND THE mountains as if it couldn't quite decide if it wanted to stay or go. I understood the feeling—that push and pull.

But I'd already tipped the way I was going. So, I kept right on walking toward the woman on the dock. Unfolding the fuzzy blanket, I wrapped it around her shoulders.

Fallon pulled it tight, the ring on her finger glinting in the twilight. *Fuck.* I loved the sight of it on her hand, the way it felt like a physical manifestation of my tether to her. The invisible tie that had always bound us.

"No furniture, but you have blankets," Fallon said, staring into the twilight.

I lowered myself to the dock next to her. "I come here sometimes. When I need to get away. Think. And you know the nights around here are cold."

She glanced over at me, her blond hair catching the fading light like her ring had. "I always wondered where you disappeared to."

One corner of my mouth kicked up. "Now you know."

"Now, I know," she echoed, turning back to the mountains. "We need to talk logistics."

I gripped the side of the dock so I wouldn't reach for Fallon. It would be hard enough having her in my space day in and day out. Too much temptation. I'd have to create distance where I could. "Probably not a bad idea."

Fal's fingers twisted in the blanket. "I'll talk to Rose tomorrow and let her know I'll be part of the custody filing. She or Mila will have to be the girls' caseworker."

"What? Why?" Anxiety flooded my system at the thought of anyone but Fal having my sisters' backs.

She glanced over at me, her expression gentle. "If I'm applying for custody alongside you, it's a conflict of interest. I can't be a part of the home inspections, the interviews, or anything else."

I pressed my palms harder against the edge of the dock, almost wishing it would tear my skin open. It would be an easier source of pain to handle. "Makes sense. I just...I need to know they're in good hands."

"Both Rose and Mila are excellent caseworkers," Fallon assured me. "But I'll ask Rose to take the case personally. She has a softer touch. For Mila, there are no shades of gray."

My jaw worked back and forth. "All right. How long will it take? The approval process, I mean."

"The house needs to be ready and approved. All your paperwork has been submitted. I just need to work on mine tonight. Could be a matter of days, or a couple of weeks. It just depends on whether it all goes according to plan."

My gut soured at that. I *hated* being dependent on anyone. The only thing I despised more was the feeling that someone could control me. That my fate was in their hands. I wanted to be the only determiner of where I was headed. But I didn't have a choice here.

"We should probably get married, too, right?" I asked.

Fal's knuckles bleached white as she gripped the blanket tighter. "Yeah. We should."

I couldn't tell what was beneath those words. But it wasn't wholehearted joy. How could it be? I was asking Fallon to lie to everyone she cared about. "We could tell the family. That it isn't real, I mean. They'd understand—"

"No." Fallon cut me off with that single word. "It would make them accessories to fraud."

Just like I was making Fallon.

She turned to me. "I want to do this. For you. For Hayden, Clem, and Gracie. But I think the fewer people who know the truth, the better. We can't risk it. And it isn't fair to ask them to lie."

I nodded slowly. "Okay." My throat worked as I struggled to swallow. "And when we end things? What do we tell them then?"

Fallon's gaze lifted to my face. "That we realized we were better as friends. And we stay in each other's lives. I stay in the girls' lives."

She made it sound so easy, but I knew it would rip me to shreds. Still, I forced myself to nod. "So when should we tell them? About the engagement, I mean."

Fallon's tongue darted out, wetting her bottom lip in that nervous habit she had. "No time like the present."

I shifted, pulling out my phone and unlocking it. I navigated to our sibling chat Rho had named *Nacho Average Siblings* yesterday.

Me: *Need a favor. Family meeting tonight at 389 Cascadia Lane. Can someone bring Nora and Lolli? And someone grab pizza? Cope, we'll video call you.*

Cope: *No, you won't.*

I glanced at Fallon in confusion, but her fingers were already flying across her phone.

Sparrow: *Why are you being a douche canoe?*

Cope sent a photo of the Monarch Mountains in answer.

Cope: *Just landed at Sparrow Falls Airport. Linc lent us his plane.*

Me: *You have practice. A game this weekend.*

Cope: *And I've got a coach and a team owner who understand the importance of family. And Linc had better understand the value of this particular family since he's going to be a part of it. They're going to let us make trips back here as much as we can. I'm not playing yet anyway.*

Cope was still recovering from being shot several months ago. While he'd mostly healed, he wasn't quite up to professional hockey strength yet. But I knew how much getting back on the ice meant to him. So, the fact that he was here, taking time away from training because he knew I'd had a rough few days, meant something.

Me: *You didn't have to.*

Cope: *I wanted to. Plus, someone's gotta get photographic evidence of you whenever Gracie or Clementine decide they need a makeover victim.*

Rhodes: *I personally think lavender is his color. And Anson and I can pick up Mom and Lolli.*

Trace: *Ellie and I have pizza. And his color isn't lavender. It's obviously periwinkle.*

Arden: *I'm so proud of you for knowing the difference, T-money.*

Trace: *Stop talking to me like I'm a rapper.*

Shep: *Ellie might've loosened him up a little, but he's still not cool enough for hip-hop. Thea and I will bring dessert. She's got extras from The Mix Up.*

Me: *Appreciate you. All of you.*

Arden: *Stop being gushy. It's freaking me out.*

A chuckle slid out of me as I typed out a new message.

Me: *Gonna give those twins of yours motorcycles when they turn sixteen. That better?*

Arden: *Kyler Blackwood, I will help Fallon rig glitter bombs in your car, Blackheart Ink, Haven, and your damn apartment.*

Sparrow: *I do have some pink unicorn glitter bombs I've been waiting to use.*

My gaze flicked up to her. "You wouldn't."

A devilish smile played over Fallon's lips. "That's just a risk you'll have to take."

"Your vengeful streak is slightly terrifying," I muttered.

Her smile widened. "Thank you."

"I didn't mean it as a compliment."

Fallon pushed to her feet. "I'm taking it as one anyway."

Pure chaos ensued as the Colson crew descended on my house. Keely leapt from Trace's SUV and came running for me. I caught her easily. "How's my Keely girl?"

She slapped both her hands on my cheeks. "Uncle Kye, is this *your* house? It's like a castle."

"It is my house. Do you like it?" I asked, trying to discern if her friend, Gracie, would like it, too.

"Kye Kye, I said it looks like a castle. I loooooooove it."

I laughed and set her down on the front steps. "I'm so glad you approve."

Ellie and Trace walked onto the porch, Trace carrying at least six pizza boxes. "You have a house you never told us about?"

"You're one to talk. You were building one without telling us," I shot back.

Ellie patted him on the chest. "He's got a point, Chief."

Trace scowled. "Because you all have big mouths, and you would've spoiled the surprise for Keely."

Shep headed up the path, both his and Thea's arms laden with bakery boxes. But he only had eyes for the house itself. "It's newish construction. Sometime in the past several years. You just buy this?"

I shook my head, knowing it would both give me away and be proof of the side of the story I was weaving with Fallon. "I had it built about seven years ago."

Shep's footsteps faltered. "You built a house and didn't have me do the work."

Rhodes let out a low whistle as she walked up with Anson at her side. Nora and Lolli followed behind. "You're in trouble now, Kye Kye."

"I'm sorry. I didn't want anyone to know." The answer felt pathetic, given the hurt I could be inflicting on Shep, who'd built an incredible construction and design business.

Shep looked up at the house again. "Incredible craftsmanship." His whole body jerked. "The house. It's..."

"The one Fal always used to draw," Nora said softly, seeking me out through the dwindling light.

All eyes shifted to me, and I fought the urge to squirm. I could feel Fallon on the step behind me, her heat bleeding into me as she stayed carefully silent. Thankfully, we were saved by a honking horn. Two sets of headlights rounded the bend, and within seconds, more of the Colson crew was descending.

Luca was out first, bounding across the driveway. "What is this place?" he called with seven-year-old wonder. "It's sick!"

"It's Uncle Kye's castle," Keely filled in helpfully.

"Bruh," Luca muttered as if that said it all.

His mom, Sutton, made her way up the path behind him and rolled her eyes. "Let me tell you that *bruh* is apparently the ultimate compliment. You have arrived."

"Good to know." I waved at our crowd as Cope, Linc, and Arden made their way toward the house. "Come on in."

I suddenly felt nervous as I stepped inside. Fallon read me like a book and reached out, hooking her pinky with mine for the briefest moment. "It's all going to be okay."

"I hope so," I whispered.

"Hot damn," Lolli called, making her way through the foyer and into the open living space. "This is a *pad*."

Fallon laughed. "Think about the parties you could throw here, Lolli."

"I'm thinking about the naked yoga sessions I could have on that patio," she said, moving to the windows and looking out at the softly lit backyard.

"Lolls," Trace warned.

Lolli turned on him. "Oh, don't you start. Because I happen to know your office got a little recreational use last week."

"Mom!" Nora chastised.

Lolli simply shrugged. "I'm just saying that Trace isn't as much of a stick in the mud as I thought, and he doesn't have a leg to stand on."

Keely looked up at her dad, her dark, artful braids swinging. "Daddy, what's rec-re-ashal mean?"

Ellie buried her face in Trace's neck. "I would like to die now."

Trace sent Lolli a scathing look.

"What?" Lolli asked with faux innocence as she turned toward the massive fireplace. "You know what would look perfect above this?"

"A fairy orgy diamond painting?" Cope suggested. "I've got one he can have."

"Copeland Colson," Nora warned. "You are not too old for me to ground you."

"I will help her," Sutton added.

"What'd I say?" Cope asked, affronted.

"Is an orgy a battle with ogres?" Keely asked, confused. "Like in a fairy tale?"

"Gotta be," Luca said with a decisive nod.

Cope grimaced. "Okay, I might've messed up there."

"You think?" Trace growled.

Linc's hazel eyes sparked with mirth as the hockey team owner slapped Cope on the shoulder. "Just wait for the call you get from Luca's teacher when he uses that one during an English lesson."

Arden choked on a laugh. "Please record the phone call."

Sutton shook her head and sighed. "It's all fun and games now, but you'll be in the same boat we are before long."

Linc's hand went to Arden's slightly rounded belly. "I'm getting the twins earmuffs."

"Make sure they're noise canceling," I muttered.

Cope chuckled as he pulled me into a back-slapping hug, holding it for a moment longer than he normally would. "You hanging in?"

I nodded as he released me. "I'll be better when my sisters are home."

God. Saying that just felt right.

"You're going to need some furniture first," Shep murmured.

His girlfriend, Thea, studied the place. "A lot of furniture. But it's going to be such a magical home for them."

I turned to Ellie. "I was actually hoping you could perform a miracle and outfit this house in the next few days."

Ellie's eyes went wide. "Days?" she squeaked.

I grimaced but nodded. "I need to get the house approved by DHS."

In a flash, all shock and doubt were gone. She fished in her tote bag and pulled out her phone. "I'm going to need you to walk me around the space. Tell me what the girls' personalities are like. What they enjoy doing. I know Gracie loves art."

"And she's really good at it, too," Arden said, burrowing into Linc's side. "I should've guessed something was off when it was always Hayden picking her up."

"I've been kicking myself all week," Cope muttered. "I should've tried harder with Hayden. Made her explain what was going on."

I couldn't help stealing a glance at Fallon, and I found her face as I expected, guilt and sadness swirling in her expression. I moved without considering the dangers or the risk to my already fraying control. Wrapping an arm around her, I pulled her into my side.

Trace crossed from the kitchen island into the living space. "There's nothing we could do. Without permission to enter the home or reports of neglect or abuse, we had no rights."

"I should've had Noah follow up again," Fallon said softly.

My fingers dug into her shoulder gently, just enough to bring her gaze to mine. "You're the reason he looked at the case to begin with. You had him circle back to their teachers twice."

"And I know you had him drop off materials about the different support programs the county offers," Trace added.

Fal shook her head. "A lot of good leaving that in her mailbox did."

My thumb ghosted back and forth across her shoulder as if memorizing the curve of the bone. I'd commit every piece of Fallon I could to memory these next months. I'd burn them into me so they'd never leave. Even if they were pieces I had no right to—stolen shards of a woman who'd never be mine but would always have my soul.

"We're doing what we can now, right?" I asked, not wanting Fallon to carry this guilt. It should belong to me. I was the one who never checked to see if Renee had other kids, never looked deeper into what she was up to. And it would've been easy. My brother was the sheriff, and I even knew a hacker through Anson, who could find anything, anywhere.

Fallon tilted her head back to meet my gaze. Waves of white-blond hair cascaded down her back, teasing my arm. Her dark blue eyes glittered with so much hurt—for my sisters, for me. Her hand lifted, and she pressed it to my chest. "I'm sorry."

"It's not on you, Sparrow." I'd never used the nickname in front of our family. It had always been something I'd tucked away, only letting it slip free when emotion got the best of me and Fal and I were alone.

"Fallon..." Rhodes began, her voice wary. "Why is there a ring on *that* finger?"

Fal's gaze didn't stray from mine, as though she thought she might lose her nerve if she looked at her family. I held that beautiful blue gaze, not letting go as I spoke. "Because I asked Fallon to marry me."

I pulled her tighter against me then, trying to bleed strength into her and apologize for making her lie to the people she loved the most.

Fallon's pink lips curved. I'd always loved watching them move: the way the highest peaks bowed when she smiled, how one corner of her mouth reached just a bit higher. She let out a silent exhale, leaned in, and stretched.

I knew what was coming as Fal rose to her tiptoes. "He asked, and I said yes."

There was stunned silence the minute my hand slid along her jaw, feeling my rough skin against her petal softness. The moment my eyes held hers, I waited one breath and then two so I could memorize her face in the light. The moment her lips met mine. Silence reigned as I finally felt what I'd been missing for fourteen years. I knew it was all pretend, a show, but I couldn't stop my tongue from sliding in for the briefest moment.

I needed to know if Fallon tasted the same or if I'd simply embellished a childhood memory. But then all my senses sparked to life as her heat blazed through my tee, and the scent of jasmine dipped in coconut swirled around me. The taste of spearmint and fresh, clean air flooded me.

That taste.

I'd happily drown in it time after time. Suddenly, I could breathe. For the first time in fourteen years, Fallon gave me air.

And then our whole world exploded.

CHAPTER SIXTEEN

Fallon

I FELT TEARS FILL MY EYES, EVEN AS THEY WERE CLOSED. BECAUSE this kiss... *This* was what I'd been waiting for. All those bad dates, the kisses that had felt like making out with a dead fish, the times I'd tried so hard to feel something, *anything*, and had come up empty. *This* was what I'd wanted.

My body pressed harder against Kye's as if it had a mind of its own. As his tongue slid in, everything in me came alive as if my nerve endings were little sparklers humming beneath my skin.

And then a voice cut in and ruined it. "What the fuck?"

I knew Cope's angry tone better than any of my other siblings. Maybe because I'd lived with him the longest. I'd memorized all the various inflections of his voice, and this one wasn't good.

"Uncle Cope, that's a bad one," Keely said.

Ellie winced. "On that note, why don't you, me, and Luca go downstairs? I heard there's a movie theater. You can tell me what movies we need to stock."

Luca sent his soon-to-be stepdad a curious look. "I don't wanna miss the good stuff."

"Luca," Sutton warned.

"Aw, man." He sighed and started after Keely and Ellie.

Cope didn't even turn to follow the boy with his eyes; he was too busy glaring at Kye. The second the door closed, he exploded. "What the hell are you thinking? That's our sister!"

"She's *your* sister," Kye corrected. "I've never once thought of her as that."

"You grew up with her," Cope snarled.

Sutton moved in closer and grabbed his arm. "Take a breath, Hotshot. You don't want to say something you'll regret."

"Are you kidding me? This is a dozen shades of wrong," he growled.

Arden looked back and forth between Kye and me. "Honestly, I'm not surprised."

"Makes a hell of a lot of sense," Shep echoed.

A little relief bled into me. "We've been seeing each other for a while but didn't want anyone to know until we were sure it had legs. Wanting custody of the girls pushed up our timetable, but it doesn't change that we're sure." My hand pressed harder against Kye's chest. "And we want to give Kye's sisters something stable. A home. We want to give them everything they haven't had."

Kye's lips brushed my forehead, and his voice dropped to a whisper. "Thank you."

My gaze searched the room. Trace was quiet and watchful, but not in a disapproving way, just an unsure one. But of all our siblings, he'd always seen the most. He'd be the hardest to fool. And I could already see him trying to peel back the layers to get to the truth beneath.

The other would be Anson. The fact that his entire job had been about profiling people would make fooling him especially difficult. I couldn't read his face; it was too carefully masked. When I turned to my sister and best friend, hers was just as unreadable.

I couldn't deny that the lack of response stung. And more than that, it was confusing. But before I could say a word, my mom rushed toward Kye and me.

She swept us up in a hug. "I knew you two always had a special bond. Something different. And you're going to give those girls such a beautiful home in all ways."

Acid surged up my throat, but I did my best to swallow it down. "Thanks, Mom."

"Hot damn," Lolli said with a grin as Mom released us. "I thought you two were making a run for the priesthood and the nunnery, but you were just getting down and dirty on the side."

Cope made a gagging noise. "Jesus. This is too fuckin' weird for me."

Sutton whirled on him. "Copeland Colson, I will do more than ground you if you don't pull your head out of your ass right this second. You, more than anyone, should know that we aren't guaranteed a certain number of moments on this Earth. And we need to make the most of them. If we find someone we love, someone who makes us feel *seen*, we can't waste it. Who cares how they came into our lives? What matters is that they're there and make us better."

The room was quiet for a moment, and then Trace started clapping. Shep let out a whistle. "You tell him, cupcake queen."

Sutton smiled at Shep. "I try."

"And you're damn right," Arden agreed, scowling at Cope.

Linc pinned his friend and star forward with a hard stare. "You would've freaked no matter who Fal ended up with. She's your little sister. But at least you know the kind of man Kye is."

I glanced up at Kye, trying to see beneath the mask he'd painted on. Lines of tension bracketed his mouth, and his amber eyes had darkened a few shades. There was hurt in there, too. Because time after time, Kye had been made to feel like he wasn't enough.

Without considering the wisdom of it, I slid my hand into his and wove our fingers together. I squeezed hard as I turned on my brother. "I love you, Cope, but if you do anything to make Kye feel like he isn't everything I deserve and more, I will do way worse than glitter bomb you. I will steal Arden's switchblade and remove any chance for you to have children in the future."

Cope's jaw went slack, and Arden stifled a laugh. Kye tugged our joined hands, so I was flush against him. "You don't have to get all vengeful for me, Sparrow."

"Trust me," I ground out. "I want to."

Sutton patted Cope's chest. "Listen to her. Not only because she's right but because I'd really love to have adorable babies with you one day."

Cope's gaze flicked to her, going soft. "You would?"

"Yeah, I would. But not if you're going to be an idiot," she murmured.

Cope's focus moved back to Kye and me. He studied us for a long moment before sighing. "I'm an ass."

"Accurate," I muttered.

Cope's lips twitched. "But I'm an ass who loves you. Both of you. And I just...I knew you two were close, but...I didn't want to see it, I guess. I don't like my baby sister growing up, and I don't want either of you taking the shit some people will give you for this."

I looked up at Kye and watched a million things pass through his eyes. A muscle fluttered in his bearded jaw, giving away some of those emotions.

"You think I'm not used to people looking at me like I'm not worth the dirt on the bottom of their shoes? I know what the people in this town think of me, of where I came from. The mistakes I've made. I *know*. And I'll take it times a million if it gives me Fal and a home for my sisters. But I will *never* let them say a damn word to your sister. Not once. And that's a goddamned oath."

Tears were welling again, this time for a whole different reason. Because the world was so damn unfair. I gripped Kye's shirt harder. "If they think that, they're just blind to the truth. Because no one has crafted hardship into something more beautiful than you. No one has taken those agonizing lessons and done more good. This town and world are just goddamned lucky you're in them."

Those emotions swirling in Kye's eyes shifted then, creating different colors and tones. Pressure mounted in that place in the center of my chest that belonged to Kye. He lifted tattooed fingers and slid them along my jaw. "Sparrow."

Beautiful pain flared again. "They should be thanking their lucky stars they live in the same town as you. That you even grace their streets. If they're idiots, they might just get a glitter bomb in the mail for their trouble."

"Vengeful," Kye whispered, so close I swore I could taste the hint of mint on his breath.

"When it comes to the people who matter."

Kye moved closer, and I thought he might close the distance entirely for more than just show this time. But a loud ringing startled us both and had us moving apart. Kye muttered a curse, and my cheeks flamed as I took in all the eyes on us.

Trace pulled out his phone and pressed it to his ear as he walked toward the entryway. "Colson."

Mom's eyes were misty. "You deserve this. Both of you. I couldn't imagine anyone better for either of you."

Rhodes wiped her thumbs under her eyes. "She's right. You both give so much to everyone around you, and you'll give that to each other, too." Her breath stuttered. "I'm just going to find the bathroom."

I frowned at her back as she retreated, trying to figure out what was going on. Anson met my eyes. "I've got her."

Cope moved in, hugging me. "You have permission to glitter bomb me."

I hugged him back. "It's no fun if you give me permission."

"Oh, I'll help you make it fun," Lolli offered. "I've got endless ideas."

"Fuck," Cope muttered.

That had Kye's lips twitching. Relief flooded my system at the sight. He grinned at Cope in that mischievous way I loved. "Whatever it is, it won't top a diamond fairy orgy."

"And for the stunt he pulled today, I'll be hanging it in our bedroom," Sutton called.

"Ooooh, that's a great plan," Lolli said, clapping her hands and making her beaded bracelets decorated with mushrooms and pot leaves jangle. "It'll help with fertility and sexual energy for sure."

"Someone save me," Cope muttered.

"I feel like my dick stick diamond painting has really helped my performance, don't you, Vicious?" Linc asked, trying to stir the pot even more.

"Cowboy," Arden warned.

Lolli adjusted her sequined shirt that read, *Save a Horse Ride a Cowboy*. "It's just a hockey stick and a pile of artfully arranged pucks. If you see more, that's on you. A buncha dirty birds, I tell you."

Linc gave her a wink. "You've got me pegged, Lolli."

Footsteps sounded as Trace headed back into the living room, but it only took one look for me to tell something was wrong. He didn't look stricken or even startled, but I'd grown to know the *sheriff* mask over the years, and he wore it now.

"What's wrong?" I asked instantly.

Trace didn't look at me. He looked straight at Kye. "You see Oren Matthews lately?"

Kye frowned. "He came into Blackheart a couple of days ago. Gave me and Jericho some shit about fighting for the MC again. I was going to tell you he hassled Jericho some after. Why?"

A muscle pulsed along Trace's stubbled jaw. "Because he's dead."

CHAPTER SEVENTEEN

Kye

MY EYES BURNED LIKE SOMEONE HAD DUNKED THEM IN GHOST pepper juice, and my entire body ached as if I'd gone a few rounds with Anderson Silva in the ring. But I still trudged my ass to Haven. I'd missed the last couple of sessions with our kids and wouldn't let myself miss another—even if I'd only managed an hour or two of sleep the night before.

Worry about what the hell had happened with Oren had swirled through my brain as I struggled to find rest. But I probably would've been better off with no sleep at all. Because when I finally managed to fall into unconsciousness, Fallon ruled my dreams. The taste of her haunted me like the ghost of everything I wanted. And in my dreams, I let myself give in to that. I let myself have every part of her.

I'd woken with a raging hard-on and enough guilt to strangle one of those sasquatches Lolli said roamed the woods around Sparrow Falls. And I'd been in a piss-poor mood ever since waking up and realizing none of it was real.

As I hauled open the gym's door, the sounds of kids and people working out met my ears. It was only three in the afternoon, but the place was busier than usual.

Serena hurried through the entryway, shooting me a grin. "I've got a pile of paperwork and checks for you to sign."

I sent her a salute. "You got it, boss."

She rolled her eyes. "You're looking a little haggard. You burning the candle at both ends?"

"Something like that." I knew I needed to fill in the rest of the people in my life about my engagement to Fallon and my sisters, but I didn't have it in me after Cope's response last night. He'd come around, but his initial reaction still stung.

"Well, look who the cat dragged in," Evan said as I made my way into the main gym. "Damn good to see you, stranger."

It had only been a couple of days, but I was usually here every day—even multiple times.

"You might take those words back." Mateo shot me a grin. "Kye is a special kind of cantankerous today."

"Dude..." Evan sent me an exasperated look. "Come out with me tonight. We'll hit up The Sage Brush, have some beers, meet some ladies."

"I still can't believe you're old enough to drink," I muttered.

Mateo wrapped Evan's neck in a fake choke hold. "They grow up so fast."

Evan shoved at Mateo. "You can come, too, Gramps." He glanced at me. "What do you say?"

"I'd say that's probably a bad idea since I just got engaged."

Mateo's hold on Evan slackened as Evan's jaw dropped. Mateo made a show of twisting a pinky in his ear as a shit-stirring smile spread across his face. "I'm sorry. What did you say?" His gaze lifted behind me. "Did you hear that, Jer? Our little Kye Kye got himself a ball and chain."

I turned to see Jericho moving toward us, shadows so similar to mine under his eyes. I knew the news about Oren was weighing on him, too. The man Oren had become might've been a stranger, but he'd once been a friend.

Jericho forced a smile. "Getting married? You don't say. And you weren't going to share this news with the class?"

I fought the urge not to scowl at my friend since he damn well knew there had been a chance of this happening.

Serena moved into our huddle. "I'm gonna have to second that question. This is something you tell your best friends."

"For real," Evan muttered, looking a little hurt.

Shit. The last thing I wanted to do was hurt any of them.

"I'm sorry. I just…it was delicate. I wasn't ready to share. The fact that I'm applying for custody of three half-sisters I just found out about sped things up."

"Wait. Did you just say you have three half-sisters?" Serena asked.

"And that he's applying for custody of them. Daddy Kye Kye in the house," Mateo added with a grin.

Evan shook his head as he scrubbed a hand over a cheek he was trying to grow stubble on. "You're straight out of a soap opera, dude."

He wasn't wrong.

Serena waved her hands at both Mateo and Evan. "You two are asking all the wrong things. *Who* did you ask to marry you? And then I also want to know when I get to meet the mini-Kyes."

A wave of nausea passed through me as I braced to tell them, waiting to hear a whole rain of bullshit. "Fallon. I asked Fallon to marry me."

All four of them went quiet. Jericho had a knowing glint in his eyes, but a huge-ass grin on his face, and Serena's eyes instantly filled as she threw herself at me. "Finally! I've been saying you two were star-crossed lovers forever. And now, Evan owes me twenty bucks."

"You two bet on me?" I asked as I released her.

Evan sent me a sheepish smile. "I really just thought you had the protective-big-bro thing going on there. I stand corrected."

"And twenty dollars poorer," Serena added.

Evan pulled me into a back-slapping hug. "Happy as hell for you, man."

"Me, too." Jericho gave me an extra hit for good measure.

"I'm a little fucking jealous—" Mateo began, only to be cut off.

"Mr. Kye," a young voice interrupted. "Why's everyone hugging you? Did you run away from home and come back? My mom hugged me like crazy when I did that. She also said a whole lotta bad words 'cause I scared her. My dad just said I was grounded till I'm twenty-five, but he still loves me."

I turned from my friends to see Benny gazing up at me with genuine curiosity. *In for a penny, in for a pound.* "They're hugging me because I asked someone to marry me."

Benny's eyes narrowed on me. "It's not Miss Arden, is it? I told Linc he could marry her for now, but you can't have her, too."

I couldn't help the chuckle that escaped. "Rest easy. It's not Arden. It's Fallon."

Another kid behind Benny scrunched his nose. "Isn't she your sister?"

Here we go.

"Nope, she's not. We've actually been friends since high school." I didn't need to make my case to an eight-year-old, but here I was.

A six-year-old powerhouse named Isabella let out an audible sigh. "That is soooooo romantic."

Evan tapped me with a set of mitts. "See? You're romantic."

Jericho snorted. "If romantic means long walks through a maze of heavy bags and brooding for hours."

Serena choked on a laugh. "He's got you pegged. I need to get back to work. But, Kye?" She pulled me into another hug. There was a lot of touching happening for someone who wasn't all that crazy about displays of affection. I took it anyway. "So damn happy for you."

"Thanks, Ser." I slid out of her embrace and straightened. When I turned, Isabella was still looking up at me with hazy eyes.

Benny, on the other hand, stared at me studiously. "You think you can teach me how to get Miss Arden to marry me?"

Evan patted the kid on the shoulder. "Benny, I'm pretty sure if you bring her a Ring Pop, she'll say yes."

I chuckled. "I have no doubt."

He looked back and forth between us. "If you're wrong, you gotta help me drown my sorrows in Yoo-hoo."

Mateo let out a strangled sound. "I'm sorry, did a six-year-old just say he might need to drown his sorrows?"

Benny looked up at Mateo. "I'm very mature for my age."

Mateo shook his head. "I got no doubt, little dude."

After we assured Benny that we'd be there for him with Yoohoo if heartbreak ensued, we got back to work. There was something magical about introducing kids to mixed martial arts. It gave them so many things I'd wished I had growing up: self-defense training, a healthy respect for the human body, practice in controlling your temper, and other physical and mental health benefits. If my introduction had been something like this and not in the fight ring, things might've turned out differently.

But it was more than just the training. It also plugged them into a community and gave them a set of adults beyond their parents who checked in. After everything that had happened lately, I found myself looking at each child more carefully.

I thought about their parents and caregivers. Were the kids too skinny? Did they have any unexplained bruises? Were they overly nervous?

As the class wrapped up, I'd come up empty when it came to any who might need intervention. But I would keep an eye on the parents.

Jericho held up a large blocking pad as the kids lined up to give it a punch and kick combo. It was one of their favorite parts of the lessons because it made them feel like they were taking on someone four times their size.

Isabella came forward, giving a jab, hook, then snap kick. She punctuated the moves with a sound fit for some over-the-top kung fu movie.

"God, she's fuckin' adorable," Evan said, coming up beside me.

"The sound effects are something else."

Evan laughed. "This is my favorite gig."

I glanced over at him, really taking in his words. "You mean that?"

He looked back at me. "That really so surprising? I just keep thinking how things would've been different for us if we'd had something like this."

Everything would've been different. Sometimes, I wondered if I would've stayed away from all that MC mess if I'd been taken out of Renee and Rex's home earlier. Maybe I'd be more like Shep, who'd been adopted by the Colsons at birth. He'd always had his shit together.

I shoved those thoughts out of my head. "We might've had our knocks, but we made it out the other side. And that means we're here to show others the path."

Evan's gaze moved back to the kids. "You're right. Hopefully, they'll never have to go through what we did."

"You know," I began, my wheels turning, "I'd like to expand the programming we offer at Haven. I've been thinking it might be nice to team up with DHS and maybe a few other county programs to offer some more classes for at-risk youth. That something you'd be interested in heading up?"

Evan's head snapped back in my direction. "Head up?"

I nodded. "You've been doing amazing with these little ones, and I think having someone closer to the teens' age might be an asset."

One corner of Evan's mouth kicked up. "You callin' me a youngin'?"

"Yeah, ya little whippersnapper."

Evan barked out a laugh. "I think your grays are showing."

"Harsh, kid. Harsh." Movement caught my attention—Trace moving into the gym through the gathering of parents waiting for class to end. He didn't come straight for me, so I knew it wasn't an emergency, but dread still pooled.

He leaned against the wall in full uniform, watching with an amused look as Benny attempted a roundhouse kick and took a tumble.

Jericho moved forward to help him up. "Good try. Let's give it one more. Pay attention to that center of gravity."

Benny nodded and tried again. The kick was wobbly at best, but he did it.

I let loose a whistle. "Way to go, Benny!"

He grinned so wide the smile took up half his face. "You make sure to tell Miss Arden about that."

"You know I will."

The last few kids went through the line, and then I moved to the center of the mat. "Amazing job today. You were focused, kind, and you seriously kicked booty." I'd learned the hard way that some parents were even opposed to the word *butt*.

The kids cheered.

"Have an amazing night, and keep up all the hard work at home," I said. "Class dismissed."

The kids ran for their parents, and Trace slowly made his way over to where I stood with Jericho and Evan. It was Jericho who spoke first. "You find out what happened to Oren?"

Trace was wearing his sheriff mask, making it hard to tell exactly what he was thinking—or know what he might be about to drop on us. But the slight flutter of the muscle I saw along his jawbone told me it wasn't good. "He was found out back behind the Steel Horse Saloon in Eagle Crest."

Eagle Crest was one town over and the Reapers MC's home. Steel Horse was a bar frequented by the MC for meetings with other clubs since it was considered neutral ground.

"What happened?" I asked, keeping my voice low.

Trace's expression went even more blank. "He was stabbed five times in the chest. The blows were brutal. Medical examiner says whoever did it must have a hell of a lot of strength."

Jericho paled and scrubbed a hand over his jaw. "Could be a rival club."

Trace lifted his chin in assent. "We're looking into that."

"Could even be internal tension," I added. "For Oren to be harping on me and Jericho to come back, something was going on. He knows we've been out since we were seventeen. Coming back around reeks of desperation."

"He probably knew that you and Jericho still have skills," Evan said. "It's no secret, given you guys do the exhibition matches here."

He had a point. Part of the reason I'd started Haven was to turn something that had been so destructive for me into something positive. And doing the occasional exhibition match was me proving to myself that I could fight and be in control.

Trace shifted his weight from one foot to the other, and his gaze zeroed in on me. "I'm sorry as hell to have to do this, but I gotta ask you and Jericho what you were doing between the hours of three and six p.m. yesterday."

The dread that'd pooled in me earlier turned ugly now. "We're suspects?"

"Respectfully, Trace," Evan began, his voice going hard, his hazel eyes along with it. "That's a bunch of bullshit. Anyone who's dealt with the rougher side of Sparrow Falls for a second knows Oren Matthews was a piece of shit with more enemies than I have parking tickets. And you know how many of those I've racked up."

That muscle in Trace's jaw started fluttering again. "I'm asking because I don't want them to be suspects."

My throat suddenly felt dry as I focused on a spot on the wall that was no longer damaged from my explosion of rage the night I'd found out about my sisters. This could ruin all of that and send my dreams of giving them a home crashing down.

Jericho gripped the blocking pad so hard I wondered if it would leave permanent damage, but I understood his anger. Oren had been messing with our lives for longer than I could remember. "I had my last client at three," Jericho said, tension radiating through each word. "I went home after that, but I don't think anyone saw me."

My voice didn't sound like mine as I answered. "I picked up Fallon around four-thirty. Before that, I went for a drive. It's possible someone saw my truck somewhere, but I doubt it."

Trace glanced between us. "It helps. And it's a hell of a lot better than nothing. Getting to Eagle Crest and back in enough time would be hard with no one seeing you."

But he didn't say it was impossible. Because it wasn't. If a judge found out I was a murder suspect? There was no way he'd give me custody of my sisters.

CHAPTER EIGHTEEN

Fallon

MY BELOVED HATCHBACK GAVE ITS FAMILIAR SPUTTER AS I eased it into a parking spot at DHS. As I shut off the engine, I let out a similar sound. Maybe we'd give out together. Give up and call it quits right here.

It had been one of those days where everything felt like it was going wrong. In family court, two of the kids from my caseload had needed to testify that they'd rather live with their aunt than their mom, who was in the throes of a meth addiction. And even though the judge had approved that transfer of care, it had broken the hearts of everyone involved.

Then I'd had three home visits, and another to one of my teens, who was in treatment for her own addiction. Even though she'd just made it through the detox period, she was desperate to get out. Telling her she'd have to stay for at least sixty more days had not gone well.

And I still had to give Rose my paperwork so I could be a part of Kye's kinship placement petition. And Rhodes hadn't answered any of the three texts I'd sent her with more than one or two-word answers. I leaned my head back on the seat rest. One of those headaches was starting to gather. Kye would be big mad if he realized I hadn't eaten since my donut this morning.

Just thinking his name added to the hardness of the day. Between telling our family about our so-called-engagement, finding out that Oren Matthews had been killed, and waiting to hear if Kye would be granted custody, he had far too much on his shoulders. And there was only so much I could do to help.

My phone dinged in my cupholder. I swiped it up and unlocked the device. A group chat alert flashed.

Cope has changed the group name to Fallon is a Felon, a Support Group.

Below that notification was a photo. It was Cope sitting in his beloved and ridiculously expensive Bentley SUV, *covered* in various shades of pink glitter.

> **Cope:** *Fallon. I will find you. And I will cover every inch of your house, car, office, and anything else I can think of with the devil's pixie dust.*

A laugh burst out of me, and it felt so damn good. Like all the tension building up in me all day had been released with the sound.

> **Me:** *You should also come for Lolli and Sutton then, because they assisted.*
>
> **Shep:** *Are there tiny penises in that glitter?*
>
> **Cope:** *Yes. There. Are. And they're fucking everywhere! I'm probably going to have dick hair for the next two weeks.*
>
> **Rho:** *I hope he has another billboard campaign scheduled. I'd pay good money to see a tiny dick sneak past some editing software.*
>
> **Arden:** *Copeland Colson, the face of menswear and men's appendages.*
>
> **Rho:** *A true dick-fluencer.*
>
> **Arden:** *A peen-thusiast.*

Cope: *None of you are allowed to use my pool anymore.*

Shep: *Eh, no big loss. I'm putting one in at my place, and Kye has that sick pond.*

Just seeing Kye's name had unease settling deep within me. I hadn't heard from him at all today, other than in the group chat with Ellie, where she told us to meet her at a local furniture store at five. Thanks to some sweet-talking the owner, he was staying open late so we could make some choices after I finished work.

Arden: *Honestly? Worth losing the pool to see you with pink penis hair.*

I wanted to laugh again, to feel more of that relief, but I couldn't quite get there. Instead, I forced myself to climb out of my vehicle and head inside. Mary Lou wasn't at her desk, but the rest of the team was gathered in the main office as I made my way in.

Noah looked up at the sound of my footsteps, and his brow instantly creased in concern. "Fal, you okay? You look a little pale."

I sent him a wobbly smile. "I've just got a little bit of a headache."

Mila frowned but stood and crossed to our fridge. She came back with one of those damned green juices. "Drink this and don't argue."

I grimaced but untwisted the cap and guzzled the thing down. I made a gagging sound after. I couldn't help it. The thing was awful. "Someone please give me some sugar. And quick."

Rose chuckled, opened my top drawer, and tossed me a bag of gummy bears. "Your system is probably in shock from all the vegetables."

I tore open the bag and immediately started gnawing on a few bears.

"You'll get used to it," Mila assured me.

My face screwed up. "Don't bank on it."

She chuckled. "It would help if your other main food source wasn't sugar."

I cradled the bag of gummy bears to my chest. "Don't even think about stealing these."

Noah touched my elbow. "You sure it's just a headache? You've been off since the Jensen case."

My stomach twisted, and I wasn't sure if it was an aversion to the junk I'd put into it, or nerves over what I needed to share next. "I actually need to loop you all in on something—a few things, really."

Three sets of eyes moved to me, looks of curiosity in all of them. "I've been seeing Kye for a while now. We didn't want to share until we knew for sure it was a forever sort of thing. But, well..." I held out my hand with the ring. I couldn't help staring at it for a beat. It still felt incredibly foreign, yet like it had always been a part of me. "It is."

Rose let out a sound that was somewhere between a squeal and a gasp, then grabbed for my hand. "Fallon. It's beautiful. And so unique."

"He gave you a black engagement ring?" Mila asked incredulously.

I would've been insulted if the question wasn't so Mila. She had no filter and could only understand things in her wheelhouse of acceptability.

"It's a black diamond. He wanted something unique," I explained. I could still hear Kye's words as if he were whispering them right in my ear. *"My battered and blackened heart will always be yours."*

"You guys are foster siblings," Noah said, the disgust clear in his voice.

My gaze cut to him, and I could feel anger stirring. "He came to live with my family at sixteen, and we already had a history."

Noah's jaw worked back and forth. "So, you guys were a thing when he came to live with you? He should've been reassigned. Or maybe he used living in your house as an excuse to start working you."

"Noah," Rose warned.

I held up a hand to her. "No, Rose. I can handle someone's small-minded bitterness. Newsflash, Noah. Life isn't perfect. You should know that better than anyone, given your job. What you should be is fucking happy for me that I found someone as amazing as Kye."

Mila made a sound that had my eyes cutting to her.

"I know you think Kye is some big, scary, tattooed monster, but he's not. He's the kindest and gentlest man I've ever known. And that's saying something because my father was one of the best." My throat constricted at the memory of the man whose tenderness with animals and children was unparalleled...until Kyler. "You haven't seen Kye playing dress-up tea party with his niece. Or having a Nerf war with his nephew. You didn't see him holding me together when grief got the best of me."

"He got to you when you were vulnerable," Noah cut in.

"The hell he did," I snapped. "He gave me a safe place to let out everything I was feeling after losing my dad and brother. And he was there for me every step of the way as I tried to move on."

Rose wrapped an arm around my shoulders and guided me toward her office. "Come on. Let's have some tea."

I didn't miss the scathing look she sent Mila and Noah, but I didn't have the energy to look for their responses. Instead, I let Rose lead me to her office and the familiar couch. As I sat, she placed two tea bags in mugs and poured water from her electric kettle into them.

Handing me one, she lowered herself to the chair next to me. "They don't see because they haven't lived through the messiness we have. Which means they also miss the miracle and gift of finding love amid all the hardship. It's sweeter for us because we've seen so much pain."

I struggled to swallow. "I can handle it. I'd battle my way through a Viking horde for Kye. But I don't want this ugliness coming down on him." Tears pressed at the backs of my eyes. "You should've heard him last night when we told our family. He *feels* how so many in this town look down on him."

Rose shook her head and swirled her tea bag. "Those fools are missing out, too."

"But those *fools* are inflicting pain." And that killed me.

Rose reached over and patted my hand. "But you'll heal it. You and those girls."

"I'm going to try." I wanted to believe I could. Wanted to think I could be the miracle for Kye he'd been for me.

"Good." She settled back in the worn chair. "You know you'll have to hand over the Jensen case."

"I know," I grumbled, wrapping my hand tighter around the mug. "I was hoping you might take it."

"Wouldn't have it any other way."

I looked up at my friend and mentor. "This world is better because you're in it, Rose. And mine, especially so."

Rose sent me a pointed look. "If you make me cry, we're gonna have problems."

I laughed. "No more emotions. Promise."

"I'm holding you to that."

"Okay," Ellie said, tapping her phone screen as we waited outside the largest furniture store in Sparrow Falls. "I've got all the rooms mapped out. I'm focusing on the girls' rooms, the primary suite, and the living spaces first. We have more time for the other guest rooms, right?"

I nodded, pulling my coat tighter around me as the sun set and a chill set in. "That's right. But could you add the library to that list? I think it might make a nice space for the girls to study, and Clem is a big reader."

Ellie grinned. "I looooove a library, so I'm sold. What do you think about going bright and bold in there? The tones of the room are dark, so I think it might be a nice case of opposites."

"I love that idea. We need to make sure Kye is willing to have all the colors of the rainbow, but I don't think he'll mind."

As if I'd conjured the man with words alone, a familiar black truck pulled into the parking lot. I couldn't take my eyes off him as he parked and slid out. I watched as he strode across the parking lot in his favorite leather jacket and a worn Colson Construction tee. As he walked, his thick thighs strained against dark denim, and I noticed the dark scruff on his jaw was even thicker.

"Girl," Ellie muttered. "You are such a goner."

My head whipped around to her, a denial bubbling up and spilling out on instinct. "I am not."

That had her bursting out laughing. "It's not a bad thing. You are marrying the man, after all."

"What's so funny?" Kye asked as he reached us.

Ellie grinned. "Just giving your fiancée a hard time about how head over heels she is for you."

My cheeks heated, and I knew they were likely the shade of a tomato. My complexion always gave me away.

Kye's lips twitched beneath his scruff as he wrapped an arm around me and kissed my temple. "Good to know."

His amusement felt real, and I couldn't help wondering if it was. I wanted him to take pleasure in the truth Ellie had given voice to. Everything in me twisted into knots, and I had a feeling this was how I'd be living for the foreseeable future—constantly wondering if the interactions between Kye and me were real.

"Okay, lovebirds," Ellie said. "We've got lots of decisions to make and not much time to make them."

I looked up at Kye. "Are you sure you're up for this? You hate shopping."

He nodded as he released me. "I want to make a home for my sisters. I want to make sure they know I helped choose the things that will be a part of that home."

Ellie sucked in a hiccupping breath. "That's so sweet. I think I'm going to cry."

"Please don't," Kye said, a slight panic in his voice. "Trace'll deck me for sure if you go home tearstained."

That had her chuckling. "I solemnly swear not to tell him it was you."

"Thank God," Kye muttered.

"Okay," Ellie said. "In we go."

She held open the door, ushering us inside and then following behind. A familiar man with a round belly and ruddy cheeks headed toward us.

"Mr. Anderson," Ellie greeted with a warm smile. "So good to see you again. Thank you for staying open a little later for us."

"Oh, I don't mind. But you may have to write my wife a note. She might think I'm fibbing and went night fishing instead."

Ellie grinned. "Happy to give a sworn statement. Do you know Fallon and Kye?"

Mr. Anderson looked at us, his smile still in place, but a wariness hit his eyes when they reached Kye. "I sure do. Good to see you kids."

"You, too," Kye said. "Appreciate you helping us out."

"Well," Ellie began, "Kye and Fallon just got engaged and are moving into a new house. And Kye's sisters will be coming to stay. We have about fifteen rooms to outfit, so we need to get busy."

"E-engaged?" Mr. Anderson asked, shock evident in his expression.

I moved into Kye's side, placing a hand over his chest. "That's right. And very happy."

I was pretty sure my accusing stare didn't exude much happiness, but I didn't give a damn.

"Oh. Well, congratulations. I'll help however I can," he said quickly.

Ellie tapped her phone screen. "I'll let you know if we need anything, but I'm just going to mark down some product numbers and colors so we can get those orders in tonight. I'm hoping you'll do us a solid and have everything delivered the day after tomorrow. I know it's a Sunday, but given the *large* order we'll be placing, maybe you can make an exception?"

I swore I saw dollar signs lighting up in Mr. Anderson's eyes. "Let me give a few of my delivery guys a call. See if they'd like to earn a little extra money."

"Thank you so much," Ellie said, then motioned Kye and me to the kids' section. "I want to tell you my vision for each girl's room. Then, we can go from there."

I looked up at Kye. His amber eyes still had smoky shadows—ones I would've given anything to sweep away. I hooked his pinky with mine. "You okay?"

His gaze dropped to our joined fingers, and his pinky curled tighter around mine. "Yeah, Sparrow. I'm okay."

I didn't completely believe him, but I held tight to my nickname on his lips and his pinky wrapped around mine. Even as he let go and moved to listen to all the things Ellie listed off, I held on to the ghost of him—like I always did.

I held on even as Ellie took us through room after room, and we got lost in so many decisions my brain swam. The sound of a text alert had me blinking away the haze. Kye pulled his phone from his pocket. "Shit. I'm going to be late for my evening appointment." He glanced at me. "Think you can make the rest of the choices?"

My brows pulled together. It wasn't unusual for Kye to tattoo people into the night, but he was pushing himself too hard with everything else going on. "You sure you're okay with that?"

He pulled out his wallet and slid out a black credit card. "I'm sure. And I had Amex send over a card for you, so you'll have one for whatever you need."

I looked at the extended card like it was some sort of snake. "I don't need that."

Kye sent me an exasperated look. "Yes, you do."

"You are getting married, Fal," Ellie said, amusement in her voice.

Kye widened his eyes, sending me a silent message. One that said, *"people are watching."*

I took the card gingerly, as if it were some sort of mini bomb. The card itself was heavier than the two cards in my wallet. I slid it into my back pocket.

One corner of Kye's mouth kicked up. "See? Was that so hard?"

"Don't you have to go stick painful needles in someone?" I shot back.

He chuckled, moving into my space with only the slightest hesitation as his gaze flicked to Ellie. "My sparrow, so averse to needles."

"I can't imagine liking them," I grumbled.

Kye wrapped his arms around me and pulled me to his chest. "Sometimes, the pain is worth the beauty in the end."

As he held me to him, I let my walls slip for just a moment. I let myself revel in the heat and strength that was Kye. I let the scents of oakmoss and amber wrap around me.

His lips dropped to my forehead. "Text me as soon as you get home. I wanna know you got there safely."

I struggled to swallow. It felt like something was twisting my throat into knots. Kye's demands to know I'd gotten somewhere safely were nothing new. Protectiveness had woven its way through our bond and remained no matter how much time had passed. But this felt different. Maybe because he was holding me, or because his lips were hovering over my skin. Whatever it was, I held on to it all, knowing the memories would be all I'd have one day.

"I will," I whispered.

He held me for a second longer before releasing me and heading to the door. I watched him go until he disappeared from sight, memorizing the cadence of his powerful steps and how his jacket hugged his broad shoulders.

When I finally forced myself to turn away, I found Ellie grinning like the Cheshire Cat. She started fanning herself and shook her head. "Damn. You two are just...damn."

My cheeks heated. "Come on. Let's finish making our choices before my head explodes."

She chuckled. "Let's do some damage to that black card. That's what they were made for, after all."

"Made for?" I asked, confused.

"You don't know the card that man just gave you?" Ellie asked.

I shook my head.

Ellie wrapped an arm around my shoulders. "Oh, my sweet, innocent friend. The card Kye handed you is an American Express Centurion card. Aka, a black card. There is no credit limit, and it comes with all the crazy perks for travel and stuff."

It suddenly felt like the credit card was burning a hole in my pocket, and I had a deep urge to throw it into the river. "I didn't know things were that good for him."

Ellie laughed. "Well, at least he knows you aren't marrying him for his money."

No, just to save his sisters.

Ellie and I hurried through the rest of the furniture selections, paid a bill with Mr. Anderson that was more than my car and a few years of rent put together, and then headed for the parking lot. Darkness had descended, but the streetlights had come on, and I could hear people making their way to The Sage Brush around the corner.

I took a deep breath, feeling my headache roaring back to life.

Ellie reached out and squeezed my arm. "You're doing great. You're making an amazing home for those girls, and they are so lucky to have you."

"Thanks, El. I really hope you're right."

"Well, if it isn't the righteous bitch herself," a female voice sneered in the distance.

I turned to see Renee striding toward me dressed in a miniskirt and tank top. She had to be freezing. I braced at the fury swirling in her amber eyes. But Renee's eyes didn't look like Hayden's, Clem's, or Gracie's. And they sure as hell didn't look anything like Kye's. Hers carried a deadness that matched her soul.

"You think you can turn my girls against me?" Renee snarled. "They love me, they *need* me, and I'll get them back."

I stared back at the woman who had done so much damage to so many innocents, trying to pull in the ugly hate swirling inside me and keep from lashing out. I wanted to tell her that they hadn't needed her for a long time but would now get what they truly needed—a real family and a home where they felt safe and cared for.

I met those dead eyes and removed every speck of emotion from my voice. "Whatever you say, Renee."

My lack of emotional response seemed to infuriate her, and red spots took shape on her cheeks. "You're gonna get yours, you uppity bitch. You're not better than me."

"I am. Not because of where I come from, but because I don't treat human beings like garbage," I clipped, a little emotion slipping free.

Her lip curled in disgust. "You think you can clean him up? Make him into someone *acceptable*. He'll always be trash. Worth nothing more than the dirt under my shoe."

Kye's words from last night echoed in my head. *"You think I'm not used to people looking at me like I'm not worth the dirt on the bottom of their shoes?"*

My heart spasmed, and for a second, I thought I might be having a heart attack. This. *This* was where he'd heard the ugly vitriol. The place that had ingrained those lies in him. From the woman who was supposed to be his mother.

"That's right," Renee snarled. "You see the nothing he is. And he'll bring you *nothing* but pain and grief—the same as he brought me. Should've known I was carrying the devil's spawn and thrown him in the trash when I had the chance."

The fury that slammed into me was almost more than I could take. I wasn't a violent person. Actually, I was quite opposed to it in ninety-nine-point-nine percent of situations. But I suddenly found myself lunging.

Only Ellie grabbing my arm saved Renee from a fist to the face. "Don't. You'll put yourself at risk."

Renee cackled. "She's mad 'cause she knows I'm right."

"You couldn't be more wrong," I growled. "Kyler is *everything*. And you missed out on the greatest gift of your life: knowing him."

Renee's nose wrinkled in disgust. "Just remember who you're getting involved with, bitch. You best be sleeping with one eye open if you're mixed up with him."

CHAPTER NINETEEN

Kye

I STOOD UP FROM MY STOOL AND SNAPPED MY GLOVES, ARCHING my back. *Fuck.* I was getting old. A two-hour session like this used to be nothing. Now, my back gave me all sorts of grief if I didn't pause for stretch breaks.

"Man, this is the best work I've ever had done," Michael said as he examined the piece curved around his left pec. "I don't know how you did it. I just told you random stuff, and you made it...perfect."

His eyes filled, and I understood why.

"You did the hard work by telling me what it needed to be. Why she was so important to you," I said quietly as he studied the piece through the clear plastic wrap.

His late wife's name, Olivia, was at the center of the piece, but it was so much more. Not unlike the murals I'd created at Haven, it wove countless other images in and around it: dahlias, her favorite flower, the Eiffel Tower, where Michael had proposed, the sweet cottage they'd shared in Carmel, nods to their two daughters, and assorted other hallmarks of their life together.

Michael's eyes glistened. "Thanks for letting me. This felt a lot like therapy."

In many ways, it was. And for me, it was where my art became magic. Where it could heal and give someone a permanent connection they'd never lose. I grinned at him. "We've got a few more sessions to finish this up. See you in a few weeks?"

He nodded and pulled on his shirt. "Thanks again. You've got a gift."

As Michael headed up to Bear to pay and check his next appointment, Penelope shoved off the wall. "He's right. You do have a gift. And there's nothing like watching you work when you're in the zone."

Apparently, she'd forgiven me for my brutal honesty the other day.

I got to work cleaning my station and tools. "It's good to do something you love, right?"

"Amen," Jericho called from the spot next to me as he worked on a woman who was getting her first tattoo at seventy-three.

Penelope didn't say anything, but I also hadn't felt her move; she simply watched me like a hawk. It set me on edge.

"You need something?" I asked, tossing a disinfectant wipe into the trash.

She shifted, jutting out a hip in a way that revealed a sliver of belly between her jeans and top. The position was awkward enough that I knew it was purposeful. It wasn't the sort of thing I usually minded, though I typically appreciated something a little more honest in an approach. But I also knew it wouldn't do a damn thing for me.

Didn't matter how stunning the woman was, if she was similar to Fal, or as different as night and day. Whoever it was, they were never *her*. And at some point, I'd just given up trying. It only made it hurt more.

"Could we get a drink and talk?" Penelope asked, that hip angling further.

"You need to talk about work stuff; we can schedule a meeting in the office," I hedged.

Her lower lip stuck out in a hell of a pout. "You never used to have a problem getting a drink with me."

She made it sound like we had history. We didn't. I used to hit The Sage Brush with her, Jericho, and Bear until Penelope made it clear she was using those opportunities for a full-court press.

"Well, Princess Pen," Jericho began, "things have changed for ole Priest." Jericho's head lifted. "I guess I can't call you Priest anymore, can I?"

"Thank fuck," I muttered.

Penelope shoved off the wall, losing her come-hither stance. "What's he talkin' about?"

"He's talking about the fact that I asked Fallon to marry me, and she said yes."

Bear let out a hoot, ambling up from his chair and crossing to me for a hard hug. "'Bout time you locked that lady down."

I gave his back a good slap. "Couldn't risk you winning her over with cookies anymore."

Bear barked out a laugh. "I had to try; she's one in a million."

"I'm not an idiot."

He gave my shoulder a good shake. "Sometimes."

"Fair enough," I said with a laugh.

Penelope was still gaping at me. "I always knew there was something weird with you two."

"Might want to watch your tone there, baby girl," Bear warned.

Her whole face scrunched. "You don't think this is fucking weird? It's like incest."

"Your bitterness is showing, Pen," Jericho called. "They only became foster siblings when Kye was sixteen. They knew each other way before then, too. Grow up."

The woman Jericho was tattooing looked up from the book in her lap. "This sounds like a hell of a love story to me."

"Trust me," Jericho said. "It is."

"Tell me all about it. I'm a sucker for an epic romance."

Jericho grinned at her. "Oh, I've got all the tea, Miss Charlotte."

"Jesus," I muttered.

"Gossip train's gonna be goin' now," Bear said.

I knew it. And everyone would have opinions.

Penelope just sent me a look of disgust and hoisted her purse over her shoulder. "I gotta get home."

I didn't say anything. I was so tired of her crap—in all ways—and I wasn't going to tiptoe around her feelings any longer.

As she headed out the door, Bear clapped me on the shoulder. "She's not your problem."

"I know she's not, but she still causes a hell of a lot of headaches."

Bear cast a look out the door and into the night. "Might want to be thinking about someone else who can do body modifications."

"You're probably right," I mumbled.

"There you go, Miss Charlotte. Bear will check you out, and you've got all your aftercare instructions. If you have any questions, just stop by or call," Jericho said.

Miss Charlotte leaned forward and gave him a smacking kiss on the cheek. "Thank you. I think I might have a thing for this now."

Jericho chuckled. "That was my devious plan all along."

As Miss Charlotte moved to check out with Bear, Jericho crossed the few steps between us and lowered his voice. "You hear anything else from Trace?"

My gut twisted at the question, but I shook my head. "Not a word."

"I mean, it's not like Oren has a shortage of enemies. We can't really be suspects, can we?"

Of course, we could. Because we had records. Nothing even close to murder, but not just public drunkenness either. "Trace'll do everything he can to clear us quickly."

Jericho squeezed the back of his neck hard. "I hope he finds someone else to be lookin' at and fast."

So did I.

"Look who decided to grace us with his presence, and at seven a.m. on a Saturday, too," Mateo called with a shit-stirring grin on his face.

I flipped him off as I walked into the main gym. "So, I'm not particularly fond of mornings. What's your point?"

"Lazy, lazy, lazy," Mateo muttered. "That'll have to change now that you're playing house."

The word *playing* had me bristling. A mix of insult and concern washed through me as Evan pulled off the mitts he'd been holding for Mateo. "Dude, you may wanna watch your word choice about Fal..."

Mateo brushed him off. "Hey, I've got nothing but respect for her. I'm just heartbroken she's off the market. I felt like she had real potential to be the future Mrs. Torres. I've been nursing my wounds since I found out."

"Get in the goddamned ring. I'll meet you there as soon as I'm warmed up." I wouldn't be pulling any punches either.

Evan turned to Mateo. "You're an idiot. You know that, right?"

The two of them started bickering like an old married couple while I did a quick treadmill warm-up. It did nothing to soothe the annoyance brought on by Mateo's words. It wasn't even his fault. He was just giving me a hard time.

The problem was, one day, months from now, some guy would make a pass at Fallon. And, eventually, she'd say yes. To the date. The ring. And the family.

Just thinking it made me feel sick. I'd had to watch it before. The guys who thought they were good enough for her. The dates. The occasional boyfriends. But it'd be worse now with the taste of Fal so fresh in my mind.

"Yo. You draggin' 'cause you're scared?" Mateo taunted.

"No, it's because that getup you're wearing is blinding," Jericho muttered as he stumbled into the gym.

Concern flashed across Evan's face. "You okay, man?"

Jericho put the sunglasses he'd had on his head back in place. "Went a little too hard last night. Gotta run it out of my system, or I'm gonna be dying all day."

Worry of my own niggled as I watched Jericho struggle onto one of the treadmills. His drinking that much did not spell good things.

"Hey. I've got fashion sense, unlike the lot of you," Mateo argued.

I shot him a grin as I climbed into the ring. "Some call it fashion sense, others call it crime."

Mateo pointed a gloved fist in my direction. "Oh, I'm gonna make you pay for that one."

"You can try."

I donned my gloves and mouthguard, and we began sparring. It started off easy as we both fully warmed up, but before long, our punches and kicks held real heat.

"Come on," Mateo goaded. "Is that the best you've got?"

I lashed out with a side kick, sending him stumbling back.

"All right, all right." Mateo righted himself and bounced on the balls of his feet. "He might have a ball and chain, but he's not dead yet."

I lunged forward with a jab-hook combo, but Mateo took the opening to land a punch to my ribs. I grunted, then straightened, trying to keep my head in the game.

"You're losing your edge, my friend," Mateo singsonged.

I sent out a cross that he dodged, and I muttered a curse.

Mateo just laughed and danced around the ring.

Movement at the gym's entrance caught my attention. A flash of white-blond hair. It only took my gaze away for the briefest of moments, but before I could refocus on the ring, a fist rammed into my jaw so hard I saw stars.

I stumbled back a few steps, trying to regain my balance and bearings.

"What in the actual hell, Mateo?" a familiar and furious voice demanded.

And Fallon didn't stop there. Before I could tell her that I was okay, she grabbed one of Evan's mitts and climbed into the ring. A second later, she was whacking Mateo with it. "That isn't the shit you pull on a friend."

Mateo held up his arms in a half-assed attempt to defend himself. "We were sparring."

She just hit him harder. "You saw that he was distracted. That's not skill, that's playing dirty."

"You tell him, Fal," Evan cheered.

"Knee him in the junk," Jericho yelled.

Fallon just smacked Mateo harder with the mitt. "You're gonna need to watch your back. You—"

I caught her around the waist and lifted her into the air. "Easy, Sparrow."

"Jesus," Mateo muttered. "You scare me."

"Good," Fallon yelled back.

I couldn't help but laugh. "Gotta watch out. This one has a vengeful streak a mile long."

"And don't you forget it," she shot at Mateo.

He rubbed the side of his head where she'd been smacking him. "All right, all right."

I slowly lowered her to the floor and then pulled out my mouthguard, dropping it into its case. "What are you doing here other than defending my honor?"

Fallon moved back into my space, tipping my head to the side to examine my face. "Are you okay? He got you good."

I worked my jaw back and forth. It definitely smarted, but nothing was broken. "Powerful lesson. Never drop your guard."

"Especially around backstabbers," she said, lifting her voice.

"Jesus," Mateo muttered again.

"Baby," I said, hooking a finger through her belt loop and pulling her to me. "Tell me why you're here."

Her face went soft at the uttered *baby*. It wasn't the same payoff as how she lit up at the nickname Sparrow, but there was a different sort of heat in those dark blues.

"Ellie heard from Mr. Anderson. All the furniture is being delivered tomorrow. She's organizing a family painting party today so we can get the murals in the girls' rooms done before it all arrives. Rose called me a bit ago and said all the paperwork looks good. If the home inspection goes well, we can take custody."

My entire body went taut, as if tiny bolts of lightning had hit me all over. "It's happening," I whispered.

A smile spread across Fallon's face, lighting her from within. "It's happening."

And she'd made it so. Had given everything to do it. I didn't stop myself from kissing her. I lied and told myself it was because we had an audience, but I knew the truth. It was because I fucking wanted to. I needed her more than anything on this Earth because she was my air. She made it so I could breathe.

My fingers sank into her hair as I took her mouth. My tongue slid in, desperate for a hit of that taste, that air. And I drank her down, grabbed anything I could get a hold of.

Evan let out a catcall that had Fallon pulling back and her cheeks flushing.

"You are a goner," he said with a laugh.

Mateo just shook his head. "Sad to see a good man go down."

Fallon's eyes narrowed on him. "I will put hot sauce in your mouthguard. Don't think I won't."

CHAPTER TWENTY

Fallon

In true Colson crew fashion, Kye's house was alive with music, voices, and a healthy dose of chaos. The battle for exactly what sort of music to play had been vicious. Arden wanted her death metal that sent most of our family running for the hills. Ellie had suggested one of her nineties pop playlists I would've loved, but Trace quickly begged her not to play it. Finally, Mom pulled rank and put on some oldies we could all enjoy, at least marginally.

Lolli spun with her paintbrush, sending pink splatters across her overalls. "This is my jam. I've got some sweet, sweet memories set to this one."

"Please, God, don't share them with us," Cope begged as he painstakingly painted the spoke of a Ferris wheel on the wall in Gracie's bedroom.

Arden and Linc had shared an art project Gracie had done in Arden's after-school program that inspired the mural. When asked to draw something that made her happy, she'd drawn herself, Hayden, and Clem at the fair. Ellie immediately set to work sketching the scene on the wall, and everyone jumped in to paint the different pieces.

"I hope you'll be making more of them with me," Walter said, his gray brows waggling as he crossed toward Lolli. The longtime cook at The Mix Up had never been deterred by her refusal to settle down.

Lolli held her paintbrush out in Walter's direction. "Oh, no, you don't, you old coot. I'm not letting you distract me from my painting mission."

His grin was smug. "Like I distracted you the other night?"

Lolli's cheeks flushed. "A moment of weakness."

"A moment of genius," Walter argued. "Marry me."

"No."

"Marry me."

"No."

I couldn't help the smile that curved my mouth. "One day, you're going to give in, Lolli."

"Hush your mouth, child," Lolli scolded. "Just because you and Kye are tying the knot doesn't mean I'm about to be tied down. I only want to be tied up."

Kye's lips twitched as he lowered his brush. "Lolls, you've got more swagger than anyone I've ever known."

Lolli shook her hips, making more paint fly. "You know it. And just wait until I bring you and Fallon my housewarming present. It is next level."

"Lolli..." I warned as I filled in part of a cotton candy machine on the mural.

"Don't even think of trying to control my muse, honey bunches. It can't be tamed," Lolli said, dipping her paintbrush and moving to one of the Ferris wheel cars.

Cope grinned as he painted a bar of the ride. "I don't know, Walter's trying pretty damn hard."

Lolli let out a huff. "That old codger doesn't have a prayer of keeping up with me."

"I'm taking that as a challenge, my love," Walter called from his spot at the mural.

I shot her a smile. "I don't know, Lolli. I'm pretty sure Walter is the only one who can keep up with you."

Lolli huffed. "He has yet to prove himself in our tantric yoga class."

Cope's whole face screwed up. "Stop. Sweet baby Jesus, please stop."

A laugh bubbled out of me as Kye moved in closer, his face going soft. He lifted a hand and swiped a thumb over my cheek. My breath caught and held. I swore I could still taste our kiss from earlier—mint and Kye—playing over my tongue.

"Paint," he whispered.

"Not you, too," Luca moaned, running into the room with Keely and Ellie on his heels.

Keely's face screwed up. "They're gonna be swapping cooties like all the time now."

"I know." Luca sighed. "It's mushy-gushy all day, every day."

A corner of Ellie's mouth kicked up. "The trauma we've put these poor children through."

Luca nodded. "There should be a no-kissing rule in this house. What do you think, Uncle Kye?"

Lolli shook her paintbrush at Luca. "Oh, no, you don't, my little ice prince. They've finally got themselves some of the good stuff. No trying to rein them in."

My face flamed. "Lolli."

"What?" she asked with faux innocence. "I can't want my granddaughter to be making the beast with two backs? That's healthy."

Keely's expression grew confused. "Why would a beast have two backs?"

"Prolly 'cause it has two heads and is real scary," Luca answered sagely.

"What's that got to do with cootie kissing?" Keely asked.

Ellie's shoulders shook with silent laughter. "Lolli, you're going to have to explain this to Trace. Have fun." She motioned to me and Kye. "You two lovebirds, with me. I've got a surprise for you."

At the word *lovebirds*, I studiously examined the floor. But Kye slid his hand into mine, weaving our fingers together. "Should I be scared?" he asked. "Did Lolli secretly bedazzle an entire wall of my house?"

"Now that's an idea," Lolli called as we followed Ellie out of Gracie's room.

"You're gonna regret putting that in her head," I muttered.

Kye groaned. "You're telling me."

"How's your jaw?" I asked, trying to see if any bruising had begun beneath his scruff, but it was hard to tell.

His chin dipped as those amber eyes searched mine, and then his lips twitched. "Sparrow, I'd take a punch over and over again to see you put the fear of God into Mateo."

My mouth curved. "Let's not put that into practice. I'll put the fear of God into Mateo for fun."

"It is good for his ego."

"No kidding," I mumbled. The fighter was a little too cocky for his own good, and it could get him into trouble. But I got the sense there was something beneath it—a need to prove himself over and over.

We made our way downstairs, where Mom and Trace were putting up wallpaper in a kitchen nook.

"Looking amazing," Ellie called.

Mom grinned. "Are you showing them the surprise outside?"

Ellie nodded. "It's all in."

Mom let out a girlish squeal. "It's perfect."

"You know both Keely and Luca will want one," Trace muttered.

Mom laughed. "Shep could start a side business after this."

My curiosity was piqued as Kye and I followed Ellie onto the back patio. While it led to the pond behind the house, you could also take a path that brought you to the side yard, which had plenty of room for kids to run and play. That was the path Ellie took.

"Shep and Anson have been working 'round the clock on this one. Building the individual pieces so they'd be ready for installation today," Ellie explained.

I only grew more confused until the structure came into sight. A gasp slipped free as I took in the play set that looked more like a castle. The wooden structure mirrored the house, with towers and turrets all painted in the same teal. There were four types of swings, two slides, a climbing wall, a rope ladder, and a bridge.

Shep and Anson grinned as we approached. Thea and Rhodes were up in the tower planting some mums in a planter box on the exterior. Thea waved, a huge smile on her face. "I think I'm going to get Shep to build one of those for me."

"I don't blame you. This is amazing," I said.

I looked up at Kye to find him struggling to swallow, emotion filling his beautiful eyes. "This..." He tried to swallow again. "This is everything they should've always had."

Shep was striding forward then. He pulled Kye into a hard hug. "And we're going to give it to them now. Everything that lets them know they're loved and supported."

Kye hugged him back as he tried to pull himself together. "Thank you."

Shep released him. "It was fun as hell to do."

Anson's mouth twitched up. "I think we should offer it on our new builds."

"That's honestly not a bad idea," Shep said.

Rhodes ran a hand over the flowers. "These probably won't last long, but we wanted a little pop of color up here for the reveal."

The deep maroon mums looked amazing against the teal.

I met Rho's eyes. "They're beautiful."

She nodded and quickly averted her gaze, sliding down the straight slide and starting for the house. "I'm going to help Trace and Nora."

I frowned, a little more worry niggling at me. I reached over and laid a hand on Kye's arm. "Be right back."

His brow furrowed for a moment, but he nodded.

I quickly jogged after Rhodes, and I needed that fast pace because she was speed-walking. "Rho!"

She didn't stop right away. Not until I grabbed hold of her elbow and halted her forward momentum.

"What's going on?" I asked as she turned to face me, her expression blank.

"What do you mean? I just said I was going to help inside."

I searched her face, trying to find what lay beneath the surface. "You've been avoiding me."

Rho's lips pressed together as if she were trying to hold everything she actually felt inside. "I'm not."

"You are. You didn't text back when I sent you the meme about a dog with anxiety poops, just like Biscuit. You always text back when I meme you."

Rho's gaze shifted to the side.

"What did I do?" I asked. "If I messed up, I want to fix it." She was my best friend, my sister, and I'd do anything for her. The idea that I may have hurt her in some way killed me.

The tension running through Rho's shoulders eased a fraction as she turned back to me. "I can't believe you didn't tell me you were seeing Kye."

Guilt hit me like an invisible freight train, nearly making my knees buckle. Rhodes and I shared almost everything with each other. I had known she might feel a little stung that I hadn't shared my so-called relationship with her, but I'd never expected this level of hurt.

A tug-of-war took root somewhere deep, a battle between protecting her and honoring the bond we'd had since she moved to Sparrow Falls at age seven.

I lowered my voice to the barest whisper. "I didn't tell you because I wasn't seeing him." Pain lit along my sternum, where all the pain, joy, and love tangled up in Kyler lived. "It's fake."

Rho's eyes went comically wide. "It's fake?"

I nodded, biting the corner of my lip.

Realization dawned in Rho's hazel eyes. "For the girls."

"For the girls," I whispered. "But..." I struggled to explain everything, wrestled with whether or not to share. But I needed someone to know everything I was carrying. More than that, I needed Rhodes to know. Because she was my person long before Kye was. "It's also not fake."

Rho's brows pulled together. "What do you mean?"

"I've been in love with him since I was fourteen. He was my first kiss. He's...he's my everything."

I saw Rhodes wading through memories, trying to pull the pieces together. Then her spine snapped straight. "The guy you were tutoring? The one you were sneaking away to see during lunch? I never thought about the fact that your MIA act stopped after Kye came to live with us."

Tears pressed against the backs of my eyes, carrying the weight of all I'd lost. They were heavy with memories that meant everything to me, suffocating with how much I missed them. Him.

I swallowed hard, my throat sticking on the movement. "He was there for me. I was struggling. Still trying to process losing Dad and Jacob, especially starting high school without them there. I used to go to the creek between the middle and high schools and scream. Because I couldn't do it at home. Couldn't do it anywhere else. He saw me one day and said, *'Let it all out, Sparrow. Don't let it drown you.'*"

"Fallon…" Rhodes whispered.

"We met now and then. I started helping him with the classes he was struggling in, and with him I could just…be. I think I gave him a place to lay down some of what he was dealing with at home, too."

Rhodes moved in closer and took my hand. "The ultimate gift."

I nodded as the tears swirled, despite me trying to fight them back. "We kissed for the first time the day he got placed with us. The day his dad tried to kill him." Just saying the words hurt on every level. "We couldn't risk it. If the social worker had found out we were together like that, they would've moved him. And you know kids with Kye's history don't have many good options for placement."

Rho's hazel eyes filled. "So, you gave up everything you ever wanted so he would be safe?"

Tears spilled over then, flowing down my cheeks and leaving tracks in their wake. "I'd do it again. I'd do it over and over if it meant he'd be safe."

Rhodes hauled me into her arms then, holding me tightly. "I'm so sorry."

"I'm not," I croaked.

"Hey," Kye said as he approached, his gait and tone cautious. "What's with all the tears?"

Rhodes straightened while still holding me. "I'm just really happy for you guys."

Kye didn't look convinced. "Girls are weird."

She laughed and hugged me harder, her mouth dropping to my ear. "Find your happy, Fal. You deserve it more than anyone I've ever known."

"He won't risk it," I whispered, so low I knew Kye couldn't hear. "He thinks he'll mess everything up."

Rho gripped me even tighter. "You'll get him to make the jump. You just have to fight." She released me with one last hard hug and raised her voice. "I have an idea."

Kye moved in, wrapping an arm around me as if to check if I was okay. "That definitely scares me."

Rhodes stuck her tongue out at him. "What do you guys think about getting married right here tomorrow afternoon before the home inspection?"

"All the furniture is being delivered tomorrow," I pointed out, even as my heart picked up its pace.

"At eight in the morning," Rhodes argued. "Ellie and Trace can handle overseeing that. Let me handle the wedding with everyone else."

I didn't want to look at Kye because I wanted it too much. It might be fake for him, something he didn't want to do, but it was everything I'd ever wanted.

Finally, I forced my gaze skyward. Up, up, up until it collided with swirling amber irises. Those eyes that always saw everything searched mine. "What do you think, Sparrow?"

"I'm ready if you are." It was a miracle my voice didn't shake. That I managed to get the words free at all.

Kye dipped his head, his lips brushing mine. It was the barest touch, with a hint of his scruff teasing my skin at the edges. But heat still flooded me. No one could make my body come alive like Kye. No one could set my soul aflame. And I knew it would always be that way.

"Let's do this, Sparrow."

CHAPTER TWENTY-ONE

Fallon

One of Ellie's nineties pop playlists filled the air as every woman in my family bustled around the primary suite of Kye's house. Sutton had somehow managed to get a few temporary makeup stations so she and Ellie could help us all with hair and makeup. Everyone chatted as they got ready, donning dresses accented with sweaters since it was only about sixty degrees outside.

"I still think we could've had a bachelorette party at the cowboy bar last night," Lolli grumbled.

Rhodes pinned our grandmother with a hard stare. "You got your round of pin the penis on the man candy last night. Just be glad we let you have that."

Thea choked on a laugh. "You make it sound like she put an actual penis on a stripper or something."

"Dear God, please do not give her any ideas," Mom begged.

Lolli beamed. "I bet I could find some gents in Vegas who'd be up for that game."

"Someone tell Linc to lock down his private jet," Sutton called from where she was working on Mom's eye shadow.

Arden grinned as Ellie wove tiny braids through her wavy strands. "Unfortunately, I think Linc would be an enabler there. He loves Lolli's shenanigans."

"Have I told you that you have the best taste of all my granddaughters?" Lolli asked.

Arden's gray-violet eyes twinkled. "Pretty sure you're not supposed to say that at your other granddaughter's wedding."

Lolli just harrumphed. "I used to be able to count on Kye, but he told me I couldn't get Fallon a stripper last night, so he's on my shit list."

Sutton stilled, makeup brush still in hand. "I'm not sure the male strippers you could find around here are ones you'd want, Lolli."

Arden let out a cackling laugh, her hand resting on her small belly. "It would certainly be interesting."

"I could've gotten Linc to send his plane to Vegas to bring some back. Only bougie strippers for my Fallon," Lolli argued.

I shook my head and adjusted my robe. "I think I'll pass on anyone shaking their junk in my face. But I appreciate the sentiment."

Thea giggled as she worked on adjusting my bouquet. "What if he could airplane propeller it?"

"Or make it dance?" Rho pressed.

"Make it stop!" I begged.

Mom laughed as she rose from her chair, her makeup done. "All right. Enough appendage conversation for one day."

"Never enough," Lolli protested.

Mom sent her a stern look and then crossed to me. "I know you were planning to wear the pale pink dress, but I wanted to give you another option."

I studied her, confused. I hadn't exactly had time to buy a wedding dress, but the pale pink one I'd worn to a friend's wedding last spring was nice enough. "You didn't have to get me anything."

"I didn't." Mom took my hand and led me into the still-empty walk-in closet—well, empty except for a single white dress hanging there. "I won't be offended if it isn't your style, but this is the dress I wore when I married your dad."

"Mom," I whispered, moving to the gown. It was simple but beautiful, with delicate cap sleeves and tiny embroidered flowers scattered across it.

"You're about my size, and this dress has so many happy memories already etched into its fabric."

I turned to find her eyes misting and pulled her into my arms. "Are you sure you want me to wear it? It was yours, and—"

"Nothing would make me happier."

She released me and lifted the gown off the hanger. I slipped out of my robe and into the dress, turning so she could help zip me up. I couldn't stop gazing down at the way the blooms were a part of the fabric itself. It was like being dressed in a field of wildflowers.

As my mom finished zipping me up, I turned. Her hand flew to her mouth. "Fallon," she rasped. "You're breathtaking." Her breath hitched. "I'd give anything for your dad to see this."

Tears pooled in my eyes. "I miss him."

She wrapped me in her comforting embrace yet again. "He's here. Because we carry him with us in everything we do."

I couldn't help but wonder what he'd think if he knew what I was really doing. That the vows I'd speak today would be as fake as the coloring on a snow cone. But as someone who would've given everything in the service and protection of others, some part of me felt he'd understand.

And, in many ways, the vows weren't a lie. This marriage might end on paper in a handful of months, but it would stay forever etched on my heart. I wouldn't want it any other way.

Mom released me and cupped my cheek. "He'd be so proud of the woman you've become. Jacob would be, too."

I swiped under my eyes, careful not to disturb the makeup Sutton had applied. "No compliment could mean more."

"It's true, my sweet girl. And so am I."

"I love you."

"More than all the stars in the sky," she whispered.

"What's taking so long?" Lolli called. "I want to see my girl."

A laugh bubbled out of me. "We can't keep her waiting."

"Patience is a virtue you could work on," Mom called back. "Along with some decorum."

Lolli made a *pssh* sound. "Where's the fun in that?"

I walked out of the closet, prepared for more of Lolli's antics. Instead, her hands flew to her face to cover her mouth.

"You're perfect," Rhodes whispered, her eyes filling.

Thea dabbed at hers with a tissue. "The most beautiful bride I've ever seen."

"Kye is gonna lose his damn mind when he sees you," Arden said with a grin.

Sutton waved both hands in front of her face. "How dare you make me cry and ruin my makeup?"

Ellie laughed at that, her smile impossibly wide. "You're glowing from the inside out."

Lolli crossed to me then, her hands lifting to my cheeks. "You are the most precious gift. You make this world a better place, and I know you bring light to Kye's."

"Lolli," I croaked.

Her thumbs tracked over the swells of my cheeks. "Can't imagine anything better than seeing you happy." She tipped her forehead to mine. "Love you to the ends of the Earth."

"Love you, too."

As she released me, it was to find everyone in the room misty-eyed. Rhodes reined us in. "Okay, everyone but Lolli and Nora downstairs so we can get started. Fal? Kye asked me to give you this."

She handed me a small box and a card. My heart stuttered as I took it. I was oblivious to the girls leaving as I opened the note.

Sparrow,

I know you always imagined your dad walking you down the aisle. I wanted to remind you that he's always with you—now and wherever your path may lead. Thank you for the gift you're giving me. It's something I'll never be able to repay. But I'll live every day trying. It's an honor to be your husband, even if only for a little while.

Kyler

My thumb traced the artful script of his name—the one he was to me then, now, and forevermore. A teardrop splashed, soaking into the thick cardstock. That familiar ache lit in the center of my chest again as I moved to open the box.

My hands trembled as I pulled the white ribbon free of the black box and lifted the lid. Inside lay an oval pendant in rose gold. It looked old, as if the metal itself had a story, and the intricate design made it absolutely stunning.

I struggled to open it, my fingers fumbling with the clasp. But when I finally did, more tears came, even as I smiled impossibly wide. A photo of my dad hoisting me in the air filled the locket, my blond hair tumbling around me as I laughed full-out. There was so much life in the image, so much love.

"He asked me for my favorite photo of the two of you," Mom whispered. "I hope I chose right."

I touched the image as the memory hit. "It was my first rodeo. I got third place in barrel racing in the kids' division, and he was so proud."

"He cheered so loud I thought he might blow out our eardrums," Lolli remembered fondly.

"Will you...?" I swallowed the emotion trying to break free. "Will you put it on me?" I asked my mom.

"Of course." Her fingers deftly fastened it around my neck, stilling on the clasp for just a moment.

Lolli handed me my bouquet. "You ready?"

I let out a long, shaky breath. "As I'll ever be."

My legs trembled as we descended the stairs, soft music wafting up. At the base, Ellie was waiting with Keely in a fairy princess gown from her dress-up collection, and Luca wore a tiny suit. Keely's eyes widened, and she clasped her hands under her chin. "Auntie Fal, you're a princess!"

I laughed, and it felt like all the nerves fled me in that moment. I crouched low so I was on her level. "Thank you. And thanks for being my flower girl." I glanced at Luca. "And my ring bearer."

"You look super pretty," Luca mumbled, pink hitting his cheeks.

"Thank you. You both look amazing."

Kye and I had decided to forgo bridesmaids and groomsmen since the wedding was so small, but I couldn't resist having my niece and nephew, in all their adorableness, walk down the aisle. I just wished Hayden, Clementine, and Gracie could've been here, too.

Ellie beamed at us all. "Okay, my beautiful people. Are we ready to make some magic?"

"We're ready," I said, pushing to my feet.

Ellie signaled to someone I couldn't see, and all of a sudden, I heard Arden's smoky voice begin singing along with a guitar. Within a handful of seconds, I recognized the song as "A Dream Is a Wish Your Heart Makes", a nod to the movie I'd watched countless times with my family growing up.

Luca and Keely started around the corner to head down the aisle, but their path was hidden by a wall. So, I just had to wait. I heard a couple of laughs and cheers as they went and hoped the photographer was getting some good shots.

Then the music changed. Arden's beautiful rasp started the lyrics to "Make You Feel My Love" by Adele, and it was all I could do not to lose it again. Lolli looped her arm through one of mine, and Mom took the other. I gripped my bouquet so hard it was a miracle I didn't snap it in two.

And then we started walking, rounding the corner into the living room with all its new furniture, and through the open French doors to the patio.

I should've taken in all the people we loved standing for us— our siblings and their significant others, Rose from work, Jericho, Bear, Serena, and Evan for Kye, and even Walter in a dapper suit and bow tie.

I should've taken in the stunning arch that Rhodes, Thea, and Shep had spent hours on, and the beautiful floral arrangements that adorned my path.

But all of that paled in comparison to the man waiting for me at the end of the aisle, dressed in a black suit complete with cowboy boots that had just the right amount of edge. His scruff was tamed but not gone, and those amber eyes glittered in the afternoon light.

My breath caught as the whole world disappeared until it was only Kyler and me. In that moment, I knew there would never be another for me. He was the only man I wanted to marry. His was the only ring I wanted to wear. He was my everything. And while this might have an expiration date in the eyes of our legal system, he would always be my forever.

CHAPTER TWENTY-TWO

Kye

I'D NEVER SEEN A MORE BEAUTIFUL HUMAN BEING. NO, THAT WAS wrong. I'd never seen a creation in this universe more stunning than Fallon. No work of art or breathtaking landscape. Nothing could compare to her as she walked down the aisle Rhodes had created.

I knew I should've taken a moment to appreciate everyone present. All the energy they'd put into this day. Arden singing. Trace standing at my side, ready to officiate. The endless blooms adorning the pathway.

But I couldn't.

I only saw Fallon.

Her pale-blond hair had been woven into an intricate braid around her crown, left to tumble over her shoulders and down her back in loose waves. Her eyes were lined in something that made them burn brighter blue as they connected with mine. And the dress hugged her willowy curves, making my fingers twitch at my sides.

Some part of me was aware that Nora and Lolli guided her down the aisle, but as Arden sang about being there for one another no matter what came your way, everything that wasn't the connection between Fal and me simply fell away. Suddenly, it was just the two of us. My favorite place to be.

My throat constricted as if a woven rope was around it, winding tighter and tighter. Because all I wanted was for this to be real. To have earned this woman walking toward me.

But I'd cherish the gift she was giving me anyway. The mercy. And I'd protect it with everything I had.

As she approached, Nora released her and moved to me, pulling me to her. "I love you, Kye. There's nothing more I want for you than a big, beautiful life."

"Thank you, Nora. For everything." She might not like me very much when this all came apart, but if Fal and I handled it the way we planned, it would all be okay.

Lolli gave me a wink. "I knew my girl could tame you."

Our friends and family laughed at that.

But then it was time. I stepped forward and held out my hands to Fallon. Her slender fingers trembled as she took mine, and I felt like the world's worst asshole. But then I wrapped my pinkies around hers, reminding her it was the same me she'd always known.

Fallon exhaled, her eyes finding mine as she smiled. "Hi."

One corner of my mouth kicked up. "You're beautiful."

A hint of sadness swept through those deep blues, but it was followed by something that looked a lot like peace. "You don't look half-bad yourself."

"Friends, family," Trace began, "we're here today to join Fallon and Kye in an everlasting bond."

My throat twisted tighter, but I didn't lose sight of Fal.

"Marriage is more than just saying 'I do.' It's a promise to be there for one another, in good times and bad. It's a vow that you can bring anything to the other, and they will help you carry the load. Your joys are higher, and your lows are never as heavy."

Fallon gripped my hands harder, her pinkies nearly strangling mine.

"Can we have the rings?" Trace asked.

Luca beamed as he carried the little pillow up to us, the wedding rings dangling from delicate ribbons.

"Thanks, little dude," I said as I forced myself to release Fallon and untie a ring.

She did the same, but I didn't miss how her hands trembled again. I hated that. Hated anything that made Fal scared or uncertain.

Trace opened his mouth to speak, but my gaze cut to him, making him pause.

"Actually, could we say our own vows?" I asked. We'd decided to go with the simple, standard ones, but that suddenly felt all sorts of wrong. I didn't want to lie to Fallon. Couldn't. The only lie I'd ever let her believe was that I didn't love her, that I'd moved on, when she was everything I wanted and all I could see.

Trace looked between us, a small smile tugging at his mouth as he stepped back. "Of course."

Fallon's eyes widened, and a slightly panicked expression crossed her face.

"I didn't want someone else's promises on my lips." I hooked my pinky with hers again. "I want to give you my own."

I took a deep breath, and the scents of jasmine and coconut washed over me, reminding me of all Fallon was to me. "You are light, breath. Air. In my darkest moments, it's always been you who lit my way."

Those dark blue eyes glistened, and I saw Fal's breath hitch.

"I promise to honor you with every step I take. To protect you with everything I have. To listen to your triumphs and your sorrows. To make sure you know you're never alone. To bring you endless packs of strawberry Sour Patch Kids and make sure you always have a dose of caffeine on standby when you get a headache."

Fallon's pinky squeezed mine even harder.

I gently tugged our joined fingers to lift her hand, mine poised to slide the diamond band into place. "I promise to be your partner and friend for all my days."

I slid the ring onto her finger, and as it clinked against the engagement ring, a sense of rightness filled every last part of me. As if this was what should've been all along.

Fallon's chest rose as she sucked in air, then she brought her gaze to mine. "You've been my safe place from the moment I met you. Safe to feel whatever I needed and give it voice. Safe to be exactly who I was without fear or anxiety. Safe in body and mind."

She swallowed hard. "But more than that. You've been my home. My resting place. Whenever the world spins too fast or things get too hard, I know I can count on you to pause it."

Fallon lifted the black band to my ring finger. "I promise to always be your defender and biggest cheerleader. I promise to bring you double-chocolate Oreo shakes after long days and make your coffee black like tar after long nights in the studio."

I couldn't help the small chuckle that slipped free.

"I promise to help you make the best home imaginable for your sisters and be with you every step of the way."

Tears pressed against the backs of my eyes, but I didn't let them fall.

"I promise to be your partner and your friend for all my days," Fallon whispered as she slid the ring onto my finger.

The moment the metal band was in place, I knew I'd made a mistake. Because I never wanted it to move. Not now, not in a few months, not ever.

Trace cleared his throat. "Well, that's a hell of a lot better than I could've done."

Everyone laughed.

"But there is one more thing I have to say." Trace grinned as he looked at me. "Kye, you may kiss your bride."

Fuck.

But there was nothing to be done. I moved in, one hand sliding along the small of Fallon's back, the other along her jaw. I leaned forward, closer and closer, stopping just shy of her pink bow lips, the ones I knew tasted like spearmint and freedom.

I didn't want to miss this moment. Not a single piece of this memory. If I was going to hell, I might as well enjoy the ride.

So, I closed the distance, my mouth meeting hers as my tongue slid in. And there she was. My sparrow. Her taste exploded on my tongue, and I drank down every drop. Because I refused to miss a single second of the time I had with her.

Fresh, clean air swirled around me, inside me, through me. And I could breathe.

Music sifted through the speakers as Keely and Luca did some ridiculous dance across what they'd decided was a makeshift dance floor. Whatever their creation was, it didn't have much rhythm. But they looked like they were having a hell of a lot of fun.

Arden pressed a hand to Linc's chest. "Luca definitely gets his moves from Cope."

My brother scowled at her. "I have incredible rhythm. Tell her, Sutton."

His fiancée burrowed into his side. "I am partial to slow dances with you."

Arden's lips twitched. "Does he do the dick propeller move?"

Trace choked on a sip of his beer, and Ellie thumped him on the back, trying not to laugh.

"Did I hear someone say dick propeller?" Lolli piped up as she hurried over to our huddle, Walter trailing behind as he struggled with a giant, paper-wrapped parcel.

Rhodes handed a ginger beer to Anson. "I swear you have the hearing of a bat when it comes to anything phallic."

One corner of Anson's mouth kicked up. "We could really dig into the meaning behind that, Lolli."

She made a *pssh* noise and waved him off. "I am at one with my sexuality. I celebrate it—unlike some of you prudes."

"Damn right, you do," Walter said with a growl.

Shep's face screwed up. "I really don't need that sort of reminder."

Thea patted him on the arm, but her shoulders shook with silent laughter. "I think it's sweet that they're in love."

Lolli straightened. "I am *not* in love. I am just using Walter for his hot bod."

Walter beamed at her like she hung the moon. "Happy to be used until you say yes to marrying me."

"Don't hold your breath," Lolli muttered as she grabbed the parcel from him. "For my favorite lovebirds."

Fallon glanced up at me as she pressed deeper into my side. "You open it. I'm scared."

I chuckled, reaching for the gift. "We'll do it together."

Our gazes met for a beat, and then we ripped the paper. It fell to the floor, revealing a canvas covered in countless glittering gemstones. *Just Married* was spelled out above and below two wedding bells with hearts and arrows scattered around.

"Lolli," Fallon began. "This is beautiful. Did you actually make us *appropriate* diamond art?"

"Wait," Cope interjected. "Look at what's coming out of the bells."

Thea choked on a laugh. "That's definitely a dick."

"She made you a dick dinger," Linc said with a triumphant smile. "I gotta admit, I'm a little jealous."

"Don't give her any ideas for our wedding," Arden warned.

"Look at the hearts," Rhodes said, her voice strangled. "The arrows have very distinctive…tips."

Damn if she wasn't right. There were tiny dicks everywhere. In the letters of just married, the hearts, the bells.

Lolli beamed at me and Fallon. "Gotta get craftier around you lot."

"Jesus," I muttered.

"That is something," Rose said as she strode up, a tablet tucked under her arm.

Fallon winced as she turned to greet her friend and mentor. "Please tell me you won't fail us over this…*gift*."

"Well, I have to say, this is my first wedding slash home

inspection," Rose said with a laugh. "And definitely my first phallic diamond art. But you're safe."

Fallon grinned. "If you stick around Lolli, it won't be your last dirty diamond art, that's for sure."

"I can make you one in any theme," Lolli offered.

Rose swallowed her chuckle. "I'll keep that in mind." She turned to us. "Ready?"

Nerves flew around in my stomach, but Fallon leaned into my side, and I felt steadier. "Ready," I said.

Cope took the canvas from me. "I'll get started hanging this over your bed."

"Don't even think about it," I growled.

He just grinned at me. "Payback."

Dammit.

But I followed Rose as she led us away from the group. Once we had a bit of privacy, she sent us a soft smile. "It was a beautiful ceremony. Those vows..." She fanned her face. "I think I have some leaky eyeballs."

I felt Fallon's gaze on me, that unique signature in the air that told me it was her. She was searching for answers I couldn't give her.

"Might want to get those eyes checked," I said, trying to lighten the mood.

Rose chuckled. "I'll be sure to do that." She flipped the case of her tablet over. "I've gone through the basement and the upstairs. Everything looks good there: smoke detectors in working order, fire extinguishers on each level, bleach and other harmful chemicals out of what will be Gracie's reach, appropriate beds and bedroom furnishings, and the pond is secured by the rock wall and the gate to the dock."

My gut twisted at the laundry list of things we'd had to consider, and I knew there were more. Yesterday, Fallon had run around the house, pointing out every possible issue to Ellie. But I had to hope we'd seen to everything.

"I know people are having wine and beer now, but we made a locked cabinet for that," I told Rose.

She sent me a reassuring smile. "You're allowed to have alcohol on the premises. We just look to make sure there isn't an excessive amount."

I glanced around at everyone at the celebration. About two-thirds of the folks had some sort of drink in their hand.

Rose laid a hand on my forearm. "You're having a wedding celebration. This is okay. Just take a breath. You're doing great."

I did as she instructed but still couldn't let go of the worry. Then, a pinky curled around mine. I looked down to find Fallon standing next to me. She'd changed out of the wedding dress and into a white sweatsuit bedazzled with the word *Bride*—a gift from Rhodes and Lolli. She still looked so stunning it stole my damn breath.

She squeezed my pinky. "We've got this."

"We've got this," I echoed.

"All right. On to the question portion," Rose said easily. "Will there be any firearms in the house?"

"No," I answered instantly.

"If that ever changes, we need to make sure you get a gun locker."

"It won't," I answered firmly. I'd seen far too much violence in my life, and I didn't need any more reminders of it. And I was sure my sisters had experienced much of the same.

"All right. What vehicles will you be transporting the girls in?" Rose asked.

Panic lit Fallon's eyes as she jerked her head in my direction. "I didn't think about cars. Your truck only fits two people, and my hatchback is in rough shape."

For once, I felt like I had my shit together. I gave her pinky a squeeze. "I actually have that covered."

"You do?"

"I do." I tugged her in the direction of the massive five-car garage. "Come on."

We moved through our friends and family and entered the attached building. I flipped on the lights, illuminating two top-of-the-line Audi Q7s. One was sparkling white, and the other was pitch black.

Fallon's jaw dropped. "You bought us cars?"

I shrugged. "I figured we'd need 'em, and that hatchback of yours should be in the junkyard."

She scowled up at me. "I was going to retire her after this winter."

I leaned in closer to her. "Well, now you can send her out to pasture a little early and not give me a heart attack every time you drive."

Rose chuckled. "That old girl was making some interesting sounds every time you parked."

Fallon blew out an exasperated breath. "Don't gang up on me."

"Only when it's for your own good," Rose shot back as she moved to walk around the vehicles.

"These models are on the list for top safety picks, and Cope recommended some super fancy booster seat for Gracie. I've got one in each vehicle, and an extra in case one of my siblings ever watches her," I explained.

Rose rounded the rear of the white SUV. "Looks like you've thought of everything. How will you handle the change to your schedules regarding after-school care?"

I nodded, appreciating the question. "I've already changed my schedule at Blackheart Ink, so I'm no longer available in the evenings."

Rose arched a brow. "That's a big change. A big sacrifice."

"They're worth it," I told her simply.

"Yes, they are," she agreed.

"You know you've already approved me to go two-thirds time for a few weeks during the adjustment period," Fallon added.

"I do." Rose made a note on her tablet. "And after that time has passed, will Kye be handling school pickups?"

"Yes," I said quickly.

Rose made another mark. "Perfect. And your background checks both cleared." She looked up at the two of us. "The official written notice will be forthcoming, but...Kye? Fallon? Congratulations. You've been approved for temporary custody of Hayden, Clementine, and Gracie."

Fallon let out a shriek and launched herself at me. I caught her on a laugh, spinning her around as her legs encircled my waist. "Told you," she whispered, her hands framing my face.

I couldn't help staring up at her, taking in the miracle she was. "None of this would've happened without you."

Her thumbs tracked across my stubble. "I'm not so sure about that."

"I am." I pulled her tighter against me. "Thank you."

Fallon's forehead dropped to mine. "You don't have to thank me. I love them already."

Because that's who Sparrow was. She was so free with her affection and care, making everyone's world brighter.

Her perfect mouth curved as her lips hovered near mine. "Ready to meet your sisters?"

Hell. My sisters.

I had sisters. Blood family that wasn't trying to kill me and didn't think I was worthless. I just hoped like hell I could be the brother they deserved.

CHAPTER TWENTY-THREE

Fallon

THE AFTERNOON SUN STREAMED DOWN ON THE PERFECTLY made bed, complete with ridiculously expensive thousand-thread-count sheets Ellie had specially ordered. But I scowled as I studied it. It wasn't because the bed was uncomfortable—it felt like sleeping on a damn cloud. And it wasn't because I didn't like the colors or the design—Ellie had done an amazing job with everything in the primary suite.

It was because it had felt so damn empty last night.

After Rose's approval, we moved the party to my place and turned it into a packing one. My siblings had helped me box up my meager belongings and schlep them over to the new house, and a friend of Mary Lou's was going to sublet from me. I'd never realized just how little I had until I saw it stacked in the corner of my new bedroom.

After that, we ate pizza, and then everyone went home. Kye had said goodnight and hightailed it to one of the many guest rooms, but that wouldn't be an option after today. It would be far too risky for the girls to see us sleeping separately and wonder what was up.

A soft knock sounded on the bedroom door—more evidence that we weren't what we should've been.

"Come in."

The door slowly swung open, and Kye stepped in. He wore his familiar scarred motorcycle boots, jeans, a worn flannel over a Haven gym tee, and that metal band around his finger. "Hey."

"Hey," I echoed lamely, struggling to take my eyes off the ring Kye now wore. *My* ring.

His dark brows pinched. "You okay?"

I finally forced my gaze to his face. "Shouldn't I be asking you that question?"

Kye shoved his hands into his pockets. "I dunno. I feel like we can ask each other."

I sighed. He was right. And it was unfair that I was salty about spending my wedding night alone. Kye had been clear about what this was and wasn't from the moment we'd entertained the crazy idea. "Sorry. I'm just...trying to get my bearings."

"Might take us a minute."

I stared back at the man who'd always given me everything—everything but the piece of him that would change it all. Was I really that greedy?

I crossed the distance and laid a hand over his heart. "We'll get there."

Kye's expression softened. "We will."

"How are *you* doing?"

"I'm scared shitless," he whispered.

God, I was such an asshole. None of today was about me. It was about him and Hayden, Clem, and Gracie. I slid my arms through Kye's and hugged him as tightly as I could. "You're going to be amazing. The fact that you're scared proves it because it means you care."

Kye's arms slowly came around me, holding me to him. "I don't think I could do this without you."

"You could," I promised. "But you don't have to."

"I want to be what they need," he rasped. "They deserve all the good. And *only* the good."

They did. But so did Kye. And the fact that he didn't see that broke my damn heart. But I knew he wouldn't be able to hear it if I told him. Wouldn't be able to feel it. So, I'd just have to give it to him through his sisters and in any tiny ways he'd accept.

"We're going to make sure they get all the good," I promised.

We stood there like that for a long moment—in the bedroom that only I had slept in the night before—and I tried to bleed into Kye everything he deserved without saying the words.

I wasn't sure how long we stayed that way, but the ringing of our phones at the same time had us pulling apart. Kye reached into his back pocket as I moved to the bed where my cell phone lay.

"It's the gate," he croaked. "They're here."

I sent him a reassuring smile. "Let them in."

Rose had thought it best to pick up the girls from school and bring them here. It would be a chance for Kye's sisters to see their new home before they officially moved in this weekend and an opportunity for them to *finally* meet their brother.

Kye tapped the screen of his phone and then shoved it back into his pocket. "I guess this is it."

I moved to him, hooking my pinky with his and squeezing. "It's going to take time. Don't take anything they say personally. They've been through a lot."

He swallowed hard. "I know. Hayden especially."

"Hayden especially," I echoed. "But I know, with time, they will love you so damn much."

"I hope you're right."

"I know I am. Now, let's get down there to welcome them."

Kye jerked his head in a nod, releasing his grip on my finger and leading the way downstairs. His hand hovered on the front door handle for a long moment. Until I laid a hand on his back. "All you can do is show up. And keep showing up—whether they're happy, sad, or pissed the heck off. Just keep showing up."

He cast a look at me over his shoulder. "Just like you always did for me."

Heat flared along my sternum. The good kind. "Just like that."

Kye opened the door.

As cold as it was outside, the Central Oregon sun blazed down, adding warmth that staved off the chill. A station wagon appeared in the distance, and my heart started beating a little faster. In a matter of seconds, Rose pulled to a stop in front of the house and opened the back door to help Gracie out.

Hayden climbed out, staring up at the massive home. Her expression was blank, but her face had gone pale. A different sort of ache flared in my chest. Because I couldn't imagine how scared she must be. Likely twice that of her sisters because she'd always had to be their protector.

I called on my smile, the one that wasn't so wide it looked forced but was welcoming, nonetheless. "Hi, guys. It's so good to see you."

That jerked Hayden out of her musings, and she hurried around the car to take Gracie's hand. Gracie's amber eyes were wide as saucers and locked solely on Kye. As if reading her apprehension, he dropped to the steps, sitting so he didn't look quite so massive.

It was a little thing, silly given how freezing the steps likely were, but Kye did it anyway.

Clementine rounded the back of the station wagon, taking everything in. She stayed quiet, but her gaze wasn't fearful. It was curious.

Rose dropped a hand to Hayden's shoulder. "I know it's a big day, and I just want to remind us all that it's okay to have big feelings to go along with it. There's been a lot of change lately."

"You're as big as a wild thing," Gracie blurted.

He cast a confused look at me. "What's a wild thing?"

"Don't say that," Clem bit out. "It's not nice."

Gracie looked panicked. "I just...like my book. The one Hay Hay reads me."

A grin broke out over Kye's face. "*Where the Wild Things Are?*"

Gracie's lower lip trembled, but she managed a nod.

"Those wild things are so freaking cool," Kye said, his smile still in place.

Gracie's lip stopped trembling. "You think so?"

"They're like monsters for good. Totally my vibe."

Her mouth curved the barest amount. "I like them, too."

Kye looked at the three girls from his perch on the steps. "I know this has gotta be scary. I've been there. Just know I want to do anything I can to make this easier for you. So, if you like or don't like something, just tell me."

He took a deep breath. "I know Renee said some stuff. Told you I knew about you guys. But I promise you I didn't. If I had, I'd have tried to have you come live with me much sooner."

Hayden's mouth pressed into a thin line, but she didn't say anything.

Clem looked between Kye and me. "Miss Rose said you guys got married yesterday."

Kye cast a quick look at me. "We did. Is that okay with you?"

"She's really pretty. And she likes chocolate," Gracie said by way of answer.

Kye chuckled. "Well, I definitely wasn't going to marry someone who didn't like chocolate."

Gracie and Clem giggled. Hayden, on the other hand, eyed me skeptically. "So much for your promise to be our microphone."

That hit me square in the chest, but I took it. "I will *never* stop being your microphone. I just get to do it in a different way now. And Miss Rose is pretty dang good at the microphone thing, too."

Rose brushed some invisible dirt off her shoulder. "Fallon did learn from the best."

Hayden's mouth just thinned further, but Gracie and Clementine didn't seem to mind the change in my relationship with their brother. Hopefully, Hayden would come around with time.

Taking a deep breath, I tried another approach. "What do you think? Want to see the inside of the house and your rooms?"

Both younger girls' smiles went wide as they nodded. Hayden's expression remained carefully blank.

Kye pushed to his feet and moved inside, all of us following. But I didn't miss how he gave the girls plenty of space. I hated that his experience meant he knew to do that. Hated that the girls probably appreciated it. But it was a beautiful gift, nonetheless.

Kye led the way upstairs, turning to the right and gesturing to an open door. "Hayden, this one is yours."

I moved into the room, trying to encourage the girls to do the same. "Gracie and Clem are right across the hall. They share a bathroom, but we thought it might be nice for you to have your own."

"Oh. My. God," Gracie said reverently as she entered the room. "Hay Hay, this is like your dream."

A queen-sized bed was on the far wall, and everything was done in shades of blue. It added to the theme, which was…hockey. Opposite the bed was a mural of an icy winter wonderland with the three girls on the ice and Hayden carrying a hockey stick.

"Is that…us?" Clem asked, her eyes wide.

I nodded. "Ellie, Trace's girlfriend, drew it, and the rest of us helped paint it."

"It's so pretty." Gracie wandered up to the wall, her fingers ghosting over one of her pigtails in the mural.

Clem plopped into one of the chairs that was a cross between a bean bag and a regular chair. "And look at this TV."

My gaze lifted to Hayden as she moved deeper into the room, quietly studying everything.

Rose and Kye followed her in. Kye still gave her plenty of space, but he watched her with cautious eyes. "If there's anything you don't like, we can change it."

"No," Hayden croaked. "This is fine."

I knew it was so much more than that. But there was only so much a fourteen-year-old could process. Especially when it was such a far cry from what she was used to.

Clem leapt from the navy chair in front of the entertainment setup. "Can I see mine?"

Kye chuckled. "You sure can."

He led the way across the hall and into a book lover's paradise. Clem's mural was a field of wildflowers with her reading under a dogwood tree—so similar to the ones in Kye's and my spot. There were plenty of bookshelves for her to fill, too, but I'd gotten her started.

"I got you some of my favorite young-adult series. But we can go to Sage Pages and pick out more because we need to fill a whole library downstairs."

Clem's head whipped around, sending her red hair flying. "There's a real, live library here?"

"We have cards to the town library," Hayden reminded her.

"Yeah, but a library in your house? That's amazing!" She spun in a circle, arms cast outward. "I'm gonna be just like Belle." She flopped onto the bed, and Gracie ran over to jump on it, too.

"It's so cozy," Gracie mumbled, running a hand over the comforter.

Hayden's jaw tightened, a muscle pulsing there. My heart cracked a little more. She was so used to providing the girls with good things that I was sure it was hard to see someone else filling in.

Clementine shoved off the bed and grabbed Gracie's hand. "Let's see your room!"

They raced through the Jack-and-Jill bathroom, oohing and awing over the deep tub, shower, and rainbow-heart towels.

"No way!" Gracie shrieked as she ran over to her mural.

Kye smiled so wide; I didn't think I'd ever seen anything like it. "Arden and Linc told us about what you drew at camp. We thought it would be fun to supersize it," he explained.

"You made my room like the fair," Gracie said, wonder coating every word.

The theme continued throughout the rest of the room with a comforter covered in balloons and a bed dotted with stuffed animals. Her window seat had brightly colored pillows, and the ceiling looked like the top of a circus tent.

"You like it?" I asked hopefully.

She beamed, revealing a tooth that looked a little loose. "This is the best thing EVER!"

Clem studied the small bookshelf loaded with children's stories Mom had given us from her old stash at the ranch. "We've never had anything like this," she whispered. "Not even close."

More cracks fractured my heart.

Movement caught my eye, and I watched Hayden shift toward the door. And then I saw it—the anger, the fear, and the grief. All battling for supremacy in her expression.

"You can't just buy us," she snapped in Kye's direction. "It doesn't change that you weren't there. You don't get to be the hero now."

CHAPTER TWENTY-FOUR

Kye

H*AYDEN'S WORDS LANDED LIKE CAREFULLY PLACED BLOWS—* daggers to my most tender spots. *"You weren't there."*

She was right. And there wasn't a damn thing I could do to change it.

Rose started to follow Hayden out the door. "Let me—"

I reached out, stopping her with a hand on her arm. "Can I try?"

Rose looked from me to the open door and then back again. "All right."

I glanced at Fallon, needing a single point of contact before I went, some of her strength and fearlessness.

"I'm right here," she mouthed.

It was all I needed—just knowing she was with me.

I looked at Gracie and Clem, who had expressions of worry carved into their tiny faces. "It's okay," I tried to assure them. "Feelings are safe here. I'd rather know everything Hayden's got going on inside her than have her not tell me."

"She's big mad," Clem muttered.

"And she should be. What you guys have been through should make us *all* mad."

Gracie studied me with curiosity in her gaze. "You're not gonna yell at her?"

I shook my head. "I promise I will do my very best never to yell. I might not get it perfect, but I promise to try. And if she needs to yell at me right now to get it all out, she can."

"I don't want her to yell at you. You're nice," Gracie whispered.

My lips twitched. "I'm big like a wild thing, remember? I can take it."

That made Gracie smile.

"I'll be right back," I assured them.

"We've got it handled up here. We need to make new room plans," Fallon said with a smile.

I left her and Rose with Clem and Gracie and hurried down the hall. I peeked into Hayden's room, but she wasn't there. I understood why. This place didn't feel like home to her. Not yet. Which gave me an idea.

Jogging down the stairs, I moved through the living room and toward the back doors. There she was, standing at the end of the dock with her arms wrapped around her too-thin frame, dark brown hair blowing in the wind.

I grabbed two blankets and headed outside. She might throw them in the pond, but I could deal with that. What I couldn't deal with was her being alone in all this.

Walking across the back patio and out onto the dock, I made a decent amount of noise. I never handled it well when someone snuck up on me, and I was sure Hayden had some of those same instincts.

She didn't look up as I made my way to her, just kept staring out at the horizon. I wanted to wrap the blanket around her shoulders, but I wasn't sure how she'd take that, so I simply handed it to her. She took it and didn't heave it into the water—but she didn't say anything either.

I wrapped my blanket around my shoulders and stood in silence with her. That had always been Fal's greatest gift to me, and I wanted to give the same to Hayden.

We stood there for a long time before I finally spoke, simply staring out at the horizon. "I might've gone too hard with the rooms," I said.

Hayden's amber gaze flicked up to mine. "Clem and Gracie love them."

I noticed that she'd left herself out of that equation. "And you're worried I'm trying to buy their affection."

"I know how that shit works. Les used to do it after he smacked Renee around, bringing her flowers and us stupid little toys. We didn't need flowers and toys. We needed parents who weren't complete garbage."

My jaw worked back and forth. "You deserve that."

"And you think you can be that?" Hayden asked, the words strained.

"I'm going to try my best to be a good brother. To give you a safe home and people around you that you can trust."

Hayden let loose a scoff.

"You don't have to believe they're trustworthy yet. That takes time. Actions, not words. But they've proven it to me with their actions." They'd done it for me time and time again. And they were doing it now with all the support they'd shown. My siblings and their partners had undergone background checks so they could babysit. Lolli and Nora, too. Nora had even gone so far as to requalify for respite care so we could leave the girls with her for a weekend if we ever needed to.

Her gaze flicked to me. "The Colsons?"

"Yes. They saved me. They gave me a home and a family when I needed it the most. And even when I kept screwing up, they didn't throw me away. They stuck with me."

"That's why you weren't around. Because you loved them so much."

Fuck. That killed me worse than a knife to the goddamned chest.

"No, I wasn't around because I didn't want anything to do with Renee. Because she hurt me, and she let someone else hurt me worse."

Hayden's eyes flared at that, her gaze running over my form as if looking for the injuries.

I tugged at the neck of my tee, stretching it so she could see the scar. Ink now surrounded it, so I could make it mine, but the wound from Rex was still there. The one Renee had watched him inflict on me.

"My dad tried to kill me while Renee watched. I wasn't ever going to have them in my life again. Not ever. But that would've changed if I'd known about you. If I had known about Gracie and Clem. It would've damn well changed. That's a promise."

A muscle fluttered in Hayden's cheek as her eyes glistened. She fought so hard to hold her tears back. "Everybody lies. Why should I believe you?"

"You're right." I released my hold on my tee. "Everybody does lie. So, I'm just going to ask you for one thing."

Hayden looked at me, not moving, but her brow arched as if to say, *What?*

"Give me a chance to prove it to you. To prove I'm here for you. That I always will be—in whatever ways you'll let me."

Hayden was quiet as she stared at me, likely trying to detect deception. But she wouldn't find any. "It's not like we have anywhere else to go," she muttered.

It wasn't exactly a resounding message of faith, but I felt like I'd just won a goddamned war regardless. Even so, I'd never stop fighting. Not for any of my sisters.

CHAPTER TWENTY-FIVE

Fallon

"I'VE GOT YOU, LITTLE G," HAYDEN SAID, PULLING GRACIE'S PLATE toward her and cutting up some of the chicken stir-fry. "But you gotta promise ten bites of veggies."

Gracie's face screwed up. "I don't like the string beans."

"I know, but they make you grow big and strong, right?" Hayden encouraged.

Kye's hand wrapped around mine under the table, squeezing it so hard I was pretty sure he stopped the blood flow. But I knew why. It had only been a matter of hours since the girls had arrived for their official move-in, and it was clear that Hayden was Clem and Gracie's only parent.

Cope shuddered. "I don't like 'em either. Especially when they're all shriveled like that. But I can seriously get down with some snap peas."

Since Gracie and Hayden knew each family, we'd invited Trace, Ellie, Keely, Cope, Sutton, and Luca over for the girls' first dinner in our new house. We thought familiar faces and some Chinese food might be the way to go.

Sutton shook her head. "These green beans are delicious." She popped one into her mouth to prove her point.

Cope leaned forward across the table, sending a stage whisper to Gracie. "Quick, sneak 'em onto her plate, and I'll give you some snap peas."

Gracie giggled. "I dunno if I've had snap peas."

Kye and I shared a look. Snap peas weren't exactly exotic, but I was sure green beans, carrots, and shelled peas were much cheaper and easier to come by.

Cope lifted one of the platters in the center of the table and dished some out to her. "I need a full report."

"Careful," Luca warned. "My dad tricked me into eating all sorts of green stuff."

My heart squeezed at Luca calling Cope *Dad*. Even though it was the norm now, it reminded me that a kid could get what they deserved after missing out on it for so long.

Cope sent Luca an affronted look. "Tricked you? You love my pesto and my broccoli rabe."

Luca wrinkled his nose. "Just no regular broccoli. That's the worst."

"I swear the whole Colson fam has waged war against vegetables," Ellie said with a sigh.

Keely giggled. "You're just the veggie queen."

Ellie tickled Keely's side. "I think I might go as a bunch of kale for Halloween next year."

"A unicorn would be way more fun," Keely argued.

"True enough," Ellie agreed.

Clementine finished the last of her milk. "Could I—?"

But Hayden was already up. "Do you want more milk or water?"

Clem eyed the few sodas on the table. "Can I have a Coke?"

Hayden shook her head. "It's way too close to bedtime."

Kye slid his chair back and rose to head into the kitchen. "We've got some flavored sparkling water with no caffeine. Strawberry, blackberry, and lime."

Hayden's mouth thinned. "She can't have that this late either. It can upset her stomach at night."

He slowed, seeming unsure of what to do.

Clem's gaze ping-ponged between the two of them. "I can just have water."

Hayden grabbed her glass, rinsed out the milk remnants, then filled it with water.

"We've got filtered on the fridge," Kye offered.

"This is fine." Hayden moved back to the table and a conversation about the volcano science project Keely and Gracie's class had been working on.

I stood, crossing to Kye and hooking my pinky with his. I led him out of the kitchen and toward the still-empty library. "You okay?" I whispered.

He looked over my head and out the door as if he could see his sisters through the wall. "She does everything for them."

I gripped his pinky harder, trying to bring his gaze back to me. "She does, and you have to let her for now."

Kye scowled, his eyes finding mine. "I know she needs to feel in control, but she has help now. She has you and me."

I simply stood in the silence with him, waiting for him to see. He didn't need me to lecture him, but he did need to understand that the girls were used to operating a certain way.

"Fuck," Kye muttered. "They don't trust me to help yet."

"They're not used to you as an option," I said, reframing the situation. "With time, especially one-on-one time, that'll shift. But they'll lock you out if you try to force it."

Pain washed through Kye's eyes, swirling in shadowy arcs, and I couldn't stop myself from moving closer. I wrapped my arms around his waist and pressed my face to his chest. His heartbeat thumped against my ear in a steady rhythm.

I'd done the same thing when he'd ended up in the hospital after a bad fight. I hadn't trusted the heart monitors to tell me the truth. I'd needed to feel it. I'd lain with my ear pressed to his chest, just waiting for him to wake up.

Kye rested his chin atop my head, arms encircling me. "I just want to magically make it better. Erase all their pain."

"But you know that's not how life works."

"No, it fucking isn't."

My fingers fisted in the soft flannel of his shirt. "But it means those moments of joy are even deeper. We feel them that much more because of the pain we've experienced. You just have to hold on until those moments start to break through."

I pulled back a fraction to see if my words had landed. Kye searched my eyes, looking for something there I couldn't identify. His fingers tangled in my blond strands. "I don't know what I'd do without you, Sparrow."

My breath caught in my throat. We were so close I could almost taste Kye. And because I'd gotten a hit of that too many times recently, I was reckless. I leaned in even closer. Stretched up, my lips hovering just shy of his. Those strong fingers tightened in my hair, waking up every nerve ending until—

"I'm heeeereeeee!" Lolli called from the entryway.

Kye and I startled apart, his hands dropping from my body as he took a giant step back and muttered a curse. "Did you give her a key?"

I tried to ignore the flare of hurt I felt at the distance Kye had put between us, knowing it was for the best. "Of course not. I'm not risking her bedazzling an angel orgy on our bedroom ceiling."

He grunted, and then a knowing look overtook his face. "I gave Cope a key so he could bring over some hockey stuff for Hayden. I bet that asshole gave it to her."

Kye was already moving back out to the living room, and I hurried to follow.

"Lolli," Ellie called. "I didn't know you were coming tonight."

"Well," she huffed, "I wasn't invited, so I just decided to invite myself."

"Because," Kye said, striding into the kitchen and living area with the massive table large enough to fit the entire Colson crew, "it's our first night. We don't want a bunch of new people all at once."

Lolli flipped her gray hair, which currently had pink streaks, over her shoulder. "But I am the *best* this family has to offer."

Trace grunted. "You're the most inappropriate this family has to offer."

"Same thing," Lolli muttered.

Gracie sent her a bashful smile. "I like your sparkles."

Lolli twirled, making her bright pink tulle skirt with sequins fly around her. She'd also donned cowboy boots with sparkly mushrooms on the sides and a shirt that read, *In Mushrooms We Trust* with an array of bedazzled fungi.

"Thank you, honey bunches. You must be Gracie."

The little girl nodded.

"I'm Clementine, but everyone calls me Clem," the redhead offered. "And I love mushrooms."

Lolli set two bags on the kitchen island and clapped. "Another fungi aficionado. I love it!"

"Pretty sure she's not into the 'shrooms you are, Lolls," Cope said wryly.

Trace held up a hand. "Please, don't make me arrest both of you. I'll make you share a cell."

Clem and Gracie giggled, but Hayden just kept staring at Lolli in pure shock.

"You must be the hockey star Cope told me about," Lolli greeted her.

A flush of pink hit Hayden's cheeks. "I think star's a stretch."

"I don't," Cope argued. "You've got what it takes if you want it."

A look passed over Hayden's face, but it was gone too quickly for me to identify it.

"Well, I'm Lolli—"

"Or Supergran," Keely cut in.

"Or Supergran," she amended. "And I brought all the fixings for my epic fairy sundaes."

Wariness entered Trace's eyes. "These sundaes aren't *special*, are they?"

Lolli waved him off. "Of course, they're special. But they're not the kind of special that would mean seeing Ellie's garden gnomes doing the macarena across your front lawn all night."

"That sounds like it would be fun," Gracie offered.

Keely nodded. "Ellie taught me the macarena and the dance to 'Bye Bye Bye'. She said it's 'portant to know your history, and the nineties is the best we got."

Trace sent Ellie a droll look. "The nineties? Really? What about the Industrial Revolution, the Civil Rights Movement, and women's suffrage?"

Ellie folded her napkin. "All vital times, but did they have frosted tips, blue eye shadow, and boy band bops that don't quit?"

Hayden choked on a laugh. "I do have a thing for 'Tearin' Up My Heart.'"

Ellie beamed at her. "I knew I liked you." She stood and motioned for Hayden to follow her. "Come on. We can set up dessert and pick the playlist."

Hayden looked uncertain for a moment, glancing at Clem and Gracie as if she wasn't sure she should leave them. But then she pushed her chair back and followed Ellie into the kitchen.

I shot Kye a look as if to say, *See?* But I couldn't help but notice the distance he'd kept between us since our moment in the library.

Lolli pawed through the two massive bags she'd set on the island. "I brought four kinds of ice cream, hot fudge, caramel sauce, rainbow sprinkles, five different mini candies, and whipped cream." She pulled out two cans of the whipped stuff and turned to Kye and me. "I brought you an extra as a honeymoon present. I'm actually working on a cannabis-infused version that will really heighten arousal, but I trust your hormones to do the trick for now."

"Lolli!" I shouted, my face flaming.

"What?" she asked innocently. "It's never too early to start the birds and the bees talk."

Kye pinched the bridge of his nose. "This is why you weren't invited."

Lolli just grinned. "But aren't you glad I came anyway?"

Hayden's lips twitched. "I am."

Lolli held out a hand to her. "My girl!"

Hayden gave her a high five across the kitchen island.

"Now, let's give us all a sugar coma!"

"Kye Kye?" Gracie asked sleepily as we made our way upstairs.

She and Keely had talked us into letting them change into jammies and watching half of the *Minions* movie while we ate sundaes, and during the process, she'd adopted Keely's nickname for Kye.

"Yeah, Gracie?" he said, a soft smile curving his mouth.

"Would you read me a bedtime story?" she mumbled.

"Can I listen, too?" Clem added.

Hayden stiffened. "I can read to you."

Gracie sent her sister a careful look. "Can Kye Kye do it?"

Hayden swallowed hard and glanced at her brother.

"Only if it's okay with you," Kye hedged, trying to give Hayden the control she needed right now.

"Sure. Yeah. I need to do some homework anyway," she muttered.

"Do you have everything you need for that?" I asked. "We can do a full school supplies shop one day this week."

"I got us everything we need for the year," Hayden clipped.

Shit.

"Okay," I said softly. "Just let me know if you need more of anything."

She jerked her head in a nod and made a beeline for her bedroom.

Clem worried the corner of her bottom lip. "She worked all summer so we could get the stuff."

A muscle fluttered along Kye's jaw. "She must love you a whole lot."

Clem nodded.

"Can you read *Wild Things*?" Gracie asked, oblivious to the new tension.

"Let me see if we have that one," Kye said.

I crossed to the small bookshelf in her room. "I know we do because it was my favorite when I was about your age. You guys get comfy, and I'll find it."

Gracie climbed under the covers and patted the spot next to her. "You gots to be in the middle so we can both see the pictures."

Kye chuckled as he kicked off his boots and settled against the pillows. "The pictures are the most important part."

"And the voices," Clem added, settling in next to them.

I found the book and handed it to Kye. "Your script."

He grinned, taking it from me with tattooed fingers. As he opened and started to read, I slowly backed away. I wanted to give them their moment, but I also couldn't find it in me to turn away. I'd heard Kye read to Keely before, but this was somehow different. He put his all into each voice and every line. He acted like he'd secretly gone to drama school or been a star of stage and screen.

Gracie's head drooped, and she leaned it against Kye's shoulder for a better view of the book. My heart clenched as Kye's gaze flicked to her before returning to the book, a look of pure love and relief on his face. Before long, Clem had an elbow leaned on his other shoulder as she giggled at his especially deep voice on one line.

They looked like they'd been doing this all their lives—exactly how it should've been.

"Everything's cleaned up downstairs," Ellie said softly as she appeared next to me. Then, she stilled. Her mouth curved as she wrapped an arm around me. "Your ovaries exploding yet?"

"They're dust," I admitted.

I'd seen Kye in many different lights over the years: fierce and protective, tender and empathetic, mischievous and troublemaking. Angry and determined to tear down the world. Kind and thoughtful. Sometimes, I even thought I caught him looking at me with love in those amber eyes, even if it wasn't the kind I'd wanted to see there.

But I'd never seen him like this. Like he was meant to be a father.

Tears gathered in my eyes, and I quickly ducked from the room. "What else needs doing downstairs?"

I started in that direction, but Ellie caught my elbow. "Everything's taken care of." She searched my face. "It's going to be a lot. This transition. But I'm here if you need to talk."

I shoved down all the feelings stirring inside me because it wasn't *about* me right now. It was about us giving the girls everything they needed. "I'm good."

"You're not, but you will be," Ellie said softly.

One corner of my mouth tugged up. "I'm an awful liar."

Ellie pulled me into a hug. "You're human."

"Here's the truth: I'm okay. I'm also not okay. But in the end, I'm okay."

Ellie laughed as she released me. "Funnily enough, I know exactly what you mean. Everything's a shit show, but you know you'll make it through. And even amid the shit show, there's beauty that can knock you sideways."

"Like Kye reading a bedtime story to his sisters—sisters who are now safe, fed, and warm." My eyes burned.

Ellie gave my hand a squeeze. "So much beauty. Just don't forget that what's happening is a lot, and you need to take care of yourself."

I let out a long breath. "I will. Right now, that means a shower."

"Good. Cope has the key, so we can lock up on our way out," Ellie said.

"Thank you. For everything."

"Always." Ellie gave my hand one last squeeze and then headed down the hall toward the stairs.

I stayed in the hallway for a moment, listening. I could still hear Kye reading. There wasn't a peep coming from Hayden's room. And there should've been. Teenagers needed music, calls with friends, and a little bit of mayhem. I just hoped she'd find that with time.

Moving down the hall, I headed for the primary suite. I did my best to ignore the massive bed in the center of the room and headed into the closet. Opening a drawer, I pawed through my pajama options and scowled.

Nothing in the assortment read: *married woman.* Everything spoke of comfort over sex appeal. And there wasn't a damn thing wrong with that, but at the same time, sometimes I wanted to be sexy. There had been minimal opportunities for that in my life.

The few times I'd tried to go further than simply fooling around, it was as if some invisible force field stopped me. Everything about it had felt…wrong, and it had left me turning that part of myself off in a way. Now, I found I was a little bitter about it.

I grabbed the set of pajamas Rhodes had gotten me for Christmas two years ago. They were covered in wrapped, brightly colored candies, and while far from alluring, they were incredibly soft.

Heading into the bathroom, I quickly showered and did my bazillion-step skincare routine until my face looked like it was covered in morning dew. I flossed and brushed, tamed my hair into loose waves, and then finally admitted I was stalling.

I took a deep breath and moved into the bedroom, where I found Kye sitting on the end of the bed wearing gray sweats and a worn Blackheart Ink tee. His gaze moved up to my face, but his expression was completely unreadable.

My tongue darted out, wetting my suddenly dry lips. "Hi."

That amber gaze swept over my face. "Gracie and Clem are asleep."

"Good. That's good. What about Hayden?" I asked, my fingers twisting in my PJ top.

"She was still reading for English, but I'm not sure I can give her a bedtime." Kye ran a tattooed hand through his hair, and I saw the lines of strain on his face.

That broke through all my awkwardness and self-centered worry. I crossed to him and ran my hands through his hair, massaging his scalp.

Kye let out a groan as my fingers hit the base of his skull. "Feels like the weight of the world is living right there. One wrong move and I'll blow it all sky-high."

"You're gonna make a wrong move," I told him softly.

Those amber eyes cut to me, full of accusation.

My fingertips dug in where Kye felt the most pain. "As far as I know, you aren't some alien life form. And all humans make mistakes."

"Those girls don't deserve any more mistakes."

"No, they don't. But teaching them how to move on from them is far more important than striving for perfection, don't you think?"

Kye's big hands wrapped around the backs of my thighs. "How'd you get so wise?"

My mouth quirked. "Lots of fucking up."

He scoffed. "Sparrow, you're as close to perfection as anything I've ever known."

Pressure built along my sternum, but I kept breathing. "Trust me, I'm not." I held on to things for too long—the good and the bad. I took on others' feelings like they were mine. I'd used people in an attempt to move on from Kye, even knowing I'd never be able to love them like I loved him. I could be selfish. And, God, could I hold a grudge.

Kye's thumbs swept up and down the backs of my legs, sending tiny sparks skittering over my skin. One corner of his mouth kicked up. "Okay, you do have a hell of a vengeful streak."

I couldn't focus on anything but Kye's fingers, but I managed to get a single word out. "True."

Amber eyes collided with mine as Kye's thumbs continued to swipe back and forth. Neither of us moved, other than those tiny ministrations. His thick, tattooed fingers shifted, swiping along my inner thighs then.

So far from where I wanted them the most, but I still thought I could come apart with this alone. My breath came in quick pants, faster and faster. And then—

Kye's phone dinged. It was as if some spell had been broken. His hands were gone, and he was suddenly on his feet, forcing me back and then creating all the distance the room could provide.

I instantly felt freezing as his fingers—fingers that had just been on my body—scrolled on his phone. "I'm gonna go to sleep," I muttered.

"'Kay," Kye said, glancing my way for only the briefest moments.

"I'll put some pillows between us when I get into bed. That way, I won't disrupt you if I thrash."

Pillows. To put those walls back in place. To keep all the distance he wanted between us.

"Okay," I whispered, pulling back the covers.

"It's just because of the nightmares," Kye hedged.

I knew he got them. He'd woken the house up more than once after he came to live with us. It broke my heart that all those demons reached him when he was asleep. But this felt like more.

"I can sneak out to a guest room if you're worried," I offered.

Kye shook his head. "No. It'll be fine."

But I knew the truth. It was anything but.

CHAPTER TWENTY-SIX

Kye

I WAS THE WORLD'S BIGGEST ASSHOLE. *FUCKING HELL.* I SCRUBBED a hand over my face in the bathroom's too-bright light. The space was far too over-the-top: the steam shower, the massive tub, the two huge sink spaces with a vanity between them.

The entire time I'd designed it with the architect, I'd imagined Fallon filling it with her trinkets, her ridiculous array of face products, her scent, and her energy.

And now that she was here? In the space where I'd always imagined her? I was fucking it up left and right.

I stared down at my hand, my fingers tingling and burning. There was no heat like Fal's heat. Everything about her scalded, leaving scars I'd wear with pride until the day I died.

Moving to the sink, I turned the water as cold as it would go and splashed some on my face. Unfortunately, it didn't do a damn thing to quench the need coursing through me. And it was only night one.

"Fuck."

I took my time brushing my teeth and trimming my scruff, which had nearly tipped into beard territory. I even gargled with the damn mouthwash I hated. But maybe burning my mouth with hellfire would stop me from imagining having it all over Fallon's damn body.

Cracking my neck, I walked into the bedroom. Only the soft light on my side of the bed was on. And it didn't do a damn thing to help me.

The day had clearly gotten to Fallon because she'd already crashed. Her blond hair cascaded over the pillow, but a few strands had fallen over her face. They fluttered with each deep exhale.

Something foreign moved in my chest, like my organs rearranging into another formation. My back teeth ground together as I took in the pillow barrier Fal had created. She didn't stop at just one to separate our two spaces. Instead, she had four different ones in place from the foot to the head of the bed.

Because I was the asshole who'd made her think she had to. The bed was large enough for us to have plenty of room without a wall, but I didn't trust myself.

Crossing to the bed, I pulled back the covers and slid inside. I turned out the light but couldn't help turning toward Fal. Even in the pitch dark of the room, she called to me. Everything about her reached out like invisible, bewitched fingers, beckoning me forward.

But I didn't let myself touch her. Didn't let myself move even a single pillow. Instead, I whispered into the dark, "I'm sorry."

Fire licked at my thigh—scarring, blazing tendrils of flames. It swirled, engulfing me and making every part of me come alive with want and need.

A soft moan had my eyes flying open. It took me a second to realize where I was: the new house, my bedroom.

And in the massive bed with me...Fallon.

Gone was the pillow wall she'd so expertly put in place last night.

Instead, Fal was curved completely around me, and I around her. It was difficult to tell where she ended, and I began.

And there was something so damn *right* about that.

One of my arms wrapped around her waist, while my other hand was tangled in those soft, blond waves. Our legs were completely intertwined, one of my thighs between hers while the other held her in place. It was like my body had entrapped hers and refused to let go.

Fallon rocked against me, the blazing heat of her core searing my thigh. A million curses flew around in my mind as she let out another moan.

Her back arched, pushing her harder against me, and those damn pajamas pulled taut over her breasts. The sleepwear was anything but suggestive, but it somehow managed to be the sexiest thing I'd ever seen a woman wear. The thin cotton revealed more than Fal realized.

Her nipples pebbled against the fabric, and I could imagine tracing them with my tongue. My fingers itched to palm the curves beneath her breasts, to feel them filling my hands as she rode me. My dick pressed hard against my sweats, against Fallon.

Fucking hell.

She moved, still asleep and blissfully unaware of what was happening here. I should've woken her or turned away. Something.

But the temptation was too great. It was as if this were the one way I could have her—in our dreams.

She was stunning as she gave in to her need. Her body moved on instinct, finding and taking the rhythm she needed. My sweats grew damp with that need, and my dick pulsed, wanting nothing more than to get to her.

It had made do with only my hand for so damn long. Now, I was about to come in my pants like I was thirteen all over again. But I didn't care. All I wanted was to watch Fallon come apart. To know what her face looked like as she shattered.

Fal's back arched again, and her body bowed as she moved back and forth, riding my thigh. Wild. Free. She was the most stunning thing I'd ever seen—taking what she needed, entirely in control of her pleasure yet totally free at the same time.

Her hip shifted, creating the most perfect friction against my cock, and it nearly made me weep. My fingers tightened in her hair. I couldn't have stopped myself if I tried.

The movement of Fallon's hips changed, picking up speed and intensity. A soft, desperate mewl left her lips, and my dick pulsed as everything in me drew up tight, almost painfully. Fallon shuddered as the first wave hit her. And as it did, her eyes flew open and met mine.

I expected panic, maybe even fury, but those deep blue eyes never left mine. Fal kept moving as my hand tightened around her waist. Her breaths came in quick pants, and there was nothing I could do to stop myself as she came again. My dick didn't have a prayer.

The orgasm hit like an uppercut to my goddamned solar plexus, stealing all the air from my lungs as my release hit almost painfully. But I didn't lose those beautiful eyes as we found it together.

As soon as the wave eased, Fallon's eyes widened, panic searing through them.

My hands released her instantly. *What the hell had I done?*

I was already moving, throwing the covers back and launching from the bed. "We were both asleep. It's not a big deal," I muttered as I took off for the bathroom.

But that was the biggest lie of all. Because now that I knew what Fal looked like when she shattered, I'd never be able to erase the image. It'd be burned into my brain for all eternity, and I'd be living in hell, having seen that and knowing I could never have it again.

CHAPTER TWENTY-SEVEN

Fallon

"Oh, fuck." They were the only words that would do in this situation. My hands flew to my face, even as the rest of my body throbbed.

What the hell had I just done? I'd mounted Kye like some breeding stallion, taking full advantage. My face flamed with shame and embarrassment. I'd never be able to look him in the eyes again. More than a little guilt niggled.

The sound of the water turning on spurred me into action. I couldn't be here when Kye got out of the shower and came out wearing nothing but a towel. I threw the covers back and leapt from the bed. The second I did, a different sort of urge hit me.

I pulled all the bedding off, leaving the comforter and pillows on the two chairs by the window but balling up the sheets to take with me. I threw them in the washer in the fancy upstairs laundry room and turned the water as hot as possible. Then I ran back for an outfit to change into. I grabbed wide-legged tan pants, a blouse, and a V-neck sweater.

As soon as I had those items, I bolted for one of the guest rooms.

Thankfully, Ellie had stocked them with plenty of toiletries. I showered and got ready as much as I could without my makeup. When I was done, I checked the time.

Seven in the morning. Time to make sure the girls were up. As I stepped into the hallway, it was to find Hayden slipping out of Clem's room.

I tried to pull myself together and smile. "I was just coming to check if everyone was up."

Hayden's eyes flashed. "I've been making sure they were up and ready for years."

I tried not to let her words sting. I knew it wasn't about me. It was about change. It was about being unsure of what her place was now.

I paused, letting all the worry and freak-outs of the morning fall away so I could focus on what was important. I took my time making sure Hayden could see my eyes, my truth. "Gracie and Clem are beyond lucky to have you as their big sister. Not everyone could've done what you did over the years. It shows how strong you are. How smart and brave."

Hayden's throat worked as she struggled to swallow.

"I'm just going to ask you for one thing."

Those amber eyes flashed again, this time with mistrust.

"If there's anything I can do to help, let me know."

Hayden shifted uneasily but managed a small nod. "Sure."

I beamed at her. "Thank you. Now, I have one more question. And this one is of the utmost importance."

That wariness was back. "What?"

"How do you feel about pancakes?"

One corner of Hayden's mouth kicked up. "Pretty sure you have to be a monster to not like pancakes."

"Phew." I slid a hand over my brow. "Marked safe from secret monsters in our midst."

"I dunno about that. You haven't experienced a morning with Gracie yet. She's pretty monstrous before nine a.m."

I chuckled. "Thank you for the warning. I will don my armor before breakfast."

Hayden smiled and then ducked back into her room. Somehow, that small smile made it feel like I'd won the biggest teddy bear at one of those impossible carnival games.

"Okay," I said, flipping a pancake. "I've got the following topping options. Raspberries, strawberries, blueberries, and bananas. And if you pick one or more of those fruitastic toppings, you also get the option of whipped cream. What'll it be?"

Hayden, Clem, and Gracie sat at stools at the counter, watching me work while Kye puttered around with coffee, a task I'd noticed was taking him ten times as long as it usually did. His avoidance game was strong. But it was better that way. Because every time our gazes collided, my face flamed as memories of this morning flared.

"I'll take all of them," Clem said as she looked up from her *Hunger Games* book.

"A girl after my own heart," I praised. "What about you, Hayden?"

"Could I have raspberries and strawberries, please?"

"Coming right up." I slid a pancake onto a plate. "What about you, Miss Gracie?"

She lifted her head from her arms, where she'd been taking a pseudo nap at the island. Instead of answering, she grunted.

"Told you," Hayden said.

"You did warn me she might turn into a mini wild thing before nine."

"She likes blueberries and strawberries," Clem added helpfully as I shifted another pancake to a plate.

Kye set a mug next to the stove. "Here you go. I'll doctor up the toppings."

When he didn't meet my eyes, the guilt I'd felt earlier turned. This was on both of us, not just me. But we couldn't let this awkwardness win. "I'm not sure you can be trusted with the right fruit-to-whipped-cream ratio, Kye." I arched a brow, waiting for him to lift his gaze.

When it finally made contact, I swore I saw relief in his eyes. And then his lips twitched. "You mean I might not have them drowning in whipped cream like the queen of sugar prefers?"

I choked on a laugh. "You say that like you aren't a sweet fiend right along with me."

Kye shook his head as he loaded up the girls' plates. "I'm pretty sure your bloodstream is ninety-nine-point-nine percent sucrose at this point."

"What's sucrose?" Gracie said sleepily as Kye handed her a plate.

"The chemical compound found in sugar," Clem said as she took her plate.

Kye's and my eyes met, both of ours flaring in surprise.

"Pretty damn—I mean dang—smart," Kye said.

Clem laughed. "We've heard that word before. And I like science."

"Well, it clearly likes you back." I plated two pancakes for myself and three for Kye.

Kye doctored his pancakes with tons of fruit and whipped cream. "I'm going to drop you off today, and Fal and I will pick you up together. Sound good?"

Hayden worked on cutting her pancake. "You don't have to pick me up. I have work after school."

Kye stiffened and spoke before I could warn him not to say anything. "You don't have to do that anymore."

Hayden's head jerked up. "I *want* to. I like earning my way. And I like working at the ice rink."

A muscle fluttered in Kye's cheek. "Okay. Then I'll drop you off, and Fal or I will pick you up at the end of your shift."

"I can take the bus," Hayden argued. "I've been doing it every day for the past year."

Kye's knuckles bleached white as he gripped the counter. "There are a lot of things you've done in the past that you don't have to do anymore if you don't want to. And while I'll let you take the lead on most of it, when it comes to your safety, you'll have to let me take the reins."

Hayden glared at Kye. "Whatever."

I let out a breath as I took the seat next to Gracie. I knew the battle could've been so much worse. We ate in silence for a while, but Clem kept casting glances at Kye. Her mouth would open like she wanted to say something, but then she'd close it again.

Kye didn't rush her. He just kept eating, waiting for her to figure out what she wanted to say and how.

Finally, she summoned the courage. "Can I go to your gym one day?"

Kye's brows rose. "You want to go to Haven?"

Clem nodded, biting her bottom lip. "It might be kind of cool to learn how to fight."

Kye beamed full-out at her. "I'd love to take you."

"Me, too?" Gracie asked hopefully, a little more awake now that she'd eaten.

"Of course," Kye told her. "We can go today after school if you want."

"Yes!" Gracie cheered. "I love your pictures on the wall outside."

"It's called a mural," Clem corrected.

Gracie's face screwed up. "I know."

"No, you didn't, or you would've said that," Clem shot back.

"Clementine," Hayden said in a warning tone.

Clem instantly snapped her mouth shut.

"I loved painting those pictures," Kye said, choosing Gracie's word so she didn't feel bad about using it.

"Painting's the best. Do you ever do it with Miss Arden? She's the bestest," Gracie said reverently.

"You know, I painted with her sometimes when we were younger. It really helped us deal with anything hard we were going through."

My heart jerked in my chest because I remembered those dark times—when Kye had let the demons grab hold, and the only way he could let them out was by fighting or painting.

Gracie studied him for a long moment. "You can draw the things in your head."

"That's right," Kye agreed. "Maybe you and I can paint together one of these days."

Gracie's grin was so wide I could see almost all her teeth. "I'd like that."

My phone dinged, and I swiped it off the counter. Noah wanted to see if I could make an extra home visit to two kids we'd placed in temporary custody with their grandmother. He wanted to make sure we had all our ducks in a row before they went before a judge for adoption.

"Everything okay?" Kye asked.

I slid off my stool. "All good. Just some extra work today."

Kye frowned. "I thought they knew you were part time for a couple of weeks."

"They do, but Noah just needs an assist with something."

At the man's name, Kye's frown deepened to a scowl. "Tell *Noah* that he can do his own work."

I rolled my eyes. "Relax. This is something I need to do. And it's fine." I rifled through my purse and slid my cell into one of the pockets. "I need to grab my car charger. Be right back."

"We've got the dishes," Kye called after me.

I sent him a wave and headed toward the front door. Unlocking it, I stepped outside, only to be hit with a wall of cold. I cursed as I ran to my car and grabbed the charger. I didn't want to admit it, but having the seat heaters in the fancy new SUV Kye had bought me would be unbelievably nice.

As I jogged back to the house, a flash of color on the front step caught my attention. I frowned. I hadn't seen it when I walked out because it was mostly tucked under the mat. It was a Polaroid. And it hadn't been there yesterday.

Maybe it fell out of Ellie's or Sutton's purse. But it was an odd thing to drop.

I bent and tugged it free. As I straightened, the whole image came into view, but it took me a second to compute what I was seeing:

a man lying on the ground, illuminated by a bad flash. Eyes wide and unblinking. Blood soaking a white shirt beneath a leather vest.

Dead.

He was dead.

And scrawled across the bottom of the Polaroid in boxy lettering, it said…

TWO DOWN. WHO'S NEXT?

CHAPTER TWENTY-EIGHT

Kye

I stared down at the Polaroid photo in the center of the table—the one now sealed in a bag with a label in big, black block letters that read, *EVIDENCE*. My throat wound itself into a rope so tight I could barely breathe.

My hand curved around Fallon's, fingers threading through hers and holding on tight. I didn't give a damn about rules or walls right now. I just needed to know she was safe.

"You should've told me immediately," I said, pitching my voice low as a handful of officers—including Trace—milled around the living space and entryway.

Fallon's dark blue gaze flicked toward me. "I couldn't, and you know it."

She hadn't said a word about the most morbid photo I'd ever seen when she came back into the house after grabbing her charger—a picture someone had broken onto our property to leave behind. Instead, she simply told us her schedule had changed for the day and called me only after I'd dropped the girls off to say she needed me back at the house. By the time I arrived, Trace and his second-in-command, Gabriel, were already here.

My hand squeezed hers tighter. "You could have pulled me aside and told me what was happening. And you sure as hell shouldn't have stayed in the house alone after someone left that shit on our front doorstep."

A fresh wave of anger washed through me. No, not just anger. Fury. Not at Fallon. At myself. This was happening because of me.

"I locked the doors," Fallon argued.

"Fal," Trace said as he walked up, the warning clear in his voice. "I know you want to protect those girls from anything that could cause them distress, mental anguish, or harm. But you can't put yourself at risk to do it."

Fallon's eyes flashed with a defiance that only made me love her more. Because I saw then just how much she cared about my sisters. She'd do anything for them. And that scared the hell out of me, too.

I squeezed her hand again, bringing her focus back to me. "I'm not saying you shouldn't protect them. We just have to do it together, okay?"

A little of the tension thrumming through her system eased, and she leaned into my side as she had countless times before. As if I was her one safe place in the universe. "Okay."

God, that trust was a gift I didn't deserve. But that wouldn't stop me from relishing it.

I glanced up at Trace. "Anything?"

"Sent the image to our medical examiner. She said it looks real, but you never know with special effects."

My jaw worked back and forth. "Feels like it'd be a hell of a lot harder to create special effects with a Polaroid camera."

"I agree," Trace said, a muscle in his jaw fluttering. "Gabriel's taking point on this. He has a few questions."

I stiffened at that. I didn't have a problem with Gabriel; he was good people—kind, hardworking, and a damn good friend to Trace. But I wanted my brother on the case. Because I trusted him, even when trust didn't come easily.

I opened my mouth to argue, but Fal squeezed my hand hard. "It's for the best. But it can't appear like you're hiding anything."

A sinking sensation took root somewhere deep. We couldn't have that because it could cause issues with my custody case.

Gabriel moved into our huddle in the living room. "I promise I'm giving this case my all."

I moved my head in a nod that felt more than a little robotic. "Thanks."

"You knew Rocco St. James?" Gabriel asked, flipping open his notepad.

I focused on Fallon. How her thumb traced circles on the back of my hand. All the pure goodness she was. "Yes. He's a member of the Reapers MC. He was the one who organized their fights when I was a teenager. Not sure if he still does it—*did* it."

Gabriel nodded, scribbling something on the paper. "When's the last time you saw him?"

"It's been years. Other than Oren, I haven't seen any of them in years. Trace put the fear of God in them when he told them to keep their distance from me."

Gabriel's lips twitched. "It's fun as hell when Trace gets scary."

My brother shook his head. "I just let them know it would put a serious crimp in their business dealings if the department had a dedicated team stationed near their clubhouse, bike shop, and bar."

Fallon's mouth curved. "You're a good brother."

Trace grinned. "I am, aren't I?"

Usually, I would've taken the opportunity to give him shit, but I didn't have it in me. "What the hell is going on?"

All humor fled Trace's face. "I don't know. But it's starting to look like someone is picking off the people involved in that fight ring, one by one."

Fallon's hand spasmed in mine. "Which means they want to hurt Kye."

I moved then, wrapping an arm around her. "If someone really wanted to hurt me, they wouldn't mess around with some threatening Polaroid. They'd just do it."

Gabriel made a sound of disagreement, and my gaze snapped to him in warning. He held up his hands. "I'm sorry, Kye. I disagree. If we've learned anything from this past year's mayhem, it's that some perps like to play with their food before they eat it."

Fallon's hand fisted in my tee. "Kye."

"I'll be fine. What about Fallon and my sisters?" I asked. "Should I be talking to their schools?" My gaze flicked to Fal as a whole new worry set in. "Is this going to hurt my case?"

"We're not letting that happen," Trace growled. "First, no one in the targets' lives has been harmed. So, I think the girls and Fallon are safe, but we'll take precautions just in case. Second, I'll make sure no judge punishes you for being the target of a monster. Worst case scenario? They have to go stay with Nora for a little while. She got approved for respite care, right?"

It didn't matter that we had Nora as a backup plan. I knew the truth. Trace couldn't do a damn thing if a judge thought the home I was creating for the girls wasn't safe.

"Cowabunga!" Gracie yelled, running full tilt at Evan, who was dressed in full-body pads. She let loose two punches and then a kick.

"Amazing, Little G," I praised. "But we might not want to give the attacker a heads-up that you're coming in hot."

Clem giggled. "You mean letting the whole neighborhood know?"

"I don't know," Fallon said, stretching out one of her thighs and then the other. "I think Gracie is pretty dang intimidating. I'd run in the other direction if I saw her coming."

She held out her hand for a high five, and Gracie smacked her palm, a huge smile on her face. But I was too caught up in Fal, dressed entirely in spandex. It was the last thing I should be thinking about. I had an adoption case to win once Renee's rights were terminated, someone was picking off people involved in the fight ring, and I had a family to make sure I didn't lose through it all.

Yet here I was, watching as Fallon bent over to touch her toes in another stretch. I took in the way the material hugged every curve, my fingers itching to glide over the globes of her ass as I—

"I think you've got a little drool there, buddy," Mateo cut into my thoughts. "Not that it isn't a beautiful sight."

"If you like your eyes in your head, get them the hell off my wife," I growled, those last two words feeling far more right than they probably should.

Fallon straightened and turned around, realizing just what our view had been. Her eyes narrowed on Mateo.

"Watch out," Evan called. "She'll take you down and not think twice."

"Especially since you're already on my s-list," Fallon clipped.

Mateo held up both hands. "I'd never. Utmost respect for the most beautiful woman I've ever seen."

Gracie glared at Mateo. "You can't say that about Fallon. She's my brother's wife, and he's way bigger than you."

My lips twitched. "What she said."

Mateo grinned. "You must be the amazing Miss Gracie."

Gracie wasn't moved by his charm. Instead, she crossed her arms and glared at Mateo harder. Evan moved to stand next to her and took up the same stance, looking ridiculous in all his padding. Then, Clem joined in, doing the same thing.

"Shit," Mateo muttered.

"Language," I warned.

His brows lifted. "You telling me I can't swear in a fighters' gym?"

"Not around my sisters, you can't."

Mateo shook his head. "Dude, you've changed."

Evan just laughed and offered high fives to both Gracie and Clem. They smacked his palm in answer.

"Okay," I said, refocusing on the girls. "Let's work on an uppercut next."

I took my time walking them through the angle and execution

of the punch. Gracie and Clem took turns practicing on Evan, who went out of his way to make epic sound effects as they connected with his pads. He was damn good with the kids, and I knew having him take charge of an additional youth program was the right move.

Fallon crossed to me, pulling her ponytail tight. "What about me, fight master? Finally going to train me on a few things?"

My dick twitched as I watched how she moved through the space with effortless grace. Damn, nothing was sexier than Fallon. Even the way her ponytail swung back and forth had me gritting my teeth. Because all I could picture was wrapping it around my fist as I took her.

Fallon moved in even closer—so close I could smell the scents of jasmine and coconut. Challenge lit those beautiful blue eyes. "So?"

She executed the punch in slow motion, her fist connecting lightly with my rib cage. "Or do you still think I don't have what it takes?"

Fallon might be giving me a hard time, but there was hurt beneath her words. And that killed me.

My fingers wrapped around her wrist, gripping it tightly. "Never thought you didn't have what it took."

Those blue eyes flashed again. "It sure as hell hasn't seemed like that."

I pulled her flush against me in a flash, not letting go of her wrist. "Did you ever consider that maybe I didn't want to be *this* close to you?" Fal's breath hitched and then picked up speed. "That I didn't trust myself to touch you like this and stop there. If I had let myself be this close, I knew I couldn't stop. I knew I'd want every damn part of you."

Fallon's mouth formed a perfect O, one I wanted to feel wrapped around my—

"Holy fucking hell! What was that?" Mateo screeched in a high-pitched voice that sounded like he was going through puberty.

I released Fallon, turning to see Mateo spitting his mouthguard onto the floor of the practice ring. He gagged and reached for his water.

"Oh, I wouldn't do that if I were you," Fallon singsonged. "I heard drinking water after ingesting something spicy just makes it burn worse."

Mateo's gaze narrowed on Fallon even as sweat broke out on his brow.

"Sparrow?" I asked, trying not to laugh. "What did you do?"

She beamed at me. "If he's going to take cheap shots at you, he runs the risk of having ghost pepper hot sauce put in his mouthguard. I warned him."

Evan burst out laughing. "I told you. Don't mess with Fal—or her dude."

"Damn straight," I echoed.

Gracie looked up at Fallon with wide eyes. "You put peppers in his mouthguard?"

Fallon shrugged. "He sucker punched your brother. He kinda earned it."

Gracie's face turned from amused to pissed the hell off. She marched over to the practice ring, ducked between the ropes, and started punching Mateo.

"Hey! Ow! Shit! She's tiny, but she's fierce," he called, trying to block her hits.

"Take it like a professional," Evan called.

"Don't you hit my brother," Gracie yelled.

Fallon leaned into me, and I wrapped an arm around her, kissing her temple. "Pretty sure she's got your vengeful streak."

Fal grinned up at me. "Don't worry. Anyone comes for you? We'll keep you safe."

My gut clenched because as much as Fallon was joking in the moment, I knew she'd do anything to protect me—even put herself at risk.

CHAPTER TWENTY-NINE

Fallon

"THIS WAS MY ABSOLUTE FAVORITE MOVIE GROWING UP," I SAID as I organized a table full of snacks in the screening room.

It had been a couple of days since the grisly photo incident, and there'd been no other threats or dead bodies. I could tell Kye was still on edge, but he was doing his best to hide it. The fact that the girls were starting to settle into their new home helped.

"It's about a garden?" Gracie asked, wrinkling her nose.

"Gracie," Clem hissed in warning.

I couldn't help but laugh. "Have I steered you wrong in either movie or snack choices yet?"

Gracie grinned, one of her teeth wiggling. "You have the *best* snacks."

One corner of Hayden's mouth kicked up. "I know why Kye said your blood is ninety-nine percent sugar."

"I actually said ninety-nine-point-nine percent sugar," Kye said as he walked into the screening room. "Which is why she's so tasty to nibble on."

He dove for me, lifting me into the air and making a show of biting my shoulder as I squealed. Gracie and Clem burst into giggles, and Hayden couldn't hold back her smile. As Kye set my feet back on the ground, we were close. Too close.

My breath hitched as those amber eyes locked with mine. I wanted him to close the distance and kiss me. It felt like it had been years since I'd tasted him. And it didn't matter that I woke with the pillow wall demolished and Kye wrapped around me each morning. It wasn't enough. Not anymore.

It was as if that stolen morning last week had reminded me of everything I was missing.

"You know you can kiss her, right?" Clem asked, amusement in her voice.

Gracie giggled. "We know you guys kiss. We're not *that* little."

Kye shifted slightly, and I waited to see what he would do, which way he'd tip. He lowered his head and kissed my cheek, his scruff ghosting across my skin.

"That's not a real kiss," Gracie complained.

Kye's callused palm skated across my jaw. "Not a real kiss, huh?"

Those amber eyes searched mine as if checking to see if it was okay. He hadn't kissed me since our wedding, and God, I missed the feel of those lips on mine, the taste of him, the heat.

I knew I should make some excuse. That I should turn this into a joke. Something. Anything to keep me from falling more in love with a man who didn't want to be mine. But I didn't. I stayed right there as Kye got closer and closer.

His mouth hovered over mine, and I could taste mint and Kye in the air between us. Then he closed the distance, his tongue stroking in. This kiss was different than the ones before. There wasn't desperation behind it. There was...something else.

A slow, stroking need. It was as if Kye was memorizing everything about my mouth.

Gracie and Clem hooted and cheered, and Kye slowly pulled back. I saw a different heat in his gaze now. We'd spent the past fourteen years shoving our connection and bond into a box that didn't fit us. I knew it could never go back there.

So, where did that leave us when this was all over?

Kye cleared his throat. "What do you say we start this movie? And please tell me it's not an ooey-gooey romance."

I rolled my eyes. "Boys," I huffed. "*The Secret Garden* is about a forbidden love and a decades-old secret."

Kye's eyes flared at that. "That's a hell of a choice, Sparrow."

I shrugged. "It's always been my favorite movie."

He studied me with a gaze that saw too much. Instead of trying to hide like I'd done for ages, I let him see. Pain lanced his features, but I still didn't hide. Finally, he grabbed my wrist and pulled me onto one of the massive couches in the screening room.

Kye didn't say a word as he wrapped an arm around me and tucked me into his side. But he didn't push me away either. Maybe that was progress.

I stayed curled into Kye on one side while Gracie, Clem, and Hayden were on the other, even after the credits rolled.

Hayden flicked on the lights, making me blink against the brightness. Clem grinned at me. "Okay, that was really good."

I shot my fist in the air. "Victory is mine!"

Gracie giggled, but her focus was on Kye's arm. She traced the line of one of his tattoos, studying the maze of shapes. "Who drew on you?"

Kye shifted to see which element Gracie was studying. "Lots of different people. But I designed all the artwork."

Gracie's amber eyes widened. "That's so cool. I really like drawing, too."

"Maybe you'll be a tattoo artist one day."

She grinned, wiggling her loose tooth. "I like the strawberry."

Kye's gaze flicked up to me. "I've always had a thing for strawberries."

My heart jerked in my chest as if it were trying to rip itself free and return to its rightful owner. Kye.

A gate alert sounded from Kye's and my phones, and I shifted to pull my cell out. Tapping the icon for the speaker box, I pressed it to my ear. "Hello?"

"Hey, Fal. It's Trace."

My stomach sank. I hated that hearing my brother's voice made me react that way, but it couldn't be helped. "Buzzing you in."

I didn't ask why he was here or for any additional details. I simply tapped the icon to open the gate. The questions I wanted to ask would've put the girls on edge, and that was the last thing I wanted when they were just starting to settle in.

"Who was it?" Kye asked.

"Trace. Probably wants to borrow your truck for something out at his new place," I lied.

Kye's mouth thinned, but he nodded. "All right, you hooligans. It's time to get ready for bed." He glanced at Hayden. "Think you can get Gracie and Clem started on bath time?"

Surprise flitted through Hayden's eyes, but she nodded. "Sure. No problem."

As the girls made their way upstairs, I realized something. Hayden wanted to feel useful and like we trusted her. There had been pride in her eyes when Kye asked her to start the other girls' baths.

Kye slowly moved toward the stairs, keeping some distance between us and his sisters. "Trace say anything?"

I shook my head.

"Fuck," Kye muttered.

He knew as well as I did that if Trace had good news, he would've led with that.

As we made our way upstairs and into the entryway, the girls laughed and squealed one floor up. Something about the juxtaposition of those two things—the dread of a sheriff's visit and the laughter of three girls we adored—felt a lot like life in a nutshell. We couldn't escape the bad. We could only hold tight to the good.

A knock sounded. Kye crossed to the front door and opened it. Trace walked in, his face unreadable. But someone else followed him in. Anson. Dread pooled.

Trace wouldn't have brought the ex-FBI profiler with him if it wasn't bad. I started walking toward the kitchen, wanting to put some distance between us and tiny ears.

"Can I get you a beer?" I asked Trace. "Soda?" I asked Anson, knowing he didn't drink.

Trace shook his head. "But I wouldn't say no to a Coke."

That told me two things. He thought he might have to go back to work, and it could be a late night. Still, I moved to the fridge and pulled out a soda for him, and a strawberry bubbly water for me.

"I'll take a ginger ale if you've got one," Anson said.

I grabbed one of those for him and then glanced at Kye in question. He just shook his head.

"What's going on?" Kye asked, pitching his voice low.

Trace popped the tab on his Coke. "Found Joker, the president of the Reapers MC, stabbed to death an hour ago."

A muscle in Kye's cheek began fluttering wildly, and I instantly crossed to him. I wrapped an arm around his waist, but he was as stiff as a board, like he was preemptively warding off any comfort I might be able to give.

"Where?" Kye ground out.

"Road on the way to his cabin. Looks like someone put down a spike strip. It sent him flying, and then whoever it was moved in to finish the job."

A wave of nausea slid through me, and I set my fizzy water down.

Kye gripped the counter's edge, and I couldn't help wishing he'd hold on to me that way, let me take some of his stress and worry. "That takes planning and knowledge," Kye said, his voice tight.

"It does," Trace agreed.

"I guess I should be thankful I have an alibi for this one," Kye muttered.

A muscle fluttered in Trace's cheek. "You know I had to dot every i and cross every t."

A sick feeling slid through me. I *hated* that Kye even had to answer a question like that, and it took everything in me not to point that pissed-off right at Trace. But I knew he was only doing his job.

Kye ran a hand through his hair, his gaze flicking to Anson. "What do you think?"

Anson tapped a finger on the top of his ginger ale before

opening it. "Someone is taking out those involved in the fight ring, one by one."

"No shit, Sherlock," Kye hissed. "Tell me something I don't know."

I squeezed his side. "Easy. This isn't Anson's fault."

Kye shrugged out of my grip. And, God, that hurt.

"I know," Kye said, slicing a hand through the air. "It's my goddamned fault. Because I'm the one who got mixed up in it all to begin with."

My jaw went slack as I stared at Kye. "You were sixteen. You made a mistake."

Kye squeezed the back of his neck and shook his head. "Thought I knew better. And even after I learned how fucked-up it all was, I thought I could get the cash to free myself. Get out. Get my own place. Start over."

His amber gaze collided with mine. His eyes were so full of pain. That's when the pieces started coming together. Just *why* he might've kept fighting after coming to live with us at sixteen—so he didn't have to stay.

"Kyler, no," I whispered.

It was the only name I could use in the moment. The only one that fit.

His throat worked as he swallowed. "I wanted to figure a way out, Sparrow. So we didn't have to throw it all away."

So, he'd taken beating after beating—one that was so bad he'd ended up in a coma, and then almost did time in juvie—all because he'd wanted a chance...to be with me.

My eyes filled. "How can you even look at me?"

Kye's eyes took on a glassy sheen. "'Cause you're the most beautiful thing I've ever seen."

"What did I miss?" Trace asked, sounding confused as he looked between us.

Anson took a pull of his ginger ale. "These two have a much longer history than people realize." He studied us. "I'd guess you met during a moment of trauma for one or both of you. A bond forged in fire."

Kye scowled at the ex-profiler. "Quit it with your mind-meld tricks."

Anson grinned. "Good to know I was right."

Trace shook his head. "None of that matters right now. What matters is figuring out who's killing these people so we can stop them."

But that's where Trace was wrong. It did matter. It meant everything.

For fourteen years, I'd thought it was as easy as breathing for Kye to throw away his feelings for me and shift us into the friend zone. But I couldn't have been more wrong. He'd given *everything* for me. And now, he was paying the price. Twice.

"What matters is how the hell we keep Kye safe," I snapped.

Anson grinned.

I glared at him. "Why are you smiling?"

"Because you love him," he said, gesturing to Kye.

Kye pinched the bridge of his nose. "A literal serial killer is running around, and you're grinning like one of those creepy bobbleheads because Fallon loves me?"

That grin only widened. "What? I can't be happy for you?"

"I swear, being in love has pickled his brain," Trace muttered.

"In case you missed the memo, that serial killer might be targeting *me*. So maybe we chill on the super smiley," Kye pointed out.

The first part of his statement had ice sliding through my veins and blood draining from my head. It wasn't like I didn't know the facts, but hearing Kye spell them out, the casualty of it, was all too much. My knees started to give way, and Kye cursed, catching me before I slid straight to the floor.

"Sorry," I mumbled.

"Don't you dare apologize, Sparrow," Kye clipped as Trace slid one of the stools toward him. "I'm the one who should apologize. I need to watch my damn words."

He settled me on the stool and popped my bubbly water. "Drink this."

I scrunched up my nose. "I don't know if I can."

"Drink it," he ordered. "I'm going to get you some cheese and crackers. You need something other than sweets. Your blood sugar probably plummeted."

Anson's lips twitched. "Love the caretaking."

"Shut up," Kye and I said at the same time.

Trace held up a hand. "All right, all right. Let's talk about what we need to do, and then we can go and let you two get some sleep."

"Not sure they're getting much—"

"Anson," Trace warned.

"Okay, okay. I just think it's nice to remember the light when things are dark," Anson said.

Kye slid a plate in front of me. "He's all well-adjusted and stuff. It's freaking me out."

"You and me both," Trace muttered. "All right. First things first. What's the update on security here and at your businesses?"

Kye leaned a hip against the counter, staying close to me. "Blackheart and Haven already have state-of-the-art systems. I've got an alarm system here, and I added cameras at the gate and the front and back doors of the house."

"That's a good start," Trace said. "Might want to reach out to Holt Hartley and see if he's got any recommendations for beefing up the system."

"Will do." Kye looked at Anson. "What do you really think?"

Anson set his ginger ale down. "I think there are a few possibilities." He ticked them off with his fingers. "One, someone is tying up loose ends from the fight ring because having it possibly starting up again puts them at risk in some way. Two, someone was hurt in the past and is looking for revenge. Or three, a competitor doesn't want a new fight ring popping up. Organized crime is rife with those sorts of operations."

"None of that sounds good," I said, breaking off a small piece of a cracker.

Kye slid a hand along my shoulders in reassuring strokes. "They all sound possible, but I'm not involved with the MC or whatever the hell they were trying to start up again."

Trace looked at Kye. "Maybe not. But I wouldn't put it past Oren to have told his club you were willing, hoping he could bring you around. You'd have been a big get for him. The famous tattoo artist walking on the dark side."

Kye scowled at the suggestion. "It might've been a big get, but he must have known I would never do it."

A phone dinged, and Kye released his hold on me to tug his device from his pocket. His fingers tapped the screen, and his whole expression turned thunderous.

Anson and Trace were already rising. "Show us," Anson demanded.

Kye's jaw worked back and forth, but he flipped his phone around. There was a new text message from an unknown number, but there were no words. Only an image.

A picture of a Polaroid.

Boxy lettering across the bottom said,

THREE DOWN. WHAT NOW?

CHAPTER THIRTY

Kye

"DOES EVERYONE HAVE HOMEWORK, BACKPACKS, LUNCH BAGS, and water bottles?" Fallon called from the front passenger seat as I pulled up to the designated drop for the elementary school. The high school was just next door, so Hayden could walk from here, which made it easier for parents corralling multiple children.

Gracie lifted her lunch bag from where she sat in her booster seat. "I gots mine." She frowned. "But it's got a little hole in the corner."

"I'll fix it tonight," Hayden said quickly.

"I can help," Fallon offered and then frowned. "I'm not the best sewer, though, so you'll have to supervise me," she told Hayden.

The older teen's lips twitched. "I suggest getting a thimble so you don't stab yourself."

Fallon winced. "Adding it to my shopping list."

The girls filed out of the SUV and headed toward their respective schools. I watched until they disappeared and the person behind me honked. I leaned over, scowling through the side mirror at the man in the sedan behind me. He took one look at me and paled.

Fallon patted my shoulder. "Let's try not to make anyone poop themselves before nine a.m., all right?"

I grunted. "I just wanted to make sure the girls got safely inside. He could have a little patience."

She rolled her lips over her teeth, trying to hide her smile. "Pretty sure he'll think twice next time."

"Good." I flipped on my blinker and pulled into the flow of drop-off traffic.

Fallon laid a hand on my thigh. "They'll be just fine. Trace has the schools on the drive-by routes, on top of the officers already stationed there throughout the day. Plus, they aren't the ones at risk."

I heard the strain in her voice as she spoke the last sentence, worry digging into each word. I dropped a hand from the wheel and twined our fingers. Touching her this much was reckless. Last night, I hadn't even put up the damn pillow wall. I'd just opened my arms and let her curl into me.

It wasn't fair or right, subjecting Fallon to the darkness that lived in me. The sort of shit I rained down on the people around me. But I couldn't seem to stop myself.

"I'll be just fine," I assured her.

Fallon nodded but didn't let go of my hand. She held it tightly as I drove through town and headed back toward our house. "Are you sure you don't want me to just drop you off at work? I can pick you up after."

She shook her head. "I need my car. I have to go and get a few things after work."

"A thimble?" I asked, quirking a brow.

Her mouth curved. "Probably not a bad idea."

I pulled up to the garage and hit a button on the remote. As the door rose, both of us slid out of my SUV. I rounded the hood and met Fallon there for a moment.

She wrapped her arms around my waist and pressed her cheek to my chest. My arms curved around her, and I rested my chin atop her head. "I'm good, Sparrow. Promise."

Her breath hitched. "I won't be able to handle it if anything happens to you."

My heart lurched. "It won't."

Fallon gripped me harder. "I'm holding you to that. Remember, if you don't make good on your word, I will glitter bomb the hell out of you."

I chuckled as I forced myself to release her. "I'll keep that in mind. Now, get your ass in that SUV. Gonna follow you to work just to be safe."

"Kye—"

"Don't argue, Sparrow. I need this."

Her entire expression softened. "Okay, Kyler."

Fuck.

That name on her lips... It was only after she'd said it the first time that I'd actually *liked* my damn name. Mostly, I'd heard it as an uttered curse...until her. Fallon made it sound like beautiful music and a solemn vow all at once.

"Get in the SUV," I said gruffly.

Her beautiful mouth dipped and bowed into one of those tentative smiles, but she did as I asked. I followed her to the DHS building and didn't leave until she was behind closed doors.

"So, I'm thinking we start the program with a few exhibition matches. We get you and Mateo, maybe Jericho and me. We show the kids that this is fun—or it can be," Evan said as he spun back and forth in Jericho's studio chair, his excitement for his vision clear.

I couldn't help but grin at him. "That's smart. I think having them see the real deal will help. I can get Linc involved, too. He's a pretty damn good fighter."

Arden's fiancé might be a billionaire, but he could hold his own in the ring.

Evan nodded. "I've seen him. He doesn't mess around. I wish Arden could fight. It'd be good for the girls to see a woman in the ring."

"The last thing we need is Linc losing it because his pregnant fiancée is trying to get into a training ring. But Serena will spar. She'd kick any of our asses."

Evan laughed as he drummed his pen on his notepad. "Truth."

The bell over the door sounded as a voice cut through the room. "Dude, what the fuck?"

I turned as Jericho strode into the studio. His expression was thunderous, and I didn't have the first clue why. "What's going on?"

"You don't think I deserve a call that Joker's fuckin' dead?" Jericho spat.

Bear's gray brows lifted at both the news and Jericho's fervor. Being a hobbyist biker, he knew the clubs in the area. He also knew what we'd gotten ourselves mixed up in during our youth.

"What?" Evan whispered.

Fucking hell.

Jericho was right. I should've called and let him know about the new developments. "I'm sorry. I just—I had Fal. My sisters. There was a lot going on."

Jericho's knuckles cracked as he fisted his hands. "I need to know you've got my back."

"You know I do. But Trace told me he was stopping by your place first thing this morning."

He nodded in a jerky, staccato beat. "Sorry. I just…this is seriously fucked. Three Reapers in as many weeks?"

Bear ambled out from behind the reception desk. "What does Trace say?"

I scrubbed a hand over my face. "That someone's picking off people from the fight ring one by one."

"Jesus," Evan muttered, his face a little pale.

"Are Fal and the girls okay?" Jericho asked, finally reining in his anger.

"My sisters don't know anything. And that's how it's going to stay if I can help it." My fingers twisted around the arm of my chair.

"Fal's seriously tweaked. And we've got other shit to worry about. My custody case. Making sure Renee doesn't pull something stupid. My head is on a permanent swivel."

"Can we do anything?" Evan asked.

I shook my head. "I wish, but we just gotta ride it out. Anson said he'll get his hacker friend, Dex, to look into the MC. He wants to see if there's any chance this could be a rival club out to squash something before it starts."

"Are you nuts?" Jericho clipped. "You know the Reapers have techies on their payroll. They'll trace him, and if they find out he's a friend of your soon-to-be-brother-in-law's, you are seriously screwed. We both are."

"Dex is one of the best. He works for the goddamned FBI. The Reapers won't know he's been in their system."

Jericho squeezed the back of his neck hard. "It's a mistake. We should both be thinking about running for the goddamned hills. That's what we should be doing."

"You know I can't." There was too much at stake for me: my sisters, the Colsons, Fallon. I'd give everything for any of them. I just hoped like hell no one had to make that kind of sacrifice.

CHAPTER THIRTY-ONE

Fallon

MY FINGERS FLEW OVER THE KEYBOARD FUELED BY CAFFEINE and the bag of strawberry Sour Patch Kids Kye had slipped into my work tote, along with a note that read: *Slay the dragons, Sparrow.* The note fueled me as much as the sugar. I loved that Kye understood just how important my job was.

The buzzer over the entry door sounded, and I glanced over to identify the newcomer. "Hey, Noah. I'm just finishing up the additional home study you needed. Give me one more second."

"Thanks, Fal," he said and crossed to his desk, sounding exhausted.

"You need some of whatever Fallon's rocking," Mila muttered. "I don't think I've ever seen someone type so fast."

I chuckled as I kept right on typing. "Diet Coke and strawberry Sour Patch Kids."

Mila's entire face screwed up like she'd just sucked on a particularly potent lemon. "That combination sounds completely disgusting."

"Don't knock it until you try it." I hit save and then attached the document to an email, shooting it off to Noah. "Done."

I turned to face our newest arrival and winced. Noah looked rough. He had more scruff around his jaw than usual and shadows beneath his eyes. "Are you okay?"

He reached for the water bottle on his desk and sent me a strained smile. "Surviving. Not thriving."

"Been there. Anything I can do?" I asked.

He shook his head. "You did it. That's the last document we need to file."

"Good." I was quiet for a moment before asking what I really wanted to. "Any updated info on terminating Renee Jensen's parental rights?"

Noah stiffened slightly. "You know I can't give you the ins and outs of a case you're personally involved in."

"I'm not asking for that. I just want to know things that are—or will be—public record. Like when the hearing is. That way, Kye and I can have our ducks in a row for filing for adoption if her parental rights are terminated."

Noah let out a long sigh. "Renee goes before the judge this week. I'll let Rose know if the judge wants to talk to Hayden, Clementine, or Gracie."

My stomach twisted. I had a pretty good feeling that Clem and Gracie would say they didn't want to live with Renee. That they wanted to live with me and Kye. But Hayden? She was a wild card. Despite the safe, stable home Kye and I provided, she might fight for the unstable one she knew because it was predictable.

"Thank you," I said, texting Kye to let him know so he could talk with his attorney.

"Fallon." Noah's voice was soft, so gentle it had my head snapping up in concern. "Are you sure this is the right move? I know you care about Kye, but are you *sure* this is what's best for those girls? For you? He hasn't exactly had a stable life, and there's some seriously messed-up shit happening with the MC he was involved with."

Fury blazed through my veins, and I knew Noah realized it when he reached out and grabbed my shoulder in an attempt to soothe me.

"I just mean—"

I jerked out of his grip and let everything I felt show in my gaze and expression. In every part of me. "Kye has been through hell on Earth. He lived with parents who abused him physically and mentally. He started fighting in a circuit that meant him getting beat to hell on a regular basis in hopes of breaking free of that life. And then he managed to get himself out of both."

I sucked in air, and the words kept right on coming. "He built a multi-million-dollar business through his gifts in tattooing. Built a mixed martial arts gym that offers programming for kids in the community *free* of charge. And he is the best brother, uncle, son, and friend I've ever seen. So, don't you ever say a word to disparage my *husband* ever again."

A slow clap sounded from the far corner of the room. Rose stood there, her eyes narrowed on Noah. "Kyler Blackwood is an example of what can happen when the system *works*. And the fact that you keep trying to belittle the man he has become and all he has achieved is really starting to piss me off."

Noah clenched his teeth, making tiny divots appear in the hollows of his cheeks. "I just wanted to make sure Fallon knows what she's getting into."

"She knows," Rose clipped. "She's known the man since she was fourteen, for God's sake."

"And he held me together when I was processing the grief of losing my dad and brother, even though his life was falling apart," I said, punctuating the point.

Rose's expression softened. "I'm so glad you had that, honey."

"Me, too," Mila said quietly. "I'm sorry I judged him based on appearances. I'm starting to see that I have some work to do in that arena."

I sent her a small smile. "Well, to be fair, he does look a little scary."

Mila chuckled. "At least it's scary hot."

I burst out laughing. "Don't tell him that. His ego's big enough."

Noah slammed his laptop shut and shoved it into a bag. "I have a dinner meeting." And with that, he stalked out of the office.

My shoulders slumped. Apparently, it was too much to ask to have both my uncertain coworkers do an about-face.

"It's not your fault," Mila said, leaning back in her chair. "I'm pretty sure he's been in love with you since the day you started here."

Anxiety grabbed at me, and my skin suddenly felt too tight for my body. "No, he's not. He just—"

"He is," Rose said with finality. "But he pissed around and lost any chance he had with you by not acting on it. And now he's mad at himself but pointing that anger outward. It's not fair to you or Kye."

I grimaced. "I didn't give him the impression that I was interested, did I?"

Rose and Mila both dissolved in a fit of giggles.

Rose wiped under her eyes. "Dear God, no."

"You seemed about as oblivious to him as you would have been if he were a monk taking a vow of silence," Mila said.

At least there was that. The last thing I wanted to do was make a friend think there was more between us than there was. Because the truth was… "It's always been Kye," I whispered, emotion clogging my throat. "Trust me. I tried to get over him. I dated. I tried fix ups and those stupid apps where every man feels the need to pose with a dead fish. But it was never…"

"Him," Rose finished for me, her eyes glassy.

Mila ripped a tissue out of the box to dab at her eyes. "Okay, I'm all in. You guys earned your HEA."

"HEA?" Rose parroted.

"Happily ever after," Mila explained. "And Fal's earned it."

"I don't know if we're there yet," I admitted. They just couldn't know how far away we truly were.

"You'll get there. Why don't you start by taking off a little early and spending some time with your new family?" Rose suggested.

I glanced at my watch. Half past two. I had a little time before school pickup. I could stop by the craft store for some lunch bag mending supplies and maybe another project like friendship bracelets.

Shoving back my chair, I grinned at them both. "Thank you. For everything."

"Go climb that scary hot man like a tree," Mila called as I grabbed my jacket and bag.

"You know," I said, glancing over my shoulder, "he has some scary hot friends."

Mila's head cocked to the side. "Color me intrigued."

I laughed, waving at both of them and heading for my SUV. I beeped the locks and double-pressed the button that started the engine. I still wasn't used to all the fancy bells and whistles on this one.

I climbed in, set my bag on the passenger seat, and turned on the seat heaters. We were slipping into official winter territory. I backed out of my spot and navigated the full parking lot. We shared a campus with other county programming, and it looked like something was happening at one of the other small buildings.

I pulled onto the two-lane road that led into town. There was hardly any traffic at this time of day, so I noticed when the motorcycle pulled onto the road behind me. A prickle of unease slid through me, but I shoved it down.

A million people drove motorcycles. Hell, Kye did. It was probably nothing.

But as I drove, the bike got closer and closer. It looked similar to Kye's, with a black body, but I couldn't tell anything about the person driving it. They wore a leather coat so bulky it could've been a man or a woman, and their helmet had a tinted visor you couldn't see through. Then again, it was freezing out, so it could've been to protect the rider from the weather.

The engine on the bike gunned, bringing them even closer. My heart hammered against my ribs as I pressed the accelerator, going well past the thirty-five-mile-per-hour speed limit. I'd honestly welcome one of Trace's deputies pulling me over right now.

The bike picked up speed behind me, matching my tempo. My mouth went dry, and I pressed the accelerator until I was going forty-five. The bike revved its engine as if in warning.

"It's broad daylight. Nothing's going to happen." I spoke the words out loud, trying to calm myself.

A truck turned in front of me, not realizing how fast I was going, and I cursed as I swerved around him. He blasted his horn at me—rightfully so. But I couldn't help but feel a surge of relief at having a vehicle between the bike and me.

Until the motorcycle rounded the truck, blazing past him and putting itself between us. My gaze jerked from the road ahead, and everything happened in snapshots. The figure on the bike pulled something from their jacket. Metal glinted in the sun. A crack pierced the air. The windshield of the truck behind me shattered.

I didn't think. I simply reacted. I slammed on my brakes, jerked the wheel to the left, and took a side street as another crack sounded.

I didn't know if the biker was shooting at me, the truck, or something else. But I wasn't sticking around to find out. I raced through a neighborhood, running two stop signs and driving at least twenty miles an hour over the speed limit.

I had no idea where I was going until I saw the building. Blackheart Ink. My tires squealed as I jerked to a stop. I didn't turn off the SUV or get my keys; I just ran for the building.

Jerking the door open, I flew inside.

Kye stood, cleaning his station, and it looked like he was the only person in the studio. He took one look at me and was already moving. He was on me in a flash, hands in my hair, skating over my body. "What happened?" he barked. "Are you hurt? The girls?"

"I think somebody just tried to kill me," I croaked.

CHAPTER THIRTY-TWO

Kye

I COULDN'T LET HER GO. I COULDN'T FORCE MYSELF TO RELEASE my grip on Fallon for a single second, even though I knew that was exactly what I should do. Because all of this was happening because of me.

Still, I kept my grip on her as I fumbled for the phone in my pocket, and I kept right on holding her as I hit Trace's contact. It rang three times before he answered.

"This an emergency? Because if not, gonna have to call you back."

"Emergency. Blackheart Ink," I clipped.

Trace cursed, a sound I still wasn't used to coming from him. "Do I need backup?"

"Gabriel."

Another curse slipped through the speaker. "On our way."

I ended the call, slid my phone back into my pocket, and then both arms were around Fallon again. She was shaking like a goddamned leaf, and I wanted to burn the whole world down.

If the asshole who'd done this had been standing in front of me, I would've ripped him limb from limb. I would've ended his life and not given a damn. That's how dark the demons inside me were. I usually did everything I could to beat them back and hide the truth of who I was. But now? I welcomed them. If it meant keeping Fallon safe, I'd be the darkest monster from the deepest parts of hell.

A siren sounded in the distance, and I knew Trace was close.

"My car," Fallon rasped. "I left the keys in the ignition."

"Don't give a damn about the SUV. If someone steals it, I'll buy you another one."

"My purse."

"Doesn't fucking matter," I growled. "You're staying right here. Not going anywhere."

The sirens got closer, then cut out. A second later, Trace burst through the door. "What the hell is going on? Fal's SUV is out there still running. Where—?"

"Enough," I barked. "Lower your goddamned voice."

Trace's green eyes flared in surprise, but he did just that. "She hurt?"

"Sparrow?" I pulled back slightly, sliding my hand along her jaw. "Does anything hurt?"

She shook her head, wisps of pale-blond hair falling into her face. "No."

"You sure?"

"I'm sure. I just—oh, God. The man in the truck. The biker shot at him. Is he—?"

"Uninjured," Gabriel said as he strode into the tattoo studio carrying Fal's bag, keys, and phone. "Scared shitless but uninjured."

Trace's jaw had gone hard as granite. "You were involved in that?"

"I-I—"

"Breathe, Sparrow. Just breathe. Like you're telling me. By the creek. Under the dogwood. Close your eyes and imagine yourself there."

Fallon's long, dark lashes fluttered as she closed her eyes and fisted her hands in my flannel. "I pulled out of the DHS parking lot, and a bike started following me."

Everything in me turned to stone. These were my worst fears realized. My old life, the one that had tainted me and marked my soul forever, was now coming for her.

"I thought maybe it was a coincidence. But when I sped up, they did, too."

Fal's breaths started coming quicker. "I went even faster, and so did they. The truck pulled out, not realizing just how fast I was going. He almost hit me because of it. He honked, and the bike swerved. It went around the truck. And then it was like..."

Her breathing was irregular now, a panic attack setting in. I framed her face, shoving down all my rage so I could gentle my voice. "Breathe, Sparrow. It's spring. The dogwoods are in full bloom. You can hear the creek. You can smell the pine trees."

Fallon's breathing slowed. "It happened so fast. Like snatches of an image. A gun. A shot. The truck's windshield shattering. I turned onto a side street and heard another shot. I didn't look back. I drove as fast as I could. I ran stop signs. I'm sorry, Trace. I didn't even know where I was going until..." Her eyes fluttered open. "Until I got here. You're always where I'm going."

Fuck. It was like a knife to the chest. A beautiful, blinding pain to be that for her, but know I was also the reason she was running.

My thumbs tracked over her cheeks, and with everything I had, I tried to keep my grip gentle. "You did exactly the right thing, Sparrow. Exactly the right thing."

"He's right," Trace said, his voice tight.

Gabriel's radio crackled, and he moved down the hall to speak into it.

"The girls," Fallon said, her body jerking slightly. "I need to get them in a few minutes."

"I'll text Arden." Trace pulled out his phone. "She and Linc can get them with a sheriff's department escort."

"Thanks," I choked.

Fucking hell. Maybe I should be begging Nora to adopt them. Even Trace. See if they could give them the safety they deserved. Because I sure as hell couldn't.

"Don't you dare," Fallon ground out, the fire returning to her eyes as if she'd read the exact thoughts running through my mind.

"What?" I hedged.

"Don't you dare take this on, Kyler. This isn't your fault."

"It is," I argued. "It's exactly my fault. It was a fucking biker, Fal. That means it was a Reaper or one of their enemies." A light dawned. "Fal's SUV is registered to me. It was easier when I bought them to just do it that way. Whoever this was might've thought it was me."

"Makes sense," a new voice said. Anson walked through the door. "This unsub has a very specific MO. They want death by stabbing. It wouldn't do to run you off the road or shoot you. My guess is they would've shot out your tires and then moved in for the kill."

Fallon's hands fisted tighter in my flannel. "Now, we know for sure. This person wants to kill you."

And anyone close to me could be collateral damage.

We made it home before my sisters. Arden and Linc had bought us some time by stopping by The Pop to order takeout, but I was sure neither Fal nor I would touch the food. I'd tried telling the rest of my family to keep their distance, but none of them would have it.

They descended on my house without delay and en masse, like they always did for the people they loved.

"Tell Linc not to skimp on the types of potatoes," Cope said, popping a piece of candy into his mouth.

Rhodes arched a brow at him from her spot on the other side of Fallon. "Shouldn't you be watching what you're eating now that you're back in training?"

Cope scowled at her. "I can have curly fries."

"But he also wants tater tots, truffle fries, *and* steak fries," Sutton said with a knowing smile.

"Hey," Cope said, affronted. "Don't forget the shoestrings. Those are important."

Luca giggled. "You're gonna turn into a potato."

"You know, I just read a book about a potato shifter," Thea said.

Shep shook his head and then kissed her temple. "That one got…saucy."

Rhodes choked on a laugh while Luca and Keely just looked confused.

"Can we go watch a movie while we wait for the food?" Keely asked hopefully.

"Come on," Ellie said, waving them toward the basement stairs. "Can't have you corrupted by potato shifters."

"You know," Lolli began, "I think I'd like to borrow that one."

"I'm warning you," Cope said, "if you ruin potatoes for me, we're gonna have problems."

"The only problem we're gonna have is you being a prude," Lolli shot back.

Cope shot up straight on the end of the sectional. "I'm not a prude." His gaze cut to Sutton. "Tell them about that thing I did the other night."

She gaped at him. "This is like when you wanted me to tell everyone you had a big dick. Not going to happen, Hotshot."

He let out a huff. "Big, kinky dick. That's all you gotta know."

Anson's face screwed up. "That makes it sound like your dick is knotted and warty."

Cope opened his mouth, but Sutton held up a hand to stop him. "I am also not telling your family how beautiful your penis is."

Cope grinned. "You heard it here. Big, beautiful dick."

Rhodes shook her head. "She didn't say anything about big."

I knew what they were doing, and I appreciated it. They were trying to steer the conversation away from anything that might veer into trauma territory. They were trying to make Fallon laugh and get me to talk shit. But neither of us could get there.

Nora rounded the couch with a tray. "Ginger tea. It soothes

the nerves." Setting it down, she patted Fallon's knee. "How are you feeling?"

"I'm fine. Really," Fallon said. But it was a lie. Her face was pale, and her hands were cold.

I leaned over and pressed a kiss to her temple. "Want me to run you a bath?"

She shook her head and burrowed deeper into me. "I want to stay right here."

"Then that's what we'll do," I said.

The front door opened, and Clem and Gracie raced in.

"Linc bought out the whole Pop!" Gracie called. "I don't think they gots any more food for anyone else."

Clem giggled. "It took 'em forever to get it ready."

"And our arms are very full," Linc called, carrying a massive box of takeout bags.

"I could've helped you," Arden said, rolling her eyes.

"I don't want you lifting anything," Linc argued.

"I'm pregnant; I don't have two broken legs. But the vast array of milkshakes is still in the car."

Anson stood and crossed to the door as Hayden moved inside. "I'll get 'em."

Hayden's expression was shuttered as she moved into the living room. "What's going on?"

I did my best to force a smile. "We just thought it might be fun to have a takeout party."

Her expression went from shuttered to pissed right the hell off. "Don't lie. You and Fallon were supposed to pick us up. You didn't. And a deputy followed us home."

Fuck.

Fallon straightened and sent a look my way. I read it instantly. As much as we wanted to protect my sisters, we couldn't lie to them. They'd see right through it, and we'd lose all the tiny pieces of trust we'd gained.

"Something happened to me on my way home from work," Fallon said as gently as possible.

Clem's face paled. "Did someone hurt you?"

God, it killed me that someone hurting Fallon was the first place Clem's mind went.

"No, they didn't," Fallon said quickly. "But someone chased me, and it scared me."

Gracie had no hesitation. She flew at Fallon, launching herself onto the couch and into Fal's arms, and started to cry.

"Oh, baby," Fal said, rubbing her back. "I'm okay. I'm better than okay because I'm surrounded by everyone I love."

"N-no one should scare you. I-it's not nice."

Fallon rocked Gracie as Clem made her way to the couch, squeezing in between us. "I know, Gracie girl. But you know what? I'm not scared anymore."

"G-good," Gracie stammered.

I looked up at Hayden, who hadn't moved an inch. Her face had gone pale, too, and her hands trembled at her sides. "I thought you were giving us back," she whispered.

"What?" I rasped.

"I thought you were giving us back." Tears pooled in her eyes. "I thought this was one last dinner, and you were gonna tell us we were too much."

I shoved to my feet, already closing the distance between us. "You are *never* too much for me. You're my sister."

"I was such a bitch to you." The tears started coming in earnest now.

"No, you weren't. You were scared."

Hayden's whole body shook with the force of her sobs. "I believed her. Renee. When she said you didn't want us. I believed her."

I couldn't stop myself. I pulled Hayden into my arms and hugged her with everything I had. "It's okay. You didn't know."

"I should've," she wailed. "I should've known."

I hugged Hayden harder. "You know now. And we're starting over. A brand-new beginning to forever."

"Forever?"

I rubbed a hand up and down her back. "Yeah. I've got my lawyer working on the paperwork so I can file for adoption once we get the okay. But only if that's all right with you."

Hayden pulled back, but she kept a hold of my flannel. "I-it's okay with me."

"You sure?"

She nodded jerkily. "I like it here. You make me feel like I could belong somewhere."

Fucking hell.

"Hayden," I rasped. "You do belong. With me. Now and always."

CHAPTER THIRTY-THREE

Kye

I RAN A TOWEL OVER MY HEAD, ATTEMPTING TO WRING THE worst of the water out of my hair. Every part of my body hurt. But it was more. The ache had settled into the very recesses of my soul.

Between Fallon's close call, Hayden's breakdown, and Clem and Gracie shedding more than a few tears, I felt like I'd been battered against a rocky shore over and over again. But the Colson crew had rallied for us all, like they always did.

We'd eaten and laughed. They'd told the girls funny stories from growing up, making my sisters feel like they were a part of us—because they were.

Hanging up my towel, I quickly brushed my teeth and then headed out into the bedroom. I came up short at the sight of Fallon slipping back into the room. She was wearing another set of ridiculous pajamas that somehow managed to be sexy.

"Are those dinosaur pajamas?" I asked, one corner of my mouth kicking up.

Pink hit the apples of her cheeks. "You know I love *Jurassic Park*."

"Because you have good taste. It's the best movie ever made."

"I thought that was *Die Hard*?" she challenged.

"*Die Hard* is the best *Christmas* movie. *Jurassic Park* is the best all-around movie."

Her perfectly plump lips twitched. "Good to know."

We stood there in the quiet of the bedroom for a moment, neither of us quite sure what to do. But when Fal twisted her fingers in the hem of her pajama top, letting her nerves show, I couldn't stop myself. I simply opened my arms.

She didn't hesitate, just walked straight into my embrace. I sometimes swore it was like our bodies were made with each other in mind. She was so small compared to my broad form, but we were like two puzzle pieces that only fit and worked with one another.

"What were you doing out there?" I asked as I held her.

"I just wanted to peek in on the girls one more time."

The invisible fist that lived inside my chest squeezed harder. "They're so damn lucky to have you."

"As hard as today was…it felt like a breakthrough."

My fingers tangled in Fallon's silky blond strands. "Sometimes, it takes the bad to wake us up to the good."

"Maybe you're right. But I'd take just living in the good for a while."

My lips skimmed the top of her head. "I wouldn't mind that either. How are you feeling?"

"Exhausted but okay," she said softly.

I maneuvered her toward her side of the bed and pulled back the covers. "In you go."

A smile played on her lips. "Gonna read me a bedtime story, too? You're pretty good at the voices."

I laughed as I rounded the bed and got in beside her. "No. But I'll put *Supernatural* on my phone until you fall asleep."

She grinned full-out, burrowing into my side. "You always know just what I need."

I pressed a kiss to the top of her head. I just wished I could be the man she deserved.

Fallon was everywhere. All around me. Her scent. The feel of her. Her sighs. My hips arched into her as my hand slid between her thighs, finding that bundle of nerves. Fire scorched my fingers. Everything about her was just short of too much.

A soft moan teased my ears, blending sleep and wakefulness. My hips flexed on instinct, and the moans deepened, changing in tenor and ferocity. A backside pressed into me, making my dick throb.

My eyes flew open.

Darkness still engulfed the room as only the first shades of pink peeked through the windows. I couldn't see what was happening, but I could feel it.

My hand was down Fallon's pajama pants, sliding through wet heat. A curse flew from my mouth, and Fallon froze, waking instantly.

I started to move my hand, even though it was the last thing I wanted to do. "I'm sorry. I—"

Fallon's fingers wrapped around my wrist, stilling. "Please. Don't. Don't take what I need from me."

Fucking hell.

My dick throbbed, wanting one thing and one thing only. Something it'd never get. But Fallon? I couldn't deny her any-damn-thing.

My hand shifted again, fingers spreading her, sliding through that wet heat and relishing every moment of it. "Sparrow," I growled.

"Please," she begged.

My resolve was dust. I slid two fingers inside her and nearly cursed again. She gripped me like a vise, so damn greedy and perfect. "Need to come?"

"Yes," Fallon breathed.

My hips flexed into her, my dick nestled between her ass cheeks. Fallon let out a moan as she pressed back, giving me the friction I was desperate for.

"Heaven," I whispered against her ear. "Gripping my fingers like you're never gonna let me go."

"I'm. Not." Fallon spoke each word between panted breaths.

And God, it felt like a promise I desperately wanted to hold on to, even though I knew I shouldn't.

My fingers pumped in and out of Fallon as her body bent and bowed. She moved so damn freely, not thinking about what she should be doing but reaching for everything she wanted.

She met me thrust for thrust, and I couldn't stop myself from sliding my other hand under her top. I palmed her breast and let out a groan, pressing harder into her backside. "So fucking perfect. Skin like warm silk. Pert little nipples my mouth is watering for."

I circled the peak with my fingers, twisting and toying.

"Kyler." My name was a prayer on her lips. And it set me aflame.

My fingers thrust deeper, circling, stretching, then curving to drag down her walls. "Tell me. Tell me what you want. What you like. Show me."

Fallon gripped my wrist, controlling my movements and speed. She circled my fingers slower and wider as her mouth formed that perfect O.

This was the thing about Fal and me. We knew the parts of each other we hid from the light. We knew each other so deeply there was no shame or shyness. We could ask for what we wanted, what we needed.

As Fallon showed me exactly what she wanted and needed, how to give her pleasure, her fingers loosened their grip. And I knew I'd learned. Learned from the beauty she'd shown me, just like always.

I followed that cadence, the circling stretch, my breaths coming faster as my dick pulsed, wanting nothing but release.

My other hand slid down from Fallon's breast to the apex of her thighs. She let out an almost pained mewling noise as I found that bundle of nerves. My finger stilled.

"Don't stop. Kyler. Don't stop."

My name was sheer command, and I did exactly as I was told. My finger circled her clit, teasing and toying as my other fingers pumped in and out. Fallon's whole body shook as she tried to hold back.

"Let go," I whispered. "Let me feel you. All of you. I don't want to miss a damn thing."

Sparks of fire lit beneath my skin as Fallon let out a sound that wasn't entirely human. She clamped down on my fingers as hers fisted the blankets. Her body arched, head thrown back, ass pressed hard into me. My dick had met its match. Her orgasm lit the fuse for mine, and I lost myself in her.

It was the best goddamned feeling, and I wasn't even inside her.

Fallon's body rocked in waves, pulling every ounce of pleasure from me, not letting me hide even one damn thing from her. Just like always.

As my eyes opened with my fingers still inside her, sheer terror set in. The force of it stole my breath and turned my muscles to stone.

No. No. No.

It was too good. Too perfect. Too pure.

Everything I wasn't.

I pulled my fingers from her, the terror digging in deep. I wouldn't ruin her. Wouldn't taint her. Wouldn't give her my darkness.

"I'm sorry," I choked out. "I can't." I tore the covers back and, like a coward, I ran.

CHAPTER THIRTY-FOUR

Fallon

"I'M SORRY. I CAN'T."

The words circled around and around in my head. Each pass leveled the kind of blow you don't recover from. It was as if each word was made of countless blades that tore at my insides.

"I'm sorry. I can't."

Pain ravaged me, even as my body still hummed. The juxtaposition of the two was enough to pull me under—the kind of depth you never emerged from.

The door to the bathroom snicked closed. Kye hadn't slammed it. He'd been in complete control as he shut the door on us.

A different emotion bubbled up. *Fury.*

He didn't get to do this. Didn't get to push me away, only to pull me close and then toss me aside again. He didn't get to have the last word, with some statement that casually dropped a bomb on my world.

I threw back the covers and shoved myself out of bed. A buzz still lived in me, vibrating beneath my skin and gathering at the apex of my thighs and the tips of my breasts.

I forced all thoughts of that down as I threw open the bathroom door. Kye's head jerked up as he scrubbed his hands. The bottle of mouthwash sat out on the counter. It was clear what he was doing. Erasing every part of what had just happened.

Two could play at that game. I snatched the bottle from the counter and tipped it back. The burn felt like a balm in a way, a distraction from the other pain still coursing through me.

I spat it out and slammed the bottle back down. "Guess what. It didn't work. I can still taste you. I still feel your hands on my skin. Your fingers moving inside me."

"Sparrow," he croaked.

"Because you live in me." The words were like missiles. "No matter how many times I've tried to dig or burn you out, you're still there. Because you're a part of me."

Sheer panic turned Kye's amber eyes a bright golden hue I'd never seen. "Fuck. I can't—I—I'll ruin you. Sparrow, I can't break you." His voice cracked, the words shattering into shards around us. "I can't taint you. You're my one good thing."

A different sort of pain crashed into me. A thunderous wave of agony as I took in the man before me. "Kyler," I whispered, moving into his space even as he tried to ward me off. "You make me the best version of myself. You make me strong and brave, unafraid to be exactly who I am. No part of you could ever ruin me."

He shook his head violently as his fingers scraped up his arms. "It's in me. That darkness. Because they bled it into me. With every beating. Every torment. I'm not saddling you with that."

I grabbed his hand, gripping it tightly and stopping him from hurting himself. "You're not the darkness. And you sharing your pain with me will only ever be one thing, Kye. An honor." I pressed his hand to my sternum, where I always felt him. "I hate that you feel it. But letting me see it is a gift, letting me hold it with you. Because it lets me truly know you. See what you've endured and the mountain you climbed after digging yourself out of the valley."

Tears filled those golden eyes. "I can't. Sparrow. I can't hurt you."

"The only thing that hurts is when you walk away. It's like you're ripping my soul out of my body."

Tears tracked down Kye's cheeks, disappearing into his scruff. "You're the only place I can breathe. You're my air."

I reached a hand up to wipe away those tears. "You've been my everything from the day you found me screaming in the woods. You gave me a safe place to land when I felt like I had nowhere to go."

"You gave me a home. In every way imaginable, you gave me a home." His hand lifted to cover mine against his face. "Do you know why I call you Sparrow?"

"You said it was because you found me singing." Only the singing had been screaming. Me letting loose all the things I'd held on to so tightly at the time.

Kye shook his head. "That's not the whole truth. They're symbols of hope. You've always been hope to me. You were my safe haven, the place I returned to again and again, even if I could only hold you in the secret places of my soul."

Every word he uttered leveled me, carved their syllables into my skin to scar me in the best way imaginable. "Kyler."

"I don't want to run from you. I don't want to run from what this could be. But I'm so damn scared I'll fuck it up. That I'll break it in a way that there's no coming back from. Sparrow, a man chased you yesterday, shot at you. Because you're in my life. You should be running for the hills."

"But I'm not." My thumb tracked over his cheek. "I'm right here, and I'm not going anywhere. You fuck something up? We'll fix it. Together. If there are dark forces in your life? We'll bury them. Put them in the ground where they'll never see the light of day. Because there is nothing—not one thing—we can't do if we tackle it together."

Kye dropped his forehead to mine, all the breath leaving him. "Sparrow. There's only ever been you. You were all I could see from the moment you walked into my life."

I pulled back, searching his face, trying to read between the lines.

"I tried," he whispered. "Anytime I let another woman close, I got physically ill."

One corner of my mouth kicked up. "I puked on Bobby Cooper's shoes when I tried to lose my virginity. Apparently, my body is repulsed by anyone but you."

Kye's body went wired. "Fallon...are you...?"

"A virgin?" Nerves bubbled up but quickly quieted because this was Kyler. The person I could tell anything without fear of judgment. "Unless a vibrator counts...I guess so."

A growl sounded in his throat as he pulled me flush against him. "I haven't had sex since I was fifteen because, apparently, when I met you, you took possession of my heart and my balls."

My jaw went completely slack. "No. You...you were always going out with Jericho and your friends. There were women around all the time."

"Yeah, around." Kye framed my face. "I won't lie. I tried a few times, knowing it would be better if we both moved on. But, Sparrow...I couldn't. There's a reason Jericho calls me Priest. Any woman's hands that weren't yours made my skin crawl. I finally gave up. Just let you think there were things where there weren't."

"Kyler Blackwood, I'm going to kill you."

A chuckle vibrated through his throat, and it sounded like pure music. "Sparrow, you've made me come in my pants twice since we moved in here, so I think we're even. And that's after fourteen years of being a walking hard-on around you."

I wanted to laugh, but a new sort of nerves settled in.

"What is it?" Kye asked, searching my eyes.

"What...what if we aren't compatible that way?" I asked, biting the corner of my lip.

Kye tugged it gently from between my teeth. "There are many things I'm scared of, but that is sure as hell not one of 'em."

"Really?"

"Really." He brushed his lips over mine. Featherlight. "You wanna test it out?"

A different feeling bubbled up inside me, swirling and stoking the fire that had already started earlier that morning. "Yes."

A curse slipped from his lips, and I frowned. "I thought yes was a good answer."

Those perfect lips brushed mine again, the scruff surrounding them sending heavenly shivers through me. Kye's callused thumb stroked my jawline. "I don't have a condom. That was the curse."

My mouth curved against his. "I'm on the pill."

Kye's thumb stilled, and he pulled back a fraction, those amber eyes searching mine. "Had a physical a couple of months ago. Are you sure? I always want to make sure you're safe—in all ways."

My heart stuttered as my fingers dropped to the hem of Kye's tee. "I want this. I want you." I tugged the tee up and over his head, letting it drop to the tiled floor. "To finally have that last piece you've been holding back from me."

"Sparrow," he rasped, his hands moving to my pajama top. "You've always had all of me."

"No. I haven't." My fingers ghosted over his bare shoulder, tracing the swirls of ink. "But now I will."

Kye tugged me closer to him by my pajama top. "You've had it all. Even if I didn't tell a soul. You've always had it all."

My eyes burned as he tugged my top over my head, letting it flutter to the floor like a feather in the breeze. My nipples pebbled at the change in temperature and the feel of those eyes I knew so well on me.

A rough palm cupped my breast, Kye's callused thumb circling my nipple. "Dreamed of what you'd look like. Painted a million different pictures in my mind. Might've even put a few down on paper."

Energy swirled somewhere deep, a surge of power engulfing me as delighted surprise hit. "You drew me?"

Kye's gaze didn't stray from mine as his thumb circled my nipple again. "Sparrow, I have six boxes of notebooks full of you and you alone in the attic."

The burn was back, but it was more beautiful this time. "Kyler."

"Love my name on your lips." He dropped his hands to my waistband and slowly tugged my pajama bottoms down, lowering right along with them. "Still fucking glistening," he growled. "Memorizing every damn inch of you. Every dip and curve."

"Kyler," I breathed again.

He was back on his feet and moving to the shower, turning it to warm as his fingers hooked into his sweats. My hands stilled as I watched him, his dick springing free, already at attention.

"But we just—I mean—you just—"

"Sparrow. I haven't had sex in a very long time. I've got some energy in reserve."

A laugh bubbled out of me as he pulled me into the shower and under the spray. His mouth met mine in a kiss without hesitation. It wasn't like the mornings we'd shared, where I'd felt his resolve crumble in a state of half-sleep. This was something else entirely. He was giving himself to me with a clear head.

I pulled back, running my hands over his broad chest, relishing the feel of his muscles under my palms and taking in the ink he always kept covered. His skin was a puzzle, one image bleeding into another, overlapping and twisting together. But as I searched, I found item after item tucked away.

Suddenly, I knew why he *never* went shirtless. Not to spar at the gym or even on pool days at Cope's. He always said the sun was bad for his ink, but I knew the truth now.

It wasn't just the sparrow behind his ear or the strawberry on his arm. Dogwood blossoms covered his chest. My necklace—the arrow—was woven around a realistic heart over where his lay. I saw packages of strawberry Sour Patch Kids and gummy bears.

There was a little first-aid kit like the one I'd carried with me to school every day to doctor his wounds. And the Band-Aids themselves were scattered over his ribs. A set of lips that were also a bow adorned his right pec. And so many other hidden gems I knew it would take me weeks—if not months—to discover.

And then I stilled completely. There was a portrait of me, my head tipped back, and my eyes closed as if I were soaking in the sun.

"Kyler," I croaked.

"I needed to feel you with me. Even when you weren't mine to touch. To have and hold. I needed to feel you." He took my hand and lowered it to his thigh.

He traced our fingers over a single band of scrawl I recognized. My handwriting. My name. Over and over around his thick corded muscles.

"You've always owned me, Sparrow. I just wanted to remember that. Have your brand on me forever."

My fingers ghosted over his thigh, my words, my writing, my name. "When?" I croaked.

"Since the day I turned eighteen."

I forced my gaze to his. "Kyler."

"I love you. I've always loved you."

Pleasure and pain warred in equal measure. "I love you, too. It's always been you."

My fingers encircled his dick, gliding up and down. Kye's eyes fluttered closed, his head tipping back. "You're my undoing."

I kissed the hollow of his throat. "And you're mine."

I tightened my grip, and he groaned. "Sparrow, you keep doing that, and it'll be over before it starts."

I grinned against his neck. "I could get used to that sort of power."

Kye's arm went around my waist, forcing me to release him as he lifted me, backing us up until we reached the bench at the rear of the glass enclosure. He lowered himself to the stone and lifted me to straddle him. His fingers found my slit as his eyes found my face. "Most beautiful creature to walk this Earth. All willowy lines and gentle curves."

His hand lifted to palm my breast, his thumb circling the hard peak. "Gonna make a study of all the ways you react to every touch. Gonna memorize the way you bend and bow."

"Kyler," I breathed as his fingers circled my opening.

"Never heard my name spoken with love until you gave me the syllables in that music that's only yours."

My eyes burned, pressure building there and everywhere. "Please."

"You ready for this, Sparrow? Finding out what we make together?"

"I've been waiting for this moment for more than half my life." Saying the words aloud made me realize it was something I could mourn. But I refused to look at it that way—as everything we'd lost. Instead, I chose to see it as what it was. Revel in the knowledge that we'd never take these gifts for granted because we'd lived without them for so long.

I steadied myself with a hand on Kye's shoulder as I lifted the other to his mouth. My fingers traced his bottom lip, wanting to feel what it did as we cemented this thing between us.

"You're leading the way," Kye rasped. "Telling me what you want, what you need. If it's too much, we can stop at any time. We have forever to find our way."

Tears filled my eyes as he guided himself to my entrance. His tip nestled there, but Kye didn't rush; he let me lead, just as he said he would. "Take your time. There's no hurry."

It was hard not to, feeling all the need I'd stored up for years bearing down on me. But I didn't want to miss a thing. My fingertips hovered over his lips as I slowly sank down onto Kye. I took it all in, the stretch, the flicker of pain, the fullness, and then I felt what I always did with Kye... *everything.*

His amber eyes didn't stray from mine as he fully seated himself in me. "Never felt more than this moment. More than knowing we're bonded in every possible way. Sparrow..."

My mouth met his as I started to move. That pressure and hint of pain shifted to pure heat, my blood coming alive under the fire Kyler lit in me.

I took and took until I had to rip my mouth from his to suck in air. My back arched as I took him deeper.

"That's my girl, finding exactly what she needs and giving it back to me." He leaned forward, sucking a nipple into his mouth. A whole new sensation lit inside me.

Sparks danced through every nerve ending as I picked up speed. Kye joined me there, in the give-and-take we created together. Everything in me spun tighter.

"The way you move," Kye ground out. "Like we were made to dance, just like this."

"Because...we...were." I struggled to get the words out with so much building inside me. There was so much feeling, it was almost pain.

"Sparrow," he croaked. "Find it with me. Let go."

His thumb circled my clit once, twice, and on the third pass, everything in me shattered. Shards of me, of him, of *us*, cascaded around us. Kye arched into me, planting himself deeper as he came. We lost ourselves in each other, but what we found was something entirely new.

And it was us. Like a camera lens finally coming into focus or a kaleidoscope dial clicking into place. The world changed in a split second, and there was only beauty.

CHAPTER THIRTY-FIVE

Kye

"WATCH ME!" GRACIE YELLED AS SHE CHARGED TOWARD Jericho, who was decked out in fight pads. Jericho's lips twitched as she leveled him with a jab, uppercut, side kick combo.

"The little fighter has some serious spunk," Mateo said as he pulled off his gloves, still breathing heavily from his workout.

Clem narrowed her eyes at him. "We both do. And don't you forget it."

I tried not to laugh.

Hayden leaned into Fallon. "You gonna tell me why my sisters hate this dude?"

"Because he made eyes at Fal," Gracie informed her. "He tried to look at her boobies."

Evan let out a strangled laugh as he crossed his arms over his chest. "These two are gonna take you out."

Mateo huffed. "I get it, I get it. Fallon is spoken for." He covered his eyes. "I'm a monk around her from now on."

Jericho scoffed. "Might need to look into becoming a eunuch for that to be true."

Gracie's face screwed up. "What's a you-you-nick?"

Fallon sent Jericho a pointed look. "Thanks for that." She turned to Gracie. "Nothing you need to worry about, Little G."

"Don't worry," Clem assured her. "I can look it up at the library."

I covered my face with my hands. "I'm so getting a call from the principal for that one."

Hayden laughed. "Good luck explaining how this all came about."

Evan scrubbed a hand over his face. "I'd pay good money to listen in on that call."

"I'd flip you off, but I'm trying to be a respectable big brother right now," I shot back.

Evan just grinned. "Do you guys wanna order pizza? We could go through everything for the new youth program."

In the two weeks since Fallon's biker incident and the two of us becoming a true *us*, Evan had pulled together the bones of an amazing program. And he'd done it largely without my help since I was focused on Fal and my sisters. Both Jericho and Mateo had stepped up big time, and despite both their occasional gripes, I knew they loved the ideas.

"I can't tonight. I'm sorry. I promised these beautiful ladies I'd take them to The Pop for a family dinner." It'd become a tradition of sorts since that's what we'd eaten the night it felt like we'd really become a family. So now, we made sure to go at least once a week.

"Throwing us over for some pretty ladies," Mateo muttered, shaking his head. "Why am I not surprised?"

I shrugged. "Your ugly mug or my family, *such* a hard choice."

Gracie giggled and then flung herself at me. "I want a double-chocolate Oreo shake."

I caught her easily and hoisted her into my arms. "That's because you have excellent taste." I glanced at Evan. "Is there anything that can't wait until our meeting next week? I can call you when we get home if there is. I know I haven't been the best team player of late."

Evan shrugged, his mouth twisting in a wry grin. "Hey, don't worry about me; I'll just be over here spending thousands of dollars on new equipment for the program while you're not looking."

Fal wrapped an arm around Hayden. "I support that."

Jericho sent me a smile, but it was slightly strained around the edges. "We've got it handled."

Mateo ambled toward the bag he'd left at the side of the ring. "I'm just making the case that I should be the face of this thing. The ladies love a man who gives back."

"So, you're not doing this out of the goodness of your heart?" Fallon asked, an amused look on her face.

Mateo shot her his most charming grin. "I can do both. Get a date and save the children."

"Jesus," I muttered as Mateo unzipped his bag.

The second he did, a pop sounded. Then magenta glitter flew into his face and all over him.

A few choice words left his mouth in Spanish before he turned, looking like he'd just gotten a glitter facial. "Fallon," he growled.

She beamed at him. "I felt like you hadn't learned your lesson *quite* yet."

"Sparrow. That crud gets everywhere. We're gonna be picking pink glitter out of the mats for months," I complained.

She simply shrugged. "Worth it."

"He looked like a pink fairy," Gracie said with glee as we headed up the steps to The Pop.

Clem grinned, making her freckles stand out on her cheeks. "It looked like a unicorn farted in his face."

"Do you think unicorn farts smell good?" Gracie asked thoughtfully.

Fallon struggled not to laugh as she opened the door and held it. "I bet they smell like cotton candy."

I just shook my head. "How is this a conversation we're actually having?"

Hayden laughed as she stepped into the restaurant. "Hey, you're the one who wanted us to come live with you. That means all unicorn fart convos are your fault."

I slid an arm around Fallon's shoulder. "It's my honor."

A familiar waitress in her mid-fifties greeted us. "Well, if it isn't the two newly minted lovebirds."

"Miss Gena. You are a sight for sore eyes," I greeted.

She waved me off. "You sweet-talker. You just love me for my double-chocolate Oreo shakes."

Fallon laughed. "I do hear the way to a man's heart is through his stomach."

"Then I should have at least twenty marriage proposals and a Lamborghini by now," Gena said with a laugh. "Little ladies, it is so lovely to see you again. Think you can make your way to that big corner booth? I'll get menus and coloring supplies."

Gracie and Clem cheered, running for the prime restaurant spot. Hayden smiled at the waitress. "Thanks, Miss Gena. Do you need me to carry anything?"

"I'm all good, sugar. You just get your booty to that booth." Gena turned to us. "They're looking good. And as polite as can be."

"That's all Hayden," I said with pride.

Gena patted my shoulder. "They're lucky to have you."

"I'm the lucky one."

Fallon burrowed into my side. "We all are."

We got settled at the table and put in our orders. As we stuffed ourselves with burgers, fries, and shakes, Clem and Gracie chatted about the new swing set that had been put in at their school, and Hayden told us about the latest hockey shot Cope was teaching her on his trips back to Sparrow Falls.

As we finished up, and I was dropping some bills on our check, Fallon stiffened beside me. I glanced over at her, trying to read the change. I followed her line of sight to a familiar man who had just taken a seat with two guys around his age.

Noah.

I'd never liked the douche canoe. Had always seen the way he looked at Fal. And there was just something disingenuous about the guy.

"Everything okay?" I asked, pitching my voice low.

Fallon's gaze jerked up to me. "Oh, yeah. Fine."

"Do you want to go say hi?"

She quickly shook her head. "That's okay."

My gaze narrowed on her. "He do something, Sparrow?"

She worried the corner of her bottom lip.

Fuck.

"He put his hands on you?" I growled.

"No, nothing like that. He just...he made his opinion of our marriage clear."

My fingers curled around the rolled silverware.

Fallon's hand glided over my thigh. "It's totally fine. Rose and Mila helped me put him in his place. I just didn't think he had that sort of judgment living inside him."

I wanted to break something, and it would've been a hell of a lot more satisfying if that something was Noah's face.

Fallon leaned into me, wrapping her arms around one of mine. "I'm good, Kyler."

"You know what it does to me when you call me that."

Her mouth curved. "Kyler."

I kissed her long and slow until Gracie hooted. Forcing myself to pull back, I grinned at my sisters. "Who's in charge of picking the bedtime story tonight?"

"Me!" Gracie cheered.

"You picked last time," Clem argued.

"How about you each pick one?" Fallon offered as we all slid out of the booth.

Hayden shot her a grin. "Way to avoid World War III."

"I try," Fallon said with a chuckle.

The girls ran ahead to get chocolate mints from Gena at the waitress station around the corner, and I slid a hand through Fallon's, trying to ignore Noah's table as we passed.

"Who knew you had a thing for incest, Fal," one of the guys I recognized as being a couple of years ahead of us in school muttered as we passed.

My body jerked to a stop as fury pulsed through me.

"Guess she had a little whore in her after all," the other one mumbled. Noah just sat there, not saying a damn word.

"What. Did. You. Call. My *wife*?" I snarled.

"Kye, don't," Fallon pleaded.

Guy number two looked up at me, suddenly rethinking his idiocy. But just when I thought he'd cave, he jutted out his chin and leaned back in his chair like a teenager showing off in class. "Just sayin' what everyone is thinking."

I moved so fast he didn't have a prayer. I kicked the legs of his chair out, making him hit the floor like a ton of bricks and spilling his water all over him.

"Oh, geez," I said, raising my voice. "Gotta be careful leaning back like that. It can be dangerous. Here, let me help you."

I grabbed him by the jacket and lifted him clean off his feet, getting in real close and lowering my voice to a lethal hiss. "If you say even one word about my wife again, I will make it my mission to ensure your pathetic life is a living hell so brutal you'll wish for death."

I righted his chair, shoved him into it, and then looked straight at Noah, who'd gone pale. "Make better friends. And stop letting the fact that you never had a chance with Fal turn you into a bitter gossip."

I wrapped an arm around Fallon and tucked her into my side.

"Well, that's one way to do it," she muttered, then looked up into my eyes. "You're not going to freak out on me, are you?"

I leaned down and brushed my lips against hers. "Nothing's taking you away from me. Never again."

CHAPTER THIRTY-SIX

Fallon

"Kye Kye," Gracie called as she bent over her open backpack. "I forgot. I made you something at school."

Kye's shoulders straightened from where he assembled pancake fixings behind the island. He'd become quite the pancake art connoisseur over the past few weeks. "You made me something?"

Gracie nodded, her pigtails swinging with the movement. "My teacher said we could save it for Christmas, but I wanna give it to you now."

"Good thing. Because if you told me you had something for me, I would've had a really hard time waiting," he admitted.

Gracie giggled and then held up her creation. I'd expected a drawing or maybe something made of clay. Instead, Gracie held out a massive, bright pink T-shirt she'd drawn on with puffy paint. Given her medium, it was remarkable how accurate her drawing was, but the subject matter had me fighting back a laugh.

She'd drawn a fluffy white cat wearing a bejeweled tiara with tons of other jewels and sparkles around it. Above the cat, in huge letters, it read, *PRINCESS*.

Everyone went silent for a moment as we took it in. Hayden started coughing in an attempt to hide her laughter, but Clem's face screwed up. "Gracie, Kye doesn't want to be a princess."

Gracie frowned. "Why not? They get way cooler clothes and jewels than the princes."

Kye beamed as he rounded the island. "Hell yeah, I want to be a princess." He pulled off his dark Blackheart Ink shirt and tugged the pink one over his head. "I'm meant to be a princess."

I couldn't help tracking the flicker of inked muscle as he made the change. "I gotta say, you as a princess is my new favorite thing."

Kye bent to me, his lips twitching. "I aim to please."

"You know Cope's gonna call you the pussy princess, right?" I whispered so only he could hear.

Kye chuckled. "Don't you dare show him this."

I snapped a quick picture with my phone.

"Sparrow," he warned.

I grinned. "You can punish me later."

"That's a goddamned promise," Kye growled as he straightened and righted his T-shirt. "Gracie, this is the best present I've ever gotten."

"Really?" she asked, smiling so wide you could see all her teeth.

Kye nodded. "Everyone's gonna be jealous and want one of their own."

Hayden squeezed Gracie's shoulder, a mischievous smile playing at her lips. "You know, we could get the supplies and make shirts for all Kye's brothers for Christmas."

My hand shot in the air. "Oh, oh. Me! I want to help!"

Hayden laughed. "This is going to be too much fun."

Gracie bent again, fishing out her lunch bag and frowning. "Uh-oh." The insulated material decorated with rainbows and unicorns had torn open wider on one corner, and her bag of carrots was trying to escape. "The hole got bigger."

Kye grabbed a squeeze bottle with pancake batter dyed a bright pink, adding a mane to the unicorn he was currently crafting on the griddle. "I'll get you a new one today."

Gracie nibbled on her bottom lip, and I moved into her side, rubbing a hand up and down her back. "Is this one special?"

She nodded. "Hay Hay got it for me. All the girls had unicorns, and I wanted one, too."

That burning sensation in my chest was back.

Hayden gave her sister a soft smile. "I bet Kye could get you one with unicorns."

"But *you* gave me this one," Gracie mumbled.

"I forgot with everything going on, but I did get some needles and thread at the craft store. We can try to fix it," I offered.

Gracie's whole face brightened. "Really?"

"Really. Give me two seconds."

"I hope you got a thimble," Hayden called, and laughter erupted behind me.

I jogged to grab the supplies from where I'd stashed them in the library and then hurried back. "I got lots of color options."

"Pink!" Gracie demanded.

"We've got all the pink." I tossed out four shades, and Gracie grabbed the brightest one.

"Here." Hayden held out her hand for the thread. In seconds, she'd gotten the embroidery thread through the needle and was studying the tear. "I bet we can make it look purposeful. Like it's part of the design."

"Like *kintsugi*," Clem offered, taking a sip of milk.

We all turned to face her.

"Kin-what?" Kye asked, sounding amused.

Clem straightened on her stool. "It's a Japanese art. They repair broken pottery with gold, silver, or platinum. They say it makes the broken beautiful. You don't disguise what the pottery went through; you honor it."

My gaze lifted and met Kye's across the island. I knew mine were glassy with unshed tears. "I love that."

"Me, too," Kye said gruffly.

"Beauty in the broken," Hayden whispered, pressing the needle through the lunch bag.

"Except no gold or silver." Gracie tapped the thread. "Only pink."

I chuckled. "Fair. Pink is far superior."

Hayden's fingers flew over the material, and before long, she'd not only repaired the corner but needlepointed a bright pink heart there. "Done."

"Hay Hay, it's beeeeeeautiful!" Gracie explained.

I wrapped an arm around the teen's shoulders. "It really is. You have a gift."

Her lips twitched. "Not gonna lie, I prefer hockey."

Kye laughed. "Well, according to Cope, you've got what it takes. He actually asked if you might be interested in something hockey-related."

Hayden's amber eyes sparked with interest. "What?"

Kye sent me a quick look as he smiled. "The Seattle Sparks host a youth workshop over schools' winter break up in Seattle. He thought you might want to attend."

Hayden's jaw went completely slack. "A hockey camp with a *professional* team? In their arena?"

Kye full-out beamed, and it hit me right in the sternum. "That's right. What do you think?"

A little of Hayden's excitement dimmed. "Would I go…by myself?"

I could practically feel her nerves. And it killed me that she was so unsure. But it made sense. She'd never left Central Oregon or been apart from her sisters. It would take time for her to gain that sort of confidence.

Reaching out, I squeezed her hand. "We were actually thinking we could make a family trip of it. We'll stay with Cope, Sutton, and Luca, and we can go to the zoo and the aquarium. Pike's Place Market and the Space Needle. There are tons of cool museums."

"They have wolf eels at the Seattle Aquarium," Clem chimed in. "I've always wanted to see one of those."

Gracie's face scrunched up. "Wolf…eels…"

I couldn't help laughing. "There will also be adorable otters."

"I'm sticking with the otters," Gracie mumbled.

Kye held out a hand to Clem for a high five. "I'm all about some wolf eels."

Clem slapped his palm. "Yes!"

Kye turned to Hayden as he slid the last pancake onto the platter. "So, what do you think?"

"I think it'd be amazing. I might not have all the right gear, though. Do you think that's okay?"

Kye grinned. "I think I might be able to help with that." He crossed to the mudroom between the garage and kitchen and came out with a *massive* gear bag. "I had Cope help me pick everything out. So, if something's wrong, blame him."

Hayden's eyes turned misty as she struggled to swallow. "Kye. It's too much."

"No, it's not," he said with finality. "You've been working so hard for so long. It's time someone helped you, too."

"He's right," Clem said softly. "You took care of us forever. Let Kye do the same for you."

She nodded and bent to unzip the bag. She pulled out workout clothes, skates, sticks, pucks, pads, and things I couldn't identify. By the time Hayden straightened, she had tears running down her face. "I've never had anything new for hockey."

And then I was crying.

She moved into Kye's space and threw her arms around him. "Thank you."

Kye hugged her hard. "You deserve all this and so much more."

"You've given me more. You've given it to all of us."

I wiped at my tears as Gracie leaned into me. "Thanks, Fallon."

God, I loved these kids.

"Okay," Kye said, dragging a thumb under his eyes. "Now, we eat pancakes."

"Yes!" Gracie cheered.

"I want the dino," Clem declared.

"Unicorn for me," Gracie begged.

Kye slid one onto my plate. "And a strawberry for the strawberry queen."

"Thank you," I said, giving him a quick kiss.

My phone dinged, and I swiped it off the counter, glancing at the alert on the screen.

Arden has changed the group name to Fallon's Hit List.

I frowned, waiting for a text to appear in the siblings' chain.

Arden: *Went with Linc to Haven this morning. Why is there pink glitter all over the mats?*

Kye sent me a meaningful stare across the island. "I told you." I winced. "Oops?"

Kyler: *Look at what she did to poor Mateo.*

A second later, a photo appeared of Mateo covered in pink glitter. "You took a picture?" I asked, incredulous.

Kye shrugged. "You never know when blackmail material might be needed."

Cope: *Fal, can you send a few of those glitter bombs to Seattle? I've got some teammates who could benefit from some good old-fashioned glitter vengeance.*

Rhodes: *I thought you were still too scarred by even the sight of glitter.*

Cope: *Don't remind me. I found more penis confetti in my Bentley the other day. AFTER it had been detailed twice. I don't even want to talk about the looks the guys who cleaned my car gave me.*

Kyler: *I always said you missed your calling as a stripper.*

Shep: *That's Trace, remember? He did all sorts of stripteases, trying to win Ellie over.*

Trace: *There was a fire. She didn't have a shirt. I had to give her mine.*

Rhodes: *The only fire was in your pants, you liar.*

Cope: *If you're feeling fiery down there, you should have that checked, T-Money.*

I choked on a laugh as my fingers flew across the screen.

Me: *I wonder if I could find stripper-themed glitter for Trace. G-strings and booties?*

Trace: *Don't you dare. Keep Satan's stardust away from me. Do you know how hard it is to clean that shit up?*

Arden: *Do it. Do it. Do it.*

"You're already planning an attack, aren't you?" Kye said as he grinned at me.

"Maaaaaaybe."

"Glitter bomb?" Hayden asked hopefully.

"You know it. Target: Trace."

Gracie looked uncertain. "I dunno. Mr. Trace really has a thing about a tidy house."

Understatement of the century. "Which is why it's going to be so freaking fun."

Gracie giggled as she finished her pancake.

"Okay, team," I said, sliding off my stool. "Wash hands, faces, and brush teeth. Kye and I will get everything in the SUV."

As the girls ran upstairs, Kye and I loaded ourselves with backpacks and lunch bags and headed out front. But we pulled up short the moment we stepped outside.

The entire front of the yard was covered in trash, and the landscaping had been destroyed. But Kye's SUV? That was the most terrifying of all. The doors were all open, the interior sliced, stuffing everywhere. And spray-painted over the side in angry, red letters, it read, YOU DON'T DESERVE ANY OF THIS.

CHAPTER THIRTY-SEVEN

Kye

EVIDENCE TECHS SWARMED THE FRONT OF MY YARD AS GABRIEL, Anson, and Trace sat at the kitchen island. A spot that, just two hours ago, was home to pancakes, a craft project, and a teenage girl who'd gotten her first brand-new hockey gear. The contrast only made me rage more.

Whoever this was didn't get what they were destroying. They didn't understand the beautiful gift I'd been given that they were endangering and threatening to collapse. But maybe they did know and didn't give a damn.

Fallon handed me a mug decorated with tiny dinosaurs. "Drink this."

My gaze dropped to the cup. "Did you get me a dinosaur mug?"

Her mouth curved. "Look on the other side."

I flipped the mug around. It read: *Being a big brother is a walk in the park—Jurassic Park.*

A laugh tore from my throat. It was the last sound I'd thought to make at the moment. I wrapped an arm around Fallon and pressed a kiss to her head. "Thank you."

"Always. And the tea is supposed to be good for soothing anxiety and promoting calm."

"Please, tell me it's not a blend Lolli gave you," Trace muttered as he eyed his mug.

Anson took a pull of his tea. "I hope it's the one that had her taste-tester seeing pink bunnies."

"I heard the second batch had folks thinking they'd turned into cats, complete with the meowing," I muttered.

Gabriel just shook his head. "How that woman hasn't ended up in lockup is beyond me."

"It's only a matter of time," Trace mumbled.

"Rest easy," Fallon assured them. "This is a blend Sutton ordered for The Mix Up. No cannabis or psychedelics on the ingredient list."

"Damn." Anson lifted his cup and took another sip.

I set my mug down and pulled Fallon in tighter against my side. "No more tiptoeing. Give it to us straight."

I knew what they were trying to do. They wanted to ease things for Fallon and me after a charged morning. We couldn't hide the state of the front yard from the girls. Or the fact that something was seriously wrong. All three of them were on edge, waiting for Ellie to pick them up.

The fact that this asshole had scared my sisters and Fallon made me want to dip into that dark side of myself. The one that would let me wipe them from the planet without a second thought.

"Dex is on his way," Anson said. "He's already tapped into your security system and is looking through the video footage to see if we can get a look at the unsub."

Anson's white hat hacker friend, who was really more of a morally gray hat, had saved our asses more than once. The fact that he was willing to take more time away from his life and his job with the FBI spoke to his character.

"What does this latest incident tell you?" I asked.

Anson's thumb traced the handle of his mug. "It says this is more personal than we first realized. Did you hurt anyone during the underground fights?"

My gut clenched as I forced myself to swallow the acid surging up my throat. "They were gloves-off fights. I hurt plenty of people."

Just saying that out loud had the darkness flaring inside me—the demons that shared the same opinion as the unsub. That I didn't deserve any of this.

Fallon's hand fisted in my tee. "That's in the past. You were doing what you had to do to protect yourself."

But that wasn't entirely true. For a time, sure. But then I'd done it hoping to earn enough money to get my own place. So I wouldn't need the Colsons' handouts. So I could be with Fallon the way I wanted to be. I'd doled out violence for selfish reasons, and that was something I'd have to live with for the rest of my days.

"Some of it was that. Some of it was selfish. I wanted to be free. Wanted you." I needed to admit it aloud. Needed her to know. Needed all of them to know.

Fallon reached up and framed my face in her hands. "I love you. Nothing you could tell me will ever change that. You were sixteen. You made some mistakes."

"I sure as hell hope no one judges *me* for the choices I made as a teenager," Gabriel muttered.

"Or way past then," Trace added.

Anson nodded. "No one who walks this Earth is perfect, Kye. The best we can do is let our mistakes shape us for the better. I see you doing that every damn day."

Fallon kissed the underside of my jaw. "He's right."

I tried to let all their kindness and understanding in. Their support.

Fallon burrowed deeper into me. "I know it's hard to go back there. But you have to remember that you've grown. Changed. But I'll never wish that boy away. He's the one I fell in love with. The fierce defender of everyone he's ever cared for. Listener to all who need an ear. Creator of safe places for all who know him."

She gripped me harder, forcing my gaze to hers. "People think I'm the empath, but it's you. You take on the feelings of everyone around you, then meet them in their darkest places and show them it's okay to face the darkness."

I dropped my forehead to hers, my mouth brushing hers. "I love you, Sparrow."

"My everything," she whispered.

"Fuck, my eyes are leaking," Gabriel muttered.

Anson slapped him on the back. "Feel those feelings, my man."

Trace shook his head. "What happened to you?"

"My question exactly," a new voice said. "He used to communicate solely with grunts and scowls. Now, he smiles."

Dex appeared, his familiar, ever-present messenger bag slung over his shoulder in the most bizarre juxtaposition I could imagine. Tall and broad with a build that made it clear he wasn't a stranger to a gym, it was as if he was a cross between a mountain man, a biker, and a professor.

Wire-framed glasses were perched on his nose, but ink peeked out from his sleeves and covered his hands and fingers. He wore jeans, hiking boots, and an outdoorsman jacket, but the T-shirt beneath read: *Hacking. Because punching people is frowned on.*

"Forget Anson's creepy-ass smiles. He tries to play *matchmaker*," Trace said, sliding off his stool and crossing to Dex.

Dex took his hand in a warm shake. "He tried to hug me the last time I was here. That's just crossing a line."

Anson stood and moved to his friend. "Prepare your soul because I'm about to do it again."

Dex laughed but gave him a back-slapping hug in return. "At least you warned me this time."

Gabriel saluted him. "Thanks for dropping everything and coming out this way."

"Well," Dex said, sliding his messenger bag off, "my tenure with the FBI has finally come to an end, so I had some time on my hands."

Anson's gray-blue eyes flared. "Seriously?"

"I promised them ten years. That ended exactly two weeks ago."

Concern made a home in Anson's expression. "How do you feel about that?"

"Honestly? It'll be nice not having them looking over my shoulder all the time."

Fallon frowned. "You didn't *want* to work for the FBI?"

One corner of Dex's mouth kicked up. "I didn't really have a choice. I got caught hacking into their files when I was in college, and they don't particularly like that."

Fallon's jaw went comically slack. "You broke into the FBI?"

He shrugged. "I was bored."

"That's what happens when you don't keep geniuses occupied," Anson muttered.

Trace's brow quirked. "Like you're one to talk. Your IQ is ridiculously high."

"I'm a reformed genius," Anson explained.

"Well, how about we put both your brains to good use and figure out what the hell is going on here," Gabriel muttered.

The levity in Dex's expression disappeared. He pulled out his tablet and lowered himself to a stool. "The way the cameras are positioned, there's no view of the unsub."

I gritted my teeth. "Not even at the gate?"

"Nope." Dex tapped a few things on his tablet. "I'm guessing he hopped the fence because he knew where the cameras were. And likely broke into your system. It's not especially hacker proof."

I muttered a curse. "You think you can remedy that?"

Dex's eyes lit up like a kid at Christmas. "It would be my pleasure."

"Oh, fuck," Anson muttered. "He's going to send some world-ending computer virus to anyone who tries to get into your system."

"Don't shit on my hobbies," Dex shot back.

"All right, all right. Stay focused," Trace ordered. "Anson, you asked if Kye had hurt anyone in the underground fights. Why?"

Anson wrapped his hands around his mug again. "This feels a lot like revenge—hurting people involved in that ring. But now this person is focused on you. Telling you that you don't *deserve* the good things in your life. That's personal."

Fallon's fingers threaded through mine. "It's okay. Just try to remember what you can."

I nodded jerkily. "I hurt plenty of people during the fights, and plenty hurt me. A couple had to go to the hospital, but I don't think I did any permanent damage to anyone."

Anson frowned. "What about someone you defeated? Someone desperate for the prize money."

I scrubbed a hand over my face. "Everyone who signed up for those fights was desperate. For money, for the release of whatever darkness lived inside them…"

"If a fight you won is linked to a traumatic event for someone, it wouldn't take much for them to focus on you. And if they've started to fixate, they've been watching you. You getting married and starting a family could have triggered them," Anson explained.

The room fell away around me as a lead weight settled in my gut. The people mixed up in the world I'd left behind were the worst of the worst. And I knew they'd do anything to tear down the people they saw as enemies—especially if that person had a glimmer of something they didn't. Happiness.

CHAPTER THIRTY-EIGHT

Kye

MY HEAD THRUMMED IN A STEADY BEAT AS I LEANED AGAINST the counter. It didn't matter that the house was now quiet. The evidence techs had gathered everything they could from the yard, and Trace, Gabriel, Anson, and Dex had headed off to the station, likely to talk more openly than they could around Fallon and me.

Maybe that was for the best. But even though it was quiet, my head still beat like the drummer of one of Arden's beloved death metal bands was playing a solo on my skull. The fact that we were now being forced to seriously consider moving the girls to Colson Ranch until this maniac was caught only intensified the pain.

Movement caught my eye, a flash of pale-blond hair and angel eyes. Fallon stepped in front of me, offering me a Coke poured over ice and two Tylenol. I took them from her outstretched hands. "How'd you know?"

"Because I know you."

I sipped the soda and swallowed the pills down, just looking my fill at the woman I'd never thought would be mine but, by some miracle, was.

Fallon hooked her fingers into my front jeans pockets. "Tell me."

It was the same thing we'd said since she was fourteen and I was sixteen. The one thing we'd never lost along the way: the invitation for brutal truth.

And maybe the permission to be whoever we truly were in the moment—even if the reality was ugly—was the greatest gift we'd ever given each other.

"Feels like stupid choices I made back then will haunt me forever. I almost lost my sisters because of it. Still could. Scared the hell out of Nora and Lolli. Lost you."

Fallon's grip on my pockets tightened. "You didn't lose me. I'm right here."

"Lost you for far too long," I whispered. "You were so close. Like I could almost reach out and touch you. But my hands were trapped behind my back. I just had to hold tight to the secret haven you were in my mind. I'd lie in bed at night, reliving those stolen moments by the creek over and over. They got me through."

Fallon searched my eyes for a long moment. "Would you do something with me?"

The response wasn't what I'd expected. One corner of my mouth kicked up. "If it's exploring the confines of that big-ass tub upstairs, the answer is yes."

A light-as-air laugh bubbled out of Fallon, as if all the darkness swirling around us didn't exist. "As tempting as that is, that's not what I had in mind."

I slid a hand along her jaw and into her silken mane. "Tell me what's in that beautiful mind of yours."

"I want you to tattoo me."

A buzz lit under my skin, energy crackling as shock and need warred in equal measure. "You hate needles."

"I do."

"You literally can't even look if you have to get a shot or need blood drawn."

Fallon sent a fierce scowl in my direction. "I don't have to look to get a tattoo."

My mouth quirked. "Well, most people like to make sure I'm not permanently defacing their skin."

She gripped my pockets harder, giving them a little tug. "I trust you. And I know whatever you do will be beautiful."

I searched those fathomless blue eyes, taking in the depths where that trust burned bright. "It's a big deal, a tattoo. Especially when you've never had one before. You sure?"

"Kyler...I'm sure."

And fuck if there wasn't pure certainty in her tone.

"You know what you want?" That was another test. Because if she didn't have a vision, something she *needed*, I wasn't setting a single needle on her skin.

Fallon's mouth curved. "I know."

"You gonna share with the class?" I pressed.

"I'll tell you once we get there."

Fuck me. I was going to mark the woman I'd loved from the moment I met her. And if that wasn't the ultimate gift, I didn't know what was.

The bell over Blackheart's door jingled as I held it open for Fallon. The moment she stepped inside, I saw Bear's whole face light up. "Now there's my queen." He moved around the desk and pulled her into a hug, then kissed both her cheeks.

"Careful where you put those lips," I warned.

Bear guffawed, his eyes twinkling. "The repercussions would be worth it."

Fallon swatted at his shoulder. "Don't go stirring up trouble."

"Who, me?"

Fallon laughed. "You stashing any cookies?"

"Well," Bear began, "it just so happens I've been testing out a new chocolate peppermint recipe."

"You know, I happen to be an excellent taste-tester," Fallon said.

My arms came around her from behind. "So am I."

Bear's lips twitched beneath his gray beard. "I trust her taste more than yours."

"Hey," I protested. "My taste is Fallon, and you seem pretty fond of her."

"Point well made." A little of the amusement slipped from Bear's face. "You guys hanging in okay? We weren't expecting you today after everything."

My gaze followed his to Jericho, who was wrapping the calf of a man who'd just gotten a list of names tattooed with some decorative Celtic elements woven around them.

"We're doing okay," I said, pitching my voice lower. "Just ready for whoever this is to be stupid and get caught."

"Amen to that," Bear echoed. "Trace got any leads?"

I shook my head. "They're working on it. Doing everything they can."

"Good, that's good. You picking up something from your office?" Bear asked.

One corner of my mouth kicked up. "Actually, my wife would like a tattoo."

A scoff sounded from down the hall, and I lifted my gaze to see Penelope walking our way, a sour look on her face. "I thought she hated needles."

"I do," Fallon said with zero animosity in her tone.

Penelope rolled her eyes. "Married to one of the most gifted men in ink, and she's a virgin. What a waste."

"Don't be a bitch, Pen," Jericho called as he straightened. "You made your play. Endless plays, in fact. You didn't win. Grow up."

"This has nothing to do with that. I was just making a point," she snapped.

"Penelope," I began.

Her multi-colored hair whipped over her shoulder as she turned back to me. "What?"

"You're fired."

She gaped at me, her sparkly lipstick only adding to the fish-like effect. "You can't fire me."

"This my business?" I asked.

"Yes, but—"

"Even if it wasn't, I'd have a case for harassment—both the sexual and the good, old-fashioned bitch kind. I probably could've kept on taking that brand of bullshit, but if you think you can make *my wife*, the woman I love more than air, feel uncomfortable in my presence, then respectfully...get fucked. And get your ass out of my shop."

Jericho snorted as he snapped off his gloves. "Respectfully? Really, Priest? Not sure that pairs with *get fucked*."

"I dunno," Bear began. "I think it has a nice ring to it."

Penelope's face turned bright red. "You're gonna regret this, Kyler."

"You don't get to call me that." My voice cracked like a whip. "Only my wife calls me that."

Fallon twisted in my arms. "Or your family when you're in trouble."

Jericho and Bear burst out laughing.

I dipped my head and kissed her. "True, Sparrow. But no one says it quite like you."

"Disgusting," Penelope spat.

"Clean out your room," I ordered, my eyes narrowing. "Bear, you wanna make sure she doesn't take anything that's not hers?"

He shot me a salute. "It'd be my pleasure."

Penelope stalked down the hall, stomping her feet the whole way.

"Jesus," Jericho said, scrubbing a hand over his face.

Fallon winced. "Sorry to be the creator of drama."

"Don't you apologize. You didn't do a damn thing," Jericho shot back. "That woman's a piranha, and it's about damn time Kye kicked her ass to the curb."

I pulled Fal into my side. "I'm sorry she was a bitch to you."

Fallon simply shrugged, a small smile on her face. "I can't

begrudge her wanting you. But I can take issue with how she went about acting on that."

"Dude," Jericho said, his mouth curving. "How did you end up with the coolest chick on the planet?"

"I do not know, brother. I'm just trying my best not to fuck it up." Jericho laughed. "That sounds like a good plan."

A frown tugged at my mouth as I really took in my best friend. The shadows under his eyes had made a home *in* his hazel eyes. But more than that, it looked like he'd lost five or ten pounds. "Are you okay?"

Jericho stiffened, pulling himself up straighter. "Yeah, man. Just tweaked about all this."

"Have you seen anything?" I asked. "Anyone following you? Feel like someone's watching?"

He shook his head. "Been moving around. Not staying at one place for too long."

"Probably not a bad idea," I muttered.

Fallon reached out and squeezed his arm. "Why don't you come over for dinner this weekend? The girls would love to see you."

Jericho forced a smile. "Wouldn't say no to a home-cooked meal."

"Good."

"You really gonna let this knucklehead take your ink card?" Jericho asked.

"I am," Fallon said with a smile. "And we'd better get a move on if we want to do it before we pick up the girls."

She started tugging me down the hall, but I gave Jericho a chin lift. "Call if you need anything, okay?"

"Will do."

But I knew he wouldn't. Not unless he was desperate. I tried to shove worry for my friend down as I let Fallon lead me down the hall. She headed straight for my private room, slipping inside and closing the door behind us. "Can I lock this?"

My brows lifted. "You plan on taking advantage of me back here?"

Fallon laughed. It was my favorite kind, the type that was full of sunshine and good, clean air. The sort that was free. "We'll have to save your tattoo room deflowering for another day." She flipped the lock on the handle. "This time, it's just so I can show you what tattoo I want."

That intrigued me. But it intrigued me even more when Fallon's slender fingers started unbuttoning her blouse.

"Sparrow..."

As she reached the last buttons, she shrugged the shirt off, dropping it to the floor, and stood there in only her jeans and a lacy, pale pink bra. Her hands reached behind her, and then that fell, too.

I couldn't help but stare at her. She was so damn beautiful. The definition of breathtaking. And I wanted to memorize every dip and curve. The way her breasts were a few shades paler than the rest of her soft gold skin, how her nipples pebbled in the room's cool air.

"Here." Fallon pressed her fingertips between her breasts in the hollow of her sternum. "I've always felt you right here. In the good times and the bad, this is where I feel you. A place that's always been yours."

Fucking hell. She slayed me in the most brutal and beautiful ways.

"Maybe it's because you've always been at the very center of everything for me. My grounding force. My haven."

"Sparrow," I croaked.

She crossed the room, lifted my palm, and held it to that spot. "It's yours. I'm yours. Just like you're mine."

"What...?" I had to take a second to swallow the rising emotion. "What do you see there?"

Fallon pressed her hand harder against mine. "*Haven.* Surrounded by dogwood blossoms and sparrows."

"I can't imagine anything more perfect. And it would be my honor to ink it into your skin."

"Forever," she whispered.

My lips ghosted over hers as I returned the promise. "Forever."

CHAPTER THIRTY-NINE

Fallon

"YOU PAINTED THE CEILING," I SAID, STARING UP AT THE MURAL I knew Kye had drawn. He'd clicked up the heat as he sketched out my tattoo, and as self-conscious as I could sometimes be, I felt none of that now as I lay on the bed in his office. Because it was Kye. There was no need to cover myself or hide a damn thing from him.

Kye's mouth curved—the uneven smile I loved. "Figured if people would be staring up at that ceiling for hours, I might as well make it beautiful."

"It's more than beautiful," I whispered as he put the finishing touches on his station and donned some black gloves. "It's enchanting."

It looked like a haunting maze of flowers and vines, with different items peeking through. You could stare at it for days and probably still discover new things.

Kye held up a stencil. "Last chance for changes or to bail."

I shook my head. "I'm ready."

"All right. Need you standing."

I swung myself up to standing, the bed hitting the backs of my thighs as I waited.

Kye set the paper on his rolling tray, folded a piece of paper towel, and wet it with something from a spray bottle. "First, just a little alcohol. It'll be cold."

I nodded, and he swiped it down my sternum and over the sides of my breasts. My nipples instantly pebbled.

"Hope this is proof of how much I love you that I'm willing to tattoo you with a hard-on."

A laugh bubbled out of me as he tossed the paper towel. "Sorry?"

He bent over and kissed me quickly. "You should be."

Kye lifted a disposable razor—the kind that came in jumbo packs. "I'll shave the area just to get any fine hairs that could get in the way of the process. That okay?"

My breaths came just a little quicker. "Sure."

Kye met my eyes. "You're in control. You want me to stop at any time, just say the word. There's no rush. We don't have to get this done all in one sitting."

I exhaled, trying to let go of my nerves. I knew he was right, but I wanted his mark on my skin, the tattoo that had taken root in my mind. Something that was Kye and me. "I'm ready."

The razor danced across my skin in featherlight strokes that felt like the kiss of fingertips. "One more alcohol application," Kye said roughly. "Then some numbing gel that will also help the stencil take."

I couldn't take my eyes off Kye as he worked. Everything about him was hypnotizing—his care and his skill, not to mention how intently he focused on each step. He gently laid the stencil between my breasts and then pressed it down along my sternum.

My mouth went dry as he smoothed the paper with a crooked finger to make sure the stencil took to my skin properly. Each little flick of his fingers had that invisible cord inside me spinning tighter, but I didn't take my eyes off Kyler, taking in the bend of his jaw as he focused, the flicker in his cheek, the way the amber tones in his irises shifted and changed.

He gently pulled back the stencil and backed up a bit to take it in. Tossing it into the trash, he reached for my hips, guiding me over two steps so I could take in our reflection in the full-length mirror he had propped against the wall. My breath caught.

There was something about this, me bare from the waist up, Kye looking at me, pure reverence in his gaze. I wanted to memorize everything about it. Burn it into my brain forever.

"Make sure you like the placement," Kye rasped.

He'd taken my body and turned it into art. The word *haven* was done in a decorative script that felt like a mix of the two of us—bold in some places, delicate in others. The dogwood flowers looked just like the ones he had inked on his own chest, but I knew mine would have pops of pale pink. And the sparrows dancing around the blooms would match the one Kye had inked behind his ear, but in colors that were my favorites, as well.

"I..." The right words weren't coming. "I feel beautiful."

"Sparrow," Kye whispered.

My gaze shot to his. "I love it. Love *you*."

"More than words."

"I'm ready," I said softly.

Kye nodded, his hands going to my hips again, but this time, he lifted me as though I weighed nothing and laid me on the bed. He hovered over me, his lips ghosting over mine as he pulled off his gloves. "A goddamned gift."

My mouth curved as he straightened, tossing the used gloves and putting on fresh ones. Then he reached for his tattoo machine. "I'm starting with a fine tip to complete the outline. We don't want the stencil to disappear before I can get those inked. But just keep checking in with me, okay?"

I swallowed hard and gripped the edge of the bed. Something about needles had always freaked me out. I knew it was more than the needles themselves, though. It was the fact that I'd woken up in the hospital at ten years old with all sorts of them poking into me and a concussion, only to find out that my brother and dad were dead. And Cope was badly injured. A deer in the road had changed everything for our family.

Kye curved his pinky around mine. "I'm right here."

"Tell me what it feels like."

"Like a deep cat scratch. It'll be the most painful when I'm going over a spot again and again. But after a while, a sort of haze will set in. Some people even think it feels good."

I squeezed his pinky. "Make me art, Kyler."

"My goddamned pleasure, Sparrow."

The first prick of the needle detonated a battle inside me. It took everything for me not to jump. But Kye was right there, talking me through each step.

"You're doing great. How does it feel on the pain scale? Zero to ten."

"Four, maybe. It's not bad," I admitted.

My heart was slowing, dipping back into its normal rhythms.

"We're almost done with the outline. It looks stunning. Your skin is the best canvas I've ever worked on. You take ink like a dream."

My mouth curved at that. "I think you're biased about my skin."

Kye pulled the tattoo machine away and bent to kiss the side of my breast opposite where he was tattooing. "Damn straight."

I laughed as he switched out the tip and poured new ink. There were more colors now. Because Kye was setting me aflame.

I lost myself in the feel of it all, the worst of the pain fading. I was starting to feel the hum Kye had talked about. The endorphin rush and high. It felt heady, the buzz of the machine, the prick of the needle. But more so the feeling of Kyler's hands dancing over me, using me as his canvas.

I slipped into a haze where space and time didn't exist; there was only us. And before long, Kye was pulling back. He set down his tattoo machine and slid closer to me. "Best work I've ever done."

He gently slathered some ointment over the fresh ink before snapping off his gloves and holding up a handheld mirror. "My Sparrow in all her colors."

My breath caught as I took in the image. If I thought I'd felt beautiful before, it had nothing on this. The way the ink curved around my breasts and became a part of me. "I've never loved something more."

His smile turned gentle as he wrapped my tattoo in clear plastic. "There's nothing like seeing my ink on you. My mark. Etched into your skin for all eternity."

My thighs pressed together in search of relief from the pressure that had been building the past several hours.

"Sparrow..." Kye warned. "You keep pressing those pretty little thighs together, we're gonna have problems."

My eyes flared, and I could feel them sparking with heat. "Maybe I want us to have problems."

Answering heat flashed in Kye's eyes, making them dance with gold flecks. "You sure about that? Because I want to taste what having my hands and needles on you has done."

"Please," I breathed, my chest rising and falling.

Kye stood, walking to the end of the tattoo bed and bringing his stool with him, but his gaze never left me. "You're going to have to be good. Lie perfectly still as I eat you. Because you can't mess up my perfect canvas."

My breaths came quicker now, not from panic like earlier but pure need.

That amber gaze never strayed as Kye pulled off one boot and then the other. Removed one sock at a time. They all hit the floor, the boots' thump echoing in the room above the strains of classic rock.

He slid his hands up my legs, eyes still locked on my face. And then he cupped me through my jeans. His eyes closed as he breathed deeply. "Sparrow, you're burning up. Could scar a man. But I'll wear those brands with pride."

I soaked in the feel of his palm and rocked my hips, searching for more. Sparks danced through me at the friction, and I knew I could come from this alone. My body felt like someone had been laying tripwires beneath my skin all day. One spark, and I would detonate.

Kye opened his eyes, and they were pure gold now. Pure need. "Tell me I can taste you."

My breath hitched, but there was only one word I could give him. "Yes."

His hand left the apex of my thighs, and deft fingers unfastened the button of my jeans. My mouth went dry as Kye pulled the zipper down. I swore I could hear every tine unfasten, even above the guitar riffs and lyrical refrains of the music in the shop. And I felt them, too—tiny vibrations echoing through me.

"On three, I want you to lift those hips, Sparrow. Careful not to move that beautiful chest too much."

"Okay," I said on an exhale.

Kye's fingers hooked in the band of my jeans and lacy underwear that matched my bra. "One…" I braced. "Two…" My muscles tensed. "Three."

I lifted my hips, and Kye pulled my jeans down my legs in one swift motion, taking my underwear with them. As he tossed them to the floor, he stared down at me, gaze flicking over every inch of my body as if he were painting it in his mind. "Could watch you forever. Never gonna get tired of memorizing every dip and curve. The way the lines blend and flare. Most beautiful work of art on this Earth and beyond."

"Kyler," I whispered.

He kicked the stool forward and sat, then lowered it and himself. My thighs pressed together on instinct.

"Don't," he growled, his fingers looping around my calves. "Don't hide from me. My favorite gift is you showing me everything. Your fire and your fear. Your tender heart and your fierce protective streak. Your body and your soul. And if you think I don't want to memorize that pretty pussy in every incarnation, you're dead wrong."

My breaths tripped over each other, trying to escape my lungs.

"Tell me I can see you, Sparrow. Every inch. I'm not above begging."

Slowly, I unclenched my thighs.

Kye sucked in air. "Fucking beautiful. You aching?"

"Yes," I breathed.

"Gonna help you through that." With one swift tug, Kye pulled me down the bed. He slung my legs over his shoulders so he was at eye level with the most vulnerable part of me. "Fucking perfect. Already weeping. My girl loves her ink."

I let out a soft laugh. "Feel like I might get addicted. Especially if it ends this way."

"I think that could be arranged." Kye ran his nose along my inner thigh, making me shiver in the best way. His fingers slid through my folds, teasing and toying, making every part of me stand at attention.

Kye's tongue flicked out, circling my clit, and then let loose a soft groan. "Tastes like freedom." Another lash of his tongue against that bundle of nerves. "Like breathing easy." His tongue swirled this time. "Like everything I've ever wanted."

My hands gripped the sides of the bed as Kye slid two fingers inside me. He glided them in and out, then circled in the way I'd guided his hand our first night together. The man didn't miss a trick.

But then he added a new move. As he circled, he curled those fingers inside me, dragging them down my walls. My mouth fell open, and I let out a sound somewhere between a mewl and a moan.

Kye hummed against my clit, sending a whole different wave of sensations through me. Then he circled his tongue, quicker moves that had my walls fluttering.

"Kyler."

He groaned against that bundle of nerves and then sucked deep, his tongue both teasing and demanding. Kye added a third finger, making my back bow.

"Still," he ordered. "Let me take care of you."

I bit the inside of my cheek but nodded. His fingers started up again. Pumping in and out, swirling and dragging. The movements were completely unpredictable, and they set me aflame.

I held on to the bed with everything I had as Kye's lips closed around my clit. As his tongue pressed down, I couldn't hold back anymore.

I broke. Fire and ice flooded me. Everything in me seized, contracting almost painfully before exploding out as if all I was fractured and then rearranged into something I'd never been before.

Kye rode every wave and shudder with me, dragging them out and making them last longer than I thought possible. Until I had nothing left to give.

My chest heaved as I opened my eyes. And all I saw was Kye's creation on the ceiling. He was everywhere. All around me, inside me, part of me.

He slowly pulled his fingers from me and licked them clean. "Goddamn, I could get used to this, Sparrow."

I grinned down at him. "I think I just became an ink addict."

CHAPTER FORTY

Fallon

"ALL MY FRIENDS WANT LUNCH BAGS LIKE ME NOW," GRACIE said as I helped her into my SUV. "Hay Hay, you think you could make theirs pretty, too?"

I glanced at a slightly panicked Hayden in the front passenger seat. "You know, you could probably start a business. Earn some money for extra ice time."

Hayden's head cocked to one side. "Not a bad idea."

The truth was, Kye would pay for all the ice time Hayden wanted. He'd be thrilled to. But we'd talked about how Hayden needed to feel useful and like she was standing on her own. It would be a difficult balance for the brother who wanted to give her everything.

"I told them it was kin-kin-ugi," Gracie said, struggling to pronounce the term.

"Kintsugi," Clem amended.

Gracie frowned. "That's what I said."

Clem rolled her eyes but still had a smile on her face. "You know, maybe we could try it with pottery."

Hayden laughed. "I don't have a lot of gold just lying around for that."

"We could mix gold paint with glue," Clem argued.

"I think that could be super fun," I said as I hopped behind the wheel. "There's a place over in Roxbury where you can break dishes for fun. We could break them and then put them back together."

"Seriously?" Hayden asked.

Clem glanced at me from the back seat. "Will we still get to go if we're staying at Miss Nora's?"

Crap. Crap. Crap.

After consulting with Rose, we'd made the hard decision to have the girls move to Colson Ranch tomorrow. We couldn't risk putting them in any sort of danger. Kye and I could still drive them to school, and Nora would bring them over for movies and dinners, but they would stay with her until this monster was caught.

"We are going to do all our things. Even bedtime stories. This is just to be sure we're extra careful," I assured Clementine.

"You mean so the stupid system thinks you're good parents," Hayden muttered. "You're the best people we've ever had in our lives."

"She's right," Gracie said softly.

My heart felt like it had been put in a vise in the best *and* worst ways. "You guys are amazing. And because you are, we all need to make extra sure you're taken care of. It won't be for long, and we'll go to the breaking-dishes place this weekend."

Gracie's head tilted to one side. "I do wanna break some things."

I couldn't help but laugh. We spent the rest of the car ride to school, making plans for the following weekend. I wasn't sure how Kye would feel about the outing, but he'd get on board when he saw how excited the girls were.

I glanced down at my phone in the holder, hoping he'd texted me. He'd had a meeting with his lawyer first thing this morning to go over his adoption filing since proceedings had begun for the state to terminate Renee's parental rights. But I hadn't heard anything from him yet.

Taking a deep breath, I tried to calm my nerves and turned into the elementary school parking lot. It didn't take long to make it to the front. I hopped out to help Gracie as Clem and Hayden got out. Gracie threw her arms around me. "I love you, Fallon."

The admission caught me off guard. It was out of the blue and completely unexpected, but it hit me right in the dang feels. I hugged her tightly. "Love you more than double-chocolate Oreo milkshakes."

Gracie beamed up at me. "Really?"

"Really," I assured her.

"Come on," Clem called. "We're gonna be late."

Gracie released me and ran off with her sister. Hayden waved as she headed to the next building over. God, they were the best kids.

I moved to climb into my SUV, but a flash of color caught my eye. A bright pink puffy jacket and a woman glaring daggers at me. Everything in me stilled. Renee.

I braced to move, to walk right into the elementary school and warn the administration, but she dipped into a sedan with a dent on the front bumper and along the side. It sputtered to life, and she took off.

Someone behind me honked, and I turned to see the same impatient man who had honked at Kye. I sent him my best death glare. Unfortunately, it didn't scare him like Kye's had, so I just climbed into my vehicle and texted Trace about the Renee sighting. He or another officer could stop by her place and issue a warning.

After taking my sweet time to get settled, I pulled away from the curb and headed for DHS. About halfway there, my phone dinged. My gaze flicked to the screen, hoping to see Kye's name. Instead, it was Rose.

I tried not to let disappointment hit me too hard. I hit a button on the steering wheel. "Read me text message."

My phone responded through my SUV's speakers in that computerized voice. "You have one new text message from Rose Hawley. Rose said, 'Morning, Fal. We got a call out for two sisters needing emergency placement. Their mother overdosed and is en route to the hospital. Can you meet Noah at 6233 Whychus Lane?'"

I pressed another button on the wheel. "No problem. On my way. About ten minutes out."

The feeling of dread simmering in me was for more than the poor girls whose mother had just been taken away by the EMTs. It was because I'd have to deal with Noah. But it would have happened sooner or later, so I might as well get it over with.

I arrived quicker than expected, but as I pulled up to the run-down cabin, only one vehicle was there—a navy sedan that looked like an unmarked law enforcement vehicle. Maybe Noah hadn't made it here yet.

Parking, I slid out of my SUV and grabbed my bag, jacket, and keys. I headed toward the front door just as the wind picked up, the cold chilling me straight to the bone. Just before I reached the door, crying started up. A baby's wails.

Poor thing was probably terrified. I tried to remember what I had in terms of supplies. I knew I had diapers and formula, but I wondered if I had toys. I knocked twice on the door, but the officer probably couldn't hear me over the crying—it had only gotten louder.

I tested the knob, and it turned. I knew I shouldn't enter until I got confirmation of law enforcement's presence, but the crying was too much for me to take. Pulling the door open, I stepped inside. It took a second for me to realize what was wrong. The cabin was too cold, too dark, and there was no furniture in it at all.

In the time it took me to realize the wrongness, I'd lost the chance to run. Something slammed into me, sending me hurtling back into a wall, hitting it so hard lights danced in front of my eyes. The blow stunned me so badly that I didn't even have a chance to defend myself.

Hands encircled my neck, squeezing as a masked face filled my vision. Some zombie with dead eyes. It kept me from seeing who might be beneath. I tried to bring my knee up, even as my vision started to tunnel.

The figure in front of me twisted, avoiding the worst of the blow, but let out a snarl. "He doesn't deserve you. He doesn't deserve happiness."

I could barely hear the words, but the growly tenor didn't hit as anyone I recognized. My ears rang, and my vision started to go black. But then I heard Kyler clear as day in my mind. *"Don't let him win. Shoot your arms straight up. Break his hold."*

It was as if my body listened before my brain caught on. I shot my arms up with everything I had, my purse clocking the guy in the face in the process. My knee came up on instinct, following through with the sequence I'd gone through with Kye countless times in the gym as Clem and Gracie practiced.

The man folded over, cupping his balls, and I didn't wait. I ran. I ran with everything I had, out the front door and into my SUV. My hand shook violently as I locked the door, but my keys were still there. My purse was still hooked on my arm.

I started the engine, gunned it, and sent gravel flying as I sped out. I didn't think. I just drove, hitting the button on my wheel as I did. "Call Kyler."

CHAPTER FORTY-ONE

Kye

MY FINGERS DRUMMED THE STEERING WHEEL AS I REPLAYED the conversation with my attorney over and over. It had a war of emotions playing out in my mind. On the upside, she felt like between Fallon and me, we had a strong case for adoption. But one thing stood in our way: the monster who had been picking off members of The Reapers MC one at a time and seemed to have targeted me.

The sooner Trace and the Mercer County Sheriff's Department could catch this guy, the better. If they didn't, she said she wasn't sure any judge would approve adoption. And the girls would be caught in limbo.

Apparently, Renee hadn't shown up for a few of her motion hearings. My lawyer assured me that it would help speed along the termination of her parental rights. Judges didn't appreciate parents being no-shows when their children were at risk of being taken away.

Honestly, that was the best gift Renee could give those girls—could give all of us. Simply letting them go. She'd never been a mother to me, and not once had she been one to them. Letting them go would be the most motherly thing she could do.

But I knew it wouldn't come without pain for my sisters. One day, they'd know she hadn't bothered to fight for them. She hadn't shown up for them. I just had to hope the family we were creating would be a balm for that.

Just like I hoped a judge could see just how much I loved my sisters and how I would put my all into giving them the permanent home they deserved.

When that happened, we were taking a trip to a private island. Maybe I'd take the whole Colson crew. We'd go for two weeks, soak up the sun, and celebrate that we were a family. Because by then, we'd damn well have earned it.

Fallon's ringtone cut through my truck's speakers, and I hit the answer button on my wheel. "Hey, Sparrow—"

"He tried to kill me—"

My blood turned to ice. "What? Who? Where are you?"

"I—I don't know who. I don't know where he is—I...I don't know where I am—"

Sheer terror shot through me as I pulled to the side of the road and pulled up Fal's location on my device.

"—I'm driving—I—off Whychus Lane—I—"

"I found you. I'm on my way. Stay on the phone. Do you see him behind you?" I barked.

"N-n-no. I d-d-don't see him." Fallon's teeth chattered violently, making it hard for her to get the words out.

"That's good, baby. That's so good. Just keep driving." I swerved back onto the two-lane road and gunned my engine. I hoped like hell one of Trace's deputies saw me because I'd lead them straight to Fallon. "You're gonna see me coming straight for you. Look for my truck."

"Wh-what i-if h-he g-g-gets me?"

"He's not gonna get you, Sparrow. I'm the only one who's getting you, okay? Just me." I pressed my foot harder against the gas, not giving a damn.

"O-o-okay," she stammered.

"I'm right here. I'm not going anywhere, and neither are you."

Rage flooded my system, terror battling for supremacy. And then I saw the white SUV.

Fallon was flying down the road at full speed, weaving slightly.

"I see you, Sparrow. I see you. Slow down. Pull over."

"I'm scared," she croaked.

"I know. But I'm here. I've got you. Like always. Just slow down."

The speed of the white SUV dwindled, and she jerked it to the side of the road. But I didn't slow until seconds before I shot across the pavement. My tires squealed as I slammed on my brakes, and then I was out of my truck and running for Fallon.

I tried to jerk her door open, but the locks were engaged. Fallon struggled with the handle for moments that felt like a lifetime. Finally, she managed to open it. She tumbled out into my hold as sirens sounded in the distance. Someone must've seen me flying like a bat out of hell.

Sobs racked Fallon's body as she climbed me like someone trying to board a life raft.

"Are you hurt? Tell me where you're hurt."

"N-not hurt," she struggled to say as the sirens got louder. Closer.

I looked down the road, trying to see if anyone had been following her, but I didn't see a soul.

I brushed a hand over the side of her face, trying to pull back so I could get a look at her. That's when I noticed it. Her skin had gone unnaturally pale, but I saw angry red marks wringing her neck. Fury lit in my veins, and it took everything in me to shove it down, way down to where the demons lived.

"Sparrow," I rasped. "Your fucking neck."

"I-I'm okay."

There she was, trying to make me feel better, when someone had strangled her—so hard they'd burst blood vessels under her skin.

"You're not okay," I snarled.

A door slammed, the closest sirens cutting off. "Kye?"

I turned, still cradling Fallon in my arms. Some part of me recognized Deputy Fletcher as the officer walking toward us, but I could only get out one thing. "Someone just tried to kill my wife."

CHAPTER FORTY-TWO

Fallon

I WATCHED KYE'S STRUGGLE PLAY OUT IN THE TATTOOED FINGERS gripping mine. The stark white hospital blanket that the kind nurse had laid over me when I started to shiver acted like a backdrop for the show. He tried his hardest to keep those fingers on mine gentle, but they'd slowly tighten, his anger or fear taking hold. Then he'd have to force them to loosen, and the process would start all over again.

I'd made a study of Kyler's fingers over the years: long and strong, callused and broad. I'd watched as he added to the ink, bit by bit. But I'd missed something.

I stared at the finger with the black metal band and the patchwork of ink beneath it. It was a tapestry of hidden designs. I saw another sparrow peeking out of a tangle of vines and leaves and initials tucked into the curve of them. *F.C.*

"You have me on your ring finger," I croaked.

The sound of my voice made Kye wince, and I didn't blame him. It had gotten worse and worse as the hours progressed. Kye's gaze dipped to his hand. "Only one person I've ever wanted there."

But there was something about the *way* Kye said those words, like a bone-deep sadness coated every syllable.

I squeezed his hand hard, wanting him to know I was strong. "I'm fine."

There'd been no argument about me going to the hospital. An ambulance had come, and Kye had gotten right in the back with me. The demons flaring in his eyes told me not to fight it.

"You don't know that. We're waiting for a CT scan to make sure there are no injuries to your goddamned brain. So, you don't know."

"Kyler," I whispered.

He scrubbed his free hand over his face. "I'm sorry. You don't need that. Don't need—"

I squeezed his hand again, putting all my force into it. "Let me tell you what I need. Right now, it's you here, holding my hand. You not hiding what you're feeling from me."

Kye met my gaze, his amber eyes blazing. "Can't give you that last part. Not right now."

I knew it was because he didn't trust himself. Thought if he let it out, it would drown him.

I traced circles on the back of his hand. "Okay. Not right now."

The curtain pulled back just as he jerked his head in a rough nod.

"Knock, knock," a feminine voice said as she entered the little cubicle. She looked to be in her mid-fifties with golden skin and black hair with hints of silver threaded through it. "I'm Dr. Alvarez. How are you feeling, Ms. Colson?"

"Please," I rasped. "Call me Fallon. My throat hurts a little, but that's it."

"She was wincing earlier," Kye argued. "Do you think you could get her some painkillers?"

Dr. Alvarez's expression softened. "Are you in pain anywhere other than your throat?"

I shook my head, regretting the move when my neck protested. "Just my throat and neck. Maybe a little sore from hitting the wall."

Kye's hand spasmed around mine.

"Okay." Dr. Alvarez crossed to me, pulling a penlight out of her pocket. "Any dizziness or nausea currently?"

"No."

She flashed the light across one eye and then the other. "Good news. Your brain looks perfectly healthy and injury-free on the CT scan. I'm not seeing or hearing any signs of concussion. Your throat should feel better in a couple of days, but it may take a couple of weeks for the bruising around your neck to go away."

She sent me a soft smile. "Lots of tea with honey for your throat. Soft foods like soup and mashed potatoes. You can take ibuprofen and Tylenol, and if it's bad, I'll send you home with a prescription for something a little stronger."

"You don't need—"

"Sparrow," Kye said, cutting me off.

I heard such pleading in his voice that I couldn't find it in me to argue.

"You don't have to take it if you don't want to, but it'll be good to have. Are there addiction concerns?" Dr. Alvarez asked. "Because we can make a plan for that."

"No, nothing like that. I just don't think I'll need it."

"Okay, then. We'll send it home with you, just in case. If the pain gets to a six on a scale of ten, I want you to take it. Sound good?"

I nodded, making the pain in my neck flare.

Kye looked up at the doctor. "You're absolutely sure there's nothing we need to be concerned about? Could there be something the CT couldn't see? Are there other tests we should do? I can pay out of pocket."

Dr. Alvarez's soft expression turned Kye's way then. "We don't see anything concerning. These types of incidents are always scary, but Fallon is lucky. She defended herself. She got away. If she seems confused, throws up, or gets dizzy, bring her back. But I don't think she'll experience any of those things."

"Maybe you should admit her just to be safe—"

"Kyler," I said gently. "I don't want to stay in a hospital. I want to go home and sleep in our bed."

"Rest is the best thing for Fallon right now. And she'll likely get more of it at home," Dr. Alvarez pointed out. "I know Dr. Avery is your personal physician. I'm sure he'd make a house call to give you a once-over tomorrow."

"I'll text him now." Kye pulled his phone out of his pocket and started angrily texting with one hand while still holding mine with the other.

I sent Dr. Alvarez a pleading look, hoping she would understand what I was asking for.

She nodded slightly and turned back to Kye. Once he'd finished his text, she said, "Fallon is going to be just fine. She's very lucky to have you looking out for her."

Kye's gaze flicked up to the doctor, a tortured look in his amber eyes. "You're right. She'll be just fine."

Neither of us missed his lack of response to the other part of Dr. Alvarez's statement. She cleared her throat. "All right. I'll just get those discharge papers ready. You have quite the crew waiting for you in the lobby. Would you like me to update them?"

Kye shoved back his chair. "I'll do it."

I opened my mouth to argue but then quickly shut it.

Kye bent, his gaze zeroed in on my neck as he moved. He brushed his lips across my temple. "Be right back."

Dr. Alvarez stayed behind for a moment as Kye strode out of the little cubicle. She sent me an understanding look. "It can be hard for those who charge themselves with our protection. When something happens to us, they can take it as a personal failure. Give him time, and make sure he talks to someone."

She spoke as if from personal experience, and that ache settled deeper in my chest. "I will… I just… none of this is his fault. But he'll take it on anyway."

She reached out and squeezed my hand. "Don't let him."

My eyes burned as the doctor left the room because I knew Kye's demons had a hold of him now. I would have to beat back every single one.

Covered in blankets, I burrowed deeper into the couch, surrounded by the entire Colson crew, minus Trace and Anson. There was no way to shelter the girls from what was happening. They would've instantly realized something had happened by looking at my neck. Ellie and Mom had done their best to prepare them, but all three had started crying when they saw me.

Endless hugs and a few jokes later, they'd settled a bit. Mom had put on a huge pot of soup, and Sutton had made two loaves of delicious bread. Rhodes had brought a ton of cut flowers over and got the girls making bouquets to "bring the happy" to the house. And it had helped to give them something to do. A purpose.

Kye's tattooed fingers pulled my blanket up a little higher. "How are you feeling now? What's the pain level?"

I glanced over at him, trying to read the thoughts swirling in those amber eyes. "I'm a lot better. The tea and soup helped. I'm probably a three."

Kye frowned, and I suddenly wished I'd said one. I lifted an arm from under the blanket. "I'm good, really. I just want you to check my tattoo and make sure nothing got messed up."

"I'm sorry, did you say tattoo?" Cope asked incredulously.

My cheeks heated a bit. "Yes. Kye gave me my first tattoo yesterday."

Lolli's eyes brightened. "I love it. But I wish you'd consulted me first. You know I have lots of ideas for artistic expression."

Rhodes snorted. "Yeah, if you wanted penis pumpkins, donut dicks, or an elven throuple on your ass cheek."

"Rhodes Stirling," Mom clipped. "Watch your language around tender ears."

Gracie frowned. "What's a throuple?"

Keely rolled her eyes. "I tried asking, and they wouldn't tell me."

Ellie pinched the bridge of her nose in a very Trace-like move. "Trace is going to have a conniption."

"Thoughts and prayers for the teachers of any of these children," Sutton called from the kitchen.

Linc rubbed Arden's belly. "Definitely investing in ear protection for these little ones."

Arden looked up at him. "I don't think there's enough ear protection in the world to protect us from Lolli."

She let out a huff. "I would've thought all your coupling up would've led to a little more living by now. I'm worried about your extracurricular activities if you're this prudish."

"You know I'll never let *our* coupling end in prudishness," Walter said, waggling his eyebrows as he set down a platter of baked goods he'd brought from The Mix Up.

"You can't pin me down, you old-timer," Lolli shot back as her cheeks pinked. "But you are a step up on the interesting meter given this lot."

Shep wrapped an arm around Thea, trying not to laugh. "If this leads to Cope talking about his dick size again, I'm out."

"Shepard Colson," Mom warned.

Thea just laughed, shaking her head. "It wouldn't be a Colson family gathering if there wasn't a phallic conversation of some sort."

Everyone laughed at that. But as they did, the front door opened. Trace, Anson, Gabriel, and Dex made their way inside, the heaviness of the day clearly still with them. But there was something more.

Kye sat up, his gaze sweeping over each of their faces. "You found something."

CHAPTER FORTY-THREE

Kye

A PHANTOM ENERGY BUZZED BENEATH MY SKIN AS IF SOMEONE had injected pure adrenaline into my bloodstream. The urge to pace was strong, but I couldn't leave Fallon. Not when she'd told me all she wanted was my hand in hers. With all the ways I'd failed her, the least I could give her was that.

It felt like it took years for Ellie, Nora, Sutton, Walter, and Lolli to get the kids downstairs for a movie. Clem had wanted to stay, but Hayden had dipped her head, speaking quiet words to her sister that had her following the rest of them. When the door to the basement finally closed, all eyes moved to our newcomers.

"Tell us what you know," I clipped.

Trace sent me a quelling look as he sat on the coffee table in front of Fallon and me. "First, we need to get a statement from Fallon." He searched Fal's face. "I can have Beth come out if you'd prefer—"

"No," Fallon said quickly. "I'd rather you do it."

"Okay," Trace said softly. "Want me to clear the room?"

Various siblings made sounds of protest at that, and Trace would have to kill me if he wanted me to leave Fallon's side.

"Enough," Trace barked, the authority he rarely used bleeding into his voice. "We will do whatever it takes to make Fallon feel comfortable, and I will kick every single one of your asses out of here if I have to."

"He's right," Thea said quietly. "It's hard enough to talk about this sort of thing out loud." Her gaze met Fallon's, so much understanding in her green eyes. "Whatever you need, we're here, Fal."

"Love you," Fallon whispered, her eyes shining. Because my sparrow was the ultimate empath, and she knew Thea was speaking from her experiences and pain.

"Love you, too," Thea whispered. "And I'll kick anyone's ass who tries to hurt you again."

"Anson's building me a murder shed, so I've got us covered for the torture portion of events," Rhodes added, completely deadpan.

"Reckless," Anson growled. "Don't say that shit in front of the cops."

"We're actually the sheriff's department," Gabriel corrected helpfully.

Fallon's lips twitched. "And how does the sheriff's department feel about murder sheds? Asking for a friend, of course."

Gabriel chuckled. "Don't make us arrest you."

Fallon smiled, then took a deep breath, her tongue darting out to wet her bottom lip. "I'm ready."

"Can I get your permission to record this?" Gabriel asked, pulling out his phone. "Trace will handle the questioning, but it will help to have a recording to refer back to."

Fallon gripped my hand harder. "Of course."

Trace leaned forward, his elbows on his knees. "If you need to stop and take a break, just say the word, okay?"

Fal nodded.

"Tell me about your morning. Walk me through what happened," Trace said, his voice gentle.

Fallon glanced at me before starting, and I nodded—as if that little movement could encourage her in some way. She swallowed, making the marks on her neck flutter. "We got up and did breakfast with the girls. Kye went to a meeting with his lawyer, and I took the girls to school."

Another failure to add to the tally. With everything going on, I never should've left them alone. I should've had one of my brothers with them or a goddamned security guard. I'd be remedying that stat. Nora would take the girls tonight, and hopefully, Fal would go, too. Then, I was getting them all a security detail until this was done and buried.

"I dropped the girls off and waited for them to get inside," Fallon continued.

"That's when you texted me?" Trace asked.

"Yes." Fallon's gaze flitted to me briefly before dropping. "Because I saw Renee outside the school, across the street."

The pulse in my neck fluttered wildly as a million what-ifs passed through my mind. *Had she been a part of this? Had she gotten someone to attack Fallon?*

"It wasn't the first time," Fallon continued.

I instantly sat up straighter. "What do you mean, it wasn't the first time?"

Fal worried her bottom lip. "The day we picked out furniture, she walked by as Ellie and I left. Said some choice things. I put her in her place. That was it. I just...there was something about her watching today. It looked like she was truly furious."

Fucking hell. Why hadn't she told me? How was she not pissed as hell that I'd brought this sort of thing into her life?

Trace drummed his fingers on his knees. "Did she say anything today? Make any threatening moves?"

"No. She just glared." Fallon looked between Trace and me. "You don't think—she wouldn't—" Fal swallowed hard again, cutting herself off.

"Let's just have you finish telling us what happened, okay? Then we'll give you all the information we have."

"A-all right."

I hated the tremor in Fallon's voice. It seeped into the air around her and then made a home in me, lighting a fury that took me out at the knees. Those demons I knew so well swirled, the ones that spoke in a language of violence and darkness. The ones that demanded blood for what had been done to Fallon.

Trace nodded and gave her a small, reassuring smile. "Tell me what happened next."

"I headed toward the DHS offices, but on the way, I got a text message from Rose about a new case. She asked me to meet Noah at an address."

Dex and Anson shared a look that had my skin prickling. There was something there. Something about that message.

The moment Deputy Fletcher arrived on the scene, Fallon begged him to send officers to the house to check on the children. But there had been none. The cabin had been foreclosed on years ago, and no one lived there.

Fallon took a deep breath. "When I got to the address, only one car was there. I didn't recognize it, but I thought it was an unmarked law enforcement vehicle."

"How come?" Trace pressed.

"Navy sedan. No markings."

"Did you happen to get a plate?"

Fallon shook her head, making wisps of blond hair flutter around her face. "Sorry, no. I should've known something was up, but I thought maybe I was late or something."

Trace leaned forward and rested a hand on Fallon's blanket-covered knee. "None of this is your fault, okay? Not one damn thing."

Fallon bit her lip but nodded. "As I walked up to the front door, I heard crying inside. It was so real. I would've bet my life that a child was in the cabin."

Dex's jaw clenched so hard the muscle in it started to flutter. "It was a recording."

"The unsub left it behind. A digital recorder," Anson explained.

"Oh, God," Fallon whispered.

Fury lit anew. The level of manipulation and deception scared the hell out of me. Because it wasn't just hatred. It was smart and calculated. They'd lured Fallon to a house with one of the few pieces of bait they knew she'd never question.

"When no one answered, I just went in." Fallon's fingers dug into the back of my hand. "I thought an officer might have had their hands full with a crying baby and couldn't get to the door. But when I stepped inside, someone flew at me. They slammed me against the wall and then started choking me."

I couldn't imagine how terrified she must've been. How out of her mind with fear and terror.

Trace's sheriff's mask was in place now, hiding everything he was battling like I was. "Did you get a look at the assailant?"

"No, I—they were wearing some sort of zombie mask. And the eyes were black. I couldn't even see that."

"What about size? Skin color?" Trace pressed.

"I-I don't know. Taller than me."

But that wasn't hard. Fallon was petite and willowy.

She twisted the blanket around her fingers. "Gloves. He was wearing gloves. And a hoodie. I didn't see any skin at all."

"What about a voice?" Trace asked. "Did he say anything to you?"

Fallon's gaze drifted to the side.

"He did," Trace surmised.

"I didn't recognize his voice," Fallon croaked.

"What did he say?" Anson asked softly. "It's important."

Fallon's fingers twisted tighter in the blanket as she stared down at her lap. "He said, 'He doesn't deserve you. He doesn't deserve happiness.'"

Everything in me went still. It was as if the world had stopped spinning. I didn't breathe, feel, or...anything else.

I knew it had to be about me. My goddamned past. The reckless choices I'd gotten Fallon mixed up in. But hearing it like this? I couldn't take it.

Trace swore.

"But I—I remembered what Kye taught me." Fallon looked up at me, all innocent trust. "I heard your voice in my head, telling me to fight, telling me exactly what to do. I broke his hold, kneed him in the balls, and ran."

"Damn straight, you did," Cope praised, but there were unshed tears in his eyes as he spoke.

Fallon squeezed my hand as if begging. "You helped me get free."

But she wouldn't have had to break free in the first place if it weren't for me. My gaze cut to Anson and Dex. "Tell me what you found out."

There was no request in my tone. It was a brutal demand, and Anson didn't wait for permission. "Someone cloned Rose's cell phone."

"What?" Fallon rasped.

"It's easier than you might think," Dex explained. "If you can get the person to click a link in a text message or email on the device, it can grant a hacker access."

My tongue stuck to the roof of my mouth as I struggled to swallow.

"They were able to text you as her and receive any responses, as well," Dex went on. "Neither of you would've known."

"That's pretty damn ballsy," Linc muttered. "What if she was already at DHS when the text came in?"

Anson and Dex shared another look.

"What?" I snarled.

Gabriel held up a hand, telling me to keep it together. "We had our evidence techs give your vehicles a once-over when we brought them back to you. The SUV that was vandalized, as well. There were trackers on both of them."

A buzzing lit in my ears as I struggled to breathe. "They knew exactly where we were at all times."

"Yes," Anson said, not pulling any punches. "It's clear that whoever this is has an obsession with you—wants to hurt you in any way they can."

"And how the hell am I supposed to keep my family safe?" I ground out.

No one spoke. Because no one had the answer. And worse, it was because of me that they were even in danger in the first place.

CHAPTER FORTY-FOUR

Fallon

I TRACED THE MARKS ALREADY TURNING PURPLE ON MY NECK. It would be a rough few weeks before they went away. At least it was winter now, so I could get away with a scarf or turtleneck. Because every time Kye looked at my throat, guilt swam in his eyes.

But there was no hiding right now. All I had was one of Kye's tees that fell to my mid-thighs. But as I inhaled deeply, the scents of oakmoss, amber, and Kye swirled. It was exactly the comfort I needed. I just wished I could give Kye the same thing.

I'd seen a piece of him die as he watched the girls pile into Mom's SUV to stay with her until this was all over. No bedtime story would soothe the fact that their lives had been disrupted again. But we would do everything we could to make sure they knew we were there for them no matter what. Even if they weren't sleeping under our roof.

Sighing, I stepped back from the vanity mirror and moved to walk back into the bedroom. As my hand closed around the knob, I took a deep breath to steady myself. The soft strains of Kye's voice seeped through the door, and I frowned as I opened it.

"Yeah, I think a four-person team would be good," Kye said into his phone as he ran a hand through his hair. "Clem and Gracie are at the same school and do many of the same activities."

He was quiet for a moment. "Thanks, Holt. I really appreciate you sending your best people. Trace has deputies on the house and schools until then." A second later, he lowered the phone.

"Something you want to tell me?" I asked.

Kye whirled around, looking so damn exhausted and ravaged that any frustration I had melted away. He gripped his phone tighter as his gaze zeroed in on my neck. "I asked Holt to refer me to his security company. I want a detail on all of you until we catch this person."

I swallowed hard, the movement painful but also keeping me from saying something I'd regret. "Okay."

Kye arched a brow. "You're not going to fight me on it?"

I stared at him for a long moment. "No. Because I know you're beating yourself up for this, and I'm not going to be mad about a few extra sets of eyes keeping us all safe."

A muscle fluttered in his jaw. "Who else should I blame? This is happening because of me." He slammed a fist against his chest. "Because *I* got mixed up in fucked-up shit." He slammed his fist again. "Because *I* thought I could have you without ruining you. But I did so much worse. I almost got you fucking killed."

A different kind of fear lit inside me, worse than when I'd been chased on the road, worse even than when I'd been strangled. But I refused to cower. I got right up in Kye's face, grabbed him by his tee, and held on.

"Don't you dare," I snarled. "You didn't kill those people. You didn't come after me. You didn't try to steal all the air from my lungs. Did you?"

"I lit the goddamned match, Fallon. Whoever this is, they're after me because of what *I* got mixed up in."

"So?" I demanded. "They're fixated on you because you were involved in some underground fights. Anson became a target because he was a profiler. Thea because she showed someone kindness. Cope because he was good at hockey. Is it their fault, too?"

"But I was fucking selfish," Kye bellowed. "I couldn't leave the promise of you alone. I couldn't be happy being safe and cared for. I needed more. I needed *you*."

"Then I guess it's my fault," I shot back.

Kye gaped at me. "Of course, it's not."

"I'm glad you think that's as stupid as it sounds, but it's just as stupid as you blaming yourself."

"I won't be the reason you get hurt. Worse," Kye rasped. "I can't—you can't ask me to—I can't lose you, Fallon."

I muttered a curse and dropped my hold on his shirt so I could reach up and frame his face. "You're not going to lose me. As long as we both keep holding on." Tears filled my eyes. "I can't lose you either. And thinking about you walking away is more than I can take."

Tears slid down Kye's cheeks. "What if walking away is the only thing that will keep you safe?"

"That's not true. This unsub, or whatever you want to call him, already knows we love each other. You think walking away will change that? It'll just ensure I'm alone as a target. What good is that?"

"Sparrow," he begged.

"I know you want to keep me safe, and you know I'd do anything to keep you that way, too, but the best way for us to do that is to stick together."

"I'm fucking terrified that I'll lose you. That everything my parents said all those years is true. That I ruin everything I touch."

Fucking hell. I wanted to do some serious damage to Renee and Rex. More, I wanted them to feel the pain they'd inflicted on their son. The agony. The demons they'd put in him.

I stretched onto my tiptoes and held my face to Kye's. "You don't ruin a damn thing. You make everything better. You're like the gold in those broken Japanese pots Clem told us about. You take broken things and make them beautiful. You take tender spots and make them strong. But most of all, you let us be exactly who we are and love us for it."

"Sparrow…" He said my name like a prayer he desperately wanted to believe in.

"Stop listening to the people who never knew you. Who never

loved you. They don't get to decide who you are. Only you can do that."

Kye lifted me, my tee riding up as my legs encircled his waist. He gently burrowed his face into the crook of my neck. "Sometimes, it feels like they're burned into me: their voices and taunts."

"Burn the truth in instead. Burn me in." My finger sifted through his hair. "Strong, fierce, kind, gentle. Funny, smart, beautiful, loving. Everything I could ever dream up for myself. Everything I could ever hope for those girls."

Kye pulled back then, his eyes wet. "Don't leave me, Sparrow."

"I'm not going anywhere."

His mouth met mine then, slow and achingly beautiful. His tongue stroked in like a promise, a vow. Kye took three long strides toward the bed before lowering us to it.

"Love you with everything I am," he whispered, gazing up as I straddled him. "I might not get it perfect—"

"No one does. What matters is that we find our way together." I reached for the hem of the tee I'd stolen from Kye and pulled it up and over my head.

Those amber eyes flared as Kye took me in, his tattooed fingers skimming my waist. "In my tee, nothing beneath except my ink. You trying to do me in, Sparrow?"

"I don't want anything on me but you."

Heat turned Kye's amber eyes golden. "You need to rest—"

I leaned over him, my hair creating a curtain around us as I took his mouth. "I need *you*."

Kye sat up in one fluid motion, ripping off his tee and maneuvering me as he shucked his sweats. "You're gonna let me do the work while you guide the show, okay?"

I pushed up to my knees, fingers closing around his length and stroking. "Sounds like a fair trade to me."

Kye's eyes fluttered closed for a moment as his fingers trailed up my inner thigh. And I knew what this was. It was the ultimate gift of trust. He trusted me not to hurt him, closing his eyes in his most vulnerable state.

As his fingers found my core, those dark eyes opened again. Heat, desire, and love had made a home there. "Love you, Sparrow." His fingers stroked in, circling in the way I loved. "Everything I have to give is yours."

"You. That's all I want. All I need." I couldn't hold in my moan as Kye's fingers curled, dragging down my walls. "Kyler."

"My name on your lips... I'll never get tired of the sound."

My hips rocked against his fingers, and I reveled in the pressure as I stroked Kye. The hint of wetness at the tip had my walls contracting around his fingers.

"She's killing me before I'm even inside her," Kye muttered.

My mouth curved. "Let's see what we can do about that."

I guided him to my entrance as his fingers slid from me. The stretch walked that line between pleasure and pain, the one we all had to walk if we wanted to live life to its fullest, but I simply let myself feel it all.

My eyes fluttered closed as I slowly slid onto him. Breathing through the stretch and the pressure. Feeling him fill me and knowing it would never change. Because I was in him just as he was in me.

"Show me those blue eyes, Sparrow. Let me see my haven," Kye coaxed.

I eased my eyes open, taking in the man below me. "I love you, Kyler."

"Never experienced anything so beautiful, hearing those words as you take me. Feeling them everywhere."

I rocked against him, testing movements to see if I was ready. Ready for more. Ready for everything.

Kye met me there, doing exactly what he'd said, taking over the effort and the strain on his shoulders but giving me all the control. He let me lead because he listened to my words, to my body. And that was Kyler. So attuned to everything about me that he could move, even before I'd stated a need.

He circled my nipple with his thumb, careful not to stray anywhere near my new ink. The peak tightened, reaching out for more of Kye. His touch, his promises.

We moved together and apart, finding something new that could only ever exist with each other. Kye powered in and out of me, stretching me and making my walls flutter around him. My fingers dug into his shoulders as my back arched and I took everything he had to give.

It was more tonight. More than ever before. Because that final wall had come down, unlocking something new in both of us.

"Sparrow," he rasped. "Let go. Together. Find it with me." His thumb circled my clit, sending sparks dancing through me and setting my blood aflame.

My walls trembled in waves as Kye thrust deeper, both of us giving each other the final piece we needed. My body fractured, and Kye's golden light filled me in every way. Just like those pieces of pottery. I took and took and took some more, and Kye rode out every wave with me, not losing my eyes for even a moment. And as the final swell peaked, I fell onto him, knowing he would catch me.

Just like always.

CHAPTER FORTY-FIVE

Fallon

"How are you feeling?" Kye asked as he carried over a tray laden with soup, mashed potatoes, tea, and, of course, a milkshake.

God, he was so damn adorable. Something about this tattooed mountain of a man making everything the doctor had suggested just melted me. "I feel like I could've gone to work." Kye opened his mouth to speak, but I kept on going. "*But* I'm not going to be mad at a day of spoiling."

"A week," Kye argued.

"Kyler…"

"Meet me in the middle. Three days."

I huffed out a breath. "I like my routine. I want to take the girls to school, go to a job I love, spend my evenings with you."

"Evenings like last night?" Kye said, a smile stretching across his face.

"Don't be cocky," I warned, but I couldn't help the smile teasing my lips at the memories of last night.

Kye's grin went slightly off-kilter in that way I loved. "Who, me? I'd never."

"Sure," I muttered.

A ringing phone cut off our conversation, and Kye shifted to pull his cell out of his pocket and hit the icon for the front gate speaker box. "Hello?"

"It's me." Trace's voice crackled over the intercom. "And I've got someone with me who has an interesting development."

I reached over and wove my fingers through Kye's, wanting him to know I was there.

"Way to be cryptic, asshole," Kye muttered.

I heard a voice chuckle in the background. Deep and husky. "Nothing like brothers."

I frowned while Kye scowled. "Come on up."

The moment he disconnected the call, he stood, giving my hand a squeeze before releasing it.

"Who do you think it is?" I asked softly.

Kye shook his head. "I have no clue."

I could see the energy crackling below Kye's surface. As if he couldn't have stayed still for all the money in the world. Looking up, I met his gaze and held it. "Whoever it is, whatever it is, we'll deal."

"Together."

"Together."

A swift knock sounded, and Kye crossed to the door, punching a button on the security panel before opening it. He held it as a parade of men entered the house. Four I recognized, and one I didn't. Trace, Dex, Anson, and Gabriel led the way, while a mysterious man brought up the rear.

He was tall, just an inch or so shorter than Kye, and broad, with dark hair and scruff lining his jaw. But what stopped me dead were his piercing, dark blue eyes.

Trace moved deeper into the living space. "How are you feeling, Fal?"

"Very pampered," I said with a small smile.

Trace chuckled. "Glad to hear it."

"You gonna tell us what's going on?" Kye muttered, shifting so he was between the stranger and me.

I tried to figure out who the man might be. He wasn't in a uniform of any kind. Instead, he wore worn cowboy boots, dark jeans, a flannel, and a thick jacket. He looked like a rancher, but that didn't make sense.

The man extended a hand to Kye. "I'm Hayes Easton. Sheriff out in Wolf Gap and the surrounding county."

I was familiar with the area with its stunning scenery of mountains and a breathtaking lake, but I didn't have the first clue why he'd be here.

"Let's sit," Trace suggested. "Hayes, this is my sister, Fallon."

Hayes dipped his chin in greeting but didn't approach, which told me a couple of things. One, he'd seen Kye's move and didn't want to appear threatening. And two, he didn't want me to feel uncomfortable. He cemented that bit when he spoke.

"I'm so sorry about what's happened to you, Fallon. If I can help in any way, know I will." There was understanding in those dark blue eyes. The kind that spoke of experience. That only piqued my interest more.

Kye settled next to me, gently pulling me into his side. "So, what does a sheriff from six hours away have to do with this case?"

Everyone went silent for a moment. Dex shifted, shadows swirling in his hazel eyes. Anson's expression had gone carefully blank. And Gabriel dropped his gaze to his shoes.

It was Trace who spoke, meeting Kye's eyes and not looking away. "Hayes has a case that looks like it might intersect with ours. Someone stabbed your birth father. Rex is dead."

Kye went unnaturally still for a long moment. I burrowed deeper against his side, placing a hand over his heart. "Same MO?" Kye croaked.

"Similar," Hayes answered. "This one looks a bit more violent. Overkill."

Kye's throat worked as he struggled to swallow. "It doesn't make sense. He had nothing to do with that fight ring."

"The profile is changing," Anson said quietly. "The unsub's devolving as his rage builds. You and your birth father look alike."

Kye reared back as if he'd been slapped, and I grabbed his hand, holding on with everything I had.

Anson waited for a moment as Kye pulled himself together. "My best guess is that your father was a surrogate for you. When the unsub killed him, in his mind, he was really killing you."

My hand spasmed around Kye's as fear dug in. "Was any evidence left behind?" I croaked. "Anything that will tell us who he is?"

Hayes scrubbed a hand over his face. "Some items are still being processed, but no prints so far. No DNA. And we think he took the knife with him."

I looked at Anson. "What about you? Anything?"

He leaned forward and rested his elbows on his knees. "Here's what I've built so far. A white male, somewhere between the ages of eighteen and thirty-five. Considerable strength. Knowledgeable with computers. There's trauma somewhere in his life. And something in the past month triggered this."

My head swam. That was practically half the population. It didn't exactly make things easier.

"You need to take precautions," Trace said.

"Anchor Security is coming tomorrow. Holt's arranging a security detail for all of us," Kye said.

Hayes's brows lifted. "You know Holt Hartley?"

Kye nodded. "Anson is friends with one of his brothers."

"No shit," Hayes said with a grin. "I've known him for years. And his company does amazing work. That's exactly who you want."

Kye dipped his head to look at me. "See? We're going to be just fine."

I wanted to believe him—wanted to so badly—but I was terrified. "Promise me."

He brushed his lips across mine. "I promise."

My hand fisted in his tee. "And you're not running?" It was a secondary fear. But a fear, nonetheless.

Kye dropped his forehead to mine. "You and me against the world, Sparrow."

"You and me," I whispered.

"*Enchanted!*" Gracie begged as Kye scrolled through movie options in the screening room while my mom knitted in the corner seat nearest a light source. Since she'd brought them over for dinner and movie time, I'd sensed them relaxing a little, trusting that we weren't going anywhere.

"Oooooh, yeah," Clem agreed.

Kye winced. "You guys don't want to watch *Spiderman* or something?"

Gracie's nose wrinkled. "He turns into a spider? No, thank you."

Hayden laughed. "He doesn't turn into a spider. He just has superhuman abilities."

"Spider abilities?" Gracie asked skeptically.

"Kind of," Hayden hedged.

"Nope. No, thank you," Gracie muttered.

Hayden laughed, shrugging as she turned to Kye. "I tried to help you."

"I appreciate the valiant effort, but *Enchanted* for the eighty-seven-millionth time it is," Kye said, resigned.

I pawed through all the candy we had stored down here in a mini concession stand. "Are we seriously out of strawberry Sour Patch Kids?"

"Sparrow, do you honestly think I'd let us be out of your favorite candy?" Kye asked, exasperation coating every word. "I've got three mega packs in the garage."

"Oh."

He laughed as Mom started to rise. "I'll get them."

I held out a hand. "I've got it. I need to move after lying around all day."

The meeting with Trace's team had lasted a while, and afterward, Kye and I had snuggled on the couch while he processed the fact that his birth father was dead. There was a whole stew of emotions: relief, guilt, fear. It would take time for him to come to terms with it all. But I wasn't sad that Rex Blackwood was no longer walking the Earth.

"Anyone need a drink?" I asked as I headed for the stairs.

"Strawberry bubbly water, please," Gracie called.

"Me, too!" Clem cheered.

I climbed the stairs, relishing the feeling of moving my muscles. Tomorrow, I was forcing Kye to go for a walk, even if we had to bring the bodyguards. I pulled drinks from the fridge and set them on the island, then went in search of my beloved candy.

Stepping into the garage, I shivered. The temperature had definitely dropped today. Flipping on the light, I crossed to the shelving unit on the far side of the garage and grinned. Kye had stacked doubles and triples of all my favorites: strawberry Sour Patch Kids, gummy bears, and Reese's peanut butter cups.

My husband was the best.

I reached out for the colorful package but stilled as I heard a squeak. I turned, but it was too late. Someone jerked me back, a hand covering my mouth. No, not just a hand, a rag. And it tasted...sweet?

I sent my elbow flying back. The person grunted but didn't release me.

"Not this time, Fallon. This time, he's going to know what it's like to lose everything."

CHAPTER FORTY-SIX

Kye

"HAY HAY, DO YOU THINK YOU COULD MAKE US PRINCESS DRESSES like this one for Halloween next year?" Clem asked as she pointed to the screen saver with a woman in a true cupcake dress.

Hayden launched a piece of popcorn at her. "Look at how poofy that thing is. It would take me five million hours to sew."

"I could help," I offered.

Hayden eyed me warily. "You want to help me…*sew*?"

"Why not?" I asked, a little affronted.

"Your hands are massive," Hayden pointed out. "I highly doubt you could thread a needle, let alone stitch all those delicate layers of tulle."

I could practically hear Ellie making a *"that's what she said"* joke in my head. She and Lolli were two peas in a pod when it came to the inappropriate remarks.

"We could get a sewing machine," I suggested. "That would probably help."

"I know the perfect starter machine," Nora suggested.

Hayden pressed her lips together, and I could tell she was trying not to laugh.

"What's so funny about me sewing? Think about all the intricate tattoos I ink on people."

That grin flew free then. "I'm just picturing you on some tiny stool covered in tulle and sewing away maniacally."

"What does man-man-eye-ack-ly mean?" Gracie asked, confused.

"Maniacally means in a loud, extreme, or wild way," Clem said instantly.

I turned to the eleven-year-old. "How'd you know that?"

She shrugged. "When I don't know what a word is while I'm reading, I look it up."

"Have I told you lately what an amazing genius you are?" I asked.

Clem's cheeks turned pink, but she nodded. "You told me."

"It's amazing," I praised. "Your brain is incredible."

Clem's gaze shifted to the side.

"What?" I pressed gently.

"Mom always said I was a freak," Clem whispered.

Anger flared somewhere deep as I remembered all the lies Renee had filled my head with over the years. That I deserved the abuse she and Rex heaped on me. That I would ruin anything I touched. It killed me that my sisters had experienced the same. It was the last thing they deserved. I opened my mouth to tell her that, but Gracie got there first.

"Mom's a big ole liar, liar, pants on fire," Gracie growled.

Hayden's mouth curved. "Little G's right. And she's not our mom. Not anymore. She never did anything a mom should do. So, I think we should stop calling her that."

My heart ached, but at the same time, I was so damn proud of them. All of them. Because they were rising up after everything they'd been through. I didn't miss Nora's eyes misting over.

Gracie twisted in her chair, her fleece blanket covered in rainbows moving with her. "Kye Kye?" she asked softly.

"Yeah, Little G?"

She pulled her tiny lip between her teeth like Fallon occasionally did, her nerves clear. But I didn't rush her. I let her take all the time she needed to get her words out. "I know you're our brother, but do you think...could we...would it be okay if we called you Dad and Fallon Mom? Or Daddy Kye Kye and Mama Fal?"

That invisible fist seized my heart in a brutal squeeze. Her wanting that was the last thing I'd ever expected. "Gracie, I'd be honored if you wanted to call me anything like that," I croaked.

"Really?"

"Really. But I am partial to Kye Kye thrown in there. And I bet Fal would feel the same about you calling her Mama Fal." I looked at my other two sisters. "That doesn't mean you have to. You can call me anything you want. Well, maybe not butthead."

Clem giggled. "I'd like to call you Dad. We never really had one of those."

My throat burned, fire racing through me. "I'd love to be that for you."

Hayden twisted her fingers in a blanket. "I think...I think I'd like that. We never had either. Not really."

"Hay, we had you," Clementine argued. "But now you don't have to be that. You can rest and play and do teenager stuff."

Fuck. Clem was so wise beyond her years. Hayden had given up her childhood to take care of her sisters. But she didn't have to anymore. She could be their sister instead of their mother.

I reached over and squeezed her hand. "It's time for you to live. Do whatever it is you want for you."

Hayden's eyes glistened as they lifted to mine. "I love you."

I pulled her into my arms and hugged her tightly. "I love you, too."

"This is even better than the movie," Clem whispered.

"We still get to watch it, though, right?" Gracie asked, worried.

I chuckled as I released Hayden. "Yes, we do. Let me go see what's taking Fal so long. Maybe she decided to make brownies." I wouldn't put it past her.

"Ooooooh, brownies," Clem said happily.

"I'm with you," Nora agreed. "I'll make some if Fal isn't."

I laughed as I climbed the stairs two at a time. Crossing toward the kitchen, I saw the drinks on the counter, but no Fallon.

"Sparrow?" I called as I walked toward the garage. The door to it was open, and the lights were on.

I stilled as I saw yet another door open. The side one to the outside. Blood roared in my ears as my gaze jumped around the space, but I didn't see Fallon anywhere.

I was already moving, my bare feet hitting the garage's cement floor and not even registering the cold. My gaze locked on the alarm panel as a chill skated down my spine. The digital screen read: *Unarmed.*

My heart hammered against my ribs. That wasn't right. It had been set twenty-four-seven since Fallon's attack. We'd taken no chances.

I strode outside, the outdoor motion lights flicking on, but no one was there. Not a single soul.

Jerking my phone from my pocket, I hit Trace's number. My entire body felt like a boa constrictor was wrapped around it, squeezing the air out of me. The life. But I still managed to run for the front of the house as the phone rang.

I knew a deputy in a squad car should be watching the place. The gravel pierced the bottoms of my feet, but I didn't give a damn. I kept right on running.

"Everything okay?" Trace asked by way of answer.

I couldn't get the words out. Not as the squad car came into view. Not as the man I'd known for years, Deputy Fletcher, lay on the ground, bleeding out.

Dropping to my knees, I felt for a pulse. "Send everyone," I croaked. "Send them now. He has Fallon."

CHAPTER FORTY-SEVEN

Fallon

AN INDISCERNIBLE SOUND POUNDED AGAINST MY SKULL, pushing me toward consciousness. My eyelids fluttered, light making its way through in short bursts that had a groan slipping from my lips. The sound I heard intensified. Not a moan. More of a muffled yell.

My eyelids fluttered earnestly as I struggled to take in my surroundings. Nothing about the place was familiar. Old, flimsy walls I guessed had once been white were now yellowed with age, and the seams told me it was an older manufactured home or trailer.

Windows were covered with tinfoil, making it impossible to see in or out. But flowery curtains that looked straight out of the eighties framed them. My frown deepened, making the ache in my head worse as I turned.

And that's when I saw her. A woman screaming through some sort of bandana gag. One I knew.

"Renee?" I croaked.

She kept right on screaming as if it would do something.

I tried to lift a hand to get her to stop and realized my

predicament. My wrists and ankles were bound to a chair. One of those metal ones with a padded seat lined in plastic so nothing would stain it—another thing straight out of the eighties.

Renee's muffled screams got louder.

"Stop," I barked, the word half-command, half-plea. But it silenced the woman opposite me. "Just give me a second." My breaths came in quick pants as I tried to orient myself.

Someone had placed us between the living room and the kitchen. Both those rooms looked straight out of the eighties, too. The couch was one of those autumn velvet deals with plenty of indiscernible stains that turned my stomach. And the TV opposite it was a tubed one framed in wood.

The kitchen also had that aged wooden look, with peeling and stained Formica countertops. But despite that, the place was as neat as if a drill sergeant was in residence. Like the house had been frozen in time. Which made no sense.

I looked for signs indicating who might live here and then saw the portrait—one of those you used to be able to get at the mall. He was only about eight in the picture, somewhere between Gracie's and Clem's age, but I would've recognized Kye anywhere. That dark hair and those amber eyes.

But there was no off-kilter smile I loved. And his whole body was stiff. I could see why. The man sitting behind him was squeezing his shoulder, and I instantly saw the evil in Rex Blackwood's eyes. Renee, on the other hand, looked out of it. Her eyes were a bit glassy and vacant. She was likely high on something.

"This was your house?" I rasped. Whatever the asshole had drugged me with had made my throat scratchy again.

Renee nodded, her eyes red and tear-filled.

"Do you still own it?" I tried to pull the pieces together, but Renee holding on to a house she could have sold for drug money or whatever else she fancied didn't seem logical.

She shook her head.

"Did you sell it?"

Another no.

"Did the bank foreclose on it?"

She nodded.

So, either the bank had turned around and sold it with everything inside, or someone was squatting.

"Did you see who took us?" I asked.

Renee nodded frantically, her eyes going wide.

"Do you know them?" I pressed.

Her mouth flattened as if she were trying to think, but then she shook her head.

So, no one who'd been involved in her and Rex's life back then. It had to be about the fight ring.

I tested the bindings on my wrists and ankles. They were so tight the plastic was cutting into my skin in places. Whoever this was, they didn't give a damn if I got hurt—not that the lack of care was a big shock.

Stilling for a moment, I *really* listened. It didn't sound like anyone else was around. With the windows covered, it would be hard to tell if anyone was close enough to hear me if I screamed or if it would just alert our kidnapper.

I looked back at Renee. "Are there any other houses around here? Anyone who could hear me if I yelled?"

Her amber-brown eyes filled with tears, and she shook her head.

Damn. I tugged at my bindings again, harder this time. All I managed to do was hurt my wrists. "Can you use your teeth to tear the bandana?"

I wasn't sure what Renee's ability to speak would accomplish, but at least we could try to come up with a plan.

She frowned around her gag but started working it with her teeth as I gazed around the room. There was a front door and a side one. Thankfully, I could easily see both and know if someone entered. And then I saw something else.

Cameras.

The kind you could get to watch your pet while you were gone. One moved, turning my blood to ice. Rhodes had gotten one of them to keep an eye on her dog, Biscuit, and I knew you could hear the people in the room, too.

I dipped my head, hoping the person watching the feed couldn't read lips. "There are cameras," I whispered.

Renee stilled.

"Keep working on your bandana," I hissed low.

She nodded but trembled as she did. She caught the fabric with her teeth, getting in a good tear and sending half the gag falling down. Enough so she could speak. "He's going to kill us."

"What does he look like?" I asked.

"I-I...he's got tattoos, and he's mean. He—"

The front door swung open and hit the wall. Hard. "Mean? I'm not mean. I'm delivering *justice*."

I struggled to pull the pieces together in my mind. I recognized the person standing in the doorway, but I also didn't. There was a look of rage in those hazel eyes I'd never seen before.

"Evan?" I croaked.

CHAPTER FORTY-EIGHT

Kye

PEOPLE. SO MANY DAMN PEOPLE. AND NOT ONE OF THEM HAD any clues that could lead to Fallon's whereabouts. Not one had any idea who this monster was.

The power source cable to the gate camera had been snipped, and the person either had my alarm code or the ability to hack it—likely the latter, given Dex's previous statement that they likely had technical know-how. He was still working on fortifying the system.

But we still had nothing. My vision went blurry as people milled around the room at the sheriff's station. It looked like a conference room typically used for meetings, but it felt like a war room now. We were battling some unknown enemy, invisible to us all.

And I couldn't feel a thing. Everything in me had turned off. Gone numb. Because no part of me could live in a world without Fal—my sparrow, my haven.

Dex sat at the conference table, two laptops in front of him. One screen changed on its own as if running a search. His fingers flew across the keyboard of the other, pausing now and then like his brain needed a moment to catch up.

Anson paced back and forth in front of an evidence board, employing a cadence similar to Dex's yet different. He stopped abruptly here and there, eyes fixed on a photo or report, silently assembling the puzzle in his mind as only he could.

Gabriel talked to a handful of his deputies in quiet tones, his mask in place. Harrison Fletcher had been rushed to the hospital, clinging to life. No one knew if he would make it or not, and their whole department was feeling that, too.

A figure moved in front of me, but it took me a moment to register who it was. I had to blink a few times to take in the dark hair, green eyes, and the familiar concern in his expression.

Trace.

"Talk to me," he said quietly.

The words were like a physical blow. He had no idea how close they were to the ones Fallon always spoke. *"Tell me."*

That gentle command was more powerful than anything I'd experienced in this life. And now, I wasn't sure I'd ever hear it again.

"I don't matter right now." My voice sounded dead, even to my ears. As if the syllables held no light or life.

"You'll always matter," Trace argued.

I stared back at him, not saying a word. Because I couldn't. The only thing that mattered in my eyes was Fallon. Her and making sure my sisters were safe. At least I knew the girls were on lockdown. Holt Hartley's crew from Anchor Security had arrived, and my house was crawling with law enforcement. The majority of the Colson crew was there, too. Waiting.

A sick feeling lit somewhere deep, the ugly voices of my past taking root in my mind. *"You ruin everything you touch. You always will."* I felt like I should believe those lies more than ever now.

But then Fallon's voice rang out in my mind. *"Strong, fierce, kind, gentle. Funny, smart, beautiful, loving. Everything I could ever dream up for myself. Everything I could ever dream up for those girls."*

Fallon would never want me to give in to the demons' lies. Would never want me to let the darkness win. So, for her, I would fight.

"I can't lose her." The words were barely audible, some foreign sound between a whisper and a rasp. Still, it felt like a roar.

Trace moved into my space and gripped my shoulders hard. "You aren't going to lose her. None of us are."

"Loved her since the moment I saw her," I croaked. "Standing by the creek and screaming. Everything in her was so raw. So real. I never knew anyone who was that authentic."

Trace's face contorted in confusion. "Screaming?"

"A few years after she lost her dad and brother. Didn't want to burden anyone with everything she was feeling. Processing. But she had to let out."

Trace's expression softened in realization. "And she could let it out with you."

It wasn't a question, but I attempted a nod anyway. "And me with her. Maybe because she was so fierce in that moment. Not afraid of the world knowing exactly how she felt. Whatever it was, I felt like I could lay everything at her feet. And she saw it all and never judged."

"So you...?" Trace swallowed hard. "You two knew each other before you came to live with Nora?"

"The day my dad tried to kill me..." My eyes burned like hellfire as I struggled to hold the tears back. "I kissed Fallon for the first time. And when I did, it was like she cleansed my damn soul. I felt like I could breathe because she gave me air."

"Kye," Trace rasped.

"You know the rules. I couldn't risk someone finding out and kicking me out of Nora's, putting me into one of those group-home situations. No one but Nora Colson would want to take on a kid with my baggage."

Trace's eyes glistened with unshed tears, but he didn't let go of me. "So, you both let go of what you wanted."

"I didn't think I deserved her. Thought I'd ruin her, taint her, and rain down all the darkness that comes with my history and my life on her. A part of me was right—"

"The hell you were." Trace gave me a hearty shake. "You've

helped her soar. No one believes in her more than you do. Cares for her more. And it's been that way for as long as I've known you."

"We make each other better." The tears crested over then, tracking down my cheeks. "I can't lose her. She's my air. She fuels everything. And she makes everyone and everything around her better."

Trace pulled me into a hard hug. "I'm not going to let either of you lose each other. Not when you finally got what you should've had all along. We're gonna find her."

I wanted to believe him. God, I wanted to trust that we'd work this all out. That we'd get a miracle. I released my grip on Trace. "I gotta get some air. Be back."

I moved through the throng of people, ignoring the looks of sympathy and concern on their faces. I stepped outside and sucked in the freezing-cold air. Only it wasn't like kissing Fallon. It didn't cleanse my soul or help me truly breathe. But maybe it would be enough to carry me through until I got my sparrow back.

My phone dinged, and I pulled it out. There were countless unread messages and missed calls, but the most recent stopped my heart cold.

Sparrow: *You want to see her alive again? Go back to the place where it all began.*

A photo was below the text: Fallon zip-tied to a chair in the house I'd grown up in. The one that had been my hell.

Blond hair. Dark blue eyes. Skin just a little too pale. Yet still so damn beautiful. My air. My everything.

Sparrow: *You breathe a word of this to Trace or any law enforcement, and I will put a bullet in her brain before you can blink.*

I was already moving, tugging my keys free and beeping the locks on my truck. It was a trap. I knew it. But I didn't have a choice. If trading my life meant setting her free, I'd let the monster put a million bullets in me. I'd take that risk—if it bought her even a second to escape.

But my brother wouldn't let me anywhere near this if he knew.

So, he wasn't going to get a choice. I started the engine and headed for a place I hadn't been to in over a decade. Somewhere I never wanted to go again.

When I was halfway there, I fumbled for my phone. I tapped the message thread I had with Trace and started a voice memo. "I knew you'd never let me go, but I had to. I can't leave her alone in this. It's always been Fallon. It will always be her. My air. I can't be in a world she's not in. He's got her at my old house. Hurry."

And then I hit send and prayed they'd make it in time.

CHAPTER FORTY-NINE

Fallon

THE FLASH ON THE BACK OF THE PHONE MADE ME REEL. A phone I realized—by the case covered in brightly colored candy—was mine. My heart thundered against my ribs.

"What are you doing, Evan?" My voice sounded like I'd smoked a pack of cigarettes and chased them with a bottle of tequila.

He lowered the device, powering it off and shoving it into his pocket. "Always with the questions. *'What are you doing? Why are you doing this?'* And then the begging. *'Please don't kill me.'* So boring. So predictable."

My brain spun in circles, trying to pull the pieces together in a way that made sense. But no matter how hard I tried, it didn't. Evan was almost a decade younger than Kye. He couldn't have been involved in the same fight ring. Maybe he'd had an older brother or father who was?

Evan grinned, a smile that showed all his teeth in an almost manic way. "I see those wheels turning, but you're not asking the right questions."

Renee made a sound—either protest or warning. I wasn't sure which.

Evan moved in a flash, pulling out a gun and leveling it at her head. "Shut up, bitch. I've had to listen to your screaming for the past two days. I'm done. I wanted you here for poetic justice, but your dead body can be just as effective."

Renee started trembling, and her jeans darkened where she'd clearly wet herself.

Evan's face contorted in disgust. "Seriously? You're pathetic. Almost as pathetic as Kye, assuming I wouldn't find the security code for his alarm system in the same damn place he keeps all his passwords in his office."

Dread pooled. That was how he'd gotten in. Kye locked his office, but Evan had always had a set of keys.

"What questions should I be asking?" I rasped, trying to pull the attention back to me and rein in Evan as much as possible.

He shifted slowly, turning in my direction and holstering his weapon. It was then that I saw the knife on his other hip. My mouth went dry as I thought about the people who'd been killed. *Stabbed.* Likely with that blade.

"You should be asking what *Kyler* did to *deserve* this, Fallon."

My breaths came a little quicker, but I shoved the anger and fear down. Time. It was the only thing I could possibly buy us. "What did he do?"

Evan's hazel eyes narrowed on me. "He sure as hell didn't appreciate me. I did *everything* for him."

My mind spun as I tried to see things from Evan's perspective. What had Kye not appreciated? "Everything you do for him at Haven?"

Evan scoffed. "That wouldn't hurt. A little thank you now and then. But I'm talking about the *real* work. I've done everything to look out for him. Everything to keep him safe."

A sick feeling swirled inside me as Evan spoke, but I tried to focus and look for advantages. I tested my bindings for what felt like the millionth time. No give. I shook the chair slightly, but it was surprisingly sturdy, given its age.

He started to pace, running a hand through his hair. "When that piece of shit Oren started messing with Kye and Jericho, *I* dealt with it."

"You killed him," I said, my voice trembling.

"Yes, I fucking killed him. Because you sometimes have to do the hard work to protect the people you love. Kye could take a lesson from me. It looks like he's gone soft."

I bit the inside of my cheek to keep from saying something stupid, and the metallic tang of blood filled my mouth. "You were trying to protect him?"

"Yes, I fucking was," Evan snarled, redness creeping into his cheeks. "That piece of shit said others still wanted Kye back. They wanted him as a full member of the MC again. Thought it would give them clout with the name Kye had built for himself."

"Kye never would've been a part of that," I said, trying to slow my racing heart.

"I wasn't taking that chance. Wasn't going to lose him to those lowlife thugs."

There was something about that. *Lose him.* As if Kye somehow *belonged* to Evan. I couldn't figure out how or why. Evan had used the word *love.* Was he in love with Kye? It didn't quite track.

"I even protected you. Made sure I tailed you after work in case any of those fucking Reapers tried to mess with who he cares about the most."

"You were on the motorcycle. You shot up that truck." The realizations came one after the other.

"That dipshit almost hit you. I was protecting *you.*" Evan's pacing picked up speed. "I wouldn't let them hurt him. Hurt what's his. I was gonna protect him like he protected me. I left him the notes, telling him what I was doing. Showing him I was looking out. I asked who else needed to go, but he wouldn't answer."

There. That piece of the puzzle helped. "You had to look out for him," I surmised.

Evan's steps halted, and then he whirled on me. "But he didn't deserve it. So much good has happened to him, and he shouldn't have any of it."

The panic was back, the fear, but I did everything I could to shove it down. "Why?"

"Why?" Evan demanded. "You've seen him lately. Where's his goddamned loyalty? I've *always* had his back. And now? He wants nothing to do with me. He's too busy with his new fucking family to remember his old one."

I struggled to pull together the threads of Evan's argument, but it wasn't logical. "You feel like Kye hasn't had time for you lately?"

The ridiculousness of my statement wasn't lost on me. *Killing people. Attacking me.* All because he wasn't getting the attention he thought he deserved?

A muscle in Evan's jaw fluttered wildly. "He threw me aside for his *new* family. I was so damn excited about Kye giving me a new job, thinking he believed in me. But he just wanted to spend time with those girls Renee spat out. With *you*. He didn't give a damn about me anymore." He slammed an open palm over his heart. "I'm his family. Me. I'm the only one who really knows."

"Of course, he's your family. Kye loves you—"

"He doesn't fucking love me. He doesn't care about me. I thought he was different. I thought he proved it when he took me in after I tagged his shop. But he's just like our dad. Selfish. Greedy. Destructive. Only cares about his goddamned self."

Everything around me slowed. I felt every beat of my heart. The two-part cadence over and over as blood roared in my ears.

"He's just like our dad."

"Your dad?" I croaked.

"Our fucking dad," Evan snarled. And then his chin started to tremble as his eyes filled. "I just wanted him to love me like a brother should. Came to find him when home got to be too much. But he had *everything*, and I just got so damn mad. I started spray-painting all over his precious tattoo studio. And then he fooled me. I thought he cared. Took me under his wing. Thought he wanted me in his life. But he just replaced me. New sisters. New wife."

"Evan," I whispered. "Kye's your brother?"

His gaze cut to me, all signs of the tears gone. "Rex Blackwood is my dad. Or he was. Kye's my half-brother. Should've been, anyway." Evan slid the knife from his belt. "Now, he's nothing to me. And he's going to feel that pain. The same way I did. How it guts you when you lose everything you thought you had."

CHAPTER FIFTY

Kye

A BRUTAL WIND CUT THROUGH MY LEATHER JACKET, CHILLING me to the bone. But it had nothing on the words I could make out through the door.

"Rex Blackwood is my dad. Or he was. Kye's my half-brother. Should've been, anyway. Now, he's nothing to me. And he's going to feel that pain. The same way I did. How it guts you when you lose everything you thought you had."

Evan. The scared and furious-at-the-world eighteen-year-old who had shown up at my gym, ready to tag the shit out of it. But he'd turned his life around. Or so I'd thought.

Evan. Who I'd spent countless hours mentoring, helping him pull his life together so he could finish high school and take community college classes.

Evan. The boy who'd become a man on my watch. Who I'd apparently failed in the worst ways imaginable.

I moved before I could consider the wisdom of it, hauling the flimsy door open—the same door Rex and Renee had slammed more times than I could count in fits of rage. Times when Rex would take off for months on end and leave me with Renee's vitriol and slaps. Times—I now knew—that he was with an entirely different family. I slid inside the house, the pain eating me up inside.

Renee had a gash on the side of her head that told me she'd been hit with something. Hope brimmed in her dull amber eyes for a moment, then disappeared when no police came in after me.

My gaze hit Fallon, and my knees wanted to give way. Zip ties cut into her wrists and ankles, and her face was unnaturally pale, but she was still breathing. Still here. I'd make sure that remained true.

She mouthed the words, *I'm okay. I love you.*

My throat twisted viciously. Bound to a chair, fighting for her life, and she was still trying to take care of *me*.

"I guess he can listen," Evan growled as he pointed his knife at Fallon, knowing she was the target I cared about the most. But he was standing equidistant from the two women. Likely making sure I didn't have an unobstructed path to either of them.

I did the mental math to see if I could tackle Evan before he could make it to Renee or Fallon.

"Don't even think about it." Evan pulled a gun holstered at his hip. He leveled it at Fallon, moving the knife to point at Renee. "You make a single move I don't like and I'll shoot them both and then you."

I took in Evan, the boy I felt I'd known forever, who was nothing but a stranger now. "You're my brother?" I whispered.

Evan jerked his head in a staccato nod.

"Why didn't you tell me? I would've wanted to know. I would've—"

"You'd want to know that Rex Blackwood's DNA runs through my veins?" Evan snarled. "The man you hate more than any other human being walking this Earth? Even more than her?" Evan thrust the knife forward, making Renee squeal in terror. The sound only made Evan laugh.

"This isn't you, Evan." I tried to keep my voice even and calm, anything that might have a prayer of defusing the situation and buying time until Trace could get here with reinforcements.

"You don't know me," Evan barked. "You don't know what I've

lived through. I had a mom who was only around when she was too high to get off the couch. And a dad who only came to see me when this bitch kicked his ass out. Even then, it was just to smack me around. Until you got his pathetic ass thrown in jail, and he was gone altogether."

"I'm sorry. I'm so damn sorry. Neither of us deserved that."

"*I* didn't deserve that," Evan bellowed. "Me. I was innocent. I thought you were, too. But you're not. You're selfish and greedy. Just like our dad. Just like this bitch. If she would've just OD'd, none of this would've happened. If she was dead, you would've lived with me. You would've protected me from him."

"I would've tried, Evan. I promise you, I would've tried," I rasped.

"Don't!" He scratched the side of his skull with the gun. "Don't mess with my head. Don't lie."

"I'm not lying—"

"Stop it!" Evan moved so fast, there wasn't anything I could do to stop it. He leveled the gun at Renee's head and pulled the trigger.

A crack lit the air, and the force of the bullet tipped her chair over and sent it crashing to the floor.

Fallon let out a strangled noise, and Evan's gun snapped in her direction.

"Don't. Please, don't," I begged. "I'll do anything. Hurt me. Not her. She doesn't deserve this. All Fallon does is try to help kids like us. She's a good person. The best."

"Stop it, Kyler," Fallon begged. "Stop."

I held up both hands, slowly walking toward Evan. "Take me. My life is yours if you'll just let her go. Please."

Something in Evan's eyes wavered, and I thought maybe I could get through to him.

Then, all at once, officers wearing tactical gear crashed through the front and side doors. "This is the Mercer County Sheriff's Department. Lower your weapon."

I recognized Gabriel's voice, the calm command of it, but my gaze was locked on Evan. Panic lit his eyes, and the gun shifted. I knew then that the only thing he wanted was to hurt me. But not in the way I hoped.

I launched into motion. Not at Evan but for Fallon. Because it was always her. My center of gravity. My air. My everything.

I dove, praying I'd reach her in time. Halfway there, a blinding, burning pain pierced my chest. It felt as if someone had driven a hot poker straight through it. But it barely registered.

The only thing on my mind was Fallon. As the darkness closed in, she was all around me. Her scent, the feel of her, her love. As it pulled me under, I knew one thing: My life was truly lived because I loved her.

CHAPTER FIFTY-ONE

Fallon

EVERYTHING HAPPENED ALL AT ONCE AS IF IN HYPERSPEED, only punctuated by brief snapshots of images, sound, and smell. The crack of a bullet. Kye in mid-air, throwing himself at me. Shouts and shots. The scent of blood in the air.

Kye hit the ground in front of me. Blood bloomed on his chest, soaking his gray Haven T-shirt. *Haven.* He was mine. He always would be.

A scream, more animal than human, left my throat. I threw myself forward, sending the chair I was tied to crashing to the floor with me still in it. I hit the floor with my arm and side, raging against the chair until the zip ties on my wrists snapped.

I hauled myself toward Kye. His eyes were at half-mast. He was fading.

"Pressure on the wound," Beth shouted as Trace rushed forward, his face deathly pale.

But I was already moving. I pressed my palms to the gaping wound, trying to stop the blood flow, trying to keep it in because

Kyler needed that blood. He needed it to live. He needed it to keep breathing.

Sirens sounded outside.

"That's the EMTs," Trace croaked, dropping to his knees.

It was then that I realized the blood had pooled. Seeping out of Kye and soaking into the knees of my jeans. I wanted to put it back. Return it to Kye, where it belonged. It was his, not mine.

"Don't," I rasped, pressing all my weight against Kye's chest. "Don't leave me. You promised."

More shouts sounded behind me. Some part of me became aware that Evan had been shot, too, blood blooming on his shoulder as officers worked on him.

"Over here," Trace barked as two EMTs charged in. I knew them. Both of them. Almost all my life. But I couldn't seem to remember either of their names right now.

I did notice how their faces went carefully blank as they registered the situation and how they moved a little faster.

"Pulse?" the woman asked.

"Faint," Trace answered.

I realized then that he must've been tracking it.

Blood seeped through my fingers as my tears fell, mixing with it, diluting it. "I can't—I can't keep it in—it needs to be in him—I—"

"It's okay," the male EMT said. "I'm going to take over for you, okay?"

"No, no, no." I shook my head violently. "I take care of Kyler. Me. Only me."

"Fal," Trace rasped. "You gotta let them help. We need to get Kye to the hospital. We—"

"I go where he goes. I protect him. I—"

"Pulse is fading," the woman barked. "We need to move."

Everything happened in a flash. Trace dove for me, hauling me into his arms as I screamed with everything I had in me. I screamed for Kyler. Shouted his name over and over as if God could hear the fervor of my battle cry and would have no choice but to listen.

"Someone get a goddamned sedative," Trace yelled as I twisted and kicked.

I screamed again. Someone grabbed my arm, and I felt a sharp sting. Everything started to feel heavy. "No," I slurred. "I can't leave him. I promised..."

I stared straight ahead as a resident who didn't look old enough to drive swiped at my wrists with a cotton swab.

"I'm sorry if this stings," he said quietly.

I didn't say a word because I didn't feel anything. Not one ounce of pain. Nor any comfort as my mom brushed her hand over my hair.

Maybe it was whatever drug the EMT had dosed me with. I should be grateful there was nothing because all I remembered from before was soul-tearing pain.

The image of Kyler's blood seeping through my fingers flashed in my mind, and I squeezed my eyes closed, trying to clear it, but I couldn't. My throat constricted as I tried to keep the scream inside. Because I knew if I started screaming, they'd just jab me again.

Someone pulled the curtain back, and Dr. Alvarez stepped inside the little cubby they'd stuck me in at the end of a row in the ER. The moment my gaze locked with hers, my mouth opened. "My husband?"

My throat was completely raw, and my voice sounded nothing like me—barely audible and like it had been roasted over an open flame.

"How are you feeling?" she asked.

"My husband." The words were a demand.

Dr. Alvarez crossed to my gurney, her gaze flicking up to my mom in question.

"Tell us," Mom said softly. "It'll only make things worse if you don't."

Dr. Alvarez turned her gaze back to me, the look in her brown eyes softening. "Kye made it through surgery, but it was touch and go. His heart stopped on the table."

Tears filled my eyes, making the doctor blurry. "I wasn't breathing for him."

"Oh, baby," Mom croaked, kissing the top of my head as she hugged me.

"We're helping him breathe now," Dr. Alvarez said. "We got his heart going again. His right lung collapsed, and we had to reinflate it. Now, we just have to wait."

"I need to see him." Tears tracked down my cheeks. "I promised him—" My voice cracked. "I promised him I wouldn't leave. That he wouldn't be alone. That it would always be him and me."

"They're getting him settled in the ICU. I can take you up there as soon as you're all fixed up," Dr. Alvarez assured me.

"I'm done, right?" I asked the teenage doctor wrapping my wrists.

He studied me. "Do you feel dizzy? We can get a wheelchair—"

"No. I'm fine. I just want to see Kyler."

"Okay," Dr. Alvarez said. "Let's go. We can take it nice and easy."

My mom braced me as I turned to get off the gurney. The scrubs they'd given me were scratchy against my skin. They weren't like my clothes. They weren't like one of Kye's worn T-shirts or his fingers trailing over my flesh.

I shoved all that into the space along my sternum, the spot Kyler had etched himself onto and into. I stood, and the world wavered a little.

Mom squeezed my hand. "I think we should get that wheelchair—"

"No. I'm good."

Still, she held on to me as we made our way down the row of cubicles and then a hall. My heart stopped as I saw a waiting room. Chairs and couches were full to bursting with everyone who loved Kye: Bear and Jericho. Serena and Mateo. Cope, Sutton, and Luca. Keely and Ellie. Shep and Thea. Linc and Arden. Rose and Mila. Lolli and Walter. Rhodes and Anson. Even Dex was there, looking unusually ravaged for someone who barely knew Kye.

And then there were my girls. They were surrounded by countless people who were holding them up. But the moment they saw me, they leapt to their feet and charged toward me. Mom held out a hand to slow them. "Gentle. She got a little banged up."

But I didn't want gentle. I hauled all three of them into my arms as we all started to cry.

"Mama Fal," Gracie croaked. "Kye...he said we could call you Mom and Dad names...even though...you're not really—"

"Nothing would make me happier than being your mom," I rasped. "Whatever you want that to be."

Clem's head lifted, her eyes rimmed in red. "If—if he doesn't make it...are you going to put us back in foster care?"

I hugged them all tighter. "You're mine, and I'm yours. We're a forever family, okay? No matter what comes our way."

Tears streamed down Hayden's face. "You need to go. Dad... he needs you now."

My tears came harder then, my heart breaking in two. I didn't want to leave them, but I knew Kyler needed me, too.

My family appeared behind them. Cope's hands landed on Hayden's shoulders. Linc hoisted Gracie into his arms as Arden took her hand. And Rhodes and Thea cocooned Clem in a hug.

"We've got them," Rho whispered. "You get Kye."

I nodded, unable to speak. But with Mom's help, I somehow managed to follow Dr. Alvarez into an elevator. I let her lead us through a closed door and allowed her to squirt hand sanitizer gel onto my palms.

"There will be a bunch of machines right now, but just know they're doing the hard work for Kye so he can recover," Dr. Alvarez informed me.

But I was already moving, heading through the open door and into the room with countless unfamiliar sounds. Beeps and whirs. Puffs and whooshes. Tubes and wires covered the man in the bed. But still...it was my Kyler. My everything.

My legs carried me to the side of the bed, trembling as I lowered myself to the chair. His arms lay on top of the blankets, one with an IV poking out of it and the other, the one closest to me, with one of those oxygen monitors affixed to his finger.

For a moment, it felt like there was no room for me. But this was Kyler. I would always fit with him.

I linked my pinky with his, holding tightly. "I'm here," I whispered. "I'm not going anywhere. Not until you come back to me. Just like you promised."

I stared at his face, willing his eyes to open. But they didn't even flutter. My throat constricted. "I'll never give up on you," I choked out. "And neither will the girls. We need you, Kyler. You make this family whole, and none of us is the best version of ourselves without you. Fight. Please."

My tears fell in earnest then, hitting our joined pinkies and soaking into our skin. I bent my head and pressed my lips to the now-wet spot. "I love you. It's always been you, and it'll always be you."

CHAPTER FIFTY-TWO

Fallon

THE SUN BEAT DOWN ON ME AS I LAY IN THE GRASS ALONG THE creek's embankment, my head resting on Kye's chest as I listened to his heart. That steady beat, without the assistance of machines, told me this was a dream. But I didn't care.

Kye felt so real in this moment. His fingers sifted through my hair, tangling in the strands. "Used to stare at you after I came to live with the Colsons and wish I could run my fingers through your silky strands."

"Kyler."

"My name on your lips...nothing better." He hauled me against him, kissing me long and deep. And when he released my mouth, he laid me half on top of him, in that spot where I fit perfectly.

With the steady beat of his heart against my cheek, I stared down at the creek and the dogwoods lining either side. "Nothing is more perfect than this."

"Love you, Sparrow. My hope in the dark. My haven."

A pressure around my pinky scattered the dream like a hand cutting through smoke. I tried to hold on, but the tendrils of hope—of Kyler—slipped right through my fingers.

The pressure around my pinky intensified, and I jerked upright, blinking rapidly. Each swish of my eyelids hurt, and my muscles protested the abrupt movement. But when I looked down at the man in the bed, I didn't give a damn about my aching muscles or gritty eyes from lack of sleep. Because for the first time in five days, amber orbs looked back into mine.

"Kyler," I croaked.

He squeezed my pinky. "Sparrow."

His voice was barely audible, but it didn't matter. He was awake, and he knew who I was. He was *here*.

The tears were instant, trailing down my face and falling onto our joined hands. "They said…they said you might not make it. But I knew better. You crawled right out of the beyond and back to me all on your own."

Kye searched my eyes, pain lacing his expression. "Not…on… my…own. With. You."

I lifted our joined hands to my lips, ghosting a kiss over his skin as if assuring my body that he was really there. "I love you."

"You taught me what love is," Kye rasped. "Never knew until you showed me. No one ever chose me…until you."

The tears came faster then.

"Sparrow." Kye shifted, and pain flashed in his amber depths.

"Let me get a nurse. They can—"

"No." His pinky spasmed around mine. "Just need a minute with my girl."

"You're here."

"I promised, didn't I?"

My heart cracked, but Kye's golden light was there, filling the broken places. "You did."

Kye's gaze roamed over my face as if he were reacquainting himself with the look of me. "How long was I out?"

A shudder raced through me. "Five days. You were breathing on your own after two, but you wouldn't wake up."

"I've never been especially fond of mornings."

I wanted to laugh or smile, but I couldn't quite get there.

"Renee?" Kye asked.

I shook my head. "Gone."

A mixture of emotions swept over his face as he struggled to swallow. "Evan?"

There was so much grief in that single word, that one name. A lifetime of unknown agony.

"He made it through surgery," I said softly. "They moved him to a prison with a hospital ward for his recovery. The facility also has psychiatric care."

Kye's eyes glittered with unshed tears. "He's so broken. I can't help but think it's my fault."

I moved then, unable to stop myself. I leaned forward and framed Kye's face in my hands, relishing the feel of his scruff against my palms. "He is broken. But that's not on you, Kyler. You gave him a haven, even when you had no idea who he was to you. How could you know his mind had twisted like that? Fixated?"

"I just...he was all alone."

My thumbs stroked across Kye's cheeks. "He wasn't. You gave him a family. His mind just...played tricks on him."

Tears crested over his lower lids and landed on my thumbs. "I can't hate him. I should, but—"

"Your heart's too good. You love too hard. You could never hate someone who means that much to you," I whispered.

"Most beautiful soul in the world, my sparrow," Kye rasped.

I brushed my lips against his. "Love you. And there are three girls who really need to see you. Can I text Mom to bring them in?"

Kye's eyes shone. "Nothing would make me happier than having all my girls together."

By the time I heard Gracie's chattering voice coming down the hall, we'd gotten Kye sitting up and cleaned him up the best we could without him being able to leave the bed. But his first glimpse of his sisters who'd become daughters did the most healing. His whole face lit up as they swept into the room.

"Daddy Kye Kye!" Gracie yelled, racing for the bed.

I caught her around the middle, hauling her onto my lap. "Careful, remember? He's got a tender chest."

"Daddy Kye Kye," she amended, dropping her voice to a whisper.

"You don't have to whisper," Clem said, rolling her eyes. "You just can't jump on him."

"'Gentle words, gentle hands,' Hay Hay says," Gracie shot back.

Mom wrapped an arm around Hayden's shoulders and brought them both closer to the bed. "Great words to live by."

Hayden was still a little pale, and dark circles shadowed her eyes. She swallowed hard. "Are you…are you really okay?"

Kye held out a hand for her, and she instantly went to him, taking it. He squeezed her hand and met her gaze. "Doc said I'm healing well. Lungs and heart look good. Apparently, I just needed an extra-long nap."

"Sometimes, I need a nap if we have a field trip at school," Gracie offered.

Kye chuckled and then winced. "Gonna need you girls to minimize the funny stuff for a bit."

Gracie frowned. "That's gonna be really hard for me. I'm hilarious."

Kye grinned. "Damn straight, you are."

Hayden's mouth kicked up. "That's one for the swear jar…Dad."

"Never gonna get tired of hearing that," Kye rasped.

"Good," Hayden said, giving his hand a squeeze before releasing it.

Kye's gaze moved to Clem. "You want to come over here?"

She pulled her lip into her mouth, worrying the corner of it with her teeth. "I don't wanna bump anything. I read about the tube that drains your chest and how they reinflated your lung and—"

"My little genius, come here. You're not gonna hurt me," Kye assured her.

Clem slowly walked toward him, standing next to Hayden before finally taking the hand he offered her. "I was scared," she admitted.

"Me, too," Kye told her. "But I felt you all with me. I heard Fallon telling me how much you all loved me. You made me strong so I could fight."

"We do love you," Hayden choked out. "So much."

"The mostest," Gracie said, bobbing her head. "Our favoritest brother-dad."

Clem laughed at that. "Maybe we could call him our Baddie."

Kye's mouth quirked. "That does make me sound like a badass." His gaze moved around the room. "I love you. All of you. Greatest gifts I've ever been given."

Hayden's eyes, so similar to Kye's, shimmered. "Thank you for giving us a family. We never had anything like this. You made us safe. Loved. You brought us home."

CHAPTER FIFTY-THREE

Kye

"I don't need a wheelchair," I grumbled as a far-too-cheery orderly pushed me toward the hospital exit.

"Dude, someone put a hole in your chest. I think you can take people up on some rides for a while," Cope muttered.

Rhodes hit him upside the head. "Sensitivity chip, Copeypants. And you're one to talk since you were pulling the same stunt not long ago."

"Yeah, Puck Boy," Fallon said, narrowing her eyes on him. "Be sensitive. Otherwise, you never know where a glitter bomb might hit."

Cope's eyes widened. "You genuinely scare me."

"Good," Fallon huffed.

"Sparrow," I said, trying to fight a laugh because it still hurt like hell, "stow your vengeful streak for a few days, would you?"

She glanced down at me as the hospital's automatic doors opened. "Now, what fun would that be?"

"I heard someone was breaking out today," Shep called, grinning as he stood in front of Cope's SUV.

I scowled at him. "Did it really take four of you to get me home?"

"When you're being a curmudgeonly idiot who tries to do way more than the doctor says you should...yes," Fallon huffed.

"A curmudgeonly idiot? Is that any way to talk to your still-recovering husband?" I demanded.

Fallon's lips twitched. "When he's being a curmudgeonly idiot, it is." She leaned down and brushed her lips across mine. "But I love you even when you rival that grumpy cat meme."

"Say it again," I whispered against her lips.

"You rival that grumpy cat meme."

I smiled against her mouth. "The other thing."

"Oh, that." Fallon kissed me again. "I love you."

"Where's Luca when you need him?" Shep muttered. "No mushy-gushy."

Rhodes threw something at him. "They're sweet."

Fallon straightened, her deep blue eyes a little hazy. "Ready to go home?"

"Get me the hell out of here." I glanced up at the orderly. "No offense, Brady."

"None taken, Mr. Kye. You get better and enjoy that sweet family of yours."

"You know I will, sir. And keep an eye on Fletcher for me," I said. Harrison wouldn't be getting out of the hospital for another week or two, but he would recover, and I was incredibly grateful for that.

Cope shook his head. "You listen to Brady. Even call him *sir*. I try to tell you to take it easy, and I get called *Puck Boy*."

"Get used to it, Puck Boy," Fallon called as she opened the SUV's front passenger door.

Rho grinned at him. "She's gonna take out all her pent-up worry on you now. You know that, right?"

"What did I do?" Cope asked as he and Shep helped me stand.

"You were a shit-stirrer. Like always," Shep said, struggling not to laugh.

Cope scowled. "Well, I learned that from Kye."

"You're welcome, buddy," I muttered.

They all bickered like usual as they got me settled in the SUV, and something about that felt comforting, like a return to a ridiculous, chaotic normal.

"You're not driving my Bentley," Cope growled, demanding the keys from Shep.

"You let me pull it around."

"Which is way different than taking this baby out on the open road," Cope shot back.

Fallon leaned forward from the back seat. "One of you had better get behind the wheel, or I'm taking my keys to this pretty leather interior."

Cope gaped at her. "You wouldn't."

She arched a brow. "Want to try me?"

Cope snatched the keys from Shep's hand and jumped behind the wheel. "Fucking terrifying."

Shep climbed into the back seat next to Fal. "Have I told you lately that I love you?"

Fallon grinned. "I'll always take an I love you."

"Yeah, at the expense of my emotional torture," Cope mumbled as he started the engine.

"Such a drama king," Rhodes muttered.

The conversation continued much like that for the entire ride home. The bumps and jostling didn't exactly equal a good time, but I'd take it over and over again if it meant being able to sleep in my own bed tonight.

As we turned onto the road toward home, Cope glanced at me as the others chatted in the back seat. "You hanging in?"

I gritted my teeth but nodded.

"I need to say something."

The pain in my chest ebbed as I took in my brother. "You okay?"

Cope's grip on the wheel tightened. "No, not really. I was a giant asshole to you and Fal when you told us you were getting married. And when you got shot, all I could think about was that those words might be some of the last I said to you."

"Cope—"

He shook his head. "I'm so fucking sorry. You are one of the best men I've ever had the privilege of knowing. And I can't imagine anyone better for Fallon. Anyone who could be a better brother, dad, son. We're all so damn lucky to have you."

"Copeypants," Rhodes whispered from the back seat as she dabbed at her eyes.

"Stop eavesdropping," he shot back.

"Then I'd miss all the good stuff," she argued.

I reached over and patted his arm. "Love you, Cope."

"Fuck, my eyes are leaking," Cope mumbled.

Shep chuckled and slapped him on the shoulder. "Feel your feelings, Puck Boy."

Cope glared as he slowed in front of my gate and punched in the code. "I hate all of you."

Rhodes grinned. "You love us. And stop stealing Trace's line."

Before long, we pulled up in front of the house, and I was being fussed over again. This time, it was Fallon on one side of me and Cope on the other. I struggled with the stairs, wheezing by the time we reached the top of just a handful of them.

Fallon squeezed my hand. "I had Ellie set up the secondary suite on the main floor, so you don't have to deal with stairs for a while."

I scowled at that bit of information. "I miss my bed."

"Kyler," she said, pausing at the threshold. My head dipped, eyes locking on her dark blue depths. "Give yourself some time to heal. Give *us* time to fuss over you. *We* need it. We lived for five days, not knowing if you'd pull through."

Fuck.

I bent, ignoring my chest's protests, and said, "Sorry, Sparrow. I'll stop being a grumpy fucker."

"I prefer curmudgeonly idiot," she whispered.

I smiled against her mouth. "You always were fancier than me."

"They're here!" I heard Gracie yell from inside.

"Let's go see our family," Fallon said.

She and Cope helped me inside, where I was greeted by a massive WELCOME HOME DADDY KYE KYE sign. There were all sorts of drawings around it, too: tattoos, boxing gloves, sparrows, and some pot leaves and little magic mushrooms.

I turned to Lolli. "Let me guess what your additions were."

She beamed. "My boy is home. I just wanted to send him some good healing vibes. I tried to make you a special healing blend, but someone"—her gaze shot to Nora—"said she'd steal my stash if I tried."

"Your healing blend had your best friend seeing pink bunnies for a week," Trace cut in.

Walter looked up from his spot on an overstuffed chair. "Forget pink bunnies. She dosed me last week, and I thought I was a T-rex. I was running all around the house with baby arms, roaring at things." He held his arms close to his chest, flinging his hands around to demonstrate.

Lolli sent her boy toy a sultry look. "But remember how much fun that role-playing was when you chased me?"

Walter grinned and rose from the chair. "Oh, I'll chase you all right…"

"Dear God, someone please make it stop," Cope moaned.

"Come on," Fallon said, leading me toward the sectional.

"Over here, Daddy Kye Kye," Gracie cheered. "We made you a nest."

I took in the spot they'd created with a bunch of blankets and a makeshift table on the cushion next to it with all sorts of things.

"I did some research," Clem explained. "Hydration is super important for recovery."

"So, we got you this cup," Hayden said, her lips twitching wildly. "Gracie picked it out, and we helped Lolli bedazzle it."

Gracie held up a bright pink cup covered in countless bedazzled hearts. In the center was a bigger heart with an arrow through it that read: *Kye + Fallon*.

Fallon made a strangled noise next to me. "I'm a little jealous."

I lowered myself to the couch with plenty of assistance. "It's perfect. I think pink's my new color."

"I know what that's like," Anson called from a chair by the fire.

Trace grimaced. "Me, too."

"Real men wear pink," I said, lifting my cup and making the girls giggle.

Arden crossed to me, a hand on her growing belly. She pulled off one of my shoes and then the other. "I've got a new appreciation for how hard that can be."

I smiled at her, even though I felt like I'd just climbed a mountain. "How are my niece and nephew in there?"

"Better now that you're home." Arden spread one of the many blankets over me and squeezed my foot. "If you ever do *anything* like that ever again, I will personally kick your ass."

"She'll do it, too," Linc said, a proud grin on his face. "I don't call her Vicious for nothing."

I reached out and threaded my fingers through Fallon's. "I think the entire Colson crew should be drama-free for a while."

Nora crossed behind the sectional and laid a hand on my shoulder. "I like that plan." She glanced at my sisters. "I think our stew is done. Want to help Sutton dish it up?"

"Yes!" Gracie cheered.

Clem sent me a pointed look. "You need to eat meat and other iron-rich foods to build up your blood supply."

"Yes, ma'am," I said, giving her a salute.

Fallon shook her head. "I should've brought Clem to the hospital. You actually listen to her."

I grinned as she released my hand and followed the girls into the kitchen.

Nora sat on the back of the sectional, studying my face. "You're going to take some pain meds with that stew. You're hurting."

"I—"

"You're going to listen to me, or I will let Lolli dose you with whatever the hell she mixed up."

I fought a laugh. "Nora, you cursed."

"Sometimes, it's necessary. And I'm not going to have my boy hurting."

A different sort of pain flared in my chest. The good kind. I laid a hand over hers. "I'm sorry I held myself back from you and the things I should've given you."

"Kye—"

"Should've called you Mom a long time ago."

Nora's eyes filled. "You know terms don't define our bond."

I swallowed hard. "But I should've given it to you anyway. I just...I didn't know how to reconcile the things I felt for Fal with who I was to the rest of you. I'm sorry if I hurt you because of it."

Nora pressed a hand to my cheek. "You've always been ours. And we've always been yours. Nothing about our family is typical, but that just makes it more special. And I couldn't be prouder to have you as my son."

The lump in my throat grew, and my eyes burned. "Love you, Mom."

"More than all the stars in the sky," she whispered.

"Fuck, my eyes are leaking again," Cope muttered.

"Swear jar!" Luca called from the kitchen.

"He's catching up to you, Uncle Kye Kye," Keely added.

"Keep it up, Puck Boy," I said with a grin.

Anson and Trace shifted the sectional so I could see out the back windows. Because that's where the fun was. While I was in the hospital, the pond had frozen solid, which meant one thing and one thing only.

Hockey.

Nearly the entire Colson crew, including Walter and Lolli, was out on the ice. They were playing some severely bastardized version of the sport that involved tripping and snowball fights.

"Jesus," Trace muttered. "Someone's going to break an arm."

"Always the safety monitor," I said with a grin.

A knock sounded on the front door before it swung open—open

because there was no reason to lock it anymore. A surprising figure stepped inside.

"Dex," Anson greeted. "I thought you'd already headed back to Virginia."

He shook his head, hazel eyes astute and glasses-free at the moment. "Heading to the airport now. I just..." His throat worked as he swallowed. "Wanted to check on Kye before I left."

Anson had shared that Dex had dealt with some pretty brutal violence growing up. Between the confrontation with Ellie's attacker and mine, it must have stirred up a lot for him.

"I'm glad you did," I said, forcing my smile wider. "I wanted to thank you in person."

"For what?" Dex asked, confused.

"Fal told me you supersized our alarm system."

He simply shrugged. "I just...I wanted to do something. When stuff like this happens, it can make you feel pretty powerless. At least I can control gear and tech."

I reached out a hand, and Dex took it as I met his gaze. "Thank you."

"It was nothing."

"Not to me. You've helped my family countless times. You need anything, just say the word."

Dex's gaze roamed over me, stopping on my chest as if he could see the wound beneath my shirt. "Your doc said you'd make a full recovery?"

"Full recovery. Just no marathons for a while."

Dex nodded but didn't smile. "Good. That's good. Take care of yourself and those girls."

"I'll do just that," I assured him. "What's next for you?"

He forced his gaze away from my injury and turned to the back windows. "I'm not sure. I need a few months to wrap up some things in Virginia, and then it might be time to go home for a while."

Anson straightened. "Back to Starlight Grove?"

Dex turned to him. "It's time. I need to get back to my brothers." He glanced at his watch. "And I need to hit the road."

Trace gave Dex a quick hug, and Anson walked him out, leaving Trace and me alone.

He lowered himself to the end of the sectional. "How are you really? No bullshitting."

"My head's a little twisty," I admitted.

"But you're not pushing Fal away. Or the rest of us."

I shook my head. "I learned. I'm so much better when she's with me. Every part of me."

The corners of Trace's mouth kicked up. "He finally learns."

I flipped him off but then sobered. "Thank you. For everything. You've had my back since you got me placed with Nora. I wouldn't have made it through any of this without you."

"Love you, brother. To the ends of the Earth," Trace rasped.

"Love you," I croaked, then shifted, pulling something out of my pocket. "Think you could do me a favor?"

"Anything."

I handed him the paper. "Take this to the jeweler. She'll know what to do."

Trace unfolded the page I'd torn from my sketchbook. "You already got Fal a ridiculously expensive ring."

"She needs this one, too. And there's nothing I wouldn't do for her."

CHAPTER FIFTY-FOUR

Fallon

SIX MONTHS LATER

THE SUN CASCADED DOWN AS SHRIEKS AND SPLASHES SOUNDED behind me.

"I don't know how they aren't freezing to death," Sutton said with a shake of her head.

Thea lifted one garden-glove-clad hand to shield her eyes while the other dropped to her swollen belly. "I put my swollen-as-hell feet in there, and it was like an instant ice bath."

Rhodes grinned. "Nothing like being young."

Arden lifted her glass of lemonade from where she sat on an outdoor chair. "Wait until you're in month nine. You can't even see your feet, and you have to pee every two seconds."

My expression softened. "Your babies are going to be besties."

Arden waved a hand in front of her face. "Don't make me cry."

Ellie laughed. "I love you being in your emo era."

"Don't you dare tell Linc," Arden threatened.

Ellie made a cross over her heart. "I'd never."

We were enjoying one of those perfect late spring days, the first glimmers of heat making it perfect for working in the garden or taking that first dip in the pond.

"Cannonball!" Luca yelled, launching himself off the dock and swimming toward the deepest water.

"I can totally splash bigger than that," Gracie called, flipping in.

"Me next," Keely called, racing down the dock.

They had become three peas in a pod, spending all their time together now that Luca, Sutton, and Cope had moved back to Sparrow Falls.

Clem had found her rhythm, too. After some academic testing, she'd been put into a gifted and talented program that challenged her beautiful brain in all sorts of wonderful ways. But my favorite way to see her was as she was now, completely relaxed, soaking up the sun and a good book.

Hayden was killing it at hockey but had also discovered a real knack for sewing. The balance of the two, and taking some MMA classes with Kye, had let her truly be a kid for the first time. And that included her very first boyfriend—one of the teens from Kye's class. Kye had put the fear of God into Mateo's cousin, Danny, but it hadn't mattered. Danny had met every challenge Kye threw at him.

And looking at them now, sprawled across the dock, I could see how much Danny cherished our girl. How could I be mad at that?

A whistle sounded, and I looked up to see Kye striding around the side of the house wearing those same scarred motorcycle boots and leather jacket he always did. I was instantly on my feet and running toward him. He caught me on the fly, and my legs encircled his waist.

"How was it?" I asked, concern bleeding into my words.

Kye's amber eyes searched mine. "Hard. Good. I think it was nice for him to see Jericho and Serena."

About a month after Kye had been shot, he'd asked me how I would feel if he went to visit Evan in prison. He'd obviously been warring with the decision, but I told him I'd be with him every step of the way if that's what he wanted to do. That first visit had turned into him going every other week. The trips always weighed heavily on Kye, but they also helped in a way.

Jericho had been more reticent to visit, today marking the first time he had. But the fact that he had told me he was doing some real healing, and throwing himself into the new program he and Kye ran for at-risk youth had helped.

I brushed through Kye's hair with my fingers. "You're the most amazing man I've ever known."

Those amber orbs sparked with gold. "Go somewhere with me?"

I glanced around. "We've got a full house."

"They won't burn the place down." Kye's gaze stilled on Hayden and Danny. "What's the teen heartbreaker doing here?"

"Kyler..." I warned.

He glanced at Arden. "You keep an eye on those two. He makes a move, choke him out."

Arden rolled her eyes but saluted him. "On it, boss."

Kye moved then, carrying me toward where he'd parked his truck.

"We have to drive?" I asked.

"Yes, but we're not leaving the property."

That piqued my interest even more. We'd made the house and grounds a home over the past seven months, doing all sorts of projects. And more than that, we'd readied it to welcome foster kids of our own. We would complete the classes for that and become eligible later this month. It was everything I'd ever dreamed of. But even with all that, I hadn't explored the entirety of the massive property Kye had purchased.

He opened the passenger door and deposited me on the seat. "Your chariot, Sparrow."

I grinned like a fool as he rounded the truck, sliding off his jacket and tossing it into the back. I took stock of his newer ink as he climbed behind the wheel. Three sparrows with *Hayden*, *Clem*, and *Gracie* etched into them. Three more symbols of hope.

Kye guided his truck toward the dirt road that cut through the property, one hand resting on my thigh. Neither of us spoke as he drove. We simply let the comfortable silence descend. But after a few minutes, his gaze flicked to me. "Close your eyes."

My mouth curved, but I covered my eyes with my hand.

The truck slowed, the engine shut off, and my door opened.

"Keep 'em closed."

"I'm not cheating," I shot back.

Kye chuckled and guided me over uneven ground. "When I first looked at this property, I found out that the creek that runs behind the schools also runs through this property."

My chest tightened at all the memories linked to that body of water. All the precious gifts it had given us.

"But it was missing something," Kye said, coming up behind me and pulling my hand from my eyes.

As my eyes fluttered open, I sucked in a breath. "Dogwoods."

The creek carved through the land, wildflowers springing up on its banks. But among all those flowers were endless dogwood trees, their white blossoms in full bloom. "I dreamt this," I croaked.

Kye shifted so he could see my face. "What?"

"I dreamed of this exact spot when you were in the hospital. Right before you woke up. But I've never seen it before. It didn't even exist."

Kye framed my face with his hands. "We made it together. It's our haven." He took my mouth in a long, slow kiss. When he leaned back, he pulled something from his pocket. "In our haven, there's both dark and light because we know you can't have one without the other. So, I needed my sparrow to have her light."

I stared as he slid a ring onto my right ring finger, a mirror to the black diamond engagement ring, but this one had a clear stone and a band made entirely of sparrows. My gaze shot to his. "Kyler..."

"I love you, Sparrow. Thank you for always being my hope in the dark."

I threw my arms around him. "Thank you for always giving me everything."

EPILOGUE

Fallon

ONE YEAR LATER

THE SUN CAST COLSON RANCH IN AN ARRAY OF GOLDS, HITTING the display of flowers Rhodes and Thea had worked on all day yesterday. They were absolutely perfect for the recipient, touching on every color of the rainbow.

Just thinking about the perfection of the gift had me seeking out the bride. She'd truly gone all out for the occasion. Lolli had given herself pink and purple highlights that matched her rainbow-sequin gown, complete with embroidered pot leaves and magic mushrooms. It was over-the-top, a little ridiculous, and perfectly Lolli.

Walter held her to him as they swayed to the band's song, gazing down at her like she was a miracle and the best thing he'd ever seen. He'd even added a few pink streaks to his hair to match her and had a rainbow-sequin bow tie.

"God, they're perfect, aren't they?" Rhodes said, sidling up next to me, one hand on her swollen belly and the other holding a glass of lemonade.

I glanced over at my best friend, my sister. She wore red, the first color of the rainbow, while the rest of us Colson crew bridesmaids donned the remaining colors, ending with me in purple. "I can't believe she actually did it. I thought for sure she'd bail the night before."

Rhodes laughed, her fingers splaying over her stomach. "She would've been in so much trouble after everything we put into this."

My lips twitched. "You mean the Vegas bachelorette party, courtesy of Linc?"

"I'm pretty sure I'm scarred for life after watching Lolli getting body rolled by Thunder Down Under."

I choked on a laugh. "What about when she danced on the bar and did body shots with the two showgirls?"

Rhodes shook her head, the red undertones of her brown hair catching the light as she did. "I still think it's the fact that she demanded a priest, pastor, rabbi, swami, *and* shaman all marry her and Walter because she wanted to be blessed by as many faiths as possible."

"I'm pretty sure they were all equally scarred when she read her own vows that included doing a strip tease for Walter every Friday night," I said, looking toward the faith leaders, who were gathered at a table eating and looking genuinely confused.

Rhodes chuckled. "That was my favorite part. But I'm pretty sure Shep almost tossed his cookies."

My gaze sought out our brother, who was curled around Thea at the edge of the dance floor as they watched the newly married lovebirds. He dipped his head to whisper something in her ear, making her smile, and then dropped a hand to the little one sleeping in Thea's arms.

"I think Trace might've beat his reaction," I said, grinning as I found him dancing with Ellie and Keely in some sort of wild, nonsensical way. They twisted and twirled in a circle, looking like they were having the time of their lives.

"Ellie has loosened him up, but not to the point where he'll enjoy hearing about the new stripper pole Lolli's having installed at her house."

This time, I couldn't hold my bark of laughter in. "How'd Anson take it when she asked him to install it for her?"

Rho's grin only widened. "He looked a little green but said yes, of course."

"He's a sucker for Lolls."

"That he is."

"Hotshot, I can carry my own plate," Sutton grumbled as Cope tried to take it from her.

"The doctor said not to lift anything heavy," Cope argued to his pregnant wife. He'd taken overprotective to a new level after she announced to him and the whole world that she was having a baby.

Rhodes shook her head. "I'd be surprised if she even gets to pee alone."

One corner of my mouth kicked up. "She begged me to have Kye kidnap Cope the other day. Said she needed two hours of peace without him hovering."

"We'll have to rescue her for a girls' day or something."

"I wouldn't put it past Cope to don a wig and try to sneak into wherever we go."

Rhodes glanced at Linc and Arden. They were each holding the hands of one of their twins, who were getting down to the music. "I'd say the overprotectiveness should end after Sutton gives birth, but Arden told me Linc wanted to hire both an on-call doctor and a full-time security detail after the twins were born."

I let out a soft snort. "Why am I not surprised he wanted to go over-the-top with the safety and protection of his family?" I looked at my bestie-sister. "How's Anson doing with it all?"

Rhodes sought out her man, who was waiting at the bar for two drinks. The moment her eyes locked on him, her whole face softened. "He's overbearing in the best ways." Her gaze flicked to me. "He tattled on me to Duncan, though. So now I can't do any physical labor at the nursery."

I grinned at that, catching sight of her Bloom & Berry boss with his arm around Thea's best friend from LA, Nikki. "Well, I hate to say it, but I agree with Anson on that one."

Rho made a scoffing sound. "You would." She sighed. "But I

can't hold it against him when he also reads to the baby every night before bed."

A lump caught in my throat as I imagined the broody ex-profiler being so tender. My fingers itched to drop to my own belly as my mind filled with images of Kye doing the same one day. "I love that you have that," I croaked.

Rho leaned into me. "I love that we all found our versions of that." She let out a squeak, her hand stilling on her belly.

"What?" I demanded. "Are you okay? The baby?"

Rho's gaze flew to my face. "They kicked." She grabbed my wrist and pressed my hand to her belly.

Just as she did, I felt a strong jab against my palm. My eyes grew glassy. "That little boy or girl is going to be a soccer player. Or an MMA star."

"Dear God, please let it be soccer," Rhodes said with a laugh.

"I'm so happy for you, Rho."

She pulled me into a hug. "Love you, Fal."

"More than all the stars in the sky," I whispered back.

"What's with the tears?" a worried voice asked as Rho and I pulled apart. Kye's amber eyes searched mine. "Are you okay?"

I quickly wiped my cheeks. "I felt her baby kick."

Relief washed through Kye's expression, and his face softened as he wrapped his arms around me. "Happy tears are allowed."

"Tears?" Anson asked, moving toward us, a scowl on his face. "Reckless, why are you crying?"

"Stow your murdery rage. I just felt the baby kick," she grumbled.

Anson's eyes widened, his hand finding her belly and his expression going soft. "I feel them."

"Told you," Rho said with a grin.

Anson quickly shook his head. "You need to sit down and eat a little more. And I got you some water to make sure you stay hydrated."

Rhodes rolled her eyes but took pity on her husband and let him guide her toward one of the tables surrounding the dance floor.

As they walked away, Kye shifted so he was behind me, his arms wrapped around me, his hands curved around my middle, and his chin resting atop my head. "Have I told you how beautiful you look today?"

My mouth curved as I watched all the people we loved milling about. "Maybe once or twice, but I'll never get tired of hearing it."

A giggle lit the air, pulling my gaze toward the source. Gracie's friend, Benny, spun her on the dance floor, her sparkly pink tutu dress matching the one Keely wore for their roles as Lolli's flower girls. I felt Kye stiffen behind me.

"Benny's been dancing with her for over thirty minutes," he grumbled.

A soft giggle left my lips. "Have you seriously been timing them?"

"Maybe."

"Kyler...they're eight and nine. I don't think they're going to run away and get married. You're safe."

"Yeah, he's *nine*. A whole *year* older than her. I don't like it. It's like Danny all over again."

My mouth curved as I caught sight of Hayden dancing with her boyfriend. Her head lay on his shoulder as he guided her around the floor like she was the world's most precious gift. "Are you really still salty about him? He looks out for her. And he makes her happy."

"I guess he's okay," Kye finally admitted.

I lifted my hand up to pat his cheek. "At least Clem still only has eyes for her books."

Even at this very moment, she was sitting beneath one of the towering aspen trees, devouring a fantasy novel in her whimsical, pale-pink dress that matched Hayden's for their roles as junior bridesmaids.

"She was my one holdout. But now she's leaving me for freaking *Yale*," Kye bemoaned.

I couldn't hold in my laugh. "It's a science summer camp. She'll be back in a few weeks."

I could practically feel Kye's frown as he held me tighter. "I just hope she doesn't get any ideas about going that far away for college. I'm gonna get Linc to take her on a visit to Stanford and hope she loves it. That's at least on the same coast."

Our beautiful Clementine was truly a genius. She'd skipped two grades already and would be starting her freshman year in the fall. Kye was incredibly proud, but he also worried nonstop about the fact that his sister would be starting college at sixteen.

"We're going to make sure she goes at her own speed. And she can always do a couple of years locally and then transfer," I suggested. "Or take classes online first."

"I vote online. Then I can really keep an eye on her."

My smile widened. Kyler was the very best father anyone could ask for. He was protective but never judgmental, kind but with gentle boundaries, and he was always a safe place for the girls and the many foster children that passed through our home to land.

Even now, I saw Levi and Frannie running around the garden as Mom looked on, making sure they didn't get into too much trouble. Levi's mom was going through treatment for alcohol addiction, and I thought there was a good chance they'd be reunited. I didn't have the same hope for Frannie's parents. But if they didn't take the steps needed for reconciliation, we'd be there with a home for her for as long as she needed.

My hands curved over Kye's that rested across my middle. "You're such a good dad."

Kye held me tighter. "You're the best mom."

I took a deep breath. "How would you feel about adding another to our brood?"

Kye stilled and then turned me to face him, searching my eyes. "You have someone who needs us?"

That was usually what happened—a particularly tough case would come across my, Rose's, Mila's, or another caseworker's desk. But no longer Noah's. He'd moved and transferred to a different county, which was for the best. But if any of the rest of us found a case that needed a gentle touch, I brought it to Kye. And he always said yes. Always put his all into caring for the child, getting them the best doctors, therapists, and whatever else was needed.

But that wasn't the case today. I shook my head, my blond waves fluttering with the motion.

Kye frowned. "Not a case?"

I swallowed hard and looked up at him. "I'm pregnant."

Those amber eyes flared wide. "Sparrow," he croaked, going stock-still.

"I know we were thinking later, but—"

Kye sank to his knees right there in the grass despite the fact that he was wearing a suit. His tattooed fingers tightened on my hips as he skimmed his lips over my belly. "Now's better." My eyes burned as Kye's gaze lifted to mine. "You're sure?"

"I, uh, went to Dr. Avery just to make sure everything was okay. I hadn't realized how many periods I'd missed, so I'm farther along than I thought. How do you feel about being the ultimate girl dad?"

Kye's amber eyes glittered with unshed tears. "It's a girl?"

I nodded, my tears falling then.

Kye's focus came back to my belly, his lips skimming the fabric of my dress once again. "I love you, baby girl. Gonna do everything I can to make your life full of only the good."

"Kyler," I whispered.

He pushed to his feet, his fingers sliding along my jaw as the pinky on his other hand hooked with mine. "I love you, Sparrow. My spark in the dark, all that's good."

"My everything." I kissed him, bleeding all the love I felt into the kiss.

"What's going on?" Hayden asked, a little worry in her voice.

"You were kissing Mama Fal's tummy," Gracie said.

"Maybe he just likes her tummy," Clem argued, but I heard a hint of apprehension in her voice.

Kye searched my eyes, and I nodded. With a huge smile on his face, he turned to the girls who had become ours in every way. "Your mom's pregnant."

Clem's eyes went wide. "You're having a baby?"

I nodded. "A girl. So I hope you'll show her the ropes."

"I'm gonna be a big sister?" Gracie shouted with glee.

"You are," Kye said with a laugh.

"I never got to be one of those before," she mumbled, looking up at Hayden. "Will you tell me how to do it good?"

A soft smile tugged at Hayden's lips as she wrapped an arm around Gracie's shoulders. "I'll tell you all the important stuff." Her focus shifted to Kye and me. "And I'll always look out for her."

Kye's hand landed on her shoulder. "We know you will. Best big sister in the world."

"Oh, shoot," I muttered, my tears coming in earnest. "It's the hormones."

Clem laughed. "I'm gonna look into that for you."

Kye engulfed us in a hug, his long arms pulling us all into a huddle. "My girls. Love you to the ends of the Earth."

And that love was exactly what Kye said I was to him. A spark in the dark. Hope in a sea of sorrow. And his love would carry us through for the rest of our days.

READ ON FOR A SNEAK PEEK AT THE MEET-CUTE IN A BRAND-NEW SERIES FROM CATHERINE COWLES

CHAPTER THREE

Dex

I MADE THE DRIVE BACK INTO TOWN MUCH FASTER THAN WHEN I'd left it, almost breaking my three-miles-an-hour-over-the-speed-limit rule. But I was desperate. Downtown was more crowded now, and I eased off the brake and put on my blinker when I saw a station wagon with bikes on the back pull out.

But before I could snag the parking spot, a maroon SUV turned in from the opposite lane.

Seriously?

My back molars clamped down as I realized it was the same damn one as earlier. Half a dozen silent expletives left my lips as the dog shoved its head out the window, tongue lolling as if sticking it out at me.

Movement a block down caught my attention, and I bolted for the new space opening up. I slid in right on the heels of the sedan, not leaving anything to chance, and made my way to the brick building that housed Blaze's rental company.

I took the wooden stairs two at a time, praying that by some miracle, he'd have an opening. I'd take a cabin with an outhouse as long as I could set up my Wi-Fi.

The door was one of those wood-and-glass deals where the glass was rippled, so you couldn't see through. The lettering read *Amazin' Blazin' Rentals*. One corner of my mouth kicked up as I knocked.

There was a long pause and then an almost musical, "Come in."

I opened the door and stepped into the sun-filled office. The rays caught on suncatchers, crystals, and an endless array of house plants, including some with distinctly shaped leaves.

Blaze stared straight ahead, his head tilting to one side and then the other as he examined a pink crystal.

"Blaze?" I asked cautiously.

His head slowly turned toward me, his long, gray hair tied back in a braid by a rainbow bandana. "Dex. Heeeeey, Little Dude. Good to see you."

Blaze had gotten his nickname for his affinity for the recreational pursuit. But he looked a little more out of it than usual.

"You okay?" I asked.

"Totally." He grinned. "That friend of yours, Lolli, asked me to sample her new blend of the good stuff, but her homemade grows might be a little stronger than mine because I don't think you have pink hair in real life."

I tried not to laugh. Connecting him with one of my best friend's soon-to-be grandmothers might have been a mistake, given her penchant for brownies with a little something extra. "I do not have pink hair, but I am hoping you can perform a miracle."

"Talk to me, Little Dude."

Blaze had called my brothers and me *Little Dude* since we came to live with my great-uncle and continued to despite the fact that I was now six foot four and over two hundred pounds.

"Do you, by any chance in tourist hell, have a cabin I could rent? Even just for the summer?" I asked.

Blaze blinked a few times, moving slowly and then suddenly speeding up, jumping out of his chair and heading to a board of keys. "Miracles abound, Little Dude. Just gotta open your eyes to truly see them."

My lips twitched. "And to see the pink hair?"

Blaze grinned. "Pink's your color. A couple just canceled on one of the Creekside Cabins. They were gonna be here all summer."

Relief washed through me fast and fierce. I loved my family.

Wanted to spend plenty of time with them. But I also needed my space—all of us Archer brothers did in our own ways.

I clapped Blaze on the shoulder. "You are my hero."

He sent me one of those lopsided grins. "I'm just happy as hell you're home. Waylon missed you."

Guilt pricked at me. Ever since I'd gotten arrested at twenty-one and was given an ultimatum by the FBI—come work for them or do the time for hacking into one of their servers—I hadn't been home much. My three-times-a-year trips had been shorter, and my stays distracted because my head was usually stuck in a case.

One for the FBI or one of the *others*—the ones my brothers and I worked in the quiet, anonymously trying to help where we could. I didn't need to be a profiler to understand why. We were doing penance for crimes that weren't ours.

"Little Dude?" Blaze pressed.

I blinked a few times, clearing away the ghosts—no, the demons. "I'm happy to be back, too."

"Good." Blaze's voice went a little dreamy again.

I shook my head and accepted the key. "How much do I owe you for first and last?"

He just waved me off. "I'll invoice you."

My brow about hit my hairline. "You using a computer now?"

"I got me one of those tablets. Granddaughter taught me."

Laughing, I shoved the key with the cabin number on the chain into my pocket. "Small miracles."

"They are *everywhere*, Little Dude."

I gave Blaze a wave as I headed out, moving down the stairs and into the sunshine. I started down the block toward my SUV, which was in a parking place much farther away, thanks to the spot-stealer.

Just as I hit the curb to step down, something hit me. Right on top of my head with a force that spoke of heat-seeking missiles or air-dropped bombs. It was a bomb, all right. As I felt the top of my head, my face screwed up in a scowl.

Bird poop.

More than half a dozen curses left my lips. But as a familiar face spotted me from down the block, a man who always looked at me and my brothers with wariness in his eyes, I shoved those curses down. Swallowed them like I did all the things I wanted to give voice to but didn't.

Instead, I climbed behind the wheel of my SUV, wiping away the worst of the bird crap with some fast-food napkins and water from the bottle in the cupholder. I ground my back molars the entire ten-minute drive to the cabins along Clover Creek. It wasn't until I saw that not another person was in sight near the three cabins along the winding water that I truly breathed.

But I still couldn't take in the beauty around me. All I could think about was a shower and some painkillers for the headache I was now rocking. I hauled the one duffel I'd need out of the back seat and started for the cabin's front door. They weren't fancy, but I knew Blaze had a crew that made sure they were clean. And he could handle any repairs.

Cabin Two was bigger than expected. Three bedrooms. Two baths. A living room and kitchen that flowed together. And a yard with an epic view of the creek, the fields, and the forest beyond.

But I only cared about the shower.

I went straight for the bathroom, dumping my bag; shucking my shoes, glasses, and clothes; and climbing into the spray. There were a couple mini-bottles of shampoo, and I washed my damn hair twice, rolling my neck under the stream and hoping it would unlock some of the knots.

Finally, the water started to turn lukewarm, and I forced myself to climb out of the antique-looking shower/tub combo. It sure as hell wasn't made for a man my size, but I made do.

A noise caught my attention as I rubbed the towel over my hair. Scraping. *Someone trying to pick a lock?*

Everything in me went on alert. I grabbed my glasses, shoving the frames onto my face as I glanced down at my open duffel and cursed. I wasn't usually this careless. I was always prepared because I knew better than anyone what could hide...in the day or dark, behind a warm smile or a sinister scowl.

It didn't matter that I hated guns—weapons of any kind, really. I'd become a master with all of them. But the small and varied arsenal I maintained was in a travel gun locker in the back of my goddamned SUV.

Hinges squeaked—the front door opening. There was no time to wait.

I wrapped the towel around my hips and stalked out of the bathroom and down the hall, only to come face-to-face with a woman whose golden-amber eyes had gone wide with shock.

The expression appeared genuine, but I knew people could be good actors. The best.

Those wide doe eyes matched lips forming a perfect O of surprise. Her hair was pulled back into a high ponytail, and the long, wavy blond strands hung around her like some sort of teasing curtain. She wore cutoffs—the denim kind with threads that dangled and danced across tanned, toned thighs—and a tank top in a dusky pink that only heightened the sun-kissed quality of her skin.

And the shoes. They looked like they'd once been white high-top Chucks, but they'd been colored all over. And not by someone with a deft hand. I could just make out what appeared to be a cookie, a heart, and something that looked like a bear.

I took in every tempting, alluring inch of the woman—took in those facts and filed them away in less than ten seconds, knowing every single one of them could be a lie.

I let the scowl rise to my lips. "What the hell are you doing in my house?"

CHAPTER FOUR

Braedyn

I HADN'T BEEN STUNNED SILENT MANY TIMES IN MY LIFE. WHEN I accidentally broke a neighbor's window at age nine. When Vincent told me he didn't want anything to do with me or my child. When I finally held Owen in my arms. The first time I saw the Pacific Ocean.

And now.

This moment. As a man who looked like some cross between a professor and a biker with mountain-man height and shoulders prowled toward me.

I should've been scared. I told my brain as much. Said to reach for the pepper spray in my pocket. To call Yeti.

But I didn't. I was too busy ogling him.

It wasn't just his rugged beauty—though he had that in spades. It was something else. An energy that clung to him. The same kind infused into his skin by way of his tattoos. It wasn't as if he was covered from head to toe, but he had a healthy dose of ink.

Art that ghosted over his forearms and hands led to bare biceps and then gave way to a piece on his chest that stole my breath. I couldn't help but study the image that pulled taut over toned muscle.

A phoenix.

My mouth went dry as the design on my own rib cage seemed to heat. The man's phoenix was surrounded by wisps of smoke and ash, and I swore the creature's eyes glowed as they burned into me.

"What the hell are you doing in my house?"

The barked words had me pulling back to the here and now, regaining some sense of sanity as I heard my little boy's laugh outside as he played with Yeti. Just because this man had a tattoo similar to mine didn't make him a friend.

But I wasn't the only one who heard the words spoken with an edge of anger. Yeti did, too. And she didn't appreciate them directed at her human.

As I pulled out the pepper spray, Yeti tore up the steps of the cabin and charged in front of me, letting loose a ferocious growl. She didn't attack the man, just stayed between him and me, but the surprise of it was enough to have him stumbling back a step— stumbling back and losing his towel.

The shock of the sequence of events was enough to have my jaw dropping right along with the terry cloth. And I suddenly didn't know where to look. I didn't want to take my eyes off him in case he made a move, but I couldn't look anywhere on his very toned body without flushing to the shade of a tomato.

The man swiped up the towel and covered himself as Yeti bared her teeth. He cursed, backing up another step as a new voice joined the chaos.

"Mom?" Owen asked.

Normally, I'd revel in the fact that my son had called me *Mom* instead of *bro* or *bruh*, but all I could think about was that this situation had just gotten so much worse.

"Why is there a shirtless dude in our new house?" he continued, completely unshaken.

ACKNOWLEDGMENTS

I will not lie. I'm looking at this blank acknowledgments page through blurry eyes because I'm more than a little emo that we've come to the end of Sparrow Falls. This series has felt so special in so many ways: in the writing of it, the reader response, and the world we created together. Thank you for being a part of that. It truly changed my life.

Now, onto *Secret Haven* and all the helping hands that brought it to life. There are many. This is my favorite book I have ever written, and that's thanks in huge part to the people who helped form it at its earliest stages.

When I embarked on a series about foster siblings, I knew I had a lot to learn. And learning about the child welfare and foster care systems has been one of the most impactful things about writing this series. My heart was broken in one moment and then inspired in the next. I am incredibly grateful for Madelyn and Jill, two incredible social workers who helped educate me and make this story as accurate as possible. Thank you from the bottom of my heart.

When I started plotting and planning this story, I wanted EPIC love for Fallon and Kye, nothing else. A massive thank-you has to go to Devyn, Jess, and Tori, who listened to all my ideas and made them stronger. Your excitement made writing this book so damn fun, and I'm so lucky to have the three of you in my corner.

To my betas: Glav, Jess, Jill, Kelly, Kristie, and Trisha, thank you for your over-the-top response to this book. It was truly the most fun I've ever had going through feedback. You all make my words and stories stronger and always help me find my way.

I have such an amazing crew of authors in my corner, and I'm incredibly grateful for all of them, but there are a few I have to shout out specifically who helped during the writing and editing of this book.

Samantha Young, who listened to worry after worry and read an early copy to make sure I was on track. I don't know what I'd do without you, but I never want to find out. Thank you for being my voice of reason and safe port in the storm.

Elsie Silver, who sprinted her ass off with me throughout the drafting and editing of this book. She held my hand on bad days, celebrated with me on the good ones, and made me laugh through it all. Love you, Gertie. Immunity necklaces for infinity.

Laura Pavlov, I'd stab a b*tch right in the kidney for you. Thank you for always having my back, getting it when things are hard, screaming from the mountaintop at every win, and always showing up when I need you. To the moon, Schmoops LLo Rocky Pavlova.

Rebecca Jenshak, pep talk queen, spiral wrangler, and the best sort of bestie you could ask for. You make life so much better. And it's been the greatest privilege to walk through this journey with you. So grateful to have you in my corner.

Willow Aster, you make this world a better place—and my world especially. Thank you for walking with me through the ups and downs, for understanding my weirdness on release days, and for being all-around amazing.

Kandi Steiner, the best cheerleader a girl could ever ask for. You make this world so much brighter, and I'm so grateful to have your sunshine in my life.

The Lance Bass Fan Club: Ana Huang, Elsie Silver, and Lauren Asher. Thanks for the endless *NSYNC giggles, the advice, and the pep talks. But most of all, for your friendship.

Jess, who hand-holds, cheerleads, and is the best friend you could hope to have. I'm so beyond grateful for you.

Paige B, my warrior, my meme queen, my Swiftie sister. Thanks for always showing up for me, in good times and bad, and for tater tots. Always tater tots.

To all my incredible friends who have cheered and supported

me through all the ups and downs of the past few months, you know who you are. Romance books have given me many things, but at the top of that list are the incredible friends I am so lucky to have in my life. Thank you for walking this path with me.

And to the most amazing hype squad ever, my STS soul sisters, Hollis, Jael, and Paige, thank you for the gift of true friendship and sisterhood. Thanks to you, I always feel supported and celebrated.

The crew that helps bring my words to life and gets them out into the world is pretty darn epic. Thank you to Devyn, Jess, Tori, Margo, Chelle, Jaime, Julie, Hang, Stacey, Katie, Jenna, and my team at Lyric, and Kimberly and my team at Park, Fine & Brower Literary Management. Your hard work is so appreciated!

To my team at Sourcebooks: Christa, Gretchen, Katie, and so many others, thank you for helping these words reach a whole new audience and making my bookstore dreams come true. And to my team at Evermore and Century in the UK, especially Claire and Jess, thank you for bringing the stories to stores across the globe.

To all the reviewers and content creators who have taken a chance on my words…THANK YOU! Your championing of my stories means more than I can say. And to my launch and influencer teams, thank you for your kindness and support, and for sharing my books with the world.

Ladies of Catherine Cowles Reader Group, you're my favorite place to hang out on the internet! Thank you for your support, encouragement, and willingness to always dish about your latest book boyfriends. You're the freaking best!

Lastly, thank YOU! Yes, YOU. I'm so grateful you're reading this book and making my author dreams come true. I love you for that. A whole lot!

ABOUT THE AUTHOR
CATHERINE COWLES

Writer of words. Drinker of Diet Cokes. Lover of all things cute and furry. *USA Today* and #1 Amazon bestselling author Catherine Cowles has had her nose in a book since the time she could read and finally decided to write down some of her own stories. When she's not writing, she can be found exploring her home state of Oregon, listening to true crime podcasts, or searching for her next book boyfriend.

STAY CONNECTED

You can find Catherine in all the usual bookish places…

Website: catherinecowles.com
Facebook: catherinecowlesauthor
Facebook Reader Group: CatherineCowlesReaderGroup
Instagram: catherinecowlesauthor
Goodreads: catherinecowlesauthor
BookBub: catherine-cowles
Pinterest: catherinecowlesauthor
TikTok: catherinecowlesauthor

ALSO AVAILABLE FROM
CATHERINE COWLES

The Tattered & Torn Series
Tattered Stars
Falling Embers
Hidden Waters
Shattered Sea
Fractured Sky

Sparrow Falls
Fragile Sanctuary
Delicate Escape
Broken Harbor
Beautiful Exile
Chasing Shelter
Secret Haven

The Lost & Found Series
Whispers of You
Echoes of You
Glimmers of You
Shadows of You
Ashes of You

The Wrecked Series
Reckless Memories
Perfect Wreckage
Wrecked Palace
Reckless Refuge
Beneath the Wreckage

The Sutter Lake Series
Beautifully Broken Pieces
Beautifully Broken Life
Beautifully Broken Spirit
Beautifully Broken Control
Beautifully Broken Redemption

Standalone Novels
Further to Fall
All the Missing Pieces

For a full list of up-to-date Catherine Cowles titles,
please visit catherinecowles.com.